YOU ARE NEXT

JAMIE MILLEN

TITLES BY JAMIE MILLEN

CLAIRE WOLFE THILLERS

YOU DID THIS
YOU MADE ME
YOU ARE NEXT

JAMIE MILLEN

YOU ARE NEXT

Copyright © 2022 by Jamie Millen

jamiemillen.com

ISBN-13: 978-1-950139-13-2 (ebook)

ISBN-13: 978-1-950139-14-9 (paperback)

ISBN-13: 978-1-950139-20-4 (large print)

ISBN-13: 978-1-950139-15-6 (hardcover)

ISBN-13: 978-1-950139-16-3 (audiobook)

FIC031080 FICTION/Thrillers/Psychological

FIC022020 FICTION/Mystery & Detective/Police Procedural

FIC022040 FICTION/Mystery & Detective/Women Sleuths

FIC031010 FICTION/Thrillers/Crime

FIC030000 FICTION/Thrillers/Suspense

FIC027110 FICTION/Romance/Suspense

Cover design by 100 Covers

First edition

CHAPTER 1

Tony Russo had been born into the wrong family. Growing up, he never got to play with the cool kids or their shiny toys. But tonight, he'd fix that error of destiny, and he had dressed up for the occasion.

He studied his reflection in his bedroom's full-length mirror and knotted his necktie for the tenth time. The new suit had cost him a large chunk of change. Was the silk tie overkill? He was aiming for "respectable," not "flashy."

The doorbell buzzed.

Tony swore under his breath. He had no time for visitors. Niccolo Moretti had invited him to dinner, and you didn't keep Nicky waiting. Not if you valued your head.

Soon, Tony would drive out to the Moretti estate in Berkley, one of Washington DC's most exclusive neighborhoods. The big boss's wife, Julia, would be there along with Nicky's powerful business associates. Nicky had asked for a favor, Tony had delivered in spades, and the head of the Moretti cartel knew how to say thank you. Tonight, he'd welcome Tony into the family. *Not bad for a butcher's son.*

The doorbell buzzed again.

Tony pulled off the tie and started from scratch. *Eleventh time lucky?*

One visit to his father's abattoir had convinced Tony not to waste his days processing dead cattle. The stench of raw meat had turned his stomach. Instead, he'd studied chemistry, a skill set Nicky Moretti appreciated. Tony suspected Nicky operated his own secret slaughterhouses. Tony pushed the thought from his mind. Plausible deniability was the key to success in the Moretti universe. What Tony didn't know couldn't hurt him. He merely provided the merchandise. What his clients did with that product was neither his business nor his responsibility.

The buzzer honked a third time.

What's this guy's problem? Tony yanked the tie from the stiff white collar of his dress shirt, tossed the silk strip on his bed, and stormed out of his room. From Tony's fancy suit, nobody would guess he lived in a dingy two-room hole-in-the-wall that stank of dry rot. Tony had invested the rest of his service fee in a downpayment on an apartment in a better neighborhood. He was moving up in the world.

He reached the front door. "Who is it?"

"Delivery," a young woman said.

Tony hadn't ordered anything. He pressed his eye to the peephole. In cut-off jeans and a black T-shirt, the delivery girl chewed gum and studied her manicured nails. She tucked a large Amazon package under her arm. A ponytail of jet-black hair stuck out the back of her black baseball cap with the retailer's familiar smile logo. *She's cute.*

His irritation subsided. This wouldn't take long. With his classy suit and charming smile, he might even get her number.

He unlocked the door and grinned. The girl's tanned skin, high cheekbones, and dark slanted eyes spoke of Native American heritage. Her smile had a naughty edge. He'd *definitely* get her number. Tony reached for the package, but she blocked him with a clipboard.

"Sign first."

He took the clipboard and fished for the pen at the end of a string. Tony had found his angle. He'd hold the clipboard hostage until she parted with her number. *Piece of cake.*

He signed his name and selected a pickup line. "So, what's a guy got to do to—"

She lunged at him, and pain flared in the back of his hand.

"Hey!"

Blood oozed from the gash on his skin. She had stabbed him with the blackened point of a switchblade.

"What the hell?"

His hand burned. A warm, tingling sensation spread up his arm and circulated through his body.

She shoved him hard on the chest, and he staggered backward. The clipboard slipped from his fingers and clattered on the tiles. His legs turned to jelly. He collapsed to the floor.

The girl followed him inside and closed the door behind her.

Tony lay flat on his back. He tried to get up, but his limbs refused to respond. He tried to speak, but his mouth wouldn't move. His lungs struggled to draw breath. He couldn't even blink. *What has she done to me?*

The girl got to work. She sliced open the Amazon package and extracted a bundle of clothing—rubber gloves, plastic coveralls, and a surgical hair cap. Within seconds, she looked like the workers at his father's abattoir. The girl climbed onto a kitchen chair and hammered a large metal ring into the ceiling joist.

Questions exploded in his feverish, captive mind. *What is she doing? Who is she, and what does she want from me?*

The girl tied his unresisting arms together at the wrists with a thick nylon cord. She threaded the rope through a metallic double pulley, hooked the contraption to the ring in the ceiling, and hoisted his arms and body upward until his feet dangled over the living room's cracked tiles. Tony's head lolled forward, his chin touching his chest.

The girl tied off the rope, wiped her brow on her sleeve, and surveyed her handiwork. She stepped closer, raised her head, and stared into his eyes.

"I know you're still in there. Don't bother trying to speak. You can't move a muscle."

She was right. She had paralyzed his body, but he could see and hear everything. His shoulders burned as his body swung gently. The girl knew exactly what she was doing.

She winked at him. "Hang in there."

Was that supposed to be funny? *Why is she doing this?* Would she clean out his apartment? Tony had few belongings worth stealing. *And what's with the medical scrubs?*

She dug around in the Amazon box again. On the kitchen table, she unrolled a plastic sheath that contained a row of sharp steel implements. They resembled a surgeon's tool kit. An involuntary shudder passed through his body. She wasn't here to steal his possessions.

"You did a bad thing, Tony."

And he understood. Tony knew why she was here and who had sent her. The knowledge sent shock waves of terror through his mind. *But that's impossible.* They were gone—all of them! Tony had seen to that.

She selected a knife from the tool kit. The curved blade reminded Tony of the tools at his father's slaughterhouse. His heart pounded like a battle drum. Sweat trickled down his forehead.

The assassin raised the skinning knife for him to see. "That's why I have to hurt you."

Tony couldn't bear to look, but he couldn't close his eyes either. She'd torture and kill him—and force him to watch. *Please, God, let me pass out!*

The girl gripped his new dress shirt and sliced the expensive fabric. But instead of gutting him with the knife, she ran a gloved hand over his chest. Goose bumps spread over his flesh. "You've got great skin, Tony. Don't worry. I won't waste it. Take comfort in that. Part of you will live on...with me."

She passed the blade over his skin, and curls of hair fell from his chest and abdomen.

His heart drummed faster. *Badum-badum-badum!* The psycho was going to skin him like an animal. But unlike the cattle of his father's abattoir, he'd be alive and conscious for the flaying.

The world swirled around him. *No! This can't be happening.* Nicky Moretti had invited him to dinner. Tony had powerful friends. Nobody could touch him.

"You'll pay for this," he wanted to say. "They'll hunt you down and kill you, nice and slow." But nobody could hear his thoughts. Nobody heard his prayers, either. His limp body hung there, his dead-fish eyes open and unmoving.

The assassin raised the skinning knife again. "I'd say 'This isn't personal. It's just business.' But I'll be honest with you, Tony." She grinned. "I love my work."

CHAPTER 2

Monday morning, Special Agent Robert Cline marched down a corridor in the CIRG building toward the most important meeting of his career and tried to keep up with his boss. The task should be easy. One of his strides matched two of hers. But Unit Chief Madeleine Alda seemed determined to arrive at the conference room early. One didn't meet the director of the FBI every day.

Director Douglas Warren's chopper had landed at the sprawling FBI Academy campus in Quantico five minutes ago, and his entourage had headed for the offices of the Critical Incident Response Group. In his second meeting of the day, the director would review Chief Alda's budget extension request. His signature was the last hurdle standing in the way of Rob's new program. The initiative would save lives and change the nation's perception of law enforcement. But the Behavioral Analysis Unit had not launched a new program in years. Skeptical managers had raised their eyebrows at his untested and unorthodox approach and referred the budget request to the director's office. Rob and Alda had to float their proposal and justify their use of taxpayer dollars, or the director would torpedo their plans and send months of hard work to a watery death.

Rob tried to lighten the mood. "I like your new suit, Chief."

Alda huffed. "Show me the financials again."

The Iron Lady seemed unusually flustered. Was Director Warren that intimidating, or was Alda having second thoughts about their new program?

Rob handed her the manila folder. "All here."

They had discussed Rob's projections in detail yesterday.

He pointed at the executive summary on the first page. "I suggest we start with how much money the program will save the Bureau over the next twenty years."

Alda nodded. "Remind me—how many candidates did we select for the trial group?"

"Five, to keep expenses low. But we've identified another twenty-four subjects for future groups."

Alda turned to the expense sheet and swore. "Team building activities? For God's sake, it sounds like we're running a summer camp."

Her assessment wasn't far from the truth. Rob had designed the treatment program with Dr. Sally Fleischer. The forensic psychiatrist had combed decades of scientific research into psychopathy and discovered hope for shepherding young offenders toward productive, law-abiding lives. Their program included neurological screening, therapy sessions, and the creation of a social environment designed to nurture empathy and a healthy moral compass. The recreational activities aimed to foster that environment.

Rob rallied to defend the program. "Sally said—"

"Never mind. Where are the psychiatric talking points?"

"Page two. Bullet format. You'll do great."

Alda scoffed. "This is a hard sell, Rob. CIRG is about critical incidents. It's in our group's freaking name. Crime prevention is completely off-brand."

Rob swallowed hard. A year ago, Alda had loved the idea. If she radiated doubt today, they'd never get the director's approval. Nine months of hard work—mostly after office hours —would go down the drain. And the missed opportunity would condemn generations of delinquents and their future victims. Rob had to inject her with positivity.

"Then it's time we rebranded. Today will go down in history as the day Madeleine Alda kicked off a new era in federal law enforcement."

Alda paused her charge to squint at him as though he'd lost his mind.

He grinned sheepishly. "Too much?"

"Agent Cline, you're an optimist."

"Thank you, ma'am."

"That wasn't a compliment." She barreled on.

Rob hurried to catch up. "So…Douglas Warren, in the flesh. We've never had a better-liked director. The media love his hard-line approach to organized crime. Rumor has it he'll run for president next year. I'm looking forward to meeting him."

"Don't. He's an asshole."

"Do you know him well?"

"We graduated together at the Academy."

"Oh."

Alda's history with the director was news to Rob. Would an old rivalry jeopardize the program?

"Would you like me to present our case today? I don't mind facing the slings and arrows."

Was this why Alda had asked him to tag along? The new program was Rob's brainchild. He knew the details by heart. He could field the director's questions and take full responsibility for the plan's flaws.

Alda tucked the folder under her arm. "Just keep quiet and let me do the talking. I know how to handle him. In fact, *you* can wait outside. I'll call if I need you."

Ouch. Rob could kick himself. His suggestion had backfired and deprived him of rare face time with the director. Had Alda misinterpreted his willingness to take the heat as an attempt to take full credit for the initiative?

Either way, he'd pissed Alda off.

"Which reminds me. Where's the girlfriend?" she asked.

She meant his *fiancée*, Claire Wolfe. Alda had attended their engagement party last week but still referred to Claire as *the girlfriend*. The habit grated on his nerves.

Chief Alda had seemed to dislike Claire from the moment she'd met her. The feeling was not mutual. Did the arrival of an attractive young agent threaten her? Alda's collection of rivalries grew by the day.

"In Newburgh. Claire took a personal day. She'll be back tomorrow."

Claire had returned to Newburgh to attend her farewell party at the local police department. Rob was supposed to be there, too, but he'd bailed when the director moved up his meeting from tomorrow.

Alda scoffed again. "Perfect timing. For her sake, I hope this meeting goes well. If Director Warren doesn't approve our budget, we'll have to delay the program, and her position will be redundant."

Rob's enthusiasm sagged. Claire had left a promising career at Newburgh PD to start over at the FBI. She had risked a lot. After the traumas she'd endured as a homicide detective, Rob had hoped the Bureau would provide a safer work environment. And running the new program in Quantico meant Rob and Claire would stay together most of the year. Their shared future hung in the balance, too.

They turned a corner. Special Agent Tom Brown, Rob's long-time partner at the BAU and a veteran Bureau hard-ass, waited for them outside the closed door of the conference room.

The older agent frowned at his wristwatch. "About time you got here," he said with his Southern drawl.

Alda gasped. "He's here already?"

"The meeting started two minutes ago."

"But he just landed!"

"He moved our meeting up. Last-minute change. Didn't you get the memo?"

Alda swore. "This is Benny's doing, I'll bet."

Benny, Rob's former boss, headed the CIRG's Crisis Negotiation Unit. *Rivalry number three.* Alda needed a twelve-step program.

"Relax," Tom said. "I saved you a seat next to the director. Follow the yellow notepad."

"Good work, Tom."

Alda steeled herself with a deep breath, knocked once on the wooden door, and let herself inside. Rob stole a fleeting glance at the director as the door closed.

Tom raised his eyebrows at Rob. "You're not invited either?"

"I'm on the bench. In case Chief Alda needs me."

Tom snorted. "She's right, by the way. Benny rescheduled the meeting. He probably wants to keep the big boss to himself. Alda won't get a word in edgeways. I'm sure the director is only happy to clear this off his schedule. He has bigger fish to fry. Haven't you heard? Serial killers are out of fashion. Transnational organized crime is the new buzzword."

Rob's optimism hit rock bottom. "Great."

"Where's the future Mrs. Cline?"

"Newburgh. She gets back tonight."

Tom grunted. "I got a peek at her New Agent Training scores. She did the Yellow Brick Road in record time."

Rob grinned. "That's my Claire."

The FBI Academy's fitness challenge included a six-mile marathon-cum-obstacle course marked by yellow bricks. Many recruits failed to complete the Yellow Brick Road. Claire had set a new record, and her Yellow Brick Award sat proudly on Rob's mantelpiece. The achievement seemed to embarrass Claire, who blamed her track team history and competitive nature.

Tom cracked a smile. "Two overachievers. You're perfect for each other." He studied Rob. "So you're finally leaving me, kiddo?"

Rob shoved his hands into his trouser pockets. "Hatchlings have to fly the nest someday."

Tom deadpanned, "I'm tearing up."

"I didn't realize you'd miss me so much."

"Don't get me wrong, Rob. The tears are for you. While I travel around the country, chasing serial killers, you'll be babysitting criminally insane teenagers."

Rob chuckled. Tom always found the silver lining.

"I can't keep jet-setting forever. Soon, I'll have a wife waiting for me at home."

"Exactly my point, Agent Cline. Travel is the main perk of the job. Heed the wisdom of an experienced married man. You might live to regret assigning your wife to your new program."

"I doubt that. But thanks for the advice."

Tom frowned at his wristwatch again. "Talking of wives, I'd love to shoot the breeze with you, but I have to call Mary back." He patted Rob on the shoulder and walked off. "Good luck, pal."

Rob opened his mouth to deliver one last witty comeback, but a deafening explosion cut him short. The floor shook beneath his feet. Then, the conference room door flew from its frame on a billowing cloud of flame. Waves of intense heat singed Rob's face. The door slammed into him like a rocket and flung him against the opposite wall. Rob crashed to the floor. A hail of smoldering debris pelted his body. And the world faded to black.

CHAPTER 3

C laire Wolfe raised her shot glass for the second toast. Platters of bagels and doughnuts covered the table of the Newburgh PD conference room, but her fellow officers hadn't touched the food yet. She'd asked both Chief Charlie Emmerso and Captain Morris Washington to keep their farewell speeches short, and both had dedicated a round of drinks in her honor. The detectives and patrol officers obliged gladly, especially Detective Brendan Mahoney. Claire had underestimated the amount of alcohol she'd needed to bring to the party.

Captain Washington called on Detective Jessica Long, who presented Claire with a bouquet of pink and white roses.

"Thanks, Jess."

The pretty young detective hugged Claire and swept a lock of blonde hair from her eyes. "I'm going to miss you, partner."

"Hey, for the next few minutes, I'm still Sergeant Wolfe."

Their friends laughed.

Detective Haruto Nakamura put his hands together. "Speech! Speech! Speech!"

The others broke into a chorus, and Claire yielded to peer pressure.

"OK, OK."

The chanting subsided. Claire had not wanted to speak at the farewell, certain she'd become emotional. The Investigations Bureau had given her no choice.

"You all know how much I love making speeches, so I'll be brief. I want to thank Chief Emmerso for taking a chance on me, and Captain Washington for the promotion."

Detective Lucas Gomez wolf-whistled. "You deserved it, Claire."

Claire blushed and turned to Jess. "Detective Long, I haven't been the easiest partner in the world. Thanks for putting up with me."

The officers watched her in expectant silence while she searched for the right words.

"It's good to see you after being away so long, even if it is to say goodbye."

Claire had spent the past nine busy months requalifying at the FBI Academy in Quantico.

"We've been through a lot of rough times together, and I've learned so much from you all. I never thought I'd leave the department. I hope this fresh start works out. But who knows, maybe I'll come back next week to beg for my old job back?" She won more laughs. "Until then, I'll miss you all."

Nakamura raised his voice. "Even Mahoney?"

His partner didn't take offense. "You kidding me? Claire loves me. I'm the reason she's having an open bar at her wedding."

The officers chuckled.

Mahoney downed his second shot of whiskey to prove his point. "We're invited to the wedding, right?"

"Of course. Rob and I are still figuring out the details. But enough talking. Those doughnuts won't eat themselves. Dig in."

The detectives and patrol officers didn't need a second invitation. Claire selected a salmon bagel and moved away from the table. *Never stand between a cop and a doughnut.*

Claire bit into her bagel. *A fresh start.* When Rob had invited her to join him at the FBI, the promising new career path had seemed too good to be true. The air of Newburgh was thick with stifling memories. She longed to explore an expansive, sunny frontier. But her troubled teenage years and her hellish brushes with violent death had cast a dark shadow over her belief in happy endings. Even now, a brooding cloud loomed over this crossroads in her life.

Lighten up, Claire. She had so much to look forward to: a meaningful new job; her marriage to the man she loved; a clean sweep in a different state. Besides, she knew what had triggered her premonitions.

During her graduation party at Tom Brown's home near Washington, a powerful explosion had sent a shock wave through the garden. The media had attributed the tremor to an accidental detonation in an industrial warehouse. Claire didn't believe in signs or portents. But the blast—seconds after she'd accepted Rob's surprise marriage proposal—had shaken her, physically and emotionally, and primed her imagination for tragedy. *Don't let that random coincidence rain on your parade, Claire.*

Jess drew near, a chocolate doughnut in her hand. "When do you start?"

"Last week. I took the day off today." Claire showed Jess her new FBI identity card.

"Cool. Remind me—what's the new program called?"

Claire had told her about Rob's initiative. The intervention aimed to turn juvenile offenders into empathic citizens instead of murderous psychopaths.

Claire swallowed a mouthful of salmon bagel. "The Youth At Risk Initiative, or YARI. The Bureau loves acronyms."

Jess licked chocolate icing from her lips. "You'll do important work there. I'm sure your mom is proud. How is she, by the way?"

"She's good. In fact..." Claire read the time off her phone. "As we speak, she's boarding a cruise ship in Boston. Frank's taking her to the Caribbean for two weeks."

"Not bad!"

"Yeah."

Claire smiled. Diane's metamorphosis still amazed her. The spiteful, alcoholic thorn in Claire's side had transformed into an energetic older woman with a budding singing career and a pampering boyfriend. Maybe happy endings did exist, after all?

"Any luck selling the house?"

"Nope."

Diane had put Claire's childhood home on the market six months ago after moving in with Frank. Renovators had repaired the bullet holes in the walls and replaced the blood-stained kitchen tiles, but the property refused to sell.

Claire shrugged. "I guess young couples aren't eager to raise their families in a crime scene. Go figure."

Mahoney drifted closer with a full shot glass. *Does he ever eat solid food?*

"Claire, darling." He slurred his words and swayed on his feet in a convincing impression of the eternally drunk pirate, Captain Jack Sparrow. "Things never have worked between us."

Jess snorted.

Nakamura joined them, tuna bagel in hand, and clapped his partner on the shoulder.

"You never stood a chance, pal. What? Don't look at me like that. Somebody's got to keep you humble."

Mahoney, still in character, knocked back his drink. "That's me wife's job, and she does it well."

The newly engaged Claire chewed her bagel in pensive silence. Mahoney had not painted a picture of marital bliss. The divorce rate among law enforcement officers was notoriously high. Claire hoped she and Rob would beat the statistics.

Jess grunted. "Talking of spouses, where's Rob?"

"He couldn't make it today. He has a meeting with Director Warren."

"Impressive."

Claire sighed. "I hope the director approves our unit's budget extension. Otherwise, I'll be unemployed."

Chief Emmerso snuck up on her. "You're always welcome back here."

"Thank you, sir."

"You're not just a colleague or friend. You're family."

Clair grinned politely. *If only that were true.* "That's nice of you to say, sir."

"I'm serious. If you ever need anything, you can count on us."

Her phone vibrated in her pocket. A Quantico number showed on the screen. "I should take this. It's probably Rob." The dark cloud loomed. *Why wasn't he calling from his phone?*

Jess brightened. "Maybe he's got good news?"

"I hope so." Claire answered. "Hey."

"Special Agent Claire Wolfe?" The man on the phone was not Rob.

"Yes?"

"This is the CIRG emergency center. What's your location?"

Emergency center? Claire's heart skipped a beat. "I'm in Newburgh, Massachusetts. Why? Is everything OK?"

"We're confirming the whereabouts of all our assets. There's been an attack at CIRG headquarters."

Claire's mind did a double take. She pictured airplanes plowing into the World Trade Center, and her heart all but sank into her stomach. *Is this 9/11 all over again?*

"What kind of attack?"

"You'll have to speak with your manager for details."

The call ended. Claire dialed Rob's number and pressed the phone to her ear. She answered her friends' worried stares.

"There's been an attack at CIRG headquarters in Quantico."

"Is Rob OK?" Emmerso asked.

"I'm trying to find out."

Rob's number was disconnected. She tried Chief Alda and got the same response. Nobody was available. *Don't assume the worst.*

Her phone shook in her hand. "I can't reach him or our unit chief."

Jess touched Claire's arm. "Maybe the cellular networks are overloaded?"

Or maybe they're all dead?

Claire drew a wavering breath. "I have to go."

CHAPTER 4

The Sentara Medical Center, with its green islands and low structures of redbrick and reflective glass, radiated sanitary and hi-tech serenity. But when Claire stormed into the Emergency Department she felt anything but serene. She'd caught the first flight from the nearest airport, Bradley International, to Manassas Regional. Details of the attack at Quantico came in vague trickles. The airport newscast screens showed external shots of the CIRG building. The bombing had gutted the offices but left the facade untouched. Talking heads speculated about terrorism. The casualties included FBI Director Douglas Warren and several high-ranking but yet unnamed agents.

Rob and Chief Alda were still unavailable when Claire landed. Special Agent Tom Brown, too. Only Dr. Sally Fleischer answered her phone. Sally had heard the blast. First responders had ordered her to evacuate the building but said nothing about her colleagues, only that ambulances had transferred the wounded to Sentara.

The linoleum passageway reeked of disinfectant and tragedy. Claire searched the jumble of incomplete facts for scraps of hope. Dispatch would have notified her if Rob had died. *No, Rob is alive.* He had to be.

Still, the sheer audacity of the attack stunned her. How had terrorists struck the secure heart of the FBI? The event would forever divide the Bureau's history into the periods before and after this unfathomable day. And for Claire, the familiar smell of guilt clung to the calamity. Part of her had expected this. Claire had left Newburgh to escape the senseless violence of her past. But a low voice in the shadows of her mind had whispered that disaster skulked around the corner.

Medical staff in blue scrubs walked by. None of them seemed to be in a hurry. Hours had passed since the blast. Rob's fate was already decided. Claire only waited to hear the verdict.

She found the information counter and flashed her brand-new FBI identity card.

"Excuse me. I'm looking for a patient, Robert Cline. He was transferred here this morning after the bombing."

Claire didn't know that for a fact, but she couldn't face the alternative. The nurse glanced at her computer monitor and searched the hospital's records. Claire tried to divine Rob's condition from her expression.

"He went into surgery three hours ago. Check with Recovery."

Recovery. Rob was alive! But he'd needed surgery. How bad were his injuries?

"Where is Recovery?"

The nurse directed Claire to the elevators in an adjoining building, and Claire marched off.

Nightmarish images floated in her mind of paraplegic wheelchairs and ventilators. Was Rob comatose? Would he be able to work again? And walk?

The dark whispers rose in her mind anew. The moment her new life had come within reach, a catastrophe had blindsided her and ruined everything. Claire had escaped Newburgh, but she couldn't outrun her family's deadly curse. First her sister, Tina. Then her father. Her mother had barely escaped. Now, that malevolent power had gone after Rob.

Knock it off, Claire. Rob is fine, and you are not cursed. There's no such thing.

She stepped into a very large elevator and drew deep breaths. The doors closed slowly. Claire had never been religious, but she moved her lips in prayer. "Please, God, let him be OK."

The elevator pinged, and the doors opened at their glacial pace. Claire slipped through the opening sideways and hurried to the nurses' station.

"The Emergency Department sent me here. I'm looking for Special Agent Robert Cline."

"Are you family?"

"I'm his fiancée."

The nurse frowned. "I'm afraid only immediate family members are allowed to visit."

"I'm the only family he's got."

Claire had raised her voice. Throwing a tantrum wouldn't grant her access to Rob. She had to calm down.

"I'm sorry. He's an only child. His father died years ago, and he's not in touch with his mother. Please. I need to see him."

"I'm sorry, the regulations are clear. We cannot—"

"It's OK," a man said. "She's with me."

Claire recognized the Southern drawl. Special Agent Tom Brown limped toward her. His left arm hung in a sling, and a surgical bandage covered his left temple. Claire had never been happier to see the older agent's weathered face.

"Tom! Thank God, you're all right. I couldn't reach you on the phone. Where's Rob?"

"He hasn't come out of surgery yet."

"But that was three hours ago."

"He went in last. Or so I heard. I guess he wasn't hurt that badly."

The tension eased from Claire's shoulders. Maybe Tom was right? Rob would be fine. *Thank God!*

Claire focused on Tom's injuries. "Are you OK?"

"I'll live. They're discharging me in a few hours. You just missed Mary. I think she was hoping to cash in my life insurance."

A nervous laugh escaped Claire's lips, but she sobered up quickly. "Tom, what happened?"

"All hell broke loose, that's what happened."

He glanced at the duty nurse, then flicked his head for Claire to follow him down the corridor and out of earshot. "What have you heard?"

"Only what the media keeps repeating. A bomb blast at CIRG. The director is dead. They suspect terrorists."

Tom grunted. "I'm still trying to piece things together. The bomb must have detonated in the conference room during the meeting. Rob and I were standing right outside."

"Rob wasn't in the room?" She added that detail to her treasure chest of hope. Maybe Rob would walk out of here today, too?

"Chief Alda changed her mind at the last minute. She saved his life. Most people in the room didn't make it: the Director; three aids; two unit chiefs."

Claire's breath caught in her chest. "And Chief Alda?"

"She survived, too." Tom shook his head in awe. "Alda was sitting right next to Director Warren. They don't call her The Iron Lady for nothing. It'll take more than a bomb to take her out." His cheek twitched, and his eyes moistened. His tough exterior had cracked. "I kept that seat for her. If I hadn't..."

"It's not your fault, Tom. You had no way of knowing."

Tom grimaced. "Somebody did. Those terrorists planted the bomb ahead of time. They knew when and where the director would be."

The deduction twisted Claire's gut into a knot. Tom was right. The attackers must have had inside help to pull off the bombing.

Tom inhaled a shaky breath. "Now the Bureau is in chaos. Nobody knows what's going on or what to do next."

Claire touched his good arm. "We'll get to the bottom of this. Whoever's responsible will get what's coming to them. Where's Alda now?"

"I'll walk you to her room."

He hobbled down the corridor.

"It's OK, Tom. Just point me in the right direction."

"Third door on the right."

She headed for Alda's recovery room. Claire had spent little time with her new boss. But Alda had believed in Rob's program and taken a chance on Claire. She wouldn't let her boss down. An enlivened sense of purpose eased the tension of Rob's uncertain future. Claire would help Chief Alda recuperate and get their team back on its feet.

On the threshold of the recovery room, Claire paused. She should buy flowers at the hospital gift shop. *Never mind*. Claire could always do that later. But when she stepped inside, she realized there was no need.

The patient on the hospital bed looked nothing like Claire's unit chief. White surgical bandages covered her body from head to toe. A sling from the ceiling suspended her right leg in a plaster cast above the bedsheets. Her left leg ended abruptly above the knee. The patient drew slow, wheezing breaths through small openings at the nose and mouth. *The Iron Lady*. Alda's condition was worse than Tom had let on.

Claire checked the clipboard at the foot of the bed. Alda

had suffered third-degree burns over her entire body and multiple internal injuries. She'd never return to the FBI or regain a semblance of normal life. At least she was breathing unassisted. Then again, maybe she was better off dead.

Claire drew near the raised bed. Alda's eyes were closed, the lids red and puffy. She had never married or had kids. The unit chief had devoted her every waking moment to her career at the FBI. What would give her the strength to go on living?

Tears welled in Claire's eyes. She turned away. *Let her sleep.* The longer Alda remained blissfully unaware of her condition the better. Claire retreated to the corridor.

Tom limped toward her. "He's here! Rob's out of surgery." He pointed behind her.

Two doors down, a male nurse wheeled a bed into a room. Claire caught sight of the patient's legs—two, full-length legs—and ran after him. After viewing Alda's injuries, two working legs were a blessing. *Please, God. Let him be whole.*

Claire ran to Rob's room. The nurse docked the bed and lowered the safety rails. A doctor, his hair still in a blue surgical cap, scribbled on a clipboard. Rob's eyes were closed. Bandages hid the side of his head. A cast covered his left arm and leg. His skin seemed unburned by the blast. Claire counted her blessings.

She drew near. "Rob?"

He didn't respond.

"Is he asleep?"

The surgeon kept his eyes on the clipboard. "Are you his wife?"

"Fiancée."

The surgeon didn't take issue with her marital status. "He has a broken leg, fractured ribs, and a nasty concussion. We managed to stop the internal bleeding, but the rest is up to him."

Claire braced for the brutal truth. "Brain damage?"

The surgeon studied her for a moment before answering. Would he soften the truth for the victim's betrothed?

"We're still waiting on the scan results."

"How long until he wakes up?"

"Hard to tell. Minutes or hours, if he's lucky. Or much longer. I'm sorry."

"Don't be. You saved his life. Thank you."

He gave her a consoling smile. "I've left instructions for pain relievers, and I'll stop by on my next shift."

Claire pulled up a visitor's chair and took Rob's hand in hers. *Minutes or hours. Or much longer.* As a beat cop, Claire had spent many shifts in hospital emergency rooms. She had escorted victims and signed over their corpses to the ME's office and funeral homes. She understood what the surgeon's words meant. Rob might never wake up again.

CHAPTER 5

The killer was putting the finishing touches to her new accessory when the phone rang. She drove the stitching awl through the fold of soft leather. Only one person called her on the burner phone.

She answered. "Hello, Daddy."

The caller wasn't her dad. Her biological father had left when she was two years old. Daddy had filled the void.

"Did you see the news?"

The voice on the phone didn't sound human. An algorithm distorted each syllable, creating an unidentifiable electronic jumble. But the words were Daddy's. People like them needed to take precautions. They were unlike other men and women. They were a different species.

"Yes, Daddy, I did."

CNN had displayed images of the CIRG building in Quantico and the steady flow of emergency workers. An update had announced the death of the FBI director and several other unnamed agents. The broadcasts had sent a thrill of pleasure through her body.

She pinched the thread at the end of the awl, creating a

loop of slack. Then, she drew the second thread through the loop and withdrew the awl from the leather. *Another perfect stitch.*

The killer took pride in her work. All good art requires sacrifice. To honor those sacrifices, she ensured her creations were flawless, and perfection demanded attention to detail. She harvested the skin while the donor was still warm. Then, she soaked the pelt in lye for twenty-four hours before scraping away the hair and residual body grease. For thread, she used only quality bonded nylon. Her early attempts had produced defective results. But she'd persevered. *If at first you don't succeed, try, try again.* Over the years, she'd honed her process until, finally, she had achieved excellence.

Daddy's synthesized voice spoke again. "Unfortunately, two birds flew the coop."

She halted her leatherwork. The code words were another precaution, but their meaning was clear. *Two of their targets had survived the blast.*

Daddy didn't like mistakes. Somebody would pay for this. She had slipped up once and faced his wrath. Would he punish her for this screw-up, too?

"How can I help?"

"They're at Sentara, rooms 219A and C. Go quietly."

She knew what he wanted. "I won't let you down." Soon, the survivors would join their fallen colleagues, but their deaths would appear natural.

"And beware the cats." The Feds were monitoring the hospital.

"Understood."

She put down the phone and ran her hand over her leather creation. Her fingertips traced the areolas and nipples. Daddy *got* her. Few people appreciated their skill sets or worldview.

The Silence of the Lambs was a case in point. Hollywood

portrayed her kind as barbaric cannibals or gender-conflicted social outcasts, preferably both. She sighed. *Sheep never understand the wolf.*

The killer returned to the task at hand. She moved the awl faster along the final seam. She derived inspiration from neither Buffalo Bill nor Hannibal Lecter. Her heroes lived not in fiction but in history. She admired the Nazis' efficiency. They had produced lampshades and soap bars from skin and fat, wasting no human resources. She fantasized about taking her art to that level. For now, her craft would remain a cottage industry. But a girl could dream.

She tied the final saddle stitch to complete the tote, slung the bag on her shoulder, and posed in her mirror. *Yes, this will do nicely.* She pressed her handiwork to her face and inhaled the glorious scent of new leather.

The killer stored the tools of her trade in her new creation and packed a few necessities in an overnight bag. With a spring in her step, she left her apartment. On the threshold, she whispered to the tote on her shoulder.

"Ready to make a fashion statement, Tony?"

She'd fulfilled her promise to Moretti's chemist. The killer giggled. Men made the best accessories.

CHAPTER 6

D r. Sally Fleischer walked into a nightmare that afternoon. The stench of smoldering wood and burnt plastic wafted from the charred walls of the corridor. Beyond the yellow crime scene tape, forensic techs in white coveralls examined the wreckage. The sight sent a shudder down her spine.

Sally was no stranger to crime scenes. Her job entailed analyzing forensic photographs and reconstructing violent crimes. But this crime scene was her workplace, the CIRG building, and the victims were her colleagues.

The impossibility of the situation dazed her. The FBI Academy campus was among the most secure locations in the country. An attack on the Bureau's inviolable premises was unthinkable. Sally had heard the blast from two floors down. The shock wave had shifted her desk chair. The FBI was no longer a safe space, and the confusion of the disaster's aftermath only added to her disorientation.

She headed toward the strip of yellow tape.

An agent in a dark suit raised his hand for her to stop. "Ma'am, this area is off-limits."

"I was told to report here."

He looked behind him and yelled, "Massoud!"

A short, pot-bellied man in a cheap brown suit stepped through the ruined wall of the conference room and eyed her. Then he picked a path through the debris toward her. Disposable blue baggies covered his shoes.

Massoud raised his hands, which were both gloved in blue latex. "We'll shake later. I wouldn't want to add your DNA to the crime scene."

"That's OK."

He smiled for a split second. "Special Agent Rafiq Massoud, Criminal Investigative Division. And you are?"

"Dr. Sally Fleischer."

His eyebrows bunched on his olive forehead. "Doctor of...?"

"Psychiatry."

He blinked at her, so she elaborated.

"Forensic Psychology. I work for the BAU. I'm supposed to assist with the investigation."

The penny dropped. "The profiler." He sounded disappointed.

"That's me."

Most people responded to her job description with interest, even fascination. Agent Massoud was a skeptic.

The investigator grunted. "I guess the BAU investigators are out of town." He glanced at the devastation around him. "Or dead."

Sally's shoulders tensed. "Or injured. Three are at Sentara, including our unit chief."

Massoud retrieved a notepad from his pocket. "That would be Unit Chief Madeleine Alda and special agents Robert Cline and Tom Brown." He put the notepad away. "I'm sorry about your friends."

Sally inclined her head. At least he had the decency to express his condolences.

He exhaled. "I'm used to working alone. But the chain of command is broken, and a higher-up decided the BAU should tag along for the ride. Congratulations, you're the lucky winner."

"What about Special Agent Wolfe? She was an experienced homicide detective before she joined the FBI."

Massoud consulted his notepad again. "There's no Wolfe on my list."

"Special Agent Claire Wolfe. She started work last week."

Massoud belched an ironic laugh. "Talk about bad timing. Never mind. You'll do."

He pointed to the boxes of latex gloves and booties on the floor. "Help yourself to the latest in forensics fashion, and I'll give you the grand tour."

Sally pulled on the disposable gear and ducked under the crime scene tape. The conference room was unrecognizable. The blast had reduced the heavy oak table to a hundred chunks of singed firewood. Shrapnel had dismantled the office chairs, shredded the leather upholstery, and ignited the stuffing. She tried not to imagine the devastation the bomb had inflicted on the soft human flesh of the chairs' former occupants.

Massoud indicated the carnage with a wave of his arm. "So what do you think, Dr. Fleischer? Is our bomber a cross-dresser with mommy issues?"

Sally already regretted this assignment. "Maybe? My specialty is serial killers, not arsonists."

Massoud grinned. "You're in luck, Doc. Arson is *my* specialty."

She folded her arms. "What can *you* tell us about the bomber, Agent Massoud?"

"I'm glad you asked, Dr. Fleischer." Massoud pointed to the

crater in the floor. "He placed two kilos of C4, commonly known as plastic explosives, at the head of the table. Apparently, Director Warren was his main target."

"You haven't answered my question."

"I haven't?"

"You described the bombing, not the bomber. Is he a cross-dresser or not?"

Massoud laughed. "I'd prefer not to speculate about his personal proclivities. Why weave colorful speculations when I can examine hard physical evidence? We'll start with an analysis of the explosive residue. The chemical composition should lead us up the supply chain to the manufacturer of the explosives. But let's not forget our good old-fashioned detective work either. For instance, how did he deliver the bomb, and how did he know when and where to plant it?" His eyebrows bunched in mock suspicion. "Which makes me wonder—when were you last in this conference room, Dr. Fleischer?"

"Last week."

Massoud smacked his lips. "Then I guess you didn't do it."

His dark humor strained her patience. "Those injured agents are my friends. Chief Alda is my boss."

Massoud shrugged. "And who doesn't think about murdering the boss now and then?" He waved the words away. "I'm just messing with you, Doc. You're not a suspect. We're looking for a professional."

Sally itched to slap him. "Excuse me?"

"I mean, this isn't his first job. But do me a favor. When we catch him, remind me to ask about his dressing habits."

"What makes you sure he's done this before?"

"You kidding me? This guy hit an FBI building—from inside. His timing was perfect. And he didn't use a pipe bomb. C4 is no toy. Its manufacture and possession are highly regulated. That bad boy is strictly for the pros." Massoud lowered his voice. "Just between you and me, I'm smelling organized crime."

Sally smirked. "The Mob has taken on the FBI?" She enjoyed playing devil's advocate.

"It makes sense. Director Warren came down hard on organized crime. They eliminated him. Means, motive, and opportunity. Don't you worry, Doc. We'll have these guys before you can say 'Jack the Ripper.'"

"You seem very sure of yourself."

Massoud grinned. "That's because they already screwed up. Luther!"

His yell startled her.

A forensic tech peeked through the hole in the wall. "You bellowed?"

"Show us that casing you found."

Luther stalked off and returned with a transparent evidence bag. "The perp padded the explosive with bags stuffed with nails and ball bearings to increase the damage. Most of the packaging vaporized on detonation, but not this piece."

Massoud snatched the bag from him. "Check out this beauty."

He handed her a blackened and badly dented metal sheet the size of a calling card.

Sally's mouth dropped open. Despite the severe damage, the metal casing displayed an etched symbol. The marking sent a tremor of fear down her spine. *But that's impossible.*

Massoud chuckled. "What do you think, Doc? V is for Vendetta?"

Sally examined the card. "That's not a V. It's a chevron."

"Whatever. Either way, it'll lead us somewhere."

Yes, it will. Sally bit her tongue. The investigator already thought she was a quack. Before she shared her suspicions, she'd better be one hundred percent sure.

CHAPTER 7

Claire woke up with a start. A door opened, and bright light poured into the room. She had slept curled on a chair and took a second to get her bearings.

A uniformed nurse switched on the ceiling fluorescents and glanced at Claire.

"Visiting hours are over. You need to leave."

Claire yawned and stretched her legs, blinking back the harsh light.

"I'm with the FBI. I'll stay the night."

"The rules are—"

Claire snapped, "My fiancé was almost killed this morning, and he's still unconscious. I'm going to be here when he wakes up."

The nurse pouted, then relented. "Can I get you anything?"

"A pillow would be nice."

"I'll see what I can do."

She left the room. Claire regretted her outburst. The nurse was just doing her job. The day's events had taken their toll on Claire. She couldn't shake this morbid sense of déjà vu. On her first day at Newburgh PD, a teenage girl had turned up dead.

When Claire had resumed active duty after recovering from a gunshot wound, a wealthy heiress was found murdered. Now, soon after she'd started her "safe" job at the BAU, the CIRG building had exploded. Violent crime hounded her every step. Each time, it struck harder and closer to home.

Claire had called her mother's mobile phone that afternoon without success. Diane had no cellular reception or Internet access on the cruise, and she probably hadn't purchased a roaming package for the islands. Her unavailability was for the best. There was no point in ruining her vacation. Diane could do nothing but worry. By the time she got home, Rob would be back on his feet. He had to be.

She stood and took a few steps to ease her stiff limbs. She approached Rob's bed and stroked his hair. An ECG beeped rhythmically. Fluids dripped from suspended plastic bags into the IV tube. Rob's body had survived the attack—battered but whole. A few weeks of rest would mend his physical wounds. But would his mind recover, too?

The surgeon had kept his promise and stopped by a few hours ago. He remained cautiously optimistic. But with Claire's track record, she feared for the worst. Rob was the gravitational center of her universe now. Losing him would jettison Claire into the dark void.

A hand knocked on the door, and a woman with long, silky hair and dark empathic eyes poked her head inside.

"Sally!"

Claire rushed over, and they embraced. Dr. Sally Fleischer had guided Claire on two intense serial killer cases in Newburgh, and she was also the scientific brains behind Rob's new program. They had started working together closely at the FBI until the bombing tossed Claire's future into the air.

"How are you holding up?"

"Barely. I yelled at the nurse."

Sally snickered. "They're tough cookies. I'm not supposed to be here either." Sally swallowed hard. "I just came from Alda's room. I'm in shock."

"Me, too."

Her friend gazed at Rob. "How's he doing?"

"I don't know. He hasn't woken up yet, but the surgeon seems optimistic."

Sally nodded. "Where's Tom?"

"Discharged this afternoon. He got off lightly—flesh wounds."

Sally scoffed. "He could have called to let me know he's all right. That's Tom for you."

Claire studied Sally for hints of news from the outside world. The waiting and helplessness were driving her crazy. Somebody had almost killed her fiancé and colleagues, and her urge to hunt the perpetrators down was boiling over.

"What's going on out there? Do we know who's behind the attack? The TV news is useless."

Sally's expression clouded over. "A CID agent from Washington is leading the investigation, Rafiq Massoud. I got roped in to assist him."

"You?"

"I know. Me—visiting an actual crime scene? I guess I was the only hand on deck."

"What do we know so far?"

Sally hesitated. "Massoud seems to know his stuff. He's confident he'll get our guy. For now, he suspects organized crime."

"Organized crime? That's a ballsy move—like Al Capone whacking J. Edgar Hoover."

"Yeah. Apparently, Director Warren had turned up the heat on organized crime."

"Wow."

The sudden anti-climax deflated Claire. The attacker had targeted the FBI director alone. Alda and Rob were collateral damage. They'd been in the wrong place at the wrong time. As far as the bomber was concerned, their lives were insignificant. The cruel injustice of the attack winded her.

A second realization added to her dejection. Claire wouldn't get near the case. Special Agent Massoud would hand over his findings to the Transnational Organised Crime group. The BAU would play no role in rounding up the criminals. Claire was helpless to bring her friends' attacker to justice. *Not completely helpless.*

"Sally, can you do me a favor?"

"Sure. Anything."

"Keep me in the loop about the investigation?"

"No problem."

"Thank you."

Sally's words calmed her. Her friend's involvement also meant Claire wouldn't have to dive into an intense homicide investigation. She could focus her energy on Rob's rehabilitation. And if Massoud was right, the attack had no connection to Claire's past. For a change, her premonitions were off target.

Sally stared at the ECG and chewed her lip. She had a lot on her mind, too. Visiting ground zero of the blast must have exhausted the sensitive psychiatrist's tolerance for human suffering. What was eating her up inside? Did she, too, fear for their new program's future?

"What do we do now?"

"We wait until order is restored. The president will appoint a new director. The Bureau will fill the other vacant positions. I'm sure our response to the bombing will be very powerful. The Senate has set up an oversight committee to manage the crisis. They'll call the shots until things are back under control. It'll take time."

Sally glanced at Rob again. "Not the best way to start your lives together."

Sally had helped Rob orchestrate his surprise marriage proposal at Claire's graduation party. Claire stared at her fiancé's prone body, and her chest shuddered.

Sally embraced her. "Rob's a fighter. He'll pull through."

Claire nodded and hoped her body language would convince her rational mind that Sally was right.

"Yeah. He'll be fine."

Sally spent a few minutes with her, then went home. Claire turned down her offer to stop by Rob's place and collect fresh clothes and toiletries. Sally had her own trauma to manage.

The nurse delivered two pillows and a thick blanket, and Claire curled up on the chair. A long night lay ahead. Claire hoped she'd fall asleep again. In the best-case scenario, Rob faced a lengthy recovery. She'd need her strength.

Claire did fall asleep because she awoke to the sound of soft groaning. She launched to her feet and placed her hand on Rob's.

She switched on a bedside light. "I'm here, Rob. Right here."

Rob opened his eyes and gazed at her. "Claire."

She almost burst with relief. Rob had emerged from his coma, and he had recognized her. Things were better than she had feared. Joyous tears wet her cheeks.

"Where are we?"

"Sentara Medical Center. There was an attack at CIRG. You were injured pretty badly."

His brow tensed, but he said nothing. *Did he remember the bombing?*

"You had me worried there. I wasn't sure you'd wake up."

Rob grinned sleepily. "You can't"—he grimaced—"get rid of me that easily."

"The surgeon prescribed painkillers. I'll call a nurse."

She followed the electric cable on the bed and pressed the call button. With some effort, Rob lifted his head to survey his body.

"What's the damage?"

"A few broken bones. Nothing that won't heal."

Rob rested his head on the pillow. "Did the director approve our budget?"

Claire hesitated, then opted for the truth. "The bomb went off during the meeting. Director Warren didn't survive."

"Geez. Is Alda OK?"

Claire chose her words carefully. "She's alive. Her room is a few doors down."

Rob sighed, then grimaced again. *Where was the nurse?*

"I go get somebody."

"Thanks. I'll just...stay here for now."

She grinned. Rob's sense of humor had survived, too. He'd be fine.

Emergency lights bathed the corridor in a soft glow. The nurses' station stood empty. An eerie silence hung over the ward, punctuated only by the electronic beeping of medical devices. Were the night staff doing their rounds, or had Claire fallen on a gap between shifts?

She drummed her fingers on the counter and looked for a buzzer. Soft footfalls drew her attention to the door of Alda's room. A woman with a jet-black ponytail hurried away, her back receding down a corridor. She had the gray tunic and matching trousers of the housekeeping staff. But the tan-colored tote bag on her shoulder snagged Claire's attention. The hairs on the back of her neck stiffened.

Claire raised her voice. "Excuse me! Can you call a nurse?"

The janitor continued on her way. *Heading home and don't care.*

"Hey! You!"

Claire stepped forward to chase after her but held back. A housekeeper couldn't help her with painkillers. Or had something else held her back—a visceral aversion to the woman? The cleaner seemed *off*. *Her bag.* Two pink circles had decorated the side of the tote, circles with identical raised points at the center. Like nipples. Human nipples. *What a creepy design.*

An electronic wail interrupted her thoughts—the monotone of an ECG flatlining. The blood in her heart chilled. Was Rob all right? She rushed toward his room, but the noise came from further down. Claire followed the sound to Chief Alda's room. The ECG beside the bed wailed, and the display drew an ominous solid line. Claire stared at her heavily bandaged boss but had no idea how to save her.

"Help! Somebody, anybody. I need help here."

Two nurses rushed into the room, a man and a woman. They jostled Claire aside and started CPR on Alda's dying body.

"What happened?" the man asked her.

"I don't know. I went to the nurses' desk and heard the ECG."

The female nurse said, "Please step outside, ma'am."

Claire did as she was told. She stood beside the door and listened.

The man spoke again. "She's not responding. Prep the defibrillator."

Bandages tore, and Claire cringed.

"Clear!"

An electric device whined.

"Clear!"

Another whine.

"Nothing. We'll use the adrenaline."

More footsteps sounded from down the corridor. Two

doctors in blue scrubs ran into Alda's room. A discussion ensued. More desperate attempts at resuscitation. Then silence. A man spoke. "Time of death, one oh seven. Notify the morgue."

Claire froze. Chief Madeleine Alda was dead. And her murderer had slipped through Claire's fingers.

CHAPTER 8

Claire slammed her hand on the counter of the nurses' station Tuesday morning.

"What do you mean, 'No?'"

The morning shift nurse kept her cool. "We cannot release him yet."

Claire counted to ten. *Don't vent your frustration on the hospital staff.* But she'd spent a sleepless night in Rob's hospital room, expecting the assassin to return for him any moment. A gossamer thread of restraint held her sanity together.

"A woman was murdered in this ward last night. We're leaving."

The nurse spoke slowly, as though Claire was an imbecile. "Your fiancé just emerged from a coma. He needs to stay a few more days for observation."

"But his life is in danger."

The nurse smiled sweetly. "I'll call security and see what they can do."

"Thank you! Call the local police department while you're at it and report a homicide."

Claire regretted declining Sally's offer last night. She

needed a shower and toothpaste. A valium wouldn't hurt either.

A short, middle-aged cleaner with tight blonde curls pushed a housekeeping trolley into Chief Alda's former room. Claire charged at her. "Hey! What do you think you're doing?"

The cleaner frowned. "Cleaning?" She spoke with a heavy Russian accent.

"You can't clean in there. It's a crime scene." Claire turned back to the desk nurse. "Where's security? They need to secure the site until the police arrive."

The nurse's smile froze over. "Please keep your voice down, ma'am. There's no need for the police. No crime was committed here."

"Madeleine Alda is dead, and she wasn't capable of committing suicide."

"Ms. Alda's death was tragic, but considering her injuries, not unlikely."

"She was stable when I saw her yesterday."

"I'm afraid her condition deteriorated rapidly. Please, let our staff handle this."

That reminded Claire. She ran after the housekeeper, who was escaping down a corridor.

"Wait!"

The cleaner halted, and Claire caught up.

"I'm looking for a housekeeper. Mid-twenties. Black hair tied back in a ponytail. Tanned skin. She had a bag..." Claire stopped herself. The tote's design was in bad taste but couldn't be actual human skin. If Claire blabbered about nipples on fashion accessories, the nurses would detain *her* for observation, too.

The Russian woman shook her head. "Don't know. There are many girls."

"Special Agent Wolfe?"

A short, plump man with a plain brown suit and thinning ash-brown hair walked toward her. Despite his Middle Eastern features, he spoke with a New York accent.

"Yes?"

"Special Agent Rafiq Massoud." He presented his identity card. "I'm investigating the CIRG incident. Can we talk?"

Dr. Sally Fleischer had mentioned the investigator yesterday evening. *Is he here about Alda's murder?*

"Yes. Of course. I'm glad you're here. I need to speak with you."

"Great." He pointed to Alda's room. "How about in there?"

"That's Chief Alda's room. She died last night."

"Yes, I know. I was sorry to hear about that."

"We need a forensics team to process the crime scene."

He wrinkled his brow. "I wasn't aware that her death involved foul play. I understand she was severely burned and lost a leg."

Claire swallowed her frustration and repeated herself. "Chief Alda was in stable condition yesterday. In the middle of the night, she went into cardiac arrest."

"There's nothing suspicious about that. The trauma she suffered—"

"I saw someone by her room just before she flatlined."

He raised his eyebrows. "You were here last night?"

"I spent the night. My fiancé, Robert Cline, is two rooms down. He was in a coma."

"How is he now?"

"Much better. He made it to the bathroom on crutches. But he can't stay here without protection."

Massoud narrowed his eyes. "Why not?"

Claire fought the urge to yell again. Had he understood a word of what she'd said?

"They came here to finish off Chief Alda. Rob might be a target, too."

Massoud scratched his chin. "Finish her off? You think your unit chief was the target of the bombing, too?"

"I didn't, at first. But now that seems like a possibility."

Massoud smirked. "And Director Warren was—what— collateral damage? No offense, Agent Wolfe, but why would anyone target the BAU?"

That was an excellent question. Claire hadn't developed the theory that far. Her anxious, sleep-deprived brain was barely functioning.

The investigator continued. "The attack at CIRG required the coordination of multiple specialized resources to acquire and plant the explosives. This was not the work of a serial killer with a grudge against forensic profilers. You were a homicide detective. Surely, you can see that?"

Claire did. Without them understanding the killer's motive, her concerns for Rob's safety sounded like a fever dream triggered by Alda's death. Were they? Either way, Massoud had done his homework. He knew more about Claire than he'd let on. But Claire had more cards up her sleeve, too.

"As I said, I saw the assassin outside Alda's room."

Massoud smiled. "The assassin? The doctors found nothing suspicious about her death."

"It was a woman—mid-twenties with long black hair and dressed in a housekeeping uniform. She must have induced cardiac arrest."

"Or she was a cleaner on her way home?"

Again, Claire pictured the tote bag of human skin but held her tongue. "The autopsy will decide that."

"There's no need for an autopsy. Alda sustained third-degree burns over her entire body. Good luck finding a needle puncture."

Right again. Claire clenched her jaw. "Blood work should be enough."

Massoud sighed. "Tell you what. I'll request a toxicology analysis. OK?"

Claire had no jurisdiction or lab resources. His offer was better than nothing.

She pushed her luck. "And the hospital's CCTV records."

He clenched his jaw but relented. "I'll look into that, too."

"Thank you."

"Now, can we talk?"

He pointed to Alda's room again, and this time Claire complied. Two steps inside, she halted, unwilling to disturb the crime scene more than necessary. Despite the flurry of medical activity in the minutes after Alda's heart attack, trace evidence of the assailant might remain.

Or not. Claire had seen the woman outside Alda's room. But had she been inside? Were Massoud and the nurses right? Had Claire's addled brain turned a lazy housekeeper into an assassin?

From his pocket, Massoud pulled a digital recorder. Claire owned a similar model.

"You don't mind, do you? My memory isn't what it used to be."

"Not at all."

He hit the Record button. "I understand you started work at the BAU last week?"

"Yes."

"But you took yesterday off, despite the meeting with the director?"

"The meeting was supposed to be today. The director moved it up on short notice. I had an event in Newburgh, Massachusetts."

"What kind of event?"

"A farewell party at my former police department."

"Where you worked as a homicide detective?"

"Yes. Have you spoken with Agent Cline? He was right outside the conference room at the time of the explosion."

"He's next on my list. Why did you join the FBI?"

"Agent Cline invited me to join his new program at the BAU."

"Was this before or after he proposed?"

Claire smiled. "Before."

She told him about meeting Rob when he'd come to Newburgh to consult on multiple homicides.

"How did Chief Alda feel about the meeting with the director?"

"I didn't discuss that with her. But we needed him to approve our unit's budget extension. The meeting was important to her."

"Why the extra budget?"

"A new program requires more funds."

"And what is this new program about?"

Claire sensed that Massoud already knew the answers. Claire had conducted dozens of interviews. Investigators used open-ended and seemingly simple questions to create rapport and paint the background scenery in broad strokes. The information offered in unguarded responses often generated useful new leads. But Massoud's line of questioning unsettled Claire. Tom Brown's words replayed in her mind. *They knew when and where the director would be.* Someone within the FBI had assisted the attackers, knowingly or not. Did Massoud consider her a suspect?

"Crime prevention. We're treating juvenile offenders who display psychopathic tendencies."

He raised his eyebrows again. "You think you can cure psychopathy?"

"Cure is a strong word. Manage. Psychological studies on adults support the idea, and teenagers should be far more receptive."

He shook his head in disbelief and pocketed his recorder. Had her description of YARI destroyed her credibility?

Claire yearned for new information about the bombing. "I'd be happy to join your investigation."

"Thank you for your offer, Agent Wolfe, but a BAU representative is already consulting on the case."

"Yes, I know. Dr. Fleischer is an excellent forensic psychiatrist. She consulted on our cases in Newburgh."

"Great. So you know the case is in good hands."

Claire wanted to point out that, unlike Dr. Fleischer, she was also an experienced homicide detective. But questioning Sally's role might get them both dropped from the investigation.

Massoud interpreted her silence as acceptance. "I'll speak with Agent Cline now."

"I'll walk you to him." Claire would beg for scraps if she had to.

"No need. I'll speak with him alone. If you don't mind."

"Of course not."

Agent Massoud left the room. Claire followed him out and lingered in the corridor. Massoud hadn't shared a drop of new information. He had blocked her attempts to insert herself into the investigation, too. But, like the nurses, he was just doing his job. *You're no longer a homicide detective, Claire. This isn't your case.* She'd have to get used to that.

A gray-haired man in a navy uniform spoke with the duty nurse at her station. She eyed Claire. The uniform followed her gaze. From their sour expressions, the staff of Sentara Medical would be glad to see the back of Claire.

The man walked over to Claire and smiled warmly. "Ms. Wolfe?"

"Special Agent." Claire hoped her title carried weight in his mind.

He offered his hand. "Jim Davidson. Director of Support Services at Sentara. I understand you have concerns about your fiancé's safety?"

Claire sighed. "Yes."

Her chat with Agent Massoud had formed cracks in her conviction about the dangers Rob faced in the hospital. But the medical center had finally responded to her protests, and she had better follow through. She told the security manager about the cleaner she had seen at Alda's room immediately before her death.

"Would you like to review photos of our housekeeping staff? Once we identify the employee, I'm sure we'll be able to set your mind at ease."

His openness surprised her. "Yes, I'd like that."

"This way."

She followed him to the nurses' station. He stepped behind the counter and, with an apology, displaced the nurse from the computer terminal. He logged on to a hospital management interface. Claire pulled up another wheeled desk chair and studied the rows of profile photographs on the screen.

Jim moved the computer mouse and set the Department filter to Maintenance. "These are our housekeeping employees. Do any of them look familiar?"

Claire scanned the faces.

He shifted sideways to give her space. "Take your time."

Claire rolled closer and grasped the computer mouse. She clicked Next to view the second page of results. None of the employees had the assassin's silken dark hair and tanned skin. Claire hadn't seen the cleaner head-on. Her ethnicity hovered somewhere between Hispanic and Asian. Did she have mixed ancestry?

Three pages later, Claire reached the end of the list.

"She's not here."

"Are you sure? Would you like to meet with our staff in person?"

The assassin's absence from the housekeeper list confirmed Claire's earlier hunch and filled the cracks in her resolve.

"She isn't a hospital employee, only dressed like one. Jim, Agent Cline needs twenty-four-hour protection."

"Our security staff monitor the entire facility. But they're not bodyguards. You're welcome to provide your own security detail. Perhaps the FBI or Prince William County Police Department will allocate the resources—if they share your concerns?"

A film of patronizing doubt coated his words. Had he spoken with Massoud? Did he know Claire had no backing from the FBI?

She forced a civil smile. "Never mind. I'll handle this myself."

"Can I help you with anything else?"

"I doubt it."

He ushered her out of the nurses' station, wished her a pleasant day, and walked off. The manager had experience deflecting the stubborn demands of anxious relatives. But he'd left her feeling helpless and exposed.

Claire dialed Tom's number. The call cut to voicemail. The BAU was a mess. Like Massoud, the local police department would treat her suspicions with skepticism. She had to conduct her own investigation.

A young doctor strolled past the nurses' desk.

Claire blocked his path. "Excuse me, Doctor. What substances induce cardiac arrest?"

His eyes narrowed with bemused curiosity at the random pop quiz.

"Um. Cocaine and methamphetamines are known to—"

Claire raised her hand. "Not narcotics. Something along the lines of lethal injection."

"Oh." He scratched his head. "Potassium chloride is what they use on death row but only after anesthetizing the inmate. It's very painful."

"Is it injected intravenously?"

"Yeah."

"How long before it takes effect?"

"About a minute."

"I see."

Alda's ECG had flatlined moments after the assassin had left the room. Either the killer had lingered by her bedside for some reason, or the poison worked faster than potassium chloride.

The doctor looked around the ward, no doubt searching for a hidden camera crew. "Why do you ask?"

"No reason. Thanks."

She returned to Alda's room. Claire had to double as a forensics team, too. Lengths of torn bandages lay on the floor along with the plastic covers of surgical needles and discarded ECG pads. Tall stands held electronic medical devices, their displays blank.

A half-empty IV bag hung on a portable metal hook. The liquid within the transparent plastic had a murky hue. Claire dropped to her haunches and peered at the short plastic finger that protruded from the bottom of the bag. Her breathing accelerated. *Bingo.*

Two minutes later, Claire pushed a wheelchair into Rob's room. Rob sat in bed and spoke to Agent Massoud. Both turned to her with surprised expressions.

Claire grinned. "Are you done?"

Massoud pocketed his recorder. "Just finished."

"Good." She tossed a white paper bag onto the bed.

The FBI investigator peeked at the half-empty IV within. "What's this?"

"Alda's IV. There's a needle hole in the injection port. Get your toxicologist to analyze the contents. If I'm right, we'll find traces of whatever killed her."

She turned to Rob. "We're going home."

CHAPTER 9

Dr. Sally Fleischer marched down a CIRG hallway Tuesday afternoon. A conviction propelled her toward her destination. A conviction and guilt. Chief Madeleine Alda had been in stable condition last night. This morning, she was dead. And it was Sally's fault.

Sally had held the bomb's metal plate in her hands. She had seen the symbol. But she'd said nothing. Had she shared her insight with Massoud or Claire, Madeleine Alda might still be alive.

She knocked on the door with no name plate. Massoud and his team of CID investigators had set up shop in the vacant office. The FBI had empowered Sally to represent the BAU in the investigation, and today she'd fulfill her duty both to the Bureau and, belatedly, to Chief Alda. But that wouldn't be easy. The folder in her hand contained a different kind of bombshell.

"Come in," Massoud called.

He and two younger agents leaned over a desk in the center of the room. Tables lined the walls. Sealed evidence bags contained shrapnel and other artifacts of the case.

Massoud straightened. "Dr. Fleischer, glad to see you."

The disappointment in his voice and irritation on his face betrayed his true feelings. Had he hoped she'd keep her distance after their cold interaction yesterday? He glanced at the folder in her hand and seemed to realize he wouldn't be able to brush her off quickly.

The investigator grinned ironically. "I'd offer you a chair, but we don't have any. CIRG likes to keep us on our feet."

The two aides chuckled.

He jerked his head at them. "Give us the room."

The agents stepped outside and closed the door.

Sally braced for Massoud's inevitable volley of doubt and derision. The chevron marking and Alda's sudden death could mean only one thing. Sally would remain silent no longer.

She got to the point. "The bombing isn't what you think."

Massoud frowned as though her declaration had impressed him. "Let me guess. It was an electrical fault."

She ignored his sarcasm. "What if Director Warren wasn't the primary target?"

Massoud snorted. "Not you, too."

"What do you mean?"

"I spoke with your colleague, Agent Wolfe, this morning. She seems to think Director Warren was in the wrong place at the wrong time. Unit Chief Alda was the real target. When the bomb didn't eliminate her, an assassin visited her hospital room to finish the job."

The news strengthened Sally's resolve. Claire had come to the same conclusion. The theory wasn't a figment of her imagination.

"I know this is counterintuitive, Agent Massoud, but we need to consider the possibility."

"Do you know what Carl Sagan said about extraterrestrial life? 'Extraordinary claims require extraordinary evidence.'"

Sally dropped her folder on the table. "I should warn you,

these images are very explicit."

Massoud opened the cover and paged through the crime scene photos: The face of a teenage girl, bludgeoned beyond recognition; letters carved into the flesh of a dead woman's back.

Sally pointed. "Note the broken A. Like the chopping marks on the victim's face, they match the symbol on the bomb's casing."

Massoud eyed her with dark interest. She'd gotten his attention.

"What does it mean?"

"The symbol represents Apex, a criminal organization we exposed in Newburgh, Massachusetts. The group was responsible for over two dozen murders, mostly paid assassinations. They used knowledge of forensic and behavioral sciences to disguise the murders as the work of isolated serial killers."

Massoud grunted. He hadn't expected her to provide solid evidence. But had she won him over?

Sally continued. "We thought we'd caught the last remaining Apex operative a year ago. It seems we were wrong."

"Did they use arson?"

"Not as far as we know."

Massoud traced the broken A with his finger. "Why leave a calling card?"

"I don't know. But they do."

Massoud scratched the stubble on his jaw. "It's a stretch. The detonation could have punched those lines into the metal plate. And why would a Massachusetts hit squad bomb the FBI in Quantico?"

"We've connected them to homicides in New York state, Connecticut, and New Hampshire. They operated across state lines. But I don't think yesterday's attack was a regular assassination."

Massoud blinked at her. "I won't even try to guess."

Sally inhaled sharply. She'd reached the most speculative link in her chain of logic.

"Chief Alda was about to launch a new BAU program."

Massoud sniggered. "The young psychopath program. Agent Wolfe told me about it."

Sally corrected him. "The Youth At Risk Initiative. Apex enlisted young offenders by posing as FBI agents. Now, we've taken a page out of their book. Our program is a direct threat to their recruitment strategy."

Massoud raised his eyebrows. "Assuming Apex still exists."

She placed her hands on her hips. "Correct."

"Remember that saying about extraordinary claims?"

"Agent Massoud, the marking on the—"

He raised his hand for her to stop. "Seeing that we're playing show-and-tell, let me share something with you."

He walked up to the corkboard. Lines of colored string connected a network of mugshots, sticky notes, and crime scene photographs.

Massoud pointed at the mugshot in the center. "Allow me to introduce Niccolo 'Nicky' Moretti, the head of the Moretti drug cartel in Washington. The bearded gentleman beside him is Stefano Bruno, a former henchman. We discovered his charred remains at a warehouse outside the capital that went up in flames two weeks ago, along with three college kids, apparently small-time dealers on campus. The bomb seems to have detonated accidentally, killing the four goons and burning a sizable amount of cash and crack cocaine."

Sally remembered the warehouse explosion well. The shock wave had shaken her during Rob and Claire's engagement party in Tom Brown's backyard. The papers hadn't mentioned large sums of money or drugs at the scene.

His hand shifted to a stapled set of papers. "Exhibit B is the chemical analysis of the residue we gathered at the CIRG crime scene. The RDX in the plastic explosives wasn't created by known manufacturers in the United States or the United Kingdom. We know this because, like the residue we found at the warehouse, the compound had no coatings or additives. This also made the explosive extra sensitive. Stefano Bruno and his young friends found that out the hard way."

Sally said, "The explosives at CIRG match those of the warehouse?"

"Exactly. You can see the picture that emerges from all this. Director Warren proposed new legislation against organized crime. Nicky Moretti felt the heat. He upgraded his arsenal by developing powerful explosives in-house. Then, he used his new weaponry to send a clear message to the FBI. 'If you mess with us, we'll get you.' Ever hear of Occam's Razor, Doc? 'The simplest explanation is usually the correct one.' There's no need to resurrect a serial killer hit squad."

He'd presented a cogent argument, but Sally wasn't ready to back down.

"Don't write off Apex. We made that mistake before, and as a result, innocent people died."

"Fine. I'll keep an open mind." He walked over to a table and patted a paper evidence bag. "Chief Alda's IV bag. Agent Wolfe claims her mystery lady poisoned your boss. Our pathologist will have a look, just in case. We have the budget, so I can afford to be generous. I'm not the bad guy here. OK?"

Sally nodded. Then she remembered her pledge to Claire.

"I'd like a copy of the case files. The warehouse explosion, too."

"Your wish is my command. But do me a favor, Doc. Don't share them with Agent Wolfe. The media is already spouting conspiracy theories. We don't need more."

CHAPTER 10

The killer watched from the shadows that afternoon. The side mirror of her car reflected a two-level home on a tree-lined suburban street. *One target down, one to go.* Or was that two?

Last night, she'd been reckless. A woman had spotted her leaving Alda's room and confronted her. The killer had fled. Now a question chewed on her peace of mind. *How much did the woman know?*

Had she seen her face? Or spotted her unique tote bag? *How could you be so stupid?* Daddy had warned her to be careful, and sloppy mistakes kindled his rage.

Never anger Daddy. His punishments were swift and lethal. Two years ago, he'd eliminated a clumsy colleague in a staged hit-and-run. The pack had learned the lesson.

That morning, the killer lay awake in her motel bed. Alda's death was supposed to appear natural. If the witness reported her, law enforcement would dig deeper. They'd uncover the true cause of the unit chief's cardiac arrest. The falling dominos might topple Daddy's master plan.

Dawn broke outside her motel window. The killer threw off

her bedsheets and showered. She'd glimpsed the witness for a split second. The woman at the nurses' desk had shoulder-length ebony curls and blue jeans. She was neither a hospital staff member nor a patient. What was she doing in the ward after visiting hours? A patient's obsessive next of kin? Was she related to the injured FBI agents? If so, the likelihood of her interfering increased.

The killer drove to the hospital and waited in the parking lot. She didn't return to the scene of the crime. Bumping into the witness would only compound her error. Instead, she watched the glass doors. Eventually, the nosy visitor would go home to freshen up. The killer had packed food and drinks for a prolonged stakeout. She'd correct her mistake and complete her mission.

Her determination paid off quicker than expected. The woman emerged through the automatic doors pushing a wheelchair. The killer smiled. *Well, what do you know?* The witness was visiting target number two, Special Agent Robert Cline. *How convenient.* She'd kill two birds with one stone.

She snapped photographs of the couple as they climbed into a white Ford Focus. The killer tailed them from a safe distance to a suburban home in North Stafford, twenty minutes away.

A Google photo search of the witness matched images from articles in *The Newburgh Herald*, a local Massachusetts daily. A reporter named Bella Winters had taken a keen interest in Agent Cline's fiancée, and her tabloid coverage provided fascinating reading. The police officer had played a key role in breaking up a clan of serial killers. *That sounds very familiar.* Did Daddy know about this?

In the side mirror, the door of the home opened, and the witness took out the trash. *Hello, Claire.* In sweatpants and a ponytail, the decorated homicide detective looked like a harried housewife. Appearances could be deceiving. With his broken leg, Agent Cline would pose no trouble. But Claire would.

Again, the question gnawed at her. *How much does she know?*

Killing them both would draw unwanted attention to Daddy's plan, and the killer had viewed only the tip of that iceberg. Then again, silencing them now might save future complications.

The world is a dangerous place. Every day, break-ins turned violent, gas leaks exploded. The killer smiled. There was more than one way to skin a cat.

CHAPTER 11

The doorbell rang a second time that evening while Claire was loading the tumble dryer in Rob's basement. *Her* basement. She and Rob were engaged to be married. This was her home, too.

Claire ran upstairs. "Coming!"

She grabbed her wallet and gun from the kitchen table. After the recent bombing and assassination, she'd raised her guard.

Claire put her eye to the peephole, and her heart rate spiked. The delivery woman's jet-black hair flowed to her shoulders. She studied the ground, her baseball cap blocking her face. Had the assassin found her?

The woman raised her head. *No.* The visitor had pasty white skin and was chubbier than the cleaner Claire had spotted outside Alda's hospital room. And she held a box of pizza.

Claire unlocked the door and accepted the delivery. "Thanks."

She balanced the box on her arm and fished in her wallet for a tip.

The woman gaped at Claire's handgun. "Never mind, I'm good." She fled to the street.

Claire called after her. "Wait. It's OK. I'm a cop. I mean, FBI."

But the delivery woman was gone. Firearms had that effect on people. Claire's fumbled explanation didn't help either.

"Whatever."

Claire peered down the street. That morning, an island-blue Subaru Impreza had lingered on the curb a few houses down. Claire knew her cars. Her dad had drilled her on the makes and models when driving around Boston. In the carefree summers of her childhood before Newburgh, she had helped him overhaul a 1957 Chevy Bel Air. The skill had served her well as a police officer, allowing her to identify vehicles at a glance, and yesterday's bombing had heightened her sensitivity to possible intruders. But the Subaru had moved on. *A neighbor's visitor?*

Claire took the pizza upstairs to Rob's bedroom. *Their* bedroom. She had propped pillows behind his back and positioned his broken leg on top of the sheets so he could watch TV in bed.

"Mm, that smells good!"

Claire joined him on the bed and placed the pizza between them. She had showered earlier but already needed another. After helping Rob upstairs and setting him up in their room, she had napped for an hour, loaded the washing machine, vacuumed the floors, and folded their clean clothes. She'd need to get used to being a homemaker and caregiver until Rob recovered his strength. Too exhausted to fix dinner—Rob wore the apron in this household—Claire had ordered pizza, and she devoured her pepperoni slice with gusto. Shower number two could wait.

CNN's "breaking news" regurgitated footage of the CIRG

bombing and interviews with emergency workers at the site. Anchors discussed the highlights of Director Warren's law enforcement career, the respect he'd earned for his zero-tolerance policy toward organized crime, and his rumored plans to run for President of the United States.

Keeping busy with household chores had kept Claire's mind off Agent Massoud's investigation and Chief Alda's death. The Iron Lady was gone. Claire struggled to wrap her head around that sudden finality. Chief Alda had seemed too indomitable and driven to ever leave this world. Her death plunged her unit into deeper uncertainty. Who did Claire and Rob report to now? What were they supposed to do?

Rob licked strands of melted mozzarella from his fingers. "This is the best pizza I've ever tasted."

Claire studied her fiancé. She was enjoying her slice, probably thanks to her ravenous appetite, but the pizza didn't make her list of all-time favorites. Rob's strange comment reminded her of his surprising response to the news of Alda's death. He'd worked closely with Alda for years. But when Claire had told him of her passing, he'd blinked at her and said nothing. People grieved in different ways. Or was Rob in denial?

He turned to her. "And you are the most beautiful woman in the world."

She snorted. With her hair tied up, reeking of sweat, and sporting baggy sweatpants, Claire doubted that assessment.

"I think the nurse was right, Rob. You should have stayed in the hospital for observation. Your head isn't right yet."

He grinned. "I've never felt better." He leaned over, pecked her on the cheek, and groaned. "Except for the pain."

Claire shook her head at his antics and wiped pizza sauce from her cheek.

Rob reached for another slice. "I'm serious. I feel like a new man. A really old man but a new one. It's so good to be alive."

Claire recalled the hours of terror when she feared she'd lost him. "I'm grateful for that, too."

The TV news loop ended, and a live camera feed showed the familiar white dome of the Capitol building.

A talking head explained. "Washington is scrambling to deal with the aftermath of the attack."

A white-haired man in an expensive suit and red tie stepped out of a limo and walked up the stairs of a pillar-fronted public building.

"Senator Arnold Schultz, the head of the oversight committee entrusted with rehabilitating the FBI's management structure, referred to the bombing in his public statement this evening."

Senator Schultz spoke at a podium crowned with microphones, the circular Seal of the United States Senate behind him.

"Our heartfelt sympathies go to the families of the agents lost and to our injured in this brazen and unprecedented attack. Initial findings indicate the involvement of local criminal elements in the bombing at the CIRG yesterday. We will take severe and immediate action, including new legislation, to hold the culprits accountable. The FBI is a core institution for the maintenance of law and order in our great nation. We will review all FBI operations to ensure the Bureau emerges from this dark hour stronger and fitter."

"Fitter?" Claire said. "What is that supposed to mean?"

Rob grunted. "He'll use this opportunity to cut the deadwood and divert budgets to serve his own agenda."

"Where does that leave us?"

Rob exhaled a deep breath. "An untested program with no unit chief to champion its cause? We'll be first on the chopping block."

Claire returned her third slice of pizza to the box. She had lost her appetite.

"And new hires."

If Senator Schultz rendered her position obsolete, Claire would be unemployed. The bomber had torn out the promising blank pages from this new chapter in her life.

Her phone rang. Sally Fleischer was calling. The forensic psychiatrist was also attached to the new program. Did she share their concerns about their future at the FBI?

Claire answered. "Did you see the news?"

"What news?"

"Senator Schultz's oversight committee is going to make the Bureau *fitter*."

"That sounds ominous. Are you at home with Rob?"

"Yeah. Why?"

"I'm on my way. There's something you need to see."

CHAPTER 12

In the kitchen, Claire added a bottle of Jack Daniel's to the tray of soda and drinking glasses, and joined Sally and Rob at the coffee table. Judging by the urgency of Sally's call, they'd need stronger stuff for this meeting.

Rob lay on the living room couch. Sally perched on the edge of the armchair and hugged a thick manilla folder. Her dark, sensitive eyes glimmered. Whatever she'd discovered had shaken her. Claire poured the drinks.

Sally sucked in a lungful of air. "I can't believe she's gone."

"Me neither. It doesn't seem real."

Rob stared at the floor but said nothing.

Sally placed the folder on the table. "If anyone asks, I was never here. Special Agent Massoud told me specifically not to share this with Claire."

Claire handed her a glass of Coke Zero. "What can I say? I make friends quickly."

"It's not personal. He wants to control the narrative, and there's enough speculation in the media."

Rob shifted his outstretched, injured leg. "It's really good to see you, Sally."

She gave Claire a questioning glance. *What's with him?* Claire shrugged.

"Thank you, Rob. It's good to see you, too."

Claire stared at the manila folder. "They're blaming organized crime. Senator Schultz made that clear in his press conference."

Sally nodded. "Massoud has evidence pointing to the Moretti drug cartel." She opened the folder. "The explosives residue at CIRG matches the warehouse bombing outside Washington last week."

Rob perked up. "The blast we heard at Claire's graduation party?"

"Correct. The blast killed a Moretti gang member, Stefano Bruno."

Claire didn't follow. "Why would the cartel blow up their own guy?"

"The detonation seems to have been accidental. Three college kids died as well. Campus dealers, apparently."

Sally handed out printed photos of the charred interior of a warehouse.

"Massoud found large amounts of cash and crack cocaine at the scene."

Rob brightened. "Case closed."

"There's more." Sally withdrew another photo. "Forensics found this among the debris at CIRG."

Claire's heart skipped a beat. Despite the dents and heat damage on the metal plate, she couldn't miss the chevron-shaped indentation.

"Apex?"

Sally nodded.

Rob frowned. "That's impossible. Apex is finished."

Sally shrugged. "Maybe not? At first, I thought the mark might be a coincidence. But after Alda's death, I couldn't ignore it. Claire, you saw the assassin, didn't you?"

"How do you know that?"

"Massoud told me when I mentioned Apex. He thinks we're crazy."

Rob waved a finger at her. "Not crazy, Sally. *Mentally ill.* You're a trained psychiatrist. Use the technical term."

Sally squinted at him, waiting for a punch line or, at least, an explanation for his comment. When none came, she turned to Claire. "What's with him?"

"I don't know. He's become a Pollyanna ever since he woke up from his coma. It's quite annoying."

"That's understandable. Survivors of near-death experiences are usually very positive afterward."

"Hello," Rob said. "I'm here, in the room, so enough of the third-person talk. And no, I didn't see any tunnels or bright lights. I'm just...happy to be alive. I love you guys. Not," he added quickly, "in the same way. But still. You rock. But," he added, "the Apex operatives in Newburgh thought they were the last of the pack. Maybe they're right?"

Claire wanted to believe that, too. But her gut refused.

"They were foot soldiers. It's possible Bill didn't tell them about the group's other activities."

"OK. Let's assume Apex is still out there. Why strike the director?"

Sally folded her arms. "Maybe he wasn't their target? YARI was about to poach their recruits. Apex targeted Alda to prevent the program from getting off the ground. When she survived the bombing, they assassinated her in the hospital."

Claire swore under her breath. Her premonitions had not failed her. All roads led back to Apex.

Sally observed her with her dark, empathic eyes. "Welcome to Samarra."

"Samarra?"

Claire glanced at Rob for a hint, but he shrugged.

Sally explained. "'The Appointment in Samarra.' It's an old Babylonian myth, popularized by W. Somerset Maugham. The servant of a merchant in Baghdad returned from the market in a panic. 'Death appeared to me in the guise of a woman and made threatening gestures.' The servant borrowed a horse from the merchant and fled to Samarra. The next day, the merchant encountered Death in the market. He asked why she'd threatened his servant. 'I didn't threaten him. But I was surprised to see him here. I have an appointment with him tomorrow in Samarra.'"

Claire smiled grimly. Sally had read her thoughts. Claire had fled Newburgh only to meet Apex in Quantico. Death, in the guise of a woman. *A woman with a tote bag of human skin.* A chill traced her spine, and Claire rubbed her arms. *No, probably not human skin.* But the choice of that creepy pattern still attested to a twisted mind.

Sally handed Claire the folder. "We'll need more evidence to convince Massoud. Alda's IV bag is a start, but we'll need more."

Claire paged through the folder. Sally had copied the FBI's file on the warehouse explosion, too.

"Did the Apex sign appear at the warehouse?"

"Not as far as I can tell."

"That makes sense if the detonation was an accident."

Rob grunted. "Hold on. Moretti produced the explosives, and Apex bombed the FBI? Are they working together?"

He'd raised a valid point.

Sally said, "Maybe the cartel is a branch of Apex?"

Claire chewed her lip. "I don't know. Apex worked under the radar. A drug cartel seems too high-profile."

She searched her memories of the Apex murders in Newburgh for hints of the connection. Had her father, William

Wolfe, known about the Moretti branch? If so, why had he kept his accomplices in the dark? The solution burst in her mind like fireworks.

"That's it! They're separate."

Rob and Sally watched her expectantly, so she explained.

"That's why they used the chevrons. Apex marked their crimes because the pack is composed of isolated cells. The symbol prevents one cell from interfering with the operations of another."

Sally's eyes sparkled. "The sign is simple enough to be go unnoticed unless you know what to look for. But why would one cell interfere..."

Her eyes widened.

Rob answered. "Apex tried to infiltrate Newburgh PD. They might have operatives in other law enforcement agencies."

The deduction dovetailed with Tom's words at the hospital. *The bomber knew exactly where and when to plant their explosives. They had access to the CIRG building.*

Claire put it all together. "The chevron tells their operatives which crimes to cover up."

Her hands trembled. Rob and Sally's horrified expressions reflected her own troubled conclusion. *Was the bomber one of their own—an Apex mole in the FBI?*

Claire closed the folder. "This has to stay in this room."

Sally nodded gravely. "Until we find extraordinary proof. Massoud won't settle for less."

"Then that's what we'll do."

Rob raised his drink. "For Alda."

They clinked their glasses together. "For Alda."

Rob drained his soda. "On the bright side, if the Apex branches are isolated, the assassin won't know we destroyed their sister cell in Newburgh. Alda was YARI's sponsor in the Bureau. The rest of us won't be on Apex's radar."

Claire's anxiety levels spiked. Rob's assessment of the threat was very optimistic.

"Let's hope so. Otherwise, they won't stop with Chief Alda. We'll be next."

CHAPTER 13

The stranger in the living room crouched so he could speak eye to eye with Karla. He held a gift box, its red wrapping covered in white teddy bears.

"I got you something."

Karla stared at him. Her hair, still damp from her bath, dripped onto her pajamas. She never received presents, and her mother had warned her against talking to strangers.

He smiled, and his cheeks dimpled. "Go on. It's OK. You can trust me."

Mom stood beside him and smiled. "It's OK, sweetie."

Karla took the box. It felt light. The mysterious contents rattled inside as they shifted.

The stranger grinned. "Go on, open it."

She tore the wrapping. The see-through packaging housed a tall plastic doll. Her shiny dark hair flowed to the leafy hem of her short green dress.

Karla jumped for joy. "It's a Barbie!"

The man winked. "Not just any Barbie, sugar. It's a Pocahontas."

Mom's smile faltered. A girl in Karla's class had called her Pocahontas, and the word had sounded mean. Mom had told her to ignore *the girl. She was just jealous. But that day Karla had learned she was different from the other kids. She'd always be different.*

The man chuckled. "A Pocahontas for our little Pocahontas." He didn't seem to think the word was bad.

Mom used her serious voice on her. "What do we say to Derek?"

"Thank you."

He smiled. "You're welcome, Karla. C'mon, give me a hug."

Karla did. Derek wasn't like her father. Dad had the tanned skin and slanted eyes of Karla and her mom, but he'd smelled bad and slept on the couch all day. One evening, he gave Mom a black eye, and Karla never saw him again. Derek smelled of flowers. He was a good man.

Derek rose to his full height and put his arm around Mom's waist. "I'm your mommy's boyfriend. She's my squaw."

He laughed again, but worry lines creased Mom's forehead.

"Are you sure you're OK with this?" she said.

"One hundred percent, babe. I love kids. And we'll be spending lots of time together. We should get to know each other."

Mom nodded, then frowned at Karla. "I have to work late tonight. Be a good girl and listen to Derek while I'm gone. OK?"

Karla promised, and Mom kissed her good night.

Derek let her stay up late to play with her new Barbie on the rug. He flopped on the couch, sipped a beer, and watched her.

"It's just you and me, Pocahontas."

His tone had changed. He seemed lost in thought. Karla focused on her Barbie.

"I can buy you more clothes for your Barbie. For you, too. Would you like that?"

Karla nodded.

Derek grunted. "Let's play a game."

Pocahontas told Derek to do things, and Karla had to do them, too. Strange, secret things. Karla didn't like this game, but she had to obey.

"Remember what Mommy said. Be a good girl and listen to Derek. *You don't want to make Mommy angry, do you?"*

Karla was trapped. A part of her ran away and observed the scene from the corner of the ceiling. She curled up in that safe place and shut out the pain and fear.

Tonight, she learned something, too. Derek was not a good man.

CHAPTER 14

Wednesday morning, Claire joined the long line of cars entering the FBI Academy grounds. Police officers with semi-automatic rifles checked the occupants' credentials at the gates. Specialists swept the undersides of the vehicles with explosives detectors while K9 handlers and their Labradors looked on. The FBI wasn't the same invulnerable institution Claire had known last week. She left her white Ford Focus in the large parking lot and headed for the main building. The rows of vehicles radiated distrust. *Did Chief Alda's murderer park here, too?*

Claire climbed the steps, passed under the triangular facade with the words FBI Academy, and waited for the physical security inspection.

The 547 acre campus housed the various units of the National Center for the Analysis of Violent Crime, a division within CIRG. Agents presented their identification cards and stepped through metal detectors. Their tense expressions mirrored Claire's inner edginess. Two days ago, the director and a handful of senior agents had lost their lives on the academy's grounds. *Who knows what today will bring?*

"Claire!"

She spun around. A freckled man with a mop of red curls grinned at her.

"Hey, Corey."

Corey Angel had graduated from the FBI Academy with Claire. The chemical engineer was about her age, and circumstances always seemed to throw them together.

He eyed the line for the inspection. "I see they've beefed up security. I stayed home yesterday." He lowered his voice. "I felt the shock wave from two floors down. Did you?"

"I wasn't here on Monday."

"Just as well. They evacuated the whole campus. I think they were expecting a second bomb. It was crazy."

"Yeah, I heard."

Claire said nothing about Rob. Her suspicions about an Apex mole had tightened her lips.

The line advanced. A woman with a beige business suit and long, dark hair presented her card to the security guard. She reminded Claire of the assassin.

Corey brightened. "I got into the BAU."

Claire kept her eyes on Beige Suit. "Me, too. Which one?"

The FBI's National Center for the Analysis of Violent Crime included five BAUs. Each unit focused on different categories of crime.

"BAU-1. I'm a CAB driver." He chuckled.

"Cab driver?"

"Counterterrorism, arson, and bombings. CAB. I guess my chemistry degree decided it."

Corey became talkative when nervous. He'd babbled nonstop throughout their tactical simulation in Hogan's Alley, and today was no different.

Claire peered around the next in line but couldn't glimpse Beige Suit's face. The guard checked the woman's small green backpack. If she was the assassin, she'd left her human-skin tote at home today.

Claire's brain processed Corey's words. *Bombing.*

"Are you investigating the attack?"

"I wish. Head Office took over. The investigators from Washington spoke with our unit's senior agents, but cooperation is a one-way street."

That sounded like Special Agent Rafiq Massoud.

Corey said, "I'd have preferred to chase serial killers with you in BAU-2."

Beige Suit passed the security check and headed for the elevators. *Which unit does she belong to?*

Claire kept her eyes on her target. "Serial murder is only part of the job now. We're applying our methods to public corruption and white-collar crime, too. I've joined a new program dedicated to crime prevention."

"YARI—the program Agent Cline started?"

Claire glanced at Corey with renewed interest. "Yeah. How do you know that?"

"I met him at your graduation party."

"Right. Sorry, that feels like ages ago."

Beige Suit stepped into the elevator. Claire couldn't see what floor she'd pressed but got a fleeting look at her face. The woman had prominent hooded eyes. She wasn't the assassin. Tracking the killer down wouldn't be easy.

Corey said, "How's he doing, by the way?"

"Rob? Much better."

"Better? What happened to him?"

"He was injured in the bombing."

"Geez. I'm sorry. I didn't know."

"Few people do. But he's OK now."

"Wow. That's crazy. Send my regards. I hope we catch these sons of bitches soon."

"Yeah. We won't know much until the investigation runs its course. If we're still here. Rumor has it, we can expect big changes at the FBI. Let's hope we get to keep our new jobs."

They cleared the security inspection, agreed to have lunch together, and went their separate ways. To Claire's relief, the elevator security sensor accepted her FBI card. Senator Schultz's bean counters hadn't canceled her access yet. She'd better use the time she had left wisely.

She made a detour past the destroyed conference room. The force of the blast had blown the door off its hinges. Forensics and housekeeping had cleaned up well. Only the ruined wall and charred plaster remained of the carnage. The Bureau was back to business as usual. But the psychological scars of the attack would remain for decades.

Claire knocked on the door of the YARI room in the BAU and entered. All three desks stood empty. Sally was shadowing Agent Massoud, and Rob was recovering at home. With an Apex assassin on the loose, Claire had not wanted to leave him unattended, but he'd assured her he'd keep the doors locked. She nudged her computer to life and searched the FBI databases for the names in Sally's file.

Stefano "Stefan" Bruno, the bearded Moretti goon, had served only two months in DC's Central Detention Facility for possessing a half kilo of cocaine. The deal he'd cut with the FBI saved him from serving five years behind bars. He didn't testify against his boss, Nicky Moretti. Apparently, Stefan had reneged on his agreement and returned to his old criminal ways. The warehouse explosion killed him one week after his release. But the circumstances of his death seemed too convenient. Did Moretti learn of Stefan's betrayal? Was the blast an accident or had Moretti whacked the unfaithful henchman? The death of the three college-aged dealers seemed to point to the former explanation.

Claire studied the little available information on the collateral damage. All of the kids were enrolled at DC's American University. Cole Williams, a sophomore with rich black skin, had studied for a BA in Political Science. Liam Wright, a first-year with a military crew cut, had just started a three-year program in Law and Criminology. Tara Patel sported a nose stud and had almost completed her master's degree in Public Policy. An African American, a Caucasian, and an Indian. All hailed from Washington, DC.

Three students. Different ages, ethnicities, and fields of study. How had these seemingly bright kids with promising futures ended up dead with a cartel goon in an abandoned warehouse? Had the promise of easy money lured them to deal drugs? Were they addicts, too?

She searched for their social media accounts but found nothing. No Facebook. No Instagram. Not even TikTok. *That's strange.* Had somebody erased them from cyberspace? The students were ghosts.

Claire called Rob and offered to bring him takeout. He refused, claiming that conquering the staircase would save him hours of physical therapy later. They reached a compromise. Claire ordered him a burger and fries, and Rob agreed to keep his service weapon near at all times.

"And don't open the door for anyone," she added.

"Not even the delivery guy?"

"I'm being serious, smart-ass. Apex might still be out there. We don't know what we're up against."

"I'll dig a moat around the house and fill it with crocodiles."

Claire sighed. His dismissive attitude exasperated her.

"Promise."

"I promise. I'll be careful. You have my word."

CHAPTER 15

R ob opened the front door. "I'm not supposed to let you in."

Tom Brown frowned at him. "Says who?"

"Claire. I promised her I wouldn't take visitors."

Tom snorted. "I warned you. The old ball and chain has imprisoned you—and you haven't even said your vows."

He limped inside, leaning heavily on a walking cane. His left arm hung in a sling.

Rob glanced up and down the street and locked the door. "She's worried I'll be next."

Tom flopped on the couch. "You're too nice, Rob. Nobody would murder you."

Rob hobbled on his crutches. *Should I tell him about Apex?* Last night, Rob had promised Claire and Sally to keep their theory about Apex *in this room.* Technically, he was still in the room. *Smart-ass.* Tom had enough to worry about without Rob entangling him in their unauthorized investigation. Besides, the Apex theory was still highly speculative.

Rob eased onto the armchair. "She's just being overprotective. After Monday, who can blame her?"

Tom nodded. He stared at the empty Burger King wrapper and ketchup-stained plate. "Glad to see your appetite is back." Was that Tom's way of saying he cared?

Rob grinned. "You should have told me you were coming over. I would have saved you some French fries."

"Nah. Junk food will kill you."

The older agent pursed his lips. Underneath the crusty exterior and gallows humor, powerful emotions raged.

"How are you holding up?" Rob asked.

Tom shrugged. "You know." He inhaled deeply. "I didn't know Director Warren. But I can't get over Chief Alda. She seemed so...indestructible."

Rob's cheek twitched. "The Iron Lady."

Tom shook his head in disbelief. "I used to say that when World War Three breaks out and the nukes fall, the only survivors will be cockroaches and Madeleine Alda."

They laughed, longer and harder than the joke merited. Their bodies released the pent-up stress of the violent attack and the disorienting shock of their new reality. Tears dripped from Rob's eyes. The convulsions hurt his broken leg. Slowly, they recovered their composure.

Tom sighed. "It's hard to see a way past this."

Rob nodded. His mind floated on mystifying emotions, too, and he tried to capture that weightless sensation in words.

"The future is a blank page. It's as though we've been given a new lease on life and can change direction."

Tom raised his eyebrows. Did Rob's sentiments sound too religious for the old cynic?

"And what direction will you choose?"

"I don't know. For the past year, YARI has been my baby. But if the Bureau canceled the program tomorrow, it wouldn't bother me so much."

"Really?"

"Yeah. Work doesn't seem so...urgent anymore. Do you know what I mean?"

Tom gazed at him. "Not in the slightest."

They laughed again. The old Tom was back. They would weather this storm.

"Can I get you a drink?"

"Don't bother. I can't take alcohol with the painkillers." He climbed to his feet. "I should get going. If I'm not home soon, Mary will send a posse after me. I'm not even supposed to drive."

Rob saw him out and locked the door. He returned to the couch. His reaction to the trauma seemed to surprise everyone, including himself. But he enjoyed the lingering sense of wonder and possibility. Something good would emerge from the chaos. He was sure of that.

The doorbell rang.

"One second," Rob called. Had Tom forgotten something?

He reached for his crutch and heaved his body upright. Claire's voice rang in his ears. *Don't open the door for anyone.*

OK, OK. Rob peered through the peephole. A woman stood on the welcome mat. A tote bag hung from her shoulder. His skin crawled.

She rang the bell again.

Rob looked around for his sidearm and swore. He'd left his gun in the bedroom, and the thought of struggling up the staircase exhausted him. The visitor seemed harmless. She probably had the wrong address. He'd get rid of her quickly. Rob unlocked the door. *Sorry, Claire.* He'd broken both promises. If Apex didn't kill him, his fiancée would.

CHAPTER 16

Claire met Corey for lunch in the FBI cafeteria. He did most of the talking. Three dead college kids haunted Claire's mind. *Why you?*

Back at her desk, she called Lieutenant Peter Edwards at the DC Metropolitan Police Department's Criminal Investigations Division.

"Don't remind me," Edwards said when Claire asked about the warehouse bombing. "I wish I could forget the smell. Since that crime scene, I can't stomach fried chicken."

"What do we know about the college students?"

"Not much. Small-time dealers. That's it."

"Any priors?"

"No, their records were clean. Seems they broke bad recently. Maybe student loans turned them? It's not as though they had any help from home."

"What do you mean?"

"They came from broken homes and had little contact with their parents. We had trouble locating their next of kin."

Claire pricked up her ears. The psychological profile for

serial killers included absent fathers and distant, critical mothers. But these three had resorted to drug dealing, not murder. "Did you interview their friends on campus?"

"Nah. By the time we notified the University Police, we'd linked the adult victim to the cartel, and the FBI criminal investigator took over the case. Speak with the Special Agent in charge. What was his name? Short guy. Middle Eastern name."

"Massoud?"

"That's him. Rafiq Massoud. He's your man."

Well, what do you know? "Thanks, I'll speak with him. You've helped a lot."

Claire leaned back in her desk chair. Massoud's name cropped up at every step of the way. That wasn't suspicious, not necessarily. He was a senior CID investigator. Based in Washington, DC, he couldn't be the Quantico bomber. But could he be an Apex mole? Was that why he refused to take the pack seriously?

The talk of disadvantaged childhoods had excited her imagination, too. The tote bag with its human nipples rose in her mind again. Was Alda's assassin somehow related to the college kids?

Don't get carried away. The chevron symbol on the bomb casing had primed Claire to see Apex in every passing cloud. Teenage pregnancy and the nation's high divorce rates meant that a quarter of US children were growing up in fatherless homes. That greatly impacted their future poverty, criminality, and mental health but didn't turn them into serial killers. Besides, these three kids had beaten the statistics and reached college. And as for Massoud—he was probably just a jackass.

Claire wrote "FBI Bombing" in the center of a notepad sheet and circled the phrase. She drew lines connecting the blast to other words: Alda; and Warehouse. She connected the latter to "Moretti" and "Students." Then, she wrote "Apex" in a bubble and scrawled large question marks over the lines connecting the pack to "FBI Bombing" and "Moretti." Did Apex belong in this mind map?

She had to consider alternative explanations. Apex might have no connection to Moretti. Maybe both criminal groups sourced their C4 from the same supplier? Claire took another step in that direction. Could Alda's death be unrelated to the bombing? Had an opportunistic killer preyed on her in the hospital? The serial killer literature Claire had studied for the BAU mentioned Hedonistic/Thrill killers. These nurses and caregivers experienced a rush when they murdered the patients in their charge. Had an "angel of death" killed Alda at random?

Claire exhaled. She was spinning her wheels. Was the Apex resurrection a figment of her and Sally's traumatized imaginations? How could she know for sure? She tapped her pencil on the notepad and reached for her phone.

Chief of Police Charlie Emmerso answered on the second ring. "Claire, how's Rob?"

Emmerso and Jess had called Claire after the attack and expressed their concern for Rob.

"Much better. He's resting at home, and I'm back at work."

She told him about Alda's passing, and he conveyed his condolences.

Claire glanced at the closed door of her room and lowered her voice.

"I need a favor, sir. Dr. Fleischer and I have reason to believe Apex is involved."

"Apex? Are you sure?"

"No. That's why I'm calling. I need to collect more evidence before I approach the FBI investigators."

Emmerso chuckled. "Once a homicide detective, always a homicide detective. How can we help?"

"I'm hoping to find corroboration from the Newburgh Slasher case."

"What do you have in mind?"

"Apex activity in the Washington area."

"Do you want to speak with Norton?"

The name chilled the blood in Claire's veins. *Johnny Norton.* The man had mutilated and murdered four women. He had shot Claire's mother in the back and almost killed Claire, too. Johnny was serving time for his crimes, but Claire had no desire to see his face again.

"No, sir. He seemed to have no knowledge of other Apex cells. But maybe William Wolfe did?"

Emmerso understood what she had in mind. "The Apex laptop?"

"Yes, sir. We analyzed the forensic copy of its hard drive last year, but we didn't know what we were looking for."

"No problem. I'll speak with Captain Washington and see what we can do."

"Thank you, sir. And, sir, can we keep this quiet?"

"That goes without saying."

Claire spent the afternoon scanning the Internet for information on the warehouse explosion. Newspaper articles provided few details about the decedents' personal lives. Where was Bella Winters's invasive reporting when you needed it?

She packed away her secret files and reviewed the list of young candidates for YARI's trial run. Sally and Rob had prepared everything the program needed to open its doors. But without sufficient funding, YARI stood frozen at the start line.

Sunlight dimmed outside her window. Claire bought groceries on her way home. She needed to schedule Rob's physical therapy. His recovery would take time. He'd need to teach Claire to cook.

The more she thought about her Apex theory, the more desperate it sounded. Claire had a dented metal plate and her dubious eyewitness report. The Loch Ness Monster had more going for it. Now she'd roped Chief Emmerso in to her clandestine investigation, too. Massoud wouldn't like that one bit. Claire had better make sure he didn't find out.

She pulled up outside Rob's house and hefted two large brown paper bags from the trunk. A white Toyota Yaris parked ten yards down the curb. Claire hadn't met any of Rob's neighbors. Were they entertaining?

She unlocked the front door. Gloomy silence shrouded the house. A side lamp burned light in the living room, but nobody was there.

"Rob?"

He didn't answer. The smell of gas wafted from the kitchen and triggered her police instincts. Had Rob left the stove on? He was in no shape to cook dinner. Claire stood still and listened. A faint sound reached her ears—metal sliding against a wooden surface. Someone had pulled a knife from the holder on the kitchen counter.

Fear gripped her. Was Rob OK? She should never have left him at home. The assassin had found him, and now Claire had walked right into her trap.

Slowly, she eased the grocery bags onto the credenza, drew her service weapon, and padded forward.

Furtive footfalls carried from the kitchen. Claire hadn't imagined the intruder, who was now moving toward her and wielding a carving knife.

Claire pounced. She rounded the doorway and aimed her weapon at the silhouette's head.

"Stop right there. Hands in the air."

The woman in the kitchen raised her hands. "Don't shoot! Please, don't shoot me."

Her voice was old and fragile. Scared. *Who is she?*

"Drop the knife!"

The old woman did nothing.

"I said, 'Drop the knife.'"

The carving knife clattered to the kitchen tiles. Claire flipped a light switch. The middle-aged intruder gaped at her. Thick makeup hid her age lines, and blonde dye concealed the gray in her straight bob hairstyle. Her wide eyes focused on the gun in terror. This was not Alda's assassin.

Claire kicked the knife away from the stranger. "Who the hell are you? What are you doing here?"

"Who am *I*?" The old woman sounded outraged, as though Claire had broken into *her* home. "Who are *you*?"

A door opened upstairs, and Rob hobbled to the railing. "Claire, you're back."

He sounded casual and relaxed. Couldn't he see what was happening?

"Stay there, Rob. We have a situation."

Rob chuckled. "I see you've met Felicity. I'm sorry, I should have called to tell you."

He knew her name. Claire frowned at him in confusion. "And Felicity is...?"

He gave her a sheepish grin. "My mother."

CHAPTER 17

Special Agent Rafiq Massoud strapped the bulky protective gear over his chest and whispered a prayer. He loved his job. But sometimes he wondered whether he should have listened to his father and joined the family convenience store business instead of the FBI. Wednesday night was one of those times.

The redbrick tenement block in Washington's Ashton Heights suburb looked deceptively ordinary and unthreatening. Rafiq joined the line of officers clad in black vests and helmets with protective visors and entered the building. Unlike him, the SWAT team was armed to the teeth. They encountered no resistance when they filed inside and climbed the stairwell. Outside the cheap wooden door of the suspect's apartment, they regrouped, and Rafiq had no idea what waited within. These might be his last seconds in this life.

Sergeant John Culley, the SWAT commander, nodded at Rafiq, the cue to start the ball rolling. At least, he thought that was Culley. *Here goes.*

Rafiq stepped forward, the search warrant in his hand, and banged on the door.

"Anthony Russo, this is the FBI. Open the door."

He stepped away from the threshold and pressed his back to the wall. His team had tracked sizable orders of formaldehyde and ammonia from two separate suppliers to the apartment's tenant. Mixed correctly, the chemicals could produce hexamine, a key component of RDX, the plastic explosive that had vaporized FBI Director Warren and his unfortunate colleagues. If Tony Russo decided to avoid capture, he might use the closest weapon at hand, and Rafiq had no intention of ending his FBI career as a red smudge on a tenement hallway.

Five seconds passed. If he had climbed out the second-floor window, the SWAT officers outside would have radioed. Tony had either fled his home earlier or he was playing hide-and-seek.

Rafiq knocked on the door a second time and repeated his demands. Still no sound issued from within the apartment.

Sergeant Culley's voice projected from the in-helmet speaker. "Stand back."

Rafiq obeyed. The sergeant waved his hand. Two of his men approached the door with a battering ram. Two swings took the door off its hinges, and the SWAT officers poured in.

Another man spoke. "Target acquired. He won't give us any trouble."

Rafiq relaxed. A K9 officer passed him with his Lab, and Rafiq followed them inside.

"Don't touch anything," he reminded them. "This brand of C4 is extremely sensitive."

Two steps into the apartment, he halted. And he winced. A large plastic bag dangled from the ceiling. The bag contained a man, suspended by his arms. Or what remained of him. Tony Russo's face had bloated but was still recognizable. The same could not be said for the rest of him. Somebody had peeled the skin from his flesh, exposing the dark muscle and white fatty tissue, leaving only his hands, feet, and head untouched. The plastic wrapper had spared his corpse from blowflies and maggots, no doubt so the neighbors wouldn't complain about the smell. A sludge of putrefying organic juices pooled at the bottom of the bag. The corpse must have hung there for at least a few days.

Sergeant Culley studied the corpse. "I guess you should speak with House Bolton."

Rafiq covered his mouth. "What?"

Culley raised his eyebrows at him, as though the answer was obvious. "The flayed man is their sigil. Didn't you see *Game of Thrones*?"

"No, I did not see *Game of Thrones*."

He shook his head with disgust. He never understood why people paid to watch violence and gore for entertainment. Rafiq got enough of that at work, and the carnage didn't amuse him.

He pulled out his phone. "I'll call in Forensics."

Culley snorted. "Tell the ME's office they got a head start on the autopsy."

Rafiq called in his request and pocketed his phone. "I was hoping he'd talk."

"Oh, he talked all right. 'A naked man has few secrets. A flayed man none.'"

"Is that another *Game of Thrones* quote?"

Culley nodded, then considered the butchered man soberly. "Think he was moonlighting for another cartel?"

Rafiq had informed Culley about their target's background during the operational briefing. Tony Russo had manufactured C4, the explosives that had blown up the CIRG building, for the Morettis.

"Maybe? Or they were covering their tracks."

"Really? Seems pretty harsh. To skin him alive?"

"Who said he was alive?" Rafiq pointed. "There are no defensive wounds. No chafing at the wrists. He didn't move a muscle. He was dead by the time they got to work on him. The flaying is a warning to others."

"I hope you're right. For his sake."

"Sergeant!" a SWAT officer called.

They followed the voice to a spare bedroom, which the late Tony Russo had converted into a laboratory, complete with large glass measuring flasks and plastic mixing tanks.

Rafiq's pulse quickened. "Any explosives?"

The K9 handler stroked the dog's head. "Only residue. Seems he moved the C4 out. But he produced it here."

Sergeant Culley whistled. "He could have blown the whole neighborhood to smithereens. Maybe the bastard got what he deserved? All right, Agent Massoud. The site is clear. We're done here."

"Thanks, I'll take things from here."

Like Stefano Bruno, Tony Russo wouldn't testify. A pattern emerged. Nicky Moretti tied up all his loose ends—and loose tongues. He'd taken his war on the Bureau to a whole new level. There was no telling what that monster could do next.

Rafiq called Agent Andrew Riddle, his lead assistant, and caught him up on the raid's outcome.

"Andy, get over here. I want you to double-check every item that Forensics bags. Our witness is dead, and I doubt Moretti left a paper trail. It's all down to forensics, and SWAT has already stomped all over the joint."

"What should I do with the shrink?"

He meant Dr. Sally Fleischer, the BAU quack and Massoud's new shadow. The forensic psychiatrist had become a pain in the ass.

"Bring her along, too. Make sure she gets a good look at the decedent. That'll teach her to follow us around."

Next up, he dialed Brenda, the ME's assistant. She was used to fielding his calls after hours.

"Please give our guy top priority. Check his stomach for swallowed papers, the works. I'm pulling my hair out here, and I don't have much left."

Brenda laughed. People in their line of work needed a sense of humor. "That toxicology analysis you ordered is in."

"Which one?"

"Madeleine Alda, the BAU chief."

"Oh, right." He'd ordered the test to pacify Special Agent Claire Wolfe. "Sorry for wasting your time."

"Don't you want to hear the results?"

Rafiq hesitated. He'd assumed they'd find nothing of interest. But he recognized a leading question when he heard one. He was the king of leading questions.

"What are you waiting for? The suspense is killing me."

She told him.

"No kidding?"

She answered his follow-up questions, too. The results had blindsided him but also provided a juicy new lead.

Brenda said, "We've updated her cause of death. Congratulations, you've landed yourself with another homicide. Good instincts, by the way."

"Just doing my job."

Rafiq thought of the flayed man and Sergeant Culley's speculation about the killer skinning Tony Russo alive, and he shuddered.

"Do me a favor, Brenda. I'll need a toxicology analysis on the new decedent, too."

"No problem."

"Thanks."

He hung up and grunted. Those good instincts weren't his. Claire Wolfe had suspected foul play in Alda's death. The new agent had avoided CIRG the day of the bombing and she'd insisted on sleeping in Alda's ward the night of her murder. Nobody's instincts were that good.

Claire Wolfe, how are you always one step ahead?

CHAPTER 18

C laire folded her arms. "I don't like this, Rob."
They had moved to their bedroom and out of earshot of Rob's estranged mother. In the kitchen, Felicity Cline chopped vegetables with the knife she had wielded at Claire minutes before.

"That woman gaslighted you as a child. She made you doubt your sanity. We don't want her living in our home."

Rob smiled. "You're right. But this is temporary. Just for a few days."

Claire hissed. "That's what she says now. I don't trust her. She's a narcissist."

Rob had told her the stories. His mother had beaten him during her drunken rages, then denied laying a hand on him in the morning. A court order had given Rob's father custody, and Rob had required years of therapy to rebuild his self-confidence.

"I know. But she's changed. She put herself through rehab. And I'm not a child anymore. You don't have to worry."

Claire shook her head. This woman was poisonous. Claire's

gut screamed the truth, and her logical brain scrambled for reasons to support her instincts.

"Why now? Why didn't she come looking for you two years ago or ten?"

"She wanted to reach out earlier but felt ashamed of what she'd done. Then she heard about the bombing at the FBI. After almost losing me, she realized she couldn't delay any longer."

Claire scoffed. "Or she figured you're weak and can't protect yourself. Now she can take advantage of you."

Rob's amused grin said Claire was being overprotective and he loved her for it.

"You won't let that happen."

"Exactly."

Rob huffed. "Maybe you're right and her reasons for being here are entirely selfish. But shouldn't I give her a chance? You made amends with your mother. All I'm asking is to give me the same opportunity before it's too late."

"My mother isn't a narcissist. She was a victim, too."

But doubt had slipped into her voice. He had a point. Claire had longed for Diane's approval all her life despite how she'd treated her. Claire had worked hard to build that bridge. How could she deprive Rob of the same reconciliation with his mother?

Rob seemed to sense the chink in her resolve. "Besides, the timing is perfect. She can help around the house while I'm on the mend. That way, you can go to work without worrying about me."

His mother living in their home gave Claire more reason to worry, but Rob's optimism was difficult to refuse.

She groaned. "Fine. But if she gets back to her old tricks, she's out of here."

"Agreed." He kissed her long and hard. "I'll make it up to you, I promise."

Claire smiled naughtily. "Why didn't you say so?"

She caught Rob up on her day and hit the shower. Claire had never imagined she'd host her future mother-in-law. Rob hadn't even bothered to notify Felicity about their engagement. Not having a mother-in-law had been one of the perks of marrying him.

But Felicity's suspicious timing gnawed on Claire's mind. Rob wasn't himself. Had the bombing impaired his judgment, too? Had she let him talk her into making a terrible mistake?

Claire toweled off and dressed. The scent of chicken soup reached her on the staircase, and her stomach rumbled.

She padded downstairs and into the kitchen. Felicity hummed to herself and stirred the soup. Claire didn't recognize the large steaming pot on the stove. Did her future mother-in-law always travel with a cauldron? Claire wouldn't be surprised if she traveled by broomstick, too.

She scanned the spices and vegetables on the counter. Paprika. Chicken broth. Salt. Pepper. No rat poison. That was a good start. She'd let Felicity taste the food first, just in case.

The soup smelled good. Claire would give her that. Rob must have inherited his cooking talent from his mother. Maybe he was right? Having a woman at home to dote on him for a few days while he healed wasn't a bad idea. Had their dramatic first meeting prejudiced Claire against her?

Rob's mother spoke without turning her head. "So you're the girlfriend?"

The girlfriend. Her tone implied Claire was a temporary and undesirable element in her son's life. Maybe Claire was reading too much into the words? She swallowed her annoyance and gave her future mother-in-law the benefit of the doubt.

"Fiancée."

Felicity scoffed. "Rob never mentioned you to me. Isn't that strange?"

Rehab hadn't cured the woman's abrasive personality. *Just a few days. You won't have to put up with her for long.*

"When was the last time you spoke?"

Felicity didn't answer the question. They both knew the answer. She hadn't spoken with Rob in years.

"Do you have an engagement ring?"

Was she asking for proof?

"Yes."

"But you're not wearing it. Don't you like it?"

Claire's shoulders tensed. Was she cataloguing her jewelry in order to steal it or searching for cracks in Claire's relationship with Rob?

"I don't wear rings."

Felicity grunted with satisfaction. "I see. I'm sure it's lovely. Rob has excellent taste. Well, in most things."

Strike three. Claire wouldn't let that pass. "But not his taste in women?"

"Your words, dear, not mine."

The woman had barely moved in and already she was plotting to get rid of her son's fiancée. Claire made her intentions clear, too.

"I think these few days will pass quickly. I'm sure you're eager to return home."

Felicity fixed her with a piercing glance. "Meanwhile, I look forward to getting to know you *very* well." Despite the smile, her words were a threat. "After all, we both want what's best for Rob. Don't we?"

CHAPTER 19

K arla padlocked the door of her locker in the high school corridor.

"Isn't he perfect?" Alice told Bethany.

Karla followed her friends' line of sight. Down the hallway, four seniors with Timberland shirts and Nike sneakers chatted with smug grins on their arrogant faces.

"Which one?"

Alice scowled at Karla as if to say she should get with the program.

"Brad Wood."

"The quarterback?"

Bethany rolled her eyes. "Duh."

Brad flicked his blow-dried blond hair and smiled his self-absorbed smile.

Alice pressed her history workbook to her chest. "One day, I'll be Mrs. Wood."

Bethany sighed.

Karla held her tongue. She should count herself lucky. The girls didn't always bother to answer her questions. Mostly, they spoke as though she wasn't even there.

At first, their invitation to hang out had excited Karla. She had always been a loner, wary of other kids and their questions about her family. But Alice and Bethany showed no interest in Karla or her life. Her excitement faded quickly. They weren't real friends. They only included her in their clique so they could brag about their poor Native American girlfriend. Each day, she found their company more excruciating. They were only interested in clothes and boys. Karla had no money for clothes and zero interest in boys.

Men are dicks. *Derek, her stepfather, had proved that point early on. Only one thing interested men, and they took it by all means necessary. Over the years, Karla's Barbie collection had grown, but her faith in mankind died.*

The boys at school were no different. They explored her body with their eyes whenever they thought she wasn't looking. The quarterback chuckled and high-fived a friend. Their alpha male posturing made her want to puke.

"I don't see why he's such a big deal." Karla hadn't meant to say that out loud.

Alice turned on her. "Why do you have to be such a bitch?"

Bethany didn't bother addressing Karla directly. "Yeah. And she never smiles either. She doesn't know how."

They laughed at her. The attack surprised Karla but didn't hurt her. Nothing hurt her anymore. She had locked away the part of her that felt pain long ago and thrown away the key. For the record, Karla could smile. She just never had a reason.

Alice turned to go. "Have a nice life, ungrateful bitch."

Bethany aped her friend. "Yeah. Later, loser. You're out."

Karla shrugged. "Whatever."

They strutted off. Good riddance. *When they passed the rich seniors, Alice said something. They all stared at Karla and laughed.* What had she told them? Another unimaginative racial slur? *Alice smirked at Karla and strolled off, the damage done. But the pack of boys didn't walk away—they sauntered toward her.*

Karla's muscles tensed. This wasn't fear. Karla hadn't registered that emotion since elementary school. But her reptile brain recognized the boy's sneers, and her body prepared for fight or flight.

Brad led the offensive, flanked by a curly-haired brute and a redhead.

"Hey, Pocahottie."

Karla had heard that one before. He wasn't hitting on her, just making fun of her. "She's been crushing on you," Alice must have said. "Poor thing doesn't realize you're out of her league."

Karla made no response.

"What's with the long face, Chief?" Curly said.

Redhead sniggered. "Brad, I think she wants to smoke your peace pipe."

They chuckled, but Karla looked them straight in the eye. They had expected a cowering, starstruck sophomore, and their confidence melted under her intense, accusatory gaze.

Brad swallowed. "Lay off her, guys. Give us a minute."

His friends shuffled off.

"I'm sorry about that. We didn't mean any harm."

Brad wasn't a complete jerk. He'd fall into Alice's web eventually. Good luck with that, bud.

"Are we good?"

He was asking Karla to let him off the hook. A racist incident wouldn't reflect well on the school's favorite jock. Karla considered her options. Fight and flight were only two. Men were all the same. Maybe she could use this opportunity to teach Alice a lesson, too?

Karla stepped forward and pressed her hand to his crotch. Brad gasped, and his eyes widened, but he didn't pull away.

She smiled. "Let's go someplace quiet."

CHAPTER 20

A wave of regret washed over Claire, Thursday morning, when she strolled through the campus of the American University in Washington, DC. Students lazed on the sunny lawns and hurried along the cement paths. Claire had planned to go to college. She'd had the grades and the ambition. But her sister's murder had rerouted her life to the police academy and, now, the FBI. As Claire approached thirty, that alternate future drifted further out of reach. Did she yearn for the uncomplicated civilian life she might have enjoyed?

After the hour-long drive from Quantico, Claire was glad to stretch her legs. She headed for the college administration buildings. If she was right, the college's innocent exterior concealed a criminal underbelly that had killed three students.

Claire settled on one of two visitors' chairs in the office of the Special Assistant to the Dean of Students. "Thank you for seeing me on short notice."

Joanne Clark closed the door and sat behind her desk. The administrator's golden-brown skin and colorful, abstract blouses resembled those in her studio photo with her husband and two young children.

"Anything for the FBI."

Claire's conscience twinged. She had no authority to investigate the FBI bombing or the warehouse explosion, and she hadn't claimed any. But her appointment at the college bordered on misrepresentation. If Agent Massoud found out she'd been sniffing around his jurisdiction, he wouldn't look the other way.

Joanne clasped her fingers. "How can I help you, Agent Wolfe?"

"I've been reviewing the warehouse incident in which three of your students died."

The assistant shook her head. "Cole Williams, Tara Patel, and Liam Wright. We were shocked by their sudden passing. Such a tragic, senseless accident."

"Yes. I'd like to find out more about them."

"Agent Massoud already went over their information. Perhaps you should speak with him?"

"I have." Claire winced at the half-truth. She had spoken with Massoud...about related matters. "I want to explore their backgrounds further to help with some unanswered questions."

"We know little about their backgrounds, only what pertained to their academic studies."

"I understand."

"OK, then. Where should we start?"

"Were there any complaints against them?"

"What kind of complaints?"

"Abuse. Fights. Any type of antisocial behavior."

"No. And I would know. All incidents pass through the dean's office."

"Did the three of them belong to clubs or campus organizations?"

"Let's see." The assistant used her computer terminal to

search the college information systems. "Two of them signed up for CSI."

"CSI?"

The words triggered Claire's Apex detectors. The criminal pack had studied the methods of law enforcement to evade apprehension. Did the students' interest in crime scene investigation point to an Apex connection?

Joanne suppressed a smile. "Not that CSI. The Center for Student Involvement is a collection of groups and events run for and by the students." She read from the computer monitor. "Tara Patel was a member of ALPA, a leadership and policy association. Liam Wright signed up for the Debate Society. But, no, the three had no groups in common."

Two leads down, two to go. The dead students had not displayed behavioral issues. They had not associated formally on campus. Sally's FBI file on the warehouse blast had speculated about narcotics-related activity, and their off-campus Drug Dealer Society remained their only shared interest. Claire needed to confirm that theory.

"Did they have drug problems?"

"No. We have a zero-tolerance policy on substance abuse."

"What about financial issues?"

"Not that I'm aware of."

"What about student loans?"

Joanne clicked her mouse button. "No. They all won full scholarships." She pressed a few more keys and grunted. "In fact, a single program sponsored them all—LFI."

"LFI?"

"The Level Field Initiative, a scholarship for disadvantaged students."

"How many other students did the scholarship fund?"

More mouse clicks. "Just them." Joanne made eye contact. "That's an interesting coincidence."

Or no coincidence. "Who runs the scholarship program?"

"We don't have that information." She clicked her computer mouse. "But they have a website."

Joanne swiveled the monitor to face Claire. The site was professionally designed, with images of smiling, ethnic children in billowing, sun-drenched wheat fields. They browsed the internal links. The independent scholarship seemed legitimate but didn't reveal its management team or funding sources.

"Anything else?"

Claire hesitated. The unifying thread she'd discovered undermined the FBI's drug theory. Financial pressures had not pushed the dead students to deal drugs. How then had their charred corpses ended up at the abandoned warehouse?

"Do you mind if I speak with their roommates?"

"No, not at all."

Joanne jotted the details on a square of colored paper and escorted Claire out.

"Send my regards to Agent Massoud."

Claire grinned. "I will."

CHAPTER 21

Special Agent Tom Brown limped toward Alda's old office. He didn't need the walking stick anymore. But if this was to be his last day at the FBI, he'd go out with pizazz.

Tom could read between the lines. Senator Schultz was using the post-bombing pandemonium to make the Bureau "stronger and fitter." His oversight committee would fire older, injured agents like Tom without blinking. The bureaucrats wouldn't understand his key role in the bigger picture or value his decades of experience.

He plodded toward the meeting, a condemned man on his way to the gallows. The walking stick might work in his favor. Worst-case scenario, he'd wallop his executioners over the head.

He paused outside Unit Chief Alda's office. Her corpse had barely cooled, but some asshole had removed her name plate already. Overnight, the Bureau had changed. The attack had not only destroyed lives and damaged property. It had shaken the institution's foundations. Tom stood at the epicenter of that earthquake, and the blame game had begun. Fingers pointed, and heads would roll.

But Tom had a strategy for contending with Senator Schultz's minions. "Gamble" was a more accurate word. Today, either way, he'd find out whether he'd survive the upheaval or start his career over.

He knocked on the door and turned the handle. The man who slouched behind Alda's desk, Special Agent Rafiq Massoud, wasn't a Senate flunky. Massoud had questioned him about the bombing yesterday. The investigator had a reputation for brutal efficiency. Tom swallowed hard. His game plan flew out the window. He'd better choose his words carefully.

"Agent Massoud, I didn't realize I'd be meeting with you today."

"Senator Schultz sends his apologies. He asked me to liaise with you in his stead."

Tom did a double take. "Senator Schultz?" He hadn't expected to meet with the senator, never mind in person. Had Tom misunderstood the meeting's agenda?

Massoud dialed a number on his phone and studied his fingernails. "Yes, sir. I'm with him now." Massoud held out the phone for Tom.

Tom cleared his throat. "Good morning, sir."

"Agent Brown, my apologies for not delivering the news in person, but things in the capital are very dynamic, as you can imagine."

"I understand."

"You've made a good impression at the Bureau and your service record is exemplary."

"Thank you, sir." Not a firing, then. Early retirement?

"I'll cut to the chase. We'd like you to take over this BAU."

"Pardon me, sir?"

"You're the new Unit Chief. Congratulations."

Tom's brain compiled a list of objections to the proposal: The position would remove him from field work; he didn't like pushing papers; he enjoyed the travel and the opportunities that provided. But the senator wasn't making an offer. He had stated a fact. And he didn't wait for Tom's reply.

"You'll get a nice salary bump, too. My office will email the details."

"Thank you, sir."

"And do me one favor, Unit Chief Brown."

"Of course." *Here's the catch.* There was always a catch.

"Assist Agent Massoud with his investigation."

Tom grinned. "That goes without saying, sir."

"Thank you. Again, congratulations."

The call ended, and Tom handed back the phone.

Massoud offered his hand. "Congratulations, Unit Chief Brown."

He vacated the chair behind the desk. Tom's desk. Not the outcome he'd expected, but he'd take it. He hung the walking stick on the edge of the table and tried out his new seat. *Alda would be pissed.*

Massoud cleared his throat. "About the investigation, everything we discuss stays in this room."

"Understood."

Massoud leaned over the desk. "Good. Now, tell me about Claire Wolfe."

CHAPTER 22

Claire climbed the stairs of the All-Gender Housing dormitory. She hadn't intended to burn two hours on the American University grounds. But nobody would miss her at the BAU today, and all three of the dead students had lived on campus. She'd use her downtime to get some answers.

She knocked on the door of the first-floor room, and a red-haired kid with bad skin answered.

"Brett?"

He took in her plain, brown work suit. Did she look like a college staff member?

"Yeah?"

"I'm Claire from the FBI." She presented her ID card. "The dean's office told me how to find you. Do you mind if I ask you a few questions? It's about your old roommate, Liam Wright."

He shoved his hands into his cargo shorts and stepped aside. "Sure. Come in."

Two single beds hugged the walls, separated by wooden closets, plywood desks, and bedside drawers. The air smelled of deodorant and dirty socks. Sci-fi film posters covered one wall: *Alien*; *Avatar*; *Star Trek*; and *Star Wars*.

"That's an impressive collection."

He smiled and stared at his feet. "Thanks."

She pointed at the empty wall above the other bed. "Did somebody come by to pick up Liam's stuff?"

"No. He didn't have much stuff."

"Not into posters?"

"No."

"I'm sorry about Liam. I know it hasn't been that long."

"Two weeks."

"What was he studying?"

"An M.A. in Law and Criminology."

Now that Claire had warmed him up, she probed deeper.

"Did you meet any of his family?"

"No."

"His friends?"

"Liam pretty much kept to himself."

"How would you describe him?"

Brett's lip twitched. Was he uncomfortable finding fault with the dead or was he hesitant to share his information with the FBI?

"He was quiet."

"Quiet?" Claire used mirroring, Rob's hostage negotiation technique. By repeating Brett's last few words, she invited him to elaborate.

"And scary."

"Scary?"

"I don't know. He didn't threaten me or anything. It was his vibe."

"Did he fight with other students?"

"Not that I know."

Claire considered how to approach the next topic without raising his defenses.

"You won't get into any trouble for answering honestly.

What you know might help us understand what happened to him. Did Liam do drugs?"

"No, I never saw him do drugs."

"Did he deal?"

Brett laughed. "Sorry. I just can't imagine him dealing drugs. He was very by-the-book. Never came late to anything."

Claire studied the tidy bed and empty desk. Was Liam straightlaced or secretive? Brett's intuition seemed to have detected something darker.

She pulled two photographs from her bag—profile shots of the other two dead kids.

"Do you know who these are?"

"The other students who died."

Claire spoke their names to jog his memory. "Did you know them?"

"Maybe I saw them around campus? I don't know."

"Did Liam hang out with them?"

"I doubt it. They were in different years and majors. That's weird, isn't it?"

"What is?"

"That they died together."

Claire nodded. "Do you mind if I look around?"

"Go ahead."

She studied Liam's shelves and opened his closets and drawers. Academic books and stationery. Jeans and a worn pair of sneakers. Tidy was an understatement. Liam's living space was sterile. He'd left no trace of a personality or personal life. The belongings might have belonged to an android. Or a spy. *What were you hiding, Liam?*

Claire's phone rang, and the caller ID showed a Newburgh PD number. She answered.

"How is Rob?" Jess asked.

"Better each day. Can I call you back?"

"Sure. I have an update on the Apex laptop."

"That was quick."

Chief Emmerso had followed through on her request, passing the task along via Captain Washington to Claire's former partner.

"A friend of mine works in digital forensics. Well, 'friend' is an exaggeration. Long story short, he resurrected a deleted email thread from five years ago."

Claire's heart skipped a beat. Had Jess found a reference to a Washington branch of Apex?

"Go on."

"The message is very short. The sender seems to have used a burner email account. He told William to delete their emails and move to more secure methods of communication. This must be an early stage of their collaboration."

Claire sighed. The message was too vague to prove anything. Jess had gotten her hopes up.

"Anything else?"

"There's more. The sender address doesn't exist anymore, but the email software stored the alias for the email address. The alias is 'alpha.' As in, 'alpha male.'"

"Hm. That fits the Apex predator theme."

Jess's voice bubbled over with excitement. "This might mean Newburgh wasn't their head office. The Apex leadership resided somewhere else."

Claire digested the information. Jess was right. The name suggested a significant collaborator outside of Newburgh. Although the alias wouldn't satisfy Agent Massoud, the detail strengthened Claire's working theory. The Apex Hydra was larger than anyone had imagined. They had destroyed only one of its heads.

"That makes sense. Thank you, Jess."

"Let me know if you need anything else."

Claire ended the call and stared at the blank wall. She'd only scratched the surface. But she was digging in the right spot.

"Did you say, 'Apex predator?'"

Claire turned to Brett. She had forgotten he was standing there. "Yes. Why?"

"I'm sure it's nothing. But Liam had a tattoo. A capital A, but without the bridge."

Claire's breath caught in her lungs. He had described the Apex symbol. "Can you draw it for me?"

"Sure."

He penciled the shape on a notepad. "It looked sci-fi, so I asked him about it. He said it stood for apex predator. I had completely forgotten about that. But then you said apex predator, and I remembered. Does that mean anything?"

Claire almost exploded with excitement. The tattoo was exactly the connecting detail she'd needed.

She smiled. "Maybe? Can I hold on to that?"

Brett tore the page from the notepad. "Sure."

Claire continued her investigation of the dorm building. She couldn't locate Tara Patel's roommate but struck pay dirt with the third student. Cole Williams had lived the same spartan life as Liam. No friends or family. No sign of drugs or bad behavior. But no tattoos either.

She drove back to Quantico. Massoud was wrong about the warehouse bombing. The college kids weren't insignificant. At least one of them belonged to another Apex cell. Was the pack in league with the drug cartel? Was Nicky Moretti the mysterious Alpha? Or had Apex infiltrated organized crime as they had law enforcement?

A blue Subaru Impreza changed lanes in the rearview mirror. A similar car had roamed the streets of North Stafford, near her house. Was the driver tailing Claire?

Her phone rang on the hands-free, and a Quantico number showed on the screen. Eager to share her discoveries with Sally, she answered.

"Agent Wolfe?" a man said.

Claire recognized the voice. "Agent Massoud. How are you?"

"I tried to reach you at your office and at home."

"Yeah, I had to step out. How can I help?"

"Can we speak—in person?"

Massoud had already interviewed her. What could he want now? Had he heard about Claire's unauthorized investigation?

"Sure. I'll be at work in twenty minutes. Is everything OK?"

"I have new information to share with you. And I think I owe you an apology."

Claire's concerns settled. Massoud wasn't hounding her. He was extending a olive branch. Her day got better by the minute.

"I'm on my way."

CHAPTER 23

Mom was in Karla's bedroom when Karla got home from school. She was shoving her clothes into a suitcase.

"Mom, what are you doing?"

Her mother dumped Karla's leather jacket—the jacket she'd bought with her own money—in the bag and reached for the Levi's.

"Hey! That's my stuff."

Karla grabbed her wrist. Then she noticed the puffy bruise under her mother's eye. That drunk bastard, Derek, had hit her again. Mom sure knew how to choose them.

"I'll kill him."

Mom shook free of her grip. "This isn't about Derek."

Karla doubted that, but she didn't argue. Her mother should have left him years ago, and Karla wasn't going to stop her.

"Where are we going?"

"Not we. Just you."

The earth seemed to fall away beneath Karla's feet. "What? Why?"

"Mr. Sweeney called again. Parents have been complaining. He threatened to call social services. I don't know what else to do. We can't afford therapy, and I won't let some stranger take you away."

Karla swore under her breath. She couldn't care less what her high school principal thought, but this time he'd gotten to Mom.

"Sweeney is a liar. Don't believe a word he says."

"Then where'd you get the money for your phones and your fancy clothes?"

"I told you, Mom. I help kids with their schoolwork and—"

"Bullshit! You almost flunked out, but now you're teaching other kids? Stop lying to me. Mr. Sweeney can't have a whore working in his school."

"Is that what he called me—a whore?"

"The word he used was prostitute."

Word had spread. Karla had seduced Brad, and now he couldn't get enough. Her revenge on Alice had succeeded beyond her wildest expectations and become a reliable source of income. Men are all the same. *But her side hustle couldn't last forever. She knew she'd get busted eventually. But she'd expected a lecture or, at worst, suspension. She never thought Mom would kick her out.*

"You stood up for me, right?"

Mom avoided her eyes.

"Tell me you stood up for me."

"I can't take care of you anymore."

"Like you took care of me until now?"

"What's that supposed to mean?"

"Don't call me a liar. You've lied to yourself for years. You know what Derek did to me. Does *to me.*"

"Don't drag him into this."

Karla scoffed. Her mother was in denial. "Derek raped me from day one."

Shame drained the color from Mom's face.

Karla kept going. "Don't pretend you didn't know. If I'm a whore, you're my pimp."

Mom slapped her, hard. She'd never hit Karla before.

Her mother's lips trembled. "You're leaving—before Derek gets home."

Karla's cheek burned. "Why? Are you afraid of the competition?"

A muscle in her mother's cheek twitched. A tear slipped from her eye. Good. She was sacrificing her daughter to keep her husband.

Mom shut the suitcase. "You need to leave now. I've already made the arrangements."

"What arrangements? Where am I going?"

"To your grandfather."

The words stunned Karla. "What grandfather?"

CHAPTER 24

C laire found Massoud sitting at the central table in his war room. The older investigator studied a document beside two Starbucks cups and a pile of sugar sachets.

He looked up and grinned. "Coffee? The instant stuff in the kitchenette is poison."

Claire laughed. "I know. Newburgh PD spoiled me with freshly ground coffee."

Massoud slid one cup toward her. "We got off to a shaky start. Consider this a peace offering."

Claire accepted the coffee. She welcomed his new attitude. Being on friendly terms would make her job easier. But what had sparked this relationship reboot? Had he uncovered evidence supporting her assassin theory—or of Apex? Would he invite her to join the investigation? The answers seemed to lie in the manila folder on the table before him.

A large corkboard showed photos of Niccolo Moretti, Stefano Bruno, and the three dead college kids along with crime scene photos related to the case. Claire recognized most of the items from the folder Sally had shared, but she pretended to scan the boards with interest. She itched to share her new findings, too, but held back. *Let him show his cards first.*

He nodded at his agents, and they left the room. "Please, sit."

Claire did.

Massoud sipped his coffee. "The toxicology results are in. You were right. Alda didn't die of her wounds. Her IV bag and blood contained traces of a rare pathogen. Any guesses?"

He watched her closely. Was this a test?

Claire shrugged. "I have no idea."

"Curare extract. Small doses disable voluntary muscle control. Large doses prevent the lungs from inflating and cause death by asphyxiation. Madeleine Alda received a large dose."

Massoud sipped his coffee again but kept his eyes on her. The report had vindicated Claire's suspicions. Why did he seem to trust her even less?

"Ever hear of curare before, Claire?"

"No."

"It's an interesting story. The indigenous peoples of Central and Southern America first discovered the plant. Caribbean hunters coated their blow darts with curare when hunting wild animals. But here's the kicker. Curare paralyzes the body but doesn't affect the mind. The animal—or human—remains fully conscious. This bit of trivia became acutely relevant when curare extract turned up in the blood of a victim we discovered yesterday."

"Yesterday? Your lab works fast."

He gazed at her. "The director is dead, Agent Wolfe. Our priorities don't get higher than this. Any guess who the unlucky victim was?"

Why was he asking her? Did he think she was somehow behind these crimes? The coffee wasn't a peace offering. It was a poor attempt at lowering her guard.

Claire folded her arms. "I have no idea."

"I'll enlighten you. The chemical trail led us to the bomb's manufacturer, a chemist working out of his apartment block in Ashton Heights, Washington DC."

He opened the manila folder and extracted a photo. "Meet Anthony Russo."

He slid the photo toward her. One look at the crime scene snapshot curdled the latte in Claire's stomach. The corpse had the bloated face of a decomposing man. From the neck down, his body resembled an abattoir cadaver. Claire didn't hide her disgust.

Massoud watched her intently. "Tony Russo was a chemical engineer and associate of the Moretti cartel. We found traces of the C4 he'd manufactured. Somebody strung him up in his apartment and skinned him alive, thanks to the wonders of curare. Flayed is the word the cool kids use, so I'm told."

"Why would Moretti do that to his chemist?"

Massoud shrugged. "'Dead men tell no tales?' Maybe the hitman had a little fun—or hit woman?"

Claire met his gaze. Was he indulging her report of the female assassin or implying that Claire killed the chemist?

A memory struck Claire so hard, she gasped. "Her bag!"

"Excuse me?"

"The woman I saw at the hospital. The assassin. She had a weird bag on her shoulder. I thought I was imagining things, but now..."

Massoud bunched his eyebrows, clearly unhappy to have lost control of the conversation.

"What bag?"

"A tote. The leather had markings like two nipples. Human nipples."

"Oh, I get it. Like in that movie, what was it called?" Massoud snapped his fingers to conjure the memory. "*The*

Silence of the Lambs. The wacko killed women to skin them and wear their boobs. Does that qualify as cross-dressing?"

"No, not like that."

He chuckled. "C'mon, Claire. There's got to be a serial killer, no? I had a closer look at your time in Newburgh, *Sergeant Wolfe.* Two serial-killer cases within a year. That's impressive. Why not repeat the success in Quantico, right?"

"I don't select the crimes I encounter, and I'm not making this up."

"Of course not. But you sell the merchandise, don't you? Does the name KillerWolfe.com ring a bell? I almost wet my pants when I found your website. Fascinating stuff. Serial killers are your personal brand, aren't they?"

Claire swore under her breath. KillerWolfe.com promoted wild conspiracy theories with her in the starring role. She'd have to send the site owner, Peter Knowles, another cease and desist order.

"I have nothing to do with that website."

"But you enjoy the attention, don't you?"

"No, I do not."

"C'mon. Not even a little? I bet you thought you'd be a star at the FBI."

"I joined the FBI to save lives. I was trying to leave Newburgh behind."

"Sure you were. And to be with your fiancé. But I hear you didn't get along with your unit chief."

"That's not true. Who told you that?"

"Does it matter? Tell me—what does your fan club say about Alda's death? Are you launching a new line of t-shirts?"

Anger exploded in her core. Claire wanted to lash him with expletives, but she reined in her temper. He'd lulled her with free coffee. Now he was goading her with insults. Both tactics aimed to crack her deceptive shell and expose the truth. But

Claire was hiding nothing. Apex wasn't a marketing ploy. More lives were at stake, including hers. She'd encountered the Apex symbol twice that week. A blue Subaru was stalking her. But Massoud only saw melodrama. Did the Subaru belong to Massoud's agents? Had he placed her under surveillance, hoping to charge her as an accessory to the crime?

Massoud waggled a finger at her and chuckled. "A tote bag with nipples. That's a good one. Remember to add that to your merchandise."

"You just told me Alda was murdered. What are you doing about it?"

"Nothing."

"You're going to ignore a homicide?"

"I didn't say that. But let's not pretend she was the target of Monday's bombing. Maybe somebody didn't like Alda and took her out? Maybe Alda knew who planted the bomb?"

His expression hardened.

That's it. He thinks you're the FBI mole! And why not? Claire had taken Monday off, she was present at the hospital the night of Alda's murder, and she spun tall tales about mysterious assassins. Was he trying to tie her to Tony Russo's murder, too? She had to break through the wall of suspicion.

"There's more going on here. You've got to believe me. Liam Wright had an Apex tattoo."

"Apex—the serial killer group from Newburgh?"

"Yes!"

"What do you know about Liam Wright?"

"I spoke with his roommate."

This time, Massoud lost his cool. "You did *what*?"

"I dropped by the American University today. Liam had a tattoo with the chevron symbol you found on the metal plate. The crimes are all connected."

Massoud stared at her in disgust. "Fleischer showed you the

files, didn't she? Well, you're both off the case. Stay out of my investigation, Agent Wolfe, or I'll charge you with obstruction."

"You're making a mistake."

"This case isn't about Apex or you. Stop muddying the waters. Drop the drama and let me do my job. Is that clear?"

Claire slammed the coffee cup on the table and stood to leave. "Crystal."

CHAPTER 25

That evening, Claire ate in silence at the dinner table. Felicity had baked tuna lasagna and prepared a green salad sprinkled with diced nuts and fruit. But gloomy thoughts distracted Claire from the home-cooked meal.

Rob moaned with pleasure. "This is delicious."

Felicity smirked. "It is, isn't it? My lasagna was always Rob's favorite."

Claire cracked an indifferent smile. "Good to know."

Rob beamed at Claire. "Thanks for putting up with this," his eyes seemed to say. "You're a trooper."

He wanted to reconnect with his mom. Despite her misgivings, Claire wouldn't stand in his way. She'd tolerate his mother for another day or two and be as cordial as possible.

Felicity raised her eyebrows at Claire. "And how was your day, dear? Did you solve any cases?"

Claire chewed slowly, considering how to answer. She needed to discuss the day's events with Rob but not with his mother present.

How much should I share with Rob? He shuffled around the house without assistance but grimaced with pain often. The simple act of sitting at the dinner table seemed to hurt. Rob needed to relax at home and recover fully. Claire's news would unsettle him. Rob wouldn't be content to twiddle his thumbs at home. He'd want to do something about it.

Claire swallowed. "I made progress on an investigation."

Rob eyed her with interest, but Claire focused on her food.

"You can tell me, dear. I'm family." Felicity had interpreted Claire's silence as an attempt to sideline her.

Rob wiped his mouth with a napkin. "It's FBI business, Mom. We can't discuss work with anyone, even family."

Felicity pouted. Her raised, stenciled eyebrows doubted the truth of his words.

"Well, if nobody else is willing to share, I'll tell you about *my* day. I did the grocery shopping, the ironing, the cooking, and the cleaning. You won't believe the amount of *filth*. It's as though nobody's ever cleaned the place properly!"

She cast an accusatory glance at Claire in case she hadn't noticed the criticism. Claire wasn't good enough for her little boy. No woman could replace his mother.

Claire shrugged. "I did the grocery shopping yesterday."

Felicity scoffed. "That processed junk hardly qualifies as food."

Claire strangled her fork. First the cleaning, now the groceries. His mother found fault with everything she did.

Rob changed the subject. "Tom stopped by this afternoon."

"That's nice."

Rob put down his fork. "He's our new unit chief."

Claire paused mid-bite. "Tom?"

"He seemed surprised, too. The oversight committee made the appointment. Senator Schultz called to congratulate him. "

"I can't see the problem," Felicity said. "Tom seems like a nice man. Rob has worked with him for years. Claire, what problem do you have with him?"

"Nothing. Tom has the experience. His appointment will be good for our new program, too. Did he say anything about our budget?"

Rob shook his head. "Everything's up in the air. He'll need time to ease into the job. But I'm sure he'll look out for us."

They resumed their meal.

"Claire," Felicity said. "How long do you intend to work for the FBI?"

Her question caught Claire off guard. "What do you mean?"

"Well, if you're serious about marrying Rob, you'll have a husband and household to care for. And children to raise. Do you want to have children or are you one of *those*?"

Claire ran out of patience. "One of *what*?"

She and Rob *had* discussed having children one day. But the topic was none of Felicity's bloody business. Claire resented the insults disguised as relationship advice from a mother who had physically and emotionally abused her young son.

"You know—*career women*. Wives who place their self-fulfillment above everything else."

Rob touched Felicity's arm. "Mom, that's enough."

"I'm only looking out for you, Rob. If she's working insane hours for the FBI, who's going to cook dinner and bathe the kids?"

"She?" Claire said. "I'm right here."

Felicity snickered. "For now."

"Mom!"

Claire had tried to play nice, but now she'd had enough. "When is your flight to Boston?"

The hint should have shut Felicity up, but instead, she smiled.

Claire shot Rob a worried glance.

He gazed at his plate. "Mom's rental fell through. She needs to stay with us a bit longer."

Claire stifled a scream. *I knew it!* Her future mother-in-law's "temporary" stay was a ploy to get her foot in the door. Why had Claire ignored her instincts? Their guest was becoming a squatter.

"How much longer?"

Felicity patted her son's hand. "I'm glad it fell through. Rob and I have bonded so well. We realized we need to stay close to build on this foundation. So, we've decided that I'll move nearby."

"*You've* decided?" Claire spat the words. How could Rob exclude her from that decision?

Felicity tittered. "Yes. I've already started looking for a rental. In addition to all the cooking and cleaning, of course. The market is difficult, but I'll be out of your hair in no time."

Claire doubted that. Felicity would never leave this house. Her Boston rental had probably been a convenient fiction, too.

"How long?"

Rob tried to control the damage. "A week, tops. Isn't that right, Mom?"

"Yes, dear. I'm on it." She gave Claire a victorious grin.

Somehow, Claire finished her dinner without strangling her future mother-in-law. Felicity volunteered to load the dishwasher. Claire locked the doors and fastened the security latches. Then, she and Rob retired upstairs.

Claire flopped on their bed. "I can't believe this."

Rob leaned his crutch against a wall and collapsed beside her. "I'm sorry about that. I really appreciate you putting up with her. This means so much to me."

"You realize there's a good chance I'll kill her before the week is up?"

Rob chuckled. "Not if she kills us first."

"Don't give her any ideas." She looked him in the eye. "Do you really think she's changed?"

He didn't answer immediately. "Time will tell. She's making an effort. That's something."

Claire shook her head. "I don't know. She's up to something. I just haven't figured out her agenda yet. People like that don't change."

"But isn't that our hope—that even psychopaths can change? YARI is built on that assumption."

"Teenagers are different. They're malleable. She's spent decades feeding off others. The circuits in her brain are hardwired to manipulate and exploit. But—whatever. We're stuck with her for now. Let's talk about something else."

Rob curled his lips into a mischievous smile. "Who wants to talk?"

He placed his hand on Claire's waist. They rolled toward each other, and their lips touched. Desire erupted within Claire, a hunger no lasagna could satisfy. She had almost lost Rob and now she wanted him, all of him, and with all of her senses. Claire pulled him close. Their bodies writhed against each other and fell into a well-rehearsed rhythm. They tore at their clothes, removing the barriers between their skin. Rob's shorts caught on the plaster cast, and he cried out.

"Are you OK?"

"Yeah. I'm good to go."

"Are you sure?"

"More than sure."

A loud knocking on the bedroom door halted their lovemaking.

Felicity said, "Rob, are you OK?"

Claire swore under her breath. His mother probably had her ear to the door.

"Yeah, Mom. I'm fine."

"It sounded like you're in pain. Should I get you a Tylenol and some water?"

The door handle turned. Claire yanked the sheet over her bare chest.

Rob reached for his boxers. "Don't come in! I'm fine. Really."

A tense silence reigned, killing Claire's libido.

Felicity released the handle. "Don't exert yourself, dear, or you won't heal well."

Claire scoffed. Rob's mother had invaded their home and now she was sabotaging their love life.

"Don't worry. I won't."

"OK, then. I'm right next door if you need me. The walls are paper-thin, and I'm a very light sleeper."

"Thank you. Goodnight."

"Goodnight." Felicity shuffled off to the second bedroom.

Claire fumed. "This is ridiculous," she hissed. "Can't she sleep downstairs?"

"On the couch? I can't do that to her."

Claire ran her hands through her hair. *This is a nightmare.* She couldn't get rid of her soon enough.

"Can't you see what she's doing? She's trying to break us up."

Rob sighed. "You're right. This was a mistake. I should kick her out right now."

Claire scoffed. "C'mon, Rob. She's your mother. We won't kick her out in the middle of the night. Just make sure she leaves, pronto, and goes as far away as possible."

They stared at the ceiling. Sex was off the menu tonight.

"You said you made progress today."

"Where do I start?"

Claire told him about her trip to the American University, where she'd learned about The Level Field Initiative, Liam Wright's Apex tattoo, and the deleted email from Alpha on the Apex laptop. Finally, Claire mentioned her meeting with Agent

Massoud and the FBI lab's toxicology report for Chief Alda and the flayed Moretti chemist.

"Massoud went ballistic when he found out Sally told me about the warehouse bombing. He's cutting her from the investigation. There goes our inside channel. When I mentioned Apex, he told me I was an attention-seeking drama queen."

"He said that?"

"Not in those words. He's convinced the cartel is to blame, and he won't listen to anything that doesn't fit that mold."

Rob knitted his brow. "You're right. Apex is still active. They're larger than we thought. But if they wanted to shut down YARI, wouldn't they come after us, too?"

Claire didn't answer.

He noticed her brooding gaze. "What?"

"Maybe they *are* coming for us?"

"What do you mean?"

"Someone's been watching us. At least, I think so. There was a blue Subaru Impreza on our street this week. It followed me back from Washington today."

"The same plates?"

"I didn't get the license number."

Rob chuckled. "There are a lot of Subarus on the roads."

"I know. You're right. It's probably nothing. Maybe Apex thinks YARI died with Alda?"

"It's a safe bet. Still, we should ask Tom to shelve YARI."

"Are you serious? You've worked so hard on that."

He shrugged. "We can always dust it off later. For now, we need to stay off the Apex radar."

Right again. If Apex murdered the FBI director to bury YARI, they'd do anything to complete the task.

Rob frowned. "Why kill the chemist?"

"Massoud thinks Moretti was covering his tracks. A

scorched-earth policy fits Apex, too. Maybe Sally's right and the cartel is an Apex branch?"

The answer didn't sit well with her. Claire still had no idea what they were up against.

"One thing is certain. Alpha predates Newburgh. If Apex is in bed with Moretti, they have money and power. And they're not afraid to use both. We can't take them on by ourselves."

"Then we won't. We'll wait out the storm. Massoud has the resources. Let him tackle Apex. He'll come around if we bring him more evidence."

"I don't know. Massoud already has it in for me. He's the kind to hold a grudge."

Claire studied the ceiling for a solution. Was there another way forward?

"Alpha. The name isn't random. He founded Apex. He's the key to destroying them, root and branch."

Rob grunted. "The surest way to kill a snake is to chop off its head."

The snake metaphor triggered other mental images. Shedding skin. The flayed man. A shudder passed down her spine. Like Apex, Alpha's minions were cold-blooded killers.

Massoud didn't respond well to ambiguous details. Claire needed to bring him a smoking gun. And she knew exactly how.

"We've hunted serial killers before," she said. "We'll do it again."

CHAPTER 26

Niccolo "Nicky" Moretti stepped out of his armored SUV at Union Square and clenched his jaw. Anger boiled in his gut. Anger and fear. Spotlights illuminated the Capitol Building. The glowing white dome reflected in the still waters of Capitol Pool. The iconic structure represented the might of the state. Nicky wielded power, too. But one organization eclipsed his strength and, it seemed, even that of the United States government. And that vicious group lurked in the shadows.

His instructions said to come alone. Nicky should obey their instructions to the letter. He'd learned that the hard way.

At first, he'd rebelled. Nicky didn't take orders—he gave them! He led the most feared cartel on the East Coast. He'd gobbled up rival gangs and consolidated his turf. But this opponent wasn't a cartel. They didn't respond to reason or abide by the rules of human decency. Their cruelty knew no bounds. He had no tools for beating that alien threat. Surrender was the only option. Tonight, he couldn't rely on their mercy. If he was lucky, he'd escape with his life.

Nicky walked along the edge of the pool and gripped the

briefcase handle tight. A late-night jogger passed by, and Nicky flinched. Those animals in human form had reduced him to a nervous wreck with a single photograph. The full-length shot of Tony Russo had turned his stomach. On the back of the photo, Nicky found instructions...and the names of his children. The message was clear, and he had no doubt they'd deliver on that threat.

He sat on a vacant bench and tucked the briefcase under the seat. Nicky imagined a sniper's crosshairs on his head. One false move and they'd end him. But he had one last card to play. *If you can't beat 'em, join 'em.*

A young woman with a sweatsuit and headphones settled beside him. He was about to say, "Beat it. This seat is taken," when she spoke.

"Eyes front, Nicky."

Her commanding tone forbade discussion. Nicky obeyed.

"Is it all there?"

Nicky swallowed hard. "Yes. Ten million. Non-sequential bills. As you said."

She reached under the bench and took the briefcase. "The price has gone up."

Nicky swore under his breath. He should have seen this coming. Torturing Tony to death had only been their way of getting his attention. He hadn't received his punishment yet.

"How much?"

"Fifty."

Nicky knew better than to argue.

"That was a bold move, what you did. I respect that. Pity Tony had to pay for your mistake. He had a strong heart. He held out for hours. And he felt *everything.* Makes you shiver, doesn't it?"

Nicky ground his molars. He wanted to throttle the sick psycho bitch. But there were more where she came from. To chew through their leash, he'd have to be smart. *Time to play that last card.*

"Fine. Bleed us dry. But the Feds are blaming us for that bombing at Quantico. When they pass their new legislation, we'll be out of business. There'll be nothing left to take."

"Oh, I know. Who do you think bombed the FBI?"

Nicky blinked at the Capitol building. "You killed the director?"

"Among others. With your explosives."

Nicky swore again. "Why would you do that?"

"To keep you honest, Nicky."

These lunatics wanted to destroy him. "Are you taking over my business—is that what this is about?"

"No, we're happy to let you run that business."

"Then why kill your cash cow?"

"Nicky, Nicky. We wanted to show you we're serious."

"I believe you. But what about the legislation?"

She chuckled. "Deliver the money. We'll take care of the rest."

"How?"

"That's your fatal mistake, Nicky. You underestimate us."

Nicky swore again. They had assassinated the FBI director. Would they bomb the Senate next?

She lifted the briefcase and made to leave. "Pay up on time, Nicky. Between you and me, I'm hoping you'll screw this up, too." She brushed her finger against his cheek. "I'm looking forward to getting under your skin."

CHAPTER 27

Friday morning, Claire arrived early at work. Skipping coffee, she slipped into her office at the BAU. A critical objective drove her. She had smashed Apex in Newburgh, and the effort had almost destroyed her. But she'd only severed the tail. The snake lived. Rob was right. To defeat the psychopathic cabal, they had to lop off its head. To do that, Claire had to smoke Alpha out before he struck again. And she knew how.

She loaded the FBI's ViCAP portal in a browser window. The Violent Crime Apprehension Program maintained a searchable database of serial and sexual crimes logged by law enforcement nationwide. When investigating the multiple homicides in Newburgh, Dr. Sally Fleischer had directed the detectives to look for similar murders. The serial killers usually struck close to home at first, and their first victims often provided the key to the perpetrator's identity. Apex nurtured serial killers. Their assassin had skinned Tony Russo alive. Would ViCAP reveal traces of her criminal past?

Claire searched for unsolved homicides during the past five years that matched the keyword "skinned." The single page of results included a child with skinned knees and an unidentified male corpse in a shipping container of skinned chicken. She deleted the suffix and reran the search. "Skin" returned three hundred results. Claire blinked at the list in dismay. She had no time—or desire—to wade through that pile of human suffering.

Another word arose in her mind, one Massoud had used. She typed the word "flayed" and pressed enter. A single result showed on the screen. She'd hit pay dirt. *Thank you, Agent Massoud.*

Claire downloaded the PDF. In the crime scene photo, a flayed corpse dangled from a hangman's noose. Not a perfect match. The Apex assassin had suspended Tony Russo by his arms, not his neck. But the unsolved homicide was tantalizingly similar. She read the crime's location, and her heart skipped a beat. *Newburgh, Massachusetts.* The brief provided no further details, not even the reporting officer's name. The find was almost too good to be true.

Claire dialed Newburgh PD on her cell phone and lowered her voice. "Jess, I need another favor."

"No problem. I hope it's not the laptop again. My contact in digital forensics is convinced we're dating, and I don't want to encourage him."

"This one should be easy. It'll only take a few seconds of desk work. ViCAP turned up a homicide in Newburgh that seems to match a cartel murder last week in Washington." Claire described the flaying and the curare extract used to disable the victim. She dictated the case number.

The patter of plastic keys echoed on the line. "I'm looking it up in the system."

Jess grunted with surprise.

"What is it?"

"The case file is only available in hard copy. I'll have to check with the archive."

Déjà vu clenched Claire's gut. Her sister's homicide file had also been omitted from the digital system. The archive officer had taken days to locate the folder. But this case was much more recent—only two years old. Why was the murder book unavailable?

"Send my regards to Officer Freeman. I hope he doesn't have to search the basement again. This might take time."

"Got it. I'll go there right away and call you back."

Claire opened another browser tab and searched for The Level Field Initiative scholarship. A website loaded—the one Joanne Clark of the American University had shown her. Among the marketing copy, Claire found no telephone numbers, postal or email addresses, only an online contact form. Who ran the fund? How did they choose their beneficiaries? Their criteria had selected the three dead students, including one suspected Apex operative.

She entered the generic Gmail address she used for potential spam sites, typed a vague request for more information, and hit Send. Then, she ran a WHOIS domain lookup. The site owner's details were not listed.

Two knocks on the door startled Claire.

"Come in."

The door cracked open, and Special Agent Tom Brown stood on the threshold. *Unit Chief* Tom Brown.

Claire minimized the browser window. "Rob told me you stopped by yesterday. Congratulations on your promotion."

Tom snorted. "You mean, 'impending crapstorm.' Management needed a fall guy. Let's see how long I last."

He cast a hangdog gaze down the corridor. "I've called a meeting to update the unit. Conference room."

He glanced at Sally's empty desk.

Claire preempted the question. "Have you seen Sally today?"

"I spoke with her earlier. She's on her way to California for a few days to consult on a case."

"California?"

"Orange County. Last-minute thing. Lucky her."

"Yeah."

Tom had sent Sally out of state. Was this a coincidence or had Agent Massoud pressured him to get her out of the way? Was Claire next on his list?

Tom's deadpan expression revealed nothing. "Coming?"

Claire stood. "Sure."

Tom marched off, and Claire kept pace.

She remembered her conversation with Rob last night. "I'm guessing YARI is on ice for now."

"Never mind YARI, the entire unit is in jeopardy. Agent Massoud thinks behavioral analysis is pseudoscience, and he has the oversight committee's ear. I'll be the shortest-serving unit chief the BAU has ever known."

Claire's energy levels dropped. Tom had plenty on his shoulders. Now was no time for speculation about an Apex plot. If Massoud dissolved their unit, they'd all lose their jobs or get transferred out. They'd be powerless to stop Alpha. *Don't give Massoud an excuse.*

A dozen agents had beaten them to the conference room. Tom called for a moment of silence in memory of Unit Chief Madeleine Alda and the other fallen agents. The gloomy faces reflected Claire's grief and her concern for the future.

"Let's keep this short." That was Tom. To the point. No frills. "I'll schedule meetings with each of you and our agents currently at field offices to discuss your expertise and caseloads. Obviously, there was no handover from Chief Alda, so this will take time. Bear with me. Questions?"

Agents raised their hands and asked about layoffs and reassignments. Tom promised to follow up. Claire's phone vibrated in her pocket. Jess was calling, but Claire didn't answer. Her job was already on the line. A clandestine investigation would place her name on a retrenchment shortlist.

The meeting dispersed. Claire hurried back to her room. A man stood at Claire's desk with his back to the door.

She recognized the mop of red curls. "Corey?"

Corey Angel spun around. "Claire, I was looking for you."

What's he doing here? Was he reading the files on my desk?

She stepped closer. "You found me. How can I help?"

Edgy as usual, Corey fidgeted with his fingers. "Um, I was wondering how Rob is doing?"

"He'd good. Stronger every day."

Corey nodded. "Great. That's great. So is YARI moving forward?"

He seemed to mention the program every time they spoke. *Why are you so interested in YARI?* Was he just making conversation?

Claire folded her arms. "No. We're in limbo for the foreseeable future."

"Oh, that's too bad." He lingered.

Why is he here? Throughout their training at the FBI Academy, Corey had hovered in Claire's vicinity. She'd suspected her classmate had developed a more personal interest in her, but she'd assumed her engagement to Rob had made her romantic intentions clear. *Some guys never give up.*

Claire considered the chemical engineer with new interest. Corey worked at BAU-1. *Counterterrorism, arson, and bombings.* Agent Massoud had tracked down Moretti's chemist by tracing the C4 manufacturing chain. Maybe Claire could use the same approach to locate Alda's assassin? Corey had chosen a perfect time for a social call.

"Corey, have you heard of curare?"

Corey blinked. "Curare? Sure, I've heard of it. Why do you ask?"

"Where is it available?"

"It isn't. Not easily. Curare is a powerful neurotoxin. It's no longer used for anesthesia, and we now use less hazardous substances for its other medical applications. You'd need a doctor's script and a very specialized pharmacy."

"I see."

Was the assassin a chemist, too? The government would monitor stock movements for regulated medications. Tony Russo had cooked C4 in his apartment to escape detection. Did the flayer synthesize the compound independently, too?

"Corey, could someone prepare curare in a home lab?"

He shrugged. "I guess so. You'd need to source plants with toxic alkaloids. Ask a botanist and make sure you know what you're doing." He squinted at her. "This is all hypothetical, right?"

Claire cleared her throat. "Yeah. Purely hypothetical."

Corey brightened. "So, um, do you want to do lunch?"

Claire sighed. "I'd love to, but I have a ton of work to get through. I'll probably just grab a sandwich." Claire hadn't lied. She had a lot of information to process...and an assassin to hunt.

Corey handled rejection well. "Another time, then. See you around." He left with a spring in his step.

Claire's phone rang.

Jess sounded breathless. "You were right. The case file wasn't in the archive."

"I guess it's back to the basement, then."

"That's the thing. They cleaned out the basement months ago. The file is missing."

Claire bit her lip. She'd hit a brick wall.

Jess continued. "That's the bad news."

"There's good news, too?"

"Hm. That depends on your definition of good. The last person to check out the file was Lieutenant O'Leary."

"Brian O'Leary?"

"The one and only."

The late Brian O'Leary had covered up a homicide and collaborated with Apex. Had he buried this case, too?

"O'Leary was dirty. We need to get hold of that file."

"Wouldn't he have destroyed it?"

"Not necessarily. Tampering with the case files would raise fewer questions. But toward the end, his conscience got to him. He'd threatened to expose Apex. Tina's file got lost in the basement. Maybe O'Leary took the file to use as leverage?"

"I'll try his home."

"Don't bother. His widow sold the house and moved to Florida."

Jess groaned. "That sucks. I'll speak with her anyway."

"Can't hurt. She was very cooperative last time. Send my regards. And ask for her chocolate chip cookie recipe."

Jess laughed. "Now I *have* to speak with her."

Claire hung up and rubbed her forehead. They were grasping at straws. The file had become a pile of ash long ago. She'd known the lead was too good to be true.

CHAPTER 28

Friday evening, Alpha poured a finger of Macallan into a tumbler and toasted the Washington skyline. Through the window, the dome on Capitol Hill burned white. Nero had fiddled while Rome burned. Alpha preferred to savor a glass of single malt. Celebrations of this kind were best kept private, far from the public eye, and tonight, he had much to celebrate.

His plans were unfolding. The prize drew near. But Alpha shunned overconfidence. Disaster could strike at any moment. Setbacks were inevitable. He made room for error and recalibrated often. Recently, he'd had to adjust course and increase his risk exposure. Nobody ever became emperor without making sacrifices.

He raised his glass at the Capitol building, the seat and symbol of power. "To Director Warren and Unit Chief Alda. Without you, none of this would be possible."

The golden liquid spilled over his tongue and excited his taste buds.

A cell phone vibrated. Only one person had the number for that line.

He answered. "Are you celebrating?"

The garbled voice didn't sound human. "In my own way."

Alpha's obfuscation software processed his voice in the same way. Digital eavesdroppers would never identify the speakers' voices or even their gender. But Alpha remembered the sound of the caller's voice. One never forgets one's children. The speaker would continue his legacy. A modern emperor had no need for harems to create heirs. Why roll the fickle dice of genetics when one can mold a disciple's heart and soul?

"But that's not why I'm calling." Despite the garbling, the voice betrayed a note of concern. "We have a problem."

Alpha knocked back his whiskey. He had kindled the flames. There was no way to extinguish the wildfire now. But he could change the inferno's course and raise the obstacles in its path to the ground.

"Does this problem have a name?"

"She does. Claire Wolfe."

CHAPTER 29

Saturday morning, Detective Jessica Long hitched her denim miniskirt up her leg and undid the top buttons of her red shirt. As a homicide detective, she'd engaged in many surprising activities, but impersonating a bimbo took the cake.

She strutted toward the cramped information office and swung her hips in case the desk jockey—hopefully, a lonely and geeky dude—was watching the security cameras. The legal foundations of her mission were shakier than her bright-red high heels. But if she reached the service window without keeling over, she might pull this off. *The things I do for Claire.*

Mrs. O'Leary had cooperated gladly on the phone yesterday. Jess attributed the widow's team spirit to Florida's balmy weather and the compliment Jess had dropped about her baking. Unfortunately, Mrs. O'Leary had found no work files among her husband's personal effects—"Brian never brought his work home"—and knew of no storage units or mysterious keys to airport lockers. But the conversation wasn't a total loss. Jess had obtained the recipe for O'Leary's famous chocolate chip cookies.

The widow had accepted her offer to swing by her old

home and check for mail. Mrs. O'Leary had canceled the utilities for her old house and notified service providers of her new address. But people tended to forget the recurring payments they accrued over the years. Jess's dad had learned that lesson when he'd canceled a stolen credit card. That act had terminated five memberships he no longer remembered or needed. In the long run, the pickpocket had saved him money. And O'Leary's widow probably had even less insight into her husband's purchasing history.

That afternoon, Jess had knocked on the door of the residence and introduced herself to the new owners. The young Asian couple had collected a pile of letters addressed to the late Brian O'Leary. Among the subscription renewal notices for Guns & Ammo and a PowerBall Season Ticket, Jess found threatening letters from Blue Flag Self-Storage. Her hunch had paid off and hatched plans for the weekend.

Jess usually did things by the book. But today, she'd push the limits of her jurisdiction and rely on her wits...and her other, more physical, talents.

She peered through the service window of the information office. A blonde, gum-chewing bimbo reflected in the reinforced glass. The hefty male inside needed a hair transplant and a shave. He stared at his Instagram feed and bit into an oversized ham sandwich—a late breakfast or an early lunch? Lady Luck had smiled on her.

Jess leaned her elbows on the ledge and raised the pitch of her voice an octave.

"Hi there!"

The attendant gazed at her and spoke with his mouth full. "Opening or closing?"

Customer service didn't feature high on the self-storage facility's list of priorities. Apparently, they didn't pay their employees to smile, either.

"Excuse me?"

He rolled his eyes. "Are you opening or closing an account?"

She squinted at the name on his shirt tag. "Neither...Daryl. I need to access a storage unit. But I don't have the code."

Jess giggled and shrugged. She ran her hand through her hair for good measure.

The desk jockey seemed impervious to female charm. "Code resets are fifty dollars a pop. I'll need your unit numbers and a photo ID."

Forget the miniskirt—Jess should have worn a ham sandwich. She slid the printed notice from Blue Flag Self-Storage through the slot in the service window.

The attendant deposited his sandwich on the desk and typed the unit number into the computer. Besides the ham sandwich lay a red and black comic book entitled *Bleed Them Dry*. On the cover, blood dripped from a girl's razor-sharp teeth, and a boy swung a gore-stained samurai sword. Not girls, then. The attendant was into stylized violence. *Wonderful.*

Daryl frowned at the computer monitor. "The account is behind on payments. You need to settle the debt before I can reset the code."

"How much?"

He clicked the mouse. "Almost a year of fees and overdue fines. That comes to one thousand and sixty-nine dollars, excluding the reset fee."

Jess balked at the amount. She wanted to help Claire out but without emptying her checking account.

"The thing is, I'm not actually the renter of the unit. They moved to Florida. I'm just doing a friend a favor."

Each sentence was true, technically, although together, they implied the renter and her friend were the same person.

He blinked at her. "Only the account owner can request a code reset."

Jess's self-esteem sagged. Over the years, her All-American good looks had opened doors effortlessly. Had her feminine charms faded already? She was only twenty-seven! Maybe the dude would respond to reason?

"I read your Terms and Conditions online. After three missed payments, the unit reverts to the service provider and the contents are sold to defray expenses. Legally speaking, the unit and its contents belong to Blue Flag. The company can do what it wants with them."

Daryl yawned. "You'll have to call head office about that."

He resumed eating his sandwich.

Jess dropped the bimbo act. "I'll level with you, Daryl. I'm a detective with the Newburgh Police Department, and this unit is related to an ongoing investigation."

The attendant snorted. "You're a cop?"

She flashed her badge. "Detective Jessica Long."

The blood-red comic book caught her eye again.

"I shouldn't be telling you this, but this is a homicide investigation. We're tracking down a serial killer."

He stopped chewing. Finally, interest sparkled in his eye. "A serial killer?"

"Yep. Nasty stuff."

His lips parted. "How nasty?"

She waved the question away. "Trust me, you do not want to know. The details will make you toss your lunch. For all we know, there's a dead body in that unit. Which means Blue Flag will have to explain why they have a corpse on their property."

"A dead body?"

Jess leaned in. "Can you keep a secret?"

"Sure."

She whispered. "The killer skins his victims alive."

"No way!"

Jess nodded. "So, how about that storage unit?"

"Um, I should probably accompany you."

"OK. But your phone stays here. No photos."

If O'Leary had hidden more than case files in his storage unit, the contents would not land up on Instagram.

The attendant dumped his sandwich in the trash can.

"Deal. I'll reset the code."

Jess sighed. Female charms, out. Blood and gore, in. Humanity was doomed.

Daryl led her inside the warehouse. With trembling fingers, he punched the temporary code into the keypad at a central terminal, and a door among a row of boxy storage units clicked.

Jess swung the door open. To Daryl's dismay, the unit contained no dead bodies, only a dusty cardboard box.

Jess pulled on a pair of disposable latex gloves and studied the contents. She'd found what she wanted...and then some.

CHAPTER 30

Saturday afternoon, Claire and Rob stood outside their unit chief's office. The evidence had reached critical mass, and they needed Tom's endorsement to move forward. *Here goes nothing.*

Rob panted softly. This was his first outing since the bombing and his first time back at the CIRG building. The crutches slowed their progress and sapped his strength.

She touched his shoulder. "Maybe this was a bad idea?"

Rob shook his head. "We need to do this."

He was right. Jess's call that morning had changed everything, and they needed to share the information with an authority they could trust. Rob had called Tom to ask him to come over, but their new unit chief was at work. Unable to explain their urgency over the phone, Claire and Rob joined him at the BAU offices.

Claire knocked on the door, and they entered. She eased Rob into a visitor's chair and leaned his crutches against the wall. Tom Brown watched the spectacle, his cynical eyebrows raised over his weathered face.

Rob sighed. "Thank you for meeting with us."

Tom snorted. "Don't get all formal on me now I'm chief."

"I'm glad to see the new role hasn't gone to your head."

Tom straightened. "You know what? I take that back. Brown-nosing will do nicely."

They laughed. After these tense and uncertain days, Claire appreciated the dash of humor. The burden of her unsanctioned investigation had weighed on her heavily. But how would Tom react to her underground project?

Claire searched for a distraction to delay her confession. "I love what you've done with the place."

Tom had evicted Alda's pot plants and replaced the portrait of J. Edgar Hoover with a still of John Wayne from *The Man Who Shot Liberty Valance*. *There's a new sheriff in town.*

Tom tipped his imaginary cowboy hat at her, then got to business. "I know why *I'm* working this weekend. What's your excuse?"

Rob gave Claire a meaningful glance and cleared his throat. "We have reason to believe Apex is still alive and kicking."

A sly grin curled the edge of Tom's mouth. "Let me guess. Apex bombed CIRG."

"Massoud told you?"

Tom chuckled at their surprise. "Sure. He wanted my blessing to fire your fiancée."

Claire's heart skipped a beat. "He tried to get me fired?"

Massoud had disagreed with her theory, but why would he destroy her career?

"His first choice was to arrest you for obstruction of justice. It isn't personal. He wanted the same for Sally, too. I sent her to California to cool off instead. Her trip seems to have appeased him for now. Don't judge him. He's under tremendous pressure to nail the people responsible for bombing a federal building and assassinating Director Warren. He needs to get all his ducks in a row, and your theory undermines his case."

"What if we're right?"

Tom sighed heavily. "What have you got?"

Rob recited their elevator pitch, then hammered home the key details.

"The RDX used at the CIRG bombing matches the warehouse explosion. The Apex symbols on the metal plate and the dead college student's tattoo tie both blasts to Newburgh. Now we've discovered an Apex connection for the flayed man, too."

"Moretti's chemist?"

Claire nodded. "Brian O'Leary of Newburgh PD covered up crimes for Apex. In a storage unit he rented, we found a stash of case files. One of the homicides is a flaying that closely resembles the chemist. We thought the case might shed light on the killer's identity, but no trace evidence was found at the scene. She'd been careful. This wasn't her first kill."

Tom steepled his fingers. "What about Moretti—what's his connection to Apex?"

"We don't know yet. But another name has surfaced. On the Apex laptop in Newburgh, there's a deleted email from Alpha, apparently the founder of Apex. He might be Moretti."

"What made you look into O'Leary?"

"ViCAP had an entry for the flaying. It's the only one that matches the chemist. Our friends at Newburgh PD did the heavy lifting."

Tom grunted. He scanned the wall behind them as he considered the facts. "If O'Leary was covering for Apex, why did he register the homicide with ViCAP?"

Rob had asked the same question. "We're guessing he uploaded the case before Apex instructed him to bury the file. Either he couldn't delete the entry or, like the case files in storage, he wanted leverage."

Tom nodded. "I understand. You'd like me to speak with Massoud and win him over. But to be honest, we're still asking for a leap of faith. If Apex is alive and kicking, they're doing a crappy job. Their operatives accidentally blew themselves up. And if their goal is to stop us from poaching their recruits, why kill the director of the FBI? The point is moot. If Moretti is Alpha then his attack on the director backfired spectacularly. Massoud is already going after him."

Claire's heart sank. Without Tom's support, they had no chance of changing Massoud's mind. She could mention the blue Subaru, but vague suspicions about a stalker would only weaken their case.

Claire blurted, "What if Moretti isn't Alpha?"

"Take my advice," Tom continued. "Keep your eyes open and your mouths shut. The Senate's oversight committee is calling the shots now, and Massoud is their gatekeeper. He didn't like the BAU to begin with, and he's got Claire in his sights. Let him figure things out. Rocking the boat now won't just sink our new program. The entire ship could go down."

Claire had heard this argument before. Tom's hands were tied. She helped Rob to his feet, and they limped back to the car.

She got behind the wheel. "So that's it? We stand down and shelve everything?"

Rob sucked in his lips. "Tom has a point. If Moretti and Apex are one and the same thing, Massoud is already onto them. Maybe we can sit this fight out?"

She shook her head in frustration. "Moretti isn't Alpha. I can feel it. I should have realized Apex was larger. The Newburgh pack didn't have the technological resources to set up a darknet assassin ring. I underestimated them. I walked into an Apex trap and barely escaped with my life. I don't want to repeat that mistake."

Rob listened in silence.

Claire squeezed the wheel. "I wish we could talk this through with Sally. Maybe she'd see something we've missed?" The forensic psychiatrist had cracked an Apex plot before, and Claire had banked on her repeating that miracle.

Rob frowned. "I don't know. Tom can't protect us if we put him in a corner."

Claire continued her rant. "Massoud's ruthless. Being closed-minded is one thing, but he actively tried to silence us. I just wish we could get around him."

Rob raised an eyebrow. "Maybe we can? Tom won't oppose Massoud publicly, but he gave us an opening."

Claire studied him with concern. Had Rob hit his head again?

"What opening?"

He smiled mischievously. "Read between the lines, Claire. When the gatekeeper locks you out, don't give up. Use the back door."

CHAPTER 31

With gloved hands, Felicity Cline opened the drawers of Claire's bedside table and rifled her personal effects. At long last, both her son and his sweetheart had left the house. Felicity had at least an hour to conduct her search and estimate the return she could expect on her investment.

So far her stash included lip gloss, a pocket pack of tissues, and a Valentine's Day card. No jewelry or wads of cash. She scanned the Valentine's Day card and grumbled with disgust. Her son was still a gushy sap. She left the items where she had found them. This venture was becoming a major disappointment.

When she'd heard about the FBI bombing, Felicity had hurried to Quantico. Rob had worked there. Was he dead? Boston had nothing left to offer. Her last three romantic partners had promised the moon but delivered pebbles. Felicity had fallen out with her parents and siblings decades ago. Her dead ex-husband had left her nothing. But their marriage had produced a single child, and she wouldn't miss out on that inheritance!

An inheritance there would be. Rob had defied her expecta-

tions and carved out a stable career in law enforcement. The
FBI provided a juicy 401(k) retirement account, no doubt. Rob
was still single. When he checked out, she would cash in. What
good were children if they couldn't make you money?

But again, Rob had defied her expectations and survived his
injuries. Without a little help, he'd outlive her, too. Felicity drew
the line at murder. Virginia had the death penalty, and Felicity
hated needles. Poisoning Rob was not an option anyway with
his wench around. No, Felicity had to find another payoff. She
had searched the house from basement to attic but found no
safes, no gold watches, or antiques. The house was a rental. All
she had to show for her efforts was spare change and Rob's
checkbook.

In desperation, she had considered blackmail. What was he
hiding? Had he taken home classified documents? She
searched his laptop as best she could, but Felicity was no
computer technician. Rob was as squeaky clean as he seemed.
She had failed as a mother.

The girlfriend was more promising. Now there was a
woman with dark secrets! Was she into kinky stuff? The Behav-
ioural Analysis Unit probably frowned on deviant sexual prac-
tices among their agents. But a Pleasure Pack of Trojan
condoms and a tube of KY Jelly didn't make the grade. Hardly
the stuff to strike fear in a young couple's hearts.

Then, just as she gave up on the project, an idea sparked.
The scam was so simple, she slapped herself for not thinking of
it sooner. The payout would be huge. But for the swindle to
work, she'd need to get rid of the bitch.

Claire Wolfe had given her the evil eye since the moment
she'd arrived. But Felicity knew how to dispatch female rivals.
Invading a man's heart and eliminating the competition were
her specialties. The former homicide detective didn't know
whom she was dealing with.

The trick was to start small. Every relationship had pressure points. Most had hairline cracks. A sharp jab in the right spot turned suspicion into jealousy and cracks into gaping chasms. With her easy temper and protective attitude toward Rob, Claire Wolfe was easy prey. The couple's working relationship provided more raw materials. At night, Felicity eavesdropped on their discussions. Their unit was in danger of closing. Claire's dark family history sounded promising, too. What was she hiding? Felicity rubbed her hands together. She'd enjoy tearing these lovebirds apart.

Sitting on the edge of their bed, Felicity unlocked her smartphone and opened a browser window. She Googled Claire Wolfe, and her mouth fell open. *Jackpot!* Felicity had all the ammunition she needed. *Claire Wolfe, say goodbye.*

CHAPTER 32

Karla woke up, shivering and confused. *The world shifted as she turned over and opened her eyes. Leafy trees rustled overhead in a chilly morning breeze. She had slept outdoors in a hammock of tough rope. A mosquito buzzed near her ear. Karla slapped her cheek but missed the pest. The moist air curled her hair. She stank of sweat. Karla had awoken in Hell.*

"Morning," a man said.

Barefoot and naked from the waist up, the wiry old man crouched on his haunches and stoked the open fire beneath a tin pot. He'd tied his white hair in a ponytail. Gray swirls dotted his tanned chest. He'd torn his cargo pants at the knee, converting them into shorts. Did he strut around in the nude when he didn't have company?

"Breakfast is ready." His voice was gravelly and monotone.

Karla needed to pee and brush her teeth, but there were no bathrooms in sight or running water, and she wouldn't expose herself in front of the stranger.

"I want to go home."

"You are home."

Karla scoffed. "I'm not a freaking animal."

His expression hardened, and he stopped poking at the burning logs. She shouldn't upset him. The old geezer lived off the grid in the middle of Prince William Forest Park. Until yesterday, she hadn't known he existed. The crazy bum was probably dangerous.

He straightened and stared her in the eye. "Correct. You are not an animal. You descend from a noble bloodline."

"I descend from shit."

He raised his voice. "You are Kalinago." He inflated his chest with pride. "And half Dakota on your father's side." He spat on the ground to express his opinion of her absentee father. "Your ancestors knew this land long before the white man arrived."

Karla rolled her eyes. "The white man? Gramps, you're living in the past."

He raised the sharp wooden poker in his hand. "And you've forgotten who you are and where you come from. But don't worry. You won't become a pretendian *like your mother. I'll educate you."*

He returned to his cooking pot and ladled a thick porridge into two bowls The scent of cinnamon wafted in the air. Karla's mouth watered. She'd pee later.

Karla disentangled her body from the hammock and joined him by the campfire. He handed her a bowl and a bent metal spoon.

"Thanks, Gramps."

"You'll call me Ichigouti."

Karla repeated the name. "What does it mean?"

"Guide. And I will call you Inhouti. Student."

Karla ate in silence. Ichigouti wasn't his real name. Let the delusional old fart call her what he liked. At the first opportunity, she'd escape the loser and return to civilization. Her mother had called her a whore. She'd refused to defend her only daughter and turned a blind eye to years of abuse. Her mother deserved Derek. Karla didn't care. Life had toughened her. She'd make her own way in the world.

Ichigouti put aside his bowl and opened the lid of a second pot on the fire. He stirred the odorless contents with a wooden spoon.

Grunting with satisfaction, he replaced the lid. Then, he removed the spoon and, taking care not to dirty his fingers, he wiped the thick, black paste on a cloth.

"I'm not eating that."

Ichigouti chuckled. "Good. Don't touch it either."

The paste wasn't edible. Was it poisonous? Curiosity poked a hole in her veil of rebellion.

"What is it?"

He bared his teeth as he smiled. "This is for the hunt."

CHAPTER 33

A wooden floorboard creaked in the early hours of Monday morning. Claire held her breath. She sat at the kitchen table. After a long silence, the creaking continued. Somebody was treading furtively on the staircase, and Claire had left her gun upstairs.

Troubled thoughts had roused her from slumber at 2 AM. Claire knew what she had to do today. But crossing that red line might end her career at the FBI. Newburgh PD might take her back, but her life was here with Rob. Was her maneuver worth the risk?

She'd tossed and turned for a half hour, then padded downstairs in her pajamas for a glass of milk. Optimistic about getting back to sleep, she hadn't turned on the downstairs lights.

Apex cast a long shadow over her future. Claire stood at a crossroads. She'd exhausted all other courses of action. Her next intervention called for a public confrontation. The daring move might blow the case open or give Agent Massoud an excuse to expel her from the Bureau.

Losing her job was the minor risk. *Apex lived.* Their operatives executed brazen assassinations: Director Warren; Chief Alda; Tony Russo; and countless unnamed victims. Claire might have escaped their attention until now. But by pouring daylight on the cabal of psychopaths, she'd draw their fire for sure.

The creak of the staircase raised another possibility. Someone was sneaking upstairs. Had Apex already gotten wind of her inquiries? Had Alpha deployed his assassins to eliminate her before she said too much?

Soundlessly, Claire rose from her chair. She lifted a hefty frying pan from the drying rack and neared the hallway, step by step. The intruder wouldn't expect a preemptive strike from behind. Another creak. She hesitated. The footsteps were moving toward her, not away.

Claire lowered the pan and stepped into view. At the bottom of the staircase, Felicity pressed her hands to her chest and swore.

"You startled me, Claire. What are you doing up so early?"

Claire turned on the kitchen light. "I was about to ask you the same thing."

Felicity's silky robe covered frilly nightclothes like a seductress from an old movie. Claire wasn't falling for her charms.

Felicity spotted the frying pan in Claire's hand and twisted her lips into a mocking smile.

"Were you going to brain me with the frying pan or cook me breakfast in bed?"

"Breakfast in bed? Don't get too comfortable here."

Felicity scoffed. As if to prove Claire wrong, she sidled past her into the kitchen and heated the kettle. She felt perfectly at home. To her mind, Claire was the intruder.

The older woman prepared a mug of coffee. "Having trouble sleeping, dear?"

Claire said nothing. Felicity didn't care about her well-being.

"I don't blame you. After this mess you've created for us, I couldn't sleep either."

"What mess?"

"Rob almost lost his life, and you're now complicating matters at work. Do you want to get him fired, too?"

Claire and Rob hadn't argued. But she pounced on Felicity's admission of guilt. "So, you've been eavesdropping on us."

"The walls are thin. You don't expect me to plug my ears day and night, do you?" She tutted. "After all he's been through, he deserves better."

"You mean after surviving a childhood with you?"

Felicity snarled at her and dropped all pretense of polite conversation.

"You know nothing about me. I'm not proud of everything I've done, but I've changed. I'm putting him first. You should do the same."

"I am."

But the fragment of truth pierced Claire's heart. Did she put his needs first? Or had she let her need to catch a criminal jeopardize their future?

Felicity scoffed again. "If you truly cared for him, you'd leave. I know all about your sordid exploits, Ms. Killer Wolfe."

Despite herself, Claire laughed. The low blow had missed its mark.

"I have nothing to do with that website. It's the creation of one seriously disturbed conspiracy theorist."

"I doubt the FBI will see things that way. Shouldn't your employers decide?"

Felicity didn't scare her. "We let you into our home, and now you're threatening us?"

"Not *us. You.* You're no good for my son. He'll realize that—sooner rather than later."

Claire folded her arms. The old hag was pathetic. "We'll see about that, mother of the year."

Felicity snapped, "And if he doesn't, I'll slit your throat while you sleep. You have no idea what I'm capable of!"

Claire laughed. Relief washed over her. The Devil had burst through Felicity's motherly facade. She had signed her own eviction notice.

"That's it. You've overstayed your welcome. I want you out of our house. Today."

Felicity sneered. "*My son's* house. And good luck with that, my girl. Blood is thicker than water."

"We'll see."

Claire marched upstairs. Felicity clambered after her, but she was too late to stop her. No amount of lasagna would save Felicity now.

Claire nudged Rob. "Rob. Wake up."

Rob moaned. "What time is it?"

"Two-thirty AM. It's your mom."

He turned on the bedside lamp and blinked back the light. "What about her?"

"She threatened to slit my throat in my sleep."

"What?" Fury knocked him wide awake.

Claire chuckled in astonishment. "Yeah, she's lost it."

She looked over her shoulder, but Felicity had disappeared. *That's it. Start packing.*

Rob reached for his crutches. "She has to go."

Claire helped him to his feet. He knocked on Felicity's door. He knocked again. A sudden doubt tugged at Claire's heart. Had the old woman jumped out the window in desperation or swallowed a bottle of sleeping pills? Claire wanted to get rid of her, but she hadn't wished her any harm.

Rob opened the door. Inky darkness filled the room.

"Mom?"

"Huh?" Felicity's voice sounded groggy with sleep. "Who's there?"

He switched on the light. "You've gone too far."

Under the covers, Felicity shielded her eyes with her arm. "What's going on?"

An astonished laugh escaped Claire. *What a nerve!* The old woman had climbed back into bed and pretended to be asleep. They wouldn't fall for that trick.

Rob folded his arms. "Apologize to Claire."

"Apologize? For what? You woke *me* up in the middle of the night."

Her self-righteous indignation almost convinced Claire, and she'd heard Felicity's threat firsthand!

Rob looked to Claire for an explanation. *No. He doesn't believe her, does he?*

Claire channeled her rage at Felicity. "You threatened to get me fired. You said you'd kill me in my sleep."

His mother screwed up her face. "Nonsense! I would never say such a thing. How could you even think that?"

"Are you calling me a liar?"

Felicity grimaced. "That doesn't even make sense. Why would I threaten to get you fired if I'm going to kill you anyway?"

The question confounded Claire for a second. Why should she explain the logic of Felicity's mean words? But the old woman had tripped up Claire's certainty and undermined her account of the event. The damage was done.

Rob raised his hands. "Hold on. Everybody calm down."

Claire swore under her breath. He was de-escalating the confrontation and trying to appear impartial. Felicity had planned her every word, and Claire had walked into her trap. Now Rob didn't know what to believe.

Felicity dismissed the fight with a wave of her hand. "Let her be, Rob. Claire had a bad dream, that's all. I forgive her. We'll forget about this in the morning."

Claire exploded. "Oh, no you don't. I want you out of the house by the time I get back from work. Do you understand?"

Felicity closed her eyes and smiled sweetly. "Perfectly."

CHAPTER 34

Claire drove to Washington's Capitol Visitor Center that morning and locked her service weapon in the trunk of her car. Unarmed, she felt naked and vulnerable, but she wanted to avoid unnecessary obstacles. During the drive, her skirmish with Felicity that night looped in her mind and boiled her blood. Claire pushed those thoughts away. She had to focus on the risky task at hand. *Use the backdoor.* Claire was following Rob's advice to bypass the gatekeeper. She'd need all her wits about her. *Don't blow your one chance at face time with the man who calls the shots.*

Inside the building, Claire handed her FBI identity card to the uniformed security guard and walked through the metal detector. The machine didn't beep. The officer returned her card. Claire relaxed. *One obstacle down, more to come.*

She entered the airy expanse of Emancipation Hall. The Statue of Freedom stood guard in her Grecian robes, helmet, and sword. Claire dodged groups of tourists and government workers and marched toward the Senate meeting rooms.

She had researched the time and location of the oversight committee's meeting online and headed down a long corridor.

Two security personnel stood guard outside the brown double doors of room SVC-217. The Senate had toughened up security after the CIRG bombing. Claire slowed her pace to a casual walk. *Act like you belong here.*

She smiled at the nearest guard, a black man with a navy suit jacket and a white earpiece.

He didn't return the smile. "This is a closed session, ma'am."

"I know. Running late." Claire handed him her FBI card. "I drove up from Quantico."

The guard checked his clipboard. "Ms. Wolfe, you're not on the list."

She feigned surprise. "Really? OK. I guess I'll wait here."

"I'm afraid you'll have to clear the area."

She weighed arguing with the man, but a debate would invite closer scrutiny. "OK."

As she turned to leave, her phone vibrated in her pocket.

"Hi, Rob." She used the call as an excuse to slow her pace.

"Have you spoken to him?"

"Not yet. I just got here. The meeting is already in session."

"Got it."

They had stuck to a safe topic and skirted the night's drama. Claire felt responsible, too. She'd fallen into Felicity's trap. She'd lost her temper and given Felicity an ultimatum. In other words, she'd placed Rob in an impossible situation. Would he side with his fiancée or his mother?

Rob cleared his throat. "I'm sorry about last night."

Was he apologizing for doubting her or did he regret the whole incident? Claire wanted to extricate him from the dilemma. Felicity had orchestrated the situation. He was her victim, too. But part of her was angry with him for not seeing through his mother's deception. Throughout his childhood, Felicity had gaslighted him, and now she had targeted Claire with the same psychological weaponry. This was a no-brainer. Why was he so blind?

Claire squeezed her phone. "Me, too."

"Mom was out of line."

"She was."

"What she did is inexcusable."

Thank God! Rob wasn't blind after all. But would he bite the bullet?

"Still, can we give her another chance?"

Claire drew a deep breath. "We've tried, Rob. It isn't working out."

"But she's really making an effort."

"Only when you're around. With me, she's a different person. She's poison. We have enough to deal with—"

The doors of the meeting room opened, and suits poured out. The session had concluded.

"I have to go, Rob. I'll call you back."

A tall, white-haired man charged ahead, and two aides hurried in his wake. She recognized him from the TV news. Senator Arnold Schultz moved with the determined stride of a much younger man. His current pace indicated he had no intention of stopping.

Claire waited until he was within six feet. "Senator!"

He turned his head, locked his eyes on hers, and raised his eyebrows. To her surprise, he slowed.

An armed guard stepped between Claire and the senator. "Ma'am! Please step aside."

"It's OK, Gavin." The senator smiled at her amiably. "I'm sure Ms..."

"Wolfe. Claire Wolfe from the BAU."

"I'm sure Ms. Wolfe means no harm. Please, walk with me."

Claire fell into step alongside him. Her throat dried up. She had a few seconds to win his confidence.

"You're the BAU's new hire, aren't you? Don't be surprised. I've reviewed every CIRG employee. That's a long list, but I haven't forgotten everything. I'm very sorry about the loss of your friends. What's on your mind, Agent Wolfe?"

"I have new information on the bombing."

"I must refer you to Special Agent Massoud. He's leading the investigation."

"Sir, I've tried Massoud, but he's not open to this angle."

The senator ground to a halt, and his eyebrows bunched. "What angle is that?"

"I have a folder of evidence."

He fixed her with a penetrating gaze. The other attendees passed them by.

Senator Schultz eyed his gold wristwatch. "You've got thirty seconds."

Claire didn't waste one. "Massoud is focusing entirely on the drug cartel."

He frowned. "That seems reasonable. Director Warren was taking action against the cartels."

"We have evidence that links the bombing to a group called Apex."

He squinted at Claire. "I'm not familiar with Apex." He glanced at his aides, who shook their heads.

"They're a covert group of killers. As a homicide detective, I encountered them in Newburgh, Massachusetts."

A smile returned to the senator's lips. "The Middle School Murderer. And the Newburgh Slasher. As I said, I read your file. Most make for boring reading. Yours didn't."

His words gave her oxygen. Senator Schultz respected her service record. Would he be sympathetic to her cause?

"We thought we'd put Apex out of commission, but now it seems there's more of them."

"What does Agent Massoud think?"

"He isn't willing to listen. I'm afraid he doesn't think highly of me."

The senator smiled warmly. "Then he's mistaken." He pursed his lips. "Though he did have solid leads on the cartel."

Within seconds, Senator Schultz had found the weak link in her theory.

Claire came clean. "The cartel's role isn't clear yet. Apex and Moretti might be collaborating. I can't say for sure."

"I see." He shook her hand. "I'll have a word with Agent Massoud and ask him to take a closer look. It's been a pleasure meeting you, Agent Wolfe."

"Thank you, sir!"

The senator receded down the corridor.

Claire floated back to her car on a cloud of optimism. *Mission accomplished.* Massoud would hate her for speaking to his superior behind his back, but the deed—and the damage—was done. If the facts proved Claire right, he'd overlook her insubordination. She'd fulfilled her duty to Alda and to herself.

On the highway back to Quantico, Claire reviewed every word of her short talk with the senator. She had to seal every hole in her theory or Massoud would make a fool of her.

How is Moretti connected to Apex? Associating with notorious groups went against the Apex DNA. The bold attack on the FBI would only draw law enforcements' fire.

Apex plans were never simple. They had layers. Claire had to tackle the problem on multiple intersecting levels if she was going to...

That's it. Claire understood. The conclusion was obvious when she viewed the puzzle from the right angle. Her encounters with Apex had uniquely prepared her for this challenge. She hadn't reconstructed the full picture, but she'd discovered an edge. Claire knew where to locate the next piece, and that step filled her with dread.

Running low on gas, Claire stopped at an Exxon in North Stafford. Petroleum fumes assaulted her nostrils while she tanked up. Rob wouldn't like the next step one bit. But she saw no other way forward.

Claire replaced the gas hose and screwed the cap on the tank. She opened the driver's door, then halted, one foot in the car. Across the street, a middle-aged woman hurried out of a Wells Fargo. Felicity shoved a fat gray purse and a checkbook into her handbag. Rob had an account at that bank branch. His mother had no business there. No *legitimate* business. *You slimy little snake.* The woman had triggered her crook detector from day one, and finally, Claire had discovered what she was up to.

Claire should buy a lottery ticket. Today was her lucky day.

CHAPTER 35

Special Agent Rafiq Massoud breezed through the lobby of the Hart Senate Office Building on Constitution Avenue without slowing. The security staff knew him well. An hour ago, Senator Schultz had brought their meeting forward by two days. The sudden change in schedule unsettled Rafiq. His next report on the investigation's progress was partial and unpolished. Jumping to conclusions would only raise the senator's expectations for a speedy arrest, and premature optimism had burned Rafiq before. But the senator always got what he wanted, and this morning he wanted to meet. Had something else come up? Was Schultz unsatisfied with Rafiq's handling of the investigation?

Rafiq's cardiologist had ordered him to take the stairs, but Rafiq's palms were already sweaty, so he chose the elevator. A nod to the secretary and a knock on the door, and Rafiq entered the senator's spacious office.

"You wanted to see me, Senator?"

"Come in, Rafiq. Have a seat."

Senator Schultz waved him to a comfy armchair. He'd kept the same office since their paths first dovetailed. In ten years, hardly anything had changed: the oriental rug; the leather visitor's chairs; the portraits of George Washington and Napoleon Bonaparte; the collection of clay and stone archaeological artifacts. His chamber combined the comforts of a drawing room with the cultural legacy of a museum. This was the senator's home away from home, and unless the voters decided otherwise, he'd never leave.

"How is our investigation going?"

Rafiq skipped the apologies and led with the meat. "Nicky Moretti hasn't made life easy. He's covered his tracks, and he's playing on our legal restrictions. Recently, he moved large sums of money, but we're still one step behind. We need that legislation more than ever. Lowering the requirements for search warrants will expedite our work."

The senator leaned back in his high-backed leather chair and pressed the tips of his fingers together as he stared out the window. Had he heard a word of Rafiq's update?

"Sir?"

"I was thinking."

Rafiq cringed. Whenever the senator had a new thought, Rafiq had to work overtime. He wished Schultz would think less and do more. But the senator headed the oversight committee, so Rafiq bit his tongue.

"Have we considered other directions?"

Rafiq smiled politely. If his wife, Nasim, had planned anything for the weekend, they'd have to cancel. "Do you have a specific direction in mind?"

"What do we know about Apex?"

Rafiq groaned within. He should have guessed. Agent Brown had exiled Dr. Fleischer, so the blame resided with the one remaining option.

"Claire Wolfe got to you, didn't she?"

Schultz grinned. "Special Agent Claire Wolfe, formerly Sergeant Wolfe, showed up after this morning's session."

Rafiq counted to ten. Claire Wolfe was the reason he'd wasted an hour on the highway this morning. The agent was a menace to society.

The senator continued. "She seems to think this clandestine group is responsible for the CIRG bombing, among other crimes."

Rafiq couldn't resist. "Do those include nine-eleven and Pearl Harbor?"

"We shouldn't dismiss her theory out of hand."

"Of course not. I mean no disrespect to Agent Wolfe, but it's a conspiracy theory."

"Have you reviewed her evidence?"

"It's circumstantial at best. A tattoo here and a mysterious dent there. Light on facts, heavy on speculation. Serial killers made her a celebrity in her hometown. Frankly, she seems to enjoy the attention and has unconventional ideas about sociopaths."

"For example?"

"She claims psychopathy is curable."

Senator Schultz grunted. Did he see the danger in that idea?

"But this Apex did exist?"

"In Massachusetts. Until a year ago. I wouldn't lean too heavily on her theories. At one point, Newburgh PD put out a BOLO for her, and I heard rumors about an embarrassing psychological evaluation. I'm betting Newburgh PD were only happy to be rid of her."

"But the FBI accepted her with open arms."

Rafiq scoffed. "Her fiancé recommended her."

Senator Schultz's face soured. He didn't seem to like Rafiq's cynical attitude. Had Schultz developed a soft spot for the pretty agent?

Rafiq softened his assessment. "To be fair, Agent Wolfe alerted us to Unit Chief Alda's assassination. Her suspicions proved right that time."

"Could she be right about Apex, too?"

"I doubt it. And any resources we divert will only help Moretti."

Senator Schultz grimaced. "Forgive me for saying this, Rafiq, but it seems you dislike Agent Wolfe personally. Could this be related to her *unconventional ideas*?"

Rafiq blinked. *Was he prejudiced against her?* The senator knew him—and his family history—better than most people. As a Muslim, Rafiq had faced his share of lazy prejudice. Had he succumbed to that character weakness, too? Had that tunnel vision blinded him to other promising leads? He had told Agent Wolfe he'd review the hospital's CCTV records but failed to follow through.

Rafiq swallowed hard. "Perhaps you're right, Senator. I'll dig deeper."

Schultz smiled with appreciation. "Thank you, Rafiq."

Maybe the senator hadn't wasted his time. By focusing on the big picture, he kept Rafiq honest. Schultz wasn't a senator for nothing.

"Anything else, sir?"

"No. I'll let you get back to work. My apologies for the disruption. And I'll get a move on that legislation."

"Thank you, sir."

Rafiq left the office. He called his aide, Andrew Riddle, from the car.

"Andy, I need you to stop by Sentara Medical and review their CCTV footage."

"Sentara? Don't you mean CIRG?"

"That, too. Delegate if you have to. Focus on Monday last week, the night after the bombing. We're looking for a twenty-something ethnic female with dark hair."

Andy fell silent for a moment. The change in direction had surprised him. "Agent Wolfe's profile for the assassin?"

"Exactly. It's time we laid eyes on Alda's killer."

CHAPTER 36

The man strutted into the killer's living room and whistled. "Nice place!"

She closed the door behind them and tossed her keys on a counter. "Thank you."

The killer had set the scene for a romantic evening. Soft lighting. A comfy leather couch. No carpets and spongy upholstery—nothing to absorb her prey's blood or other forensic traces.

Her work required caution. Daddy had taught her all she needed to know. The home setup allowed her to hone her skills without worrying about getting caught.

Daddy had called off the hit on Robert Cline last week. The special agent was no longer a threat to Apex, and his death might cause more trouble than good. She'd told Daddy about the potential danger Cline's fiancée posed, but he'd advised restraint. *Daddy knows best.*

The downtime allowed her to focus on her hobby. Her prototype had turned out wonderfully. Now, she'd ramp up production. Fortunately, a new batch of raw materials had just walked into her lair.

The man's name was Tristan, and he reeked of margarita. He admired the living room. His muscular neck shimmered with sweat from the dance floor. But she wasn't interested in his athletic physique.

Her guest grinned. "Are you into TRX?"

"What?"

He pointed at the metal hook in the ceiling. "You know, suspension training?"

"Yeah, that's it."

None of the other men she'd brought home had noticed the hook. She'd picked Tristan up in downtown Washington. She preferred noisy, dark nightclubs packed with young, fit specimens. Nobody had seen them leave together. Tristan had visited DC for a two-day conference and had an early flight home tomorrow. The plane would leave without him. But his memory would live on forever in her creations.

The killer shed her leather jacket and unbuttoned her shirt, revealing a bra of black lace.

Tristan feasted his eyes on her exposed flesh and smiled. "You don't waste any time."

"Life's too short to waste time."

"I agree."

He leaned in for a kiss, but she wagged her finger at him.

"Uh-uh. Clothes first."

Tristan pulled his shirt over his head and dropped it on the floor. She ran her fingers over his chest and bulging abs. The six-pack was useless to her, but she appreciated the shaved chest. *How considerate.* She ran her tongue over his pecks, and he shuddered with delight.

"You have great skin."

She'd developed an eye for dermal quality. Nothing frustrated her more than bringing home defective material. Tonight, she'd hit the jackpot.

Her prepping equipment—a fruit knife and a vial of curare extract—lay in a discreet drawer. She stored the other tools of her trade rolled in a plastic sheath because often she had to travel for work on short notice. The guest room housed reams of plastic sheeting and tubs of industrial-strength acid. By dawn, only choice sections of her guest's hide would remain.

Tristan grabbed her shoulders and drew her near. His body had responded to her. He could overpower her easily, but he wouldn't. Tristan was a gentleman. She knew how to choose them. Once, an impatient donor had tried to force himself on her. She'd neutralized the threat, but the scuffle had ruined his skin. The killer had learned her lesson. Since that incident, she only selected docile candidates. Women had domesticated men over thousands of years, and she reaped the rewards.

She dodged Tristan's kiss again. "I have a surprise for you."

She handed him a red blindfold.

Doubt flickered in his eyes. "A surprise?"

She knew what he was thinking. *We met minutes ago. Can I trust her?*

The killer had a surefire remedy for cold feet. She kicked off her shoes and peeled away her jeans, revealing the delicate lingerie bottoms. Visual stimuli alleviated most men's fears, and Tristan was no different.

He grinned, and his qualms melted. She tied the red sash over his eyes. Sexual desire had blinded him, literally. *Men are so predictable.*

She unbuckled his belt and slid his jeans down to his shoes. "Nice boxers."

He laughed. "Thanks."

She'd destroy his clothes, too. She kept no mementos or trophies of her subjects, only their leather. *Daddy knows best.*

Tristan's breathing picked up. *Good.* The poison would spread quickly in his bloodstream, shortening that awkward moment when the sheep realized he'd entered the slaughterhouse.

"No peeking."

He crossed his fingers. "Scout's honor."

She opened the drawer. Did he think she was reaching for a condom or lubricant? Someday, her youthful looks would fade. How would she lure young men to her lair? She'd cross that bridge later.

She dipped the tip of the knife in the black paste. "Just a few more seconds."

"I'm waiting."

"It'll be worth it. I promise."

He licked his lips and shifted on his feet.

The killer stepped around her guest. She always took them from behind in case they stole a glance at the blade. She hated cheaters. Their cries might alarm the neighbors, and her landlord was an asshole.

She aimed the blade at the back of Tristan's naked arm as though administering a vaccine.

The phone rang. She swore. Hadn't she turned her phone off? She recognized the ringtone. Someone was calling her special phone.

"I'm sorry. I need to take this."

"OK. It's cool."

She answered. "Hello, Daddy. I'm kind of busy."

"I'll be quick," the garbled voice said. "Take care of our friend."

She smiled. "Understood."

Daddy had a new target for her—Claire Wolfe. *What had changed his mind?*

The killer hid her knife in the drawer. She'd been looking forward to her date tonight, but the stars had aligned for her, and Daddy's orders demanded immediate execution.

Tristan bobbed his head, still blindfolded. "Are we good to go?"

She pulled the red sash from his head. "Something's come up. You have to leave."

"Seriously?"

"Now." She shoved his shirt into his hands. "Sorry, it's work."

"But didn't you say, 'Daddy?'"

"It's a family business."

He put on his jeans and shirt, and she herded him outside.

"Man! I thought I was getting lucky tonight."

She shut the door on him. "You did, pal, You did."

CHAPTER 37

R ob paced the bedroom on his crutches and rehearsed his speech while Claire showered. She'd arrived home that evening all smiles. *Perfect.* He needed her in a good mood because Claire wouldn't like what he had to say.

"I've been thinking," he whispered. "Maybe we should slow down and all get to know each other better." *No.* That sounded like he was breaking up with her. *Wrong impression.* He wanted to build relationships, not destroy them. He and Claire were creating a family, and families meant children...and grandparents. Despite the bickering, Rob had made genuine progress with his mom. Couldn't Claire give her a second chance?

The showerhead turned off. His mouth dried up, too. He had a few seconds of grace before the confrontation. No, not a confrontation—a discussion. He sighed. Why was this so complicated? He'd trained as an FBI hostage negotiator, for crying out loud. Why was making peace between family members harder than wrangling with hardened criminals?

Claire emerged from the bathroom, a towel wrapped around her midsection and another covering her hair like a turban. She beamed at him.

"Today was a good day."

Rob forgot about his speech. "You spoke with Schultz?" He had assumed the senator would blow Claire off. That was the best-case scenario. The worst-case involved a summary firing for obstructing justice.

Claire selected underwear from the closet. "He only gave me thirty seconds, but they were enough. He said he'll tell Massoud to reconsider the Apex angle."

"What does Massoud have to say about that?" Would the risky tactic return to bite them in the ass?

"Nothing yet. That's why we need to work fast to fix our theory's weakest link—the Apex-Moretti connection. I read up on Nicky Moretti. His cartel is grassroots and very involved in local communities. Moretti presents himself as a man of the people. He's not the kind to attack the FBI or join with Apex. And his dead goon, Stefano Bruno, had signed a plea bargain to rat on the cartel. His death was too convenient to be accidental."

Her excitement was infectious.

"So...what's his connection to Apex?"

Claire grinned mysteriously. "Maybe? I've been thinking. Alpha founded Apex. Their lots consist of multiple layers. So far, we've focused on the inner purpose—what they really aim to achieve with the bombing. But there's also the outer layer, too—the public deception. That's how Sally identified the Newburgh Slasher's final target."

"Yes, I know. And?"

"The FBI thinks Moretti is behind the attack. Maybe that's exactly what Apex wants? And if that's their plan—"

Rob completed her sentence. "Apex isn't working with Moretti. They're rivals. But we considered that before."

"Not rivals. Something else."

"What?"

"I don't know. But I'm going to find out."

Claire selected a fresh work suit.

Rob had a bad feeling about this. "Dressing up for dinner?"

"I'm going out."

"Why?"

"To get answers from the horse's mouth."

"From Moretti? You can't be serious."

This was Rob's fault. He'd encouraged her to bend the rules. But this gamble might be a suicide mission.

Claire shrugged. "The enemy of my enemy is my friend. The cartel is our ally."

"You're making a lot of assumptions. If the cartel whacked the FBI director, they'll add you to their hit list without blinking."

Claire buttoned her blouse. "I'll be careful." She headed for the bedroom door.

"Wait, Claire. There's something we need to discuss. I've been thinking, too."

She sighed. "She's still here. I saw her car out front. We'll deal with Felicity later. I don't have time for her now." Claire brightened. "What's for dinner?"

Felicity served shepherd's pie. Both women sat at the dinner table and pretended that their late-night altercation hadn't happened. Rob's mom spooned minced meat and mashed potatoes onto his plate and smiled at him. He returned a weak grin. Claire hadn't let him share his proposal with her. *Too late now.*

They ate in silence. Neither woman looked at the other. *Silence is better than death threats.* Were they on the road to a chilly truce?

He swallowed. "This is very good."

"Thank you, son. Wait till you taste what I've planned for next week. We'll have—"

Claire snorted.

Felicity smiled. "Is something the matter, dear?"

"I wouldn't bank on being here next week, if I were you."

Claire glanced at Rob, and he almost choked on his mouthful. He should have stuck with silence.

Felicity smirked at Claire. "Didn't get the memo, dear? I'm staying."

Claire shot Rob a piercing glance. "What is she talking about?"

Rob hesitated. "Um. I've been thinking." The rest of his speech evaporated from his mind.

"Rob, we were going to discuss this later."

He found his tongue. "Mom and I have made progress."

Felicity nodded and touched his hand. "Tell her, Rob. This is our chance to start over—to get to know each other again."

Claire slammed her hand on the table, and the cutlery tinkled. "I've gotten to know your mother well enough, Rob. She hasn't changed. She's taking advantage of you."

Felicity scoffed. "I've done nothing but slave away since I arrived. I'd hardly call that taking advantage."

Mom's victimized tone wasn't helping.

Rob stammered. "Sh-she's trying—"

Claire reddened with rage. "It's an act. She's manipulating you. Can't you see that?"

Felicity gasped. "Rob, are you going to let her speak to your mother like that?"

Rob felt hot and confused. This was his parent's divorce all over again. Only this time, he was caught between his mother and his fiancée. Each used him to strike at the other and forced him to take sides. Why couldn't they all be on *his* side?

"Can't we just ...get along—for my sake?"

Felicity folded her arms. "I will. For your sake, Rob, I'll put aside all my concerns about this *hussy*."

Rob cringed. She'd slipped in another insult and implied Claire didn't care about his well-being. Mom had a talent for rubbing people the wrong way.

Claire huffed incredulously, which only kindled his mother's wrath. It was like watching a train wreck—from inside the train.

Felicity lifted her nose in the air. "I'm even prepared to overlook the incident with my earrings."

Claire's knuckles whitened around the knife. "What incident?"

"Go on—pretend you don't know. I found my earrings in your bedside drawer."

"You went through our drawers?"

"Only to find my earrings. They were a gift from my late mother—Rob's grandmother."

Claire glared at Rob as if to ask: Are you swallowing this nonsense? He didn't believe for a moment that Claire had stolen anything. But was he supposed to call his mother a liar?

Claire gazed at Felicity through fiery eyes. "I don't even wear jewelry."

Mom shrugged. "Of course you don't. But they're pure gold. You'd get a fat wad of cash for them at any pawnshop."

Claire huffed again. "Fine. I wasn't going to say anything since you were already leaving, but you forced my hand." She turned to Rob. "I saw her leaving Wells Fargo today—your branch."

Felicity tittered. "Now she's following me around like a common criminal."

Claire ignored her. "She put a checkbook in her bag, and I'm willing to bet it's yours. That's why she's been hanging around, Rob. Not"—she drew air quotes—"to reconnect. She's using your injury and good heart to steal from us."

Mom sneered. "She talks like it's her money already. Don't say I didn't warn you, Rob."

Claire's stare could cut diamonds, but Rob had to tell her the truth.

"Claire, I gave Mom my checkbook. I sent her to get cash for groceries."

Claire's cheeks turned a deeper scarlet as the news hit home. She'd only been protecting him. With his mother's track record, Claire's suspicions were well-founded. But the rebuttal made a fool of Claire. A little voice at the back of his mind whispered: *Felicity set Claire up for the fall.* He had to act quickly to calm her down.

"I'm sorry, Claire. I know how that must have looked. I should have told you. But you were busy."

Felicity snorted. "Busy following me around, apparently."

"Mother!"

Mom raised her hands in surrender. "I take that back." She zipped her mouth, clearly knowing the damage was done.

Claire placed her cutlery on the table. "I'm through with her. When I get back, she'd better not be here."

She grabbed her car keys and stormed out into the night.

CHAPTER 38

Claire parked on the dark, tree-lined street corner and left the engine running.

"Do you know what you're doing?" Talking to oneself was a sign of madness. *Have I gone insane?*

Claire snatched a sidelong glimpse at her destination as she drove by. Nicky Moretti's mansion resembled the other residences of Berkley, the luxury Washington, DC neighborhood. The three-story brick edifice boasted Grecian columns and carved gables but also high walls and electric fencing. The owners flaunted their wealth but guarded their privacy. Unlike the other homes, the Moretti estate used cement barriers and armed guards to keep booby-trapped vehicles and snoopy neighbors away.

During the drive north, hurt had simmered in Claire's chest. How could Rob take Felicity's side after all she'd done to him? Did he honestly believe she had changed? Maybe Agent Massoud was right. Psychopaths didn't change. They didn't heal. They only got better at destroying others' lives.

Claire sucked in a deep breath to calm her mind. She had to focus on the task ahead. Once she stepped behind those walls, she'd need her wits about her. Nicky Moretti was not in bed with Apex. He hadn't killed his valuable asset, Tony Russo. The only way to unlock Alpha's identity was to speak with Nicky Moretti, face-to-face. With luck, Moretti would provide the missing key and empower Claire to behead the snake. And she knew just how to convince him.

She checked the magazine of her Glock, killed the motor, and got out of the car.

Claire understood Rob's opposition to her gutsy move, but she had no choice. She'd alerted the investigation to the existence of Apex. Alpha had a mole in the FBI. His wolves were already circling her, ready to pounce. If Claire didn't expose Alpha soon, those wolves would silence her forever.

She crossed the street and headed for the gates of the Moretti mansion. A security guard blocked her path.

"Stop there, ma'am. This is private property."

Thick body armor covered his torso. He held a semi-automatic rifle loosely in both hands.

Claire presented her FBI identity card. "Special Agent Claire Wolfe. I'm here to see Niccolo Moretti."

The guard took her card. "Wait here, please."

He retreated to the guard shack and spoke into a telephone. Claire counted four security cameras. Beyond the tall iron gates, a cobblestone driveway led through manicured gardens, all illuminated by floodlights. Without the expensive trappings, the mansion could be mistaken for a high-security prison.

The guard put down the phone and signaled her to be patient. Claire hoped she'd get her FBI card back. She didn't want to explain to FBI security how Moretti had acquired her access card. Soon enough, a golf cart hummed along the driveway toward them. The driver was not Nicky Moretti but a henchman in a suit. A pedestrian gate buzzed open. The suit walked over to the guard, examined Claire's card, and approached her.

"How may I help you, Special Agent Wolfe?"

He had a heavy New York accent and Mediterranean tan. His sarcastic tone implied they were playing a thinly disguised game that he happened to enjoy. He hid his muscular bulk well under his suit but not the pistol at his waist. The thug dressed his intimidation tactics in fine Italian clothes and called himself a civilized man. Behind him, a security camera swiveled toward them. *Let the show begin.*

"I'm here to see Niccolo Moretti."

Henchman smiled. "Mr. Moretti is a very busy man, Ms. Wolfe. Why don't you speak with me? I'm Vinny."

"I need to speak with your boss."

"Did you make an appointment?"

As if I can schedule an appointment with the drug lord.

"This isn't an official visit. I'm not really here."

He laughed and rubbed his nose. "Do you have a warrant?"

"Do I need one?"

He handed back her card. "Mr. Moretti thanks you for stopping by."

With a parting nod, he swaggered back to the golf cart. Claire swore under her breath. She didn't even get past the front gate.

"I'm here about Apex."

Vinny stopped in his tracks. Did he think Alpha had sent her? Would he deny all knowledge of the group? Or had the unfamiliar word simply aroused Vinny's curiosity?

The suit pressed his finger to his ear, as though adjusting a miniature speaker. When he turned around, the sarcasm had fled from his features.

He held out his hand. "Hand over your weapon. Mr. Moretti will see you now."

CHAPTER 39

"You've got balls, Agent Wolfe, I'll give you that."

Nicky Moretti stoked the burning logs in the fireplace of his den with a long silver-handled poker. Claire interpreted his statement as a compliment.

Vinny had driven her in the golf cart to the house, then led her through the Grecian pillars and along marble corridors to a cozy study, where the cartel overlord tended the fire.

Nicky Moretti had more gray hairs than his FBI profile photo. At the lacquered bar cabinet, he poured eighteen-year-old whisky into two glass tumblers. Claire settled on an armchair of aged leather. Books lined the oak shelves from floor to ceiling. The spines of leather-bound titles carried familiar names. *Don Quixote. A Christmas Carol.* First editions and collector's items, no doubt. Moretti probably hadn't read any of them. The books, like his house and community service, were the trappings of a violent man who, having defeated his criminal rivals, longed for the warm embrace of civil society. Her intuitions flared again. She was right about him. Nicky Moretti was no friend of Apex.

He handed her a tumbler, eased onto the chair opposite her, and sipped his drink.

"I'm not exactly in the FBI's good books after the bombing."

"I don't believe you did that."

He studied her and seemed to accept her words at face value. "Thank you, for what it's worth. Nobody will believe the truth, anyway." He eyed the untouched drink in her hands. "Go on, I'm not trying to poison you. I promise."

Agent Massoud believed Moretti had ordered the execution of Chief Alda and Tony Russo. But Claire had to trust him.

She sipped her drink. Three seconds later, she could still move her fingers and draw breath. Moretti maintained his innocence, but he'd stopped short of fingering the bombing's true culprit. His hesitance bolstered her convictions.

"I know about Apex."

Fear flickered in his eyes. "Then you know you're as good as dead for speaking that name." The drug lord seemed unwilling to pronounce the word Apex.

"I've taken them out before. I'll do it again. But I need information."

"This isn't Newburgh, Special Agent Wolfe."

First Senator Schultz, now Niccolo Moretti. How had she appeared on the radar of these heavy hitters? Her surprise must have shown on her face because he laughed.

"I like to know who I'm dealing with. And any new agent at the Bureau so close to the blast is of particular interest to me."

"Then you know of my track record?"

He shrugged. "How do I know you're not Apex? After you moved to the Bureau, somebody got to Director Warren. Could that be you?"

A dark thought troubled her. Was that Agent Massoud's working assumption, too? No wonder he'd stonewalled her.

Once again, Claire found herself surrounded by accusations she couldn't disprove.

She pushed onward. "They've gotten to you."

Niccolo didn't deny the claim. "Maybe they're checking up on me right now to make sure I'm playing by their rules?"

The balance of power emerged from his words. Apex commanded. Niccolo obeyed. The Mafia boss surely chafed at the master-slave relationship. But he resisted the urge to shake off their yoke. He feared them.

"If I was their operative, I wouldn't throw their name around in public. Apex thrives in the shadows. Help me light them up."

Niccolo grunted. His mouth worked as he considered her proposition.

Claire needed to seal the deal before he balked at the danger. "I can't get rid of them alone. I need information."

He shook his head. "I tried that. Crush one tentacle, two more take its place. Their vengeance has no limits."

Claire connected his words with other facts. "The warehouse bombing. Stefano Bruno's death was no accident."

Moretti's jaw clenched. "They sent kids, at first. Like an idiot, I underestimated them."

"The college kids who died at the warehouse?" Claire had been right—the students were members of Apex.

"We got wind of the deal Bruno cut with the Feds and gave him a choice. Either he took one for the team or his family would pay the price. He made the honorable decision. Tony provided the explosives, and Bruno wiped the kids out."

Niccolo knocked back his whisky. "That was a mistake. They skinned Tony alive and sent me a photo. He was like family to me. Then they stole Tony's C4 and took out the director of the FBI. Now the Feds want my head on a pike."

Claire's thoughts raced. She had thought Apex had targeted

Chief Alda to bury YARI and protect their recruitment strategy. Had Alpha killed two birds with one stone?

He continued. "These people are animals. They respect no code, no rules. I should have done as they said and counted my blessings."

"What do they want from you?"

Niccolo laughed. "What does anybody want? Money."

Claire leaned back on the luxurious upholstery of the chair. The audacity of the move rendered her speechless. Apex wasn't moving into the drug trade. They were extorting the Mob. They'd given organized crime a taste of their own medicine. And they were getting away with it.

"How much?"

Nicky snorted. "Five times what they were asking before."

Apex had jacked up their fee. Were they squeezing Moretti for all they could, or did they need the money for a big operation?

"Why so much? What are they up to?"

"They don't exactly share their plans with me. But whatever it is, it's big. The FBI bombing will seem like the good old days."

Claire leaned forward. Stopping Alpha had become much more urgent.

"Go on record. Tell us everything you know about Apex. Let the Bureau root them out."

"Haven't you been listening? These people are animals."

"We can protect you."

"The way you protected Director Warren? Ha! You can't save me. The FBI can't even save itself. I received that message loud and clear. If I snitch, they'll come after me, and when they do, Tony Russo's death will seem merciful compared with what they'll do to me—and my family."

Claire sighed. "My colleagues are convinced Apex is a fairy tale. Your testimony is the only thing that will convince them

Apex exists. I need your help. You know what they're capable of. Think about what they'll do with your money. We have to stop them."

Niccolo Moretti, Washington's most powerful gangster, shrugged in defeat. "Be my guest. But this conversation never happened."

Claire ground her molars in frustration. The FBI didn't believe Apex existed, and Nicky Moretti refused to prove them wrong. Claire was on her own.

She downed her whisky, too, and got to her feet. Nicky Moretti stared at the dying embers of the coals in the fireplace, obviously lost in thoughts of doom.

"I'll show myself out."

"Agent Wolfe," he said as she touched the doorknob.

She turned, hoping that the cartel lord had changed his mind.

"Good luck."

Claire marched down the driveway. No golf cart escorted her out. The guards buzzed the gate open and returned her identity card and firearm.

She crossed the street and fished her car keys from her pocket. Eleven o'clock on a Monday night, Claire still had an hour's drive back home. She climbed into the driver's seat, inserted the key into the ignition, and hesitated.

Home. Was Rob's house still her home? Would Felicity be there when she got back? His mother was a snake. She'd slithered into his heart and taken over his life. Couldn't he see what she was doing to him—to them?

Was her move to Quantico a mistake? Shortly after she'd started work at the FBI, her life had imploded—her career and now her relationship with Rob. Did she belong here? Claire never thought she'd miss Newburgh, but at least she had friends in the Investigations Bureau.

Claire slumped on her seat. *Friends only get you so far.* Felicity was right about that. Blood was thicker than water. Diane had sailed off into her bright new life, but fate had stranded Claire in shark-infested waters. She needed Rob's lifeline more than ever, but she'd never felt so alone.

She started the car and drove off. Claire should never have given Rob that ultimatum. She'd swallowed Felicity's bait again —hook, line, and sinker. She should give him space. He needed to work things out with his mother. Claire would stay out of their way.

Claire stopped at a red light. The streets were desolate. Berkley was known for its high realty prices, not its nightlife.

Rob was right—he wasn't a child. If Felicity was up to no good, Rob would figure it out and wake from his slumber. Either way, he'd find his way back to Claire. And if he didn't—

Sharp pain in her shoulder shattered her thoughts. "Ow!"

Behind her, fabric rustled. Somebody—or something— moved in the backseat. Claire reached for her weapon, but her arms refused to move. Her seat belt clicked open. The backrest lowered. Claire flopped on the reclining seat. Hands grasped her arms and pulled her backward.

A woman's face hovered over hers, upside down. Olive skin. Slanted eyes. Silky black hair, tied back. The assassin from the hospital!

The killer heaved Claire's body onto the backseat like a sack of potatoes. But Claire's mind remained sharp. Terrified thoughts bubbled to the surface. *Curare extract. Tony Russo. Skinned alive.* Claire screamed. *Somebody! Anybody! Help me!* But her mouth failed to budge. Her tongue lay limp in her mouth. Nobody could hear her cries.

CHAPTER 40

The white-tailed deer grazed on a tuft of wild grass. Karla aligned the string of the bow with the groove at the back of the arrow and oriented the fletching feathers away from the flexible wooden staff. She placed her feet shoulder-width apart, raised the bow, and pulled the shaft back toward her face, forming a T with her arms and shoulders. Then, she aimed the metal tip of the arrow at the center mass of the chewing animal.

Karla had never shot a bow and arrow before today. Ichigouti, her guide and grandfather, had taught her how. Within a half hour, she could hit a tree trunk at twenty feet. But hitting a stationary object was one thing. Killing a moving creature was quite another.

Her heart pounded. Her senses heightened. Ichigouti nodded, and she released the fingers of her string hand. With a familiar whoosh, the arrow launched. The deer leaped at the sound. The arrow ricocheted off the animal's raised hind leg and landed in the undergrowth.

Karla swore. Her prey had escaped into the wild landscape. Ichigouti chuckled at her frustration and stalked toward the spot where the deer had stood.

"Come on."

Karla remained put. She'd collected enough misfired arrows for one day. The old man slipped the arrow into a tube-shaped quiver and stepped deeper into the brush.

"Come on!"

"What's the point? I missed."

"No, you didn't."

Moved by a sudden hope, Karla hurried after him. Forty paces away, her grandfather crouched over the motionless body of the deer. He pointed at the scratch on the animal's hind leg.

"You broke the skin. That's enough."

Karla stared in amazement. Ichigouti had smeared the thick, black paste on the tip of the arrow and instructed Karla not to touch the substance. Now she understood why. The poison was incredibly powerful.

He stroked the deer's neck. We'll get a nice jacket out of this one.

The deer's leg twitched once.

"Is it alive?"

"Oh, yes. He cannot move, but his senses are functional. He can see and hear everything."

Karla drew near. He was right. The animal's chest rose and fell softly as it breathed. She hadn't killed the beast, only paralyzed it. Karla stared at the downed animal at her feet. A sense of beauty and power filled the moment. She and the deer shared a deep connection. Both understood the nature of their relationship. Karla was its master. The deer was at her mercy.

Ichigouti reached for the leather sheath strapped to his thigh and withdrew a large, serrated hunting knife.

"The curare will wear off in a few minutes." He put the knife to the animal's neck.

"Wait." She scanned the brush for onlookers. "Won't we get into trouble for killing it?"

He craned his neck to gaze at her. "White-tail deer breed out of control. They're considered pests in these parts. Park rangers hunt them with rifles and feed them to the homeless. They won't miss this one. We'll put her to better use."

He slaughtered the deer, tied its legs to a large branch, and they carried the carcass back to camp. Ichigouti removed the hide. He seasoned long strips of meat and hung them to dry behind fly nets. The rest of the meat ended up in a venison stew.

That night, they ate by the light of the crackling campfire. Karla dug into her food and enjoyed the warmth of the fire. Her hair was still damp from bathing in a stream of icy water.

"Where did you learn all this?"

Ichigouti stared at the flames. "My grandfather taught me. His grandfather taught him. Our ancestors understood the world." He'd become philosophical at the end of the day's work. "We're all a part of nature. The strong eat the weak. When Columbus arrived in the Caribbean, most of the indigenous tribes perished. Our ancestors didn't. Do you know why?"

Karla shook her head.

"Because they fought back. When Columbus's men reached our villages, they found human flesh on the spit. They'd never encountered ritual cannibalism before. We scared the shit out of them, and they kept their distance." He chuckled, and Karla joined in.

Ichigouti's words comforted her. Karla had never fit in. She'd spent her life thinking she was worthless. But now she'd learned the liberating truth. Karla wasn't a whore. She wasn't a friendless, unsmiling outcast. Karla descended from a long, noble line of survivors. In a world of the weak, she was strong. And the strong devoured the weak.

Her eyes moistened. "Teach me, Ichigouti. Teach me everything."

CHAPTER 41

Under a blanket on the backseat, Claire's limp body lurched as the car moved. Her attacker had climbed into the driver's seat and pulled off. Claire's mind writhed in terror. *Where is she taking me?*

"Crush one tentacle," Nicky Moretti had said, "two more take its place." The tentacles had closed around Claire. There was no way she'd escape alive.

The sound of her galloping heart filled her mind like a siren.

You're still breathing. Don't give up hope. Claire focused on the pain in her shoulder to ease her panic attack. The wound stung, and oozing blood wet the surrounding skin. Her attacker had used a knife not a needle.

How much curare did she use? The dose hadn't killed Claire. To survive, she had to regain control of her body. When would the paralysis wear off? Claire should have researched the poison more seriously while she had the chance. She cursed her complacency. *Too late now.* But the assassin was no amateur. She knew her tools well and would have adjusted the dosage for her needs. Claire wouldn't regain her motor functions in the nick of time. She needed help.

Nobody's coming to save you. Claire had told Rob she planned to visit Moretti. But even if Rob sent a SWAT team to the mobster's residence, they wouldn't find her. Claire was no longer there. And after their last angry conversation, Rob would be cautious. She had stormed out of their home. Did he think she wanted space? By the time he realized she was missing, Claire would be dead. *Or worse.*

Claire's phone vibrated in her pocket, but she couldn't answer. *Rob, is that you?* The phone cut out. Did he think she was screening his calls? A tear dripped from her eye and slid down her temple. She'd never see him again. *Don't think that. Stay focused!*

The car negotiated a corner, and Claire's body shifted softly. The driver was in no hurry. No patrol officers would stop her for speeding. *Smart.* Apex hadn't survived so long in complete anonymity without exercising caution. The killers had left Tony Russo's corpse in his apartment to send a message to Moretti. Claire's murder would be different. They'd dispose of her body without a trace. Detectives working her missing person case would conclude she'd run away or committed suicide. *The mentally unstable FBI recruit snaps after a heated lovers' quarrel.* Her mysterious disappearance would be a cliché.

This is all your fault. Claire had sensed she was being followed. She should never have approached Moretti alone. But who could she have taken with her? Rob's injuries had put him out of action. Sally was out of town and untrained for physical confrontations. Tom had warned them to stay out of trouble.

You're on your own, kiddo. Claire tried to scream again. While her murderer ferried her to an excruciating death, Claire lay on the dusty floor of her car, her gun and phone within reach, but unable to lift a finger to save her life. *I have to get away from here.* She had to get word to Rob about Alpha's big operation. But how?

The car turned a sharp corner, and the g-forces shoved her body over the edge of the seat. The floor shook. They had left the paved road? *Time is running out.*

Her head banged against the passenger seat, and her eyes blinked once. Was the poison wearing off? Claire tried to repeat the movement but failed.

The car stopped. Doors opened. Hands grabbed Claire's ankles and hauled her out of the vehicle. She hit the hard, smooth floor without breaking her fall, like a human sandbag. If she lived long enough, she'd have a nice fat bruise on the side of her head.

Claire gawked at her car's undercarriage. No street sounds reached her ears. No wind brushed her skin. A fluorescent light buzzed to life and spread a white glow. She lay on a cement floor marred by faded oil stains.

The killer found Claire's phone in her jacket pocket and powered it down. She reached under Claire's armpits and heaved her onto a wheelchair. The woman tied a rope around Claire's chest to prevent her from falling over and propped her feet on the chair's plastic supports. The killer had prepared for this. Was this how she had abducted other victims? How many had she brought here? Claire tried to study her environment, but her head lolled forward.

The wheelchair rolled onto a large sheet of thick plastic. They passed through the flaps of an expansive tent-like structure made of the same translucent material. Claire came to a halt. Her journey had ended.

The woman bound Claire's wrists together with a cable tie —completely unnecessary—then she looped a rope through the gap. Chains clinked. The rope tightened. An upward force raised Claire's arms over her head, then hoisted her body into the air. When the toes of her shoes grazed the plastic carpet, her movement halted. Her attacker had strung her up like a carcass in an abattoir, ready for skinning. Again, the vision of Tony Russo's flayed body rose unbidden in her mind. Her heartbeat accelerated. Sweat beaded on her forehead. Saliva trickled from her mouth.

Her attacker stepped into view. Chief Alda's assassin smiled at her. "Hello, Claire. We've met before. Well, sort of."

The killer knew Claire could hear her. She was talking to her. *That's a good sign, isn't it?*

"Be right back." She walked off.

Where has she gone? Claire strained her peripheral vision. The room was an isolated warehouse or garage. The plastic sheeting prevented a more accurate assessment.

Wheels squeaked. The assassin reappeared, dressed in a surgeon's plastic coveralls, complete with disposable booties and a shower cap.

The woman rolled a metal trolley into view. She unfurled a plastic sheath of tools to reveal a row of sharp steel implements within: scalpels and hooks. The killer set up her equipment, a surgeon preparing her instruments for an operation. But this professional didn't save lives. She snuffed them out.

The woman pulled up a plastic chair and studied Claire, inspecting her body. "To be honest, I prefer men. Their skin is more robust and even. Anthony Russo was a prime specimen. I got an entire bag out of him. You might have seen it at the hospital. The female dermis is too warped and stretchy, especially one like yours." The killer gestured at Claire's breasts. "There's not much material to work with."

A grim realization chilled Claire to the bone. The assassin

would turn her into another tote bag like Tony Russo. Nicky Moretti was right. These killers were animals.

The assassin unbuttoned Claire's blouse and ran her fingers over her stomach. Goose bumps spread over Claire's flesh.

The woman sighed. "I guess, we'll make do with what we've got."

CHAPTER 42

Rob lay on the couch with his leg up. News reports cycled on the living room TV, but he couldn't focus. Black dread pooled in his heart. Claire had left three hours ago. He'd called her cell phone a dozen times. His text messages went unanswered, too. Was Claire still angry with him? They'd had their share of arguments. But they always kept an open channel of communication. They always resolved their differences before the end of the day. Tonight, Claire had severed contact. He scrolled the list of messages on his phone. The single check marks indicated she hadn't read any of them. The pool of dread deepened. This wasn't like Claire. Was she in trouble?

Before dinner, Claire had talked about visiting Nicky Moretti. She believed his drug cartel wasn't in league with Apex. Claire hoped Moretti would provide the missing information they needed to implicate the covert pack of killers in the FBI bombing. But what if she was wrong? Had she walked into a kill zone?

By refusing to pick sides at the dinner table, Rob had pushed her away. He'd practically goaded her into reckless behavior. If anything bad happened to her, he'd never forgive himself. But what was he supposed to do? With his constant pain and plaster cast, he was in no shape to rescue her. Alerting Tom and calling in the big guns would end their careers at the FBI. And what if Claire was simply punishing him with the silent treatment? She'd chosen the worst possible moment to give him the cold shoulder.

"Shouldn't you get some sleep?"

The voice startled him. Mom had a habit of sneaking up on him. She stood behind the couch in her frilly pajamas and robe and with curlers in her hair.

"I'm worried about Claire."

Felicity stroked his head. "My poor little boy. Don't lose any sleep over that tramp."

"Mom!"

She pouted. "I'm just looking out for you. I know her type."

His shoulders tensed at her words. "What type is that?"

His tone was harder than he had intended. But with Mom's track record, she had no right to criticize the other woman in his life.

"The type who runs off when the going gets tough. I know I wasn't a model mother, but at least I stuck around. Until your father took you from me."

Rob let the comment pass. She had doctored their family history into a more flattering version. Felicity had always been flexible about the truth. But Rob remembered. His mother had caused those tough times. His father had rescued him from her at great personal expense.

But once she got started, she couldn't stop. "What kind of a woman walks out on her injured fiancé in the middle of the night? You deserve better than her. I told her so—to her face—and I think she realized I'm right. That's why she left." She smirked.

"You wanted her to leave, didn't you?"

The smirk disappeared. "For your sake, Rob. I'm only looking out for your best interests."

"Is that why you went through our things?"

The question froze her expression. "I was searching for my diamond earrings. I didn't want to suspect Claire, but after I exhausted all other options—yes, I searched her room, too. And I'm sorry I did because now I've upset you."

Her lower lip trembled as though she was on the verge of tears. "I only wanted to do right by you, Rob, for once in my life. But now I've gone and ruined everything." A single tear leaked down her cheek.

Rob sighed. "You haven't ruined anything." He wasn't convinced of that, but he had no energy for more drama. He smiled. "You should go to bed. I'll follow soon."

"Do you need help with the stairs?"

"No, I need to practice. I'll be fine."

"OK. Goodnight, my dear. Everything will look better in the morning, I promise."

She patted him on the shoulder and went upstairs.

Rob reached for his phone and called Claire again. Still no answer. Why had she turned off her phone? Did she want him to suffer? No, that behavior suited his mother, not Claire. Like searching his personal space and guilt-tripping him when he caught her.

What have I done? Claire had warned him about Felicity. After his brush with death, he'd been so desperate to reconcile with her. Now Claire was gone. She'd been wrong about the bank, but was she right about his mother's endgame?

He'd chosen a bad time to have second thoughts about Felicity. He could have searched her room while she'd taken a bath. He'd have to wait until she went out tomorrow to get another chance. Rob swore under his breath. *This can't wait until morning.*

An idea popped into his head. If Mom was plotting to swindle him, she'd hide the evidence well. The criminal mind expected others to search for dirt, too.

Rob lowered his injured leg to the floor and, leaning on his crutch, got to his feet. Slowly and quietly, he entered the kitchen. His mother had never spent a red cent on him when he was a child, but she'd always had cash for alcohol. She had stashed money where she thought her little boy would never look. Rob had found her secret troves. But he'd stolen nothing, and so she'd never learned of his discoveries.

He paused at the kitchen counter and listened. Felicity moved about in her room. Then he pulled a thick cookbook from a shelf and turned the pages. He held the spine and shook the book over the counter. Nothing fell from the pages. He reached for a second cookbook, and this time, papers fluttered to the counter. *Bingo*. Not twenty-dollar bills, but a wad of documents. Rob studied them, and his resolve hardened.

Claire was right. His mother hadn't reached out from the goodness of her heart. She was back to her old tricks, and this time, she intended to wipe him out.

CHAPTER 43

Claire dangled by her raised arms. Her shoulders burned. Her anguish reached a fever pitch. Soon, she'd witness her living autopsy. She'd feel every incision. *This is too much.* She had to escape. Claire wasn't a religious person, but she prayed for deliverance, or at least a quick death.

The assassin strolled leisurely to her equipment table and inspected her surgical implements. But instead of dissecting Claire with her scalpels, the killer pulled up a plastic chair and sat by her victim's dangling feet. She glanced at her cheap digital wristwatch.

What is she waiting for?

The BAU's profiling literature mentioned Power/Control serial killers who enjoyed dominating their victims. Was she drawing out Claire's suffering? The assassin seemed more interested in removing Claire's skin than inducing terror. Was something else holding her back? Hope sprouted in the thin, dry soil of the blessed delay. Was Claire's fate still undecided? Would she survive this ordeal to die another day?

The assassin checked her watch again. "Can you feel it yet?"

I feel everything, you psycho bitch.

"I pricked myself once by accident. The paralysis wears off eventually. I gave you a small dose. Your fingers and toes will tingle as your mobility returns. Which reminds me."

She fetched a cable tie and secured Claire's ankles together. "No surprises, Claire. OK? Or the next dose will stop your heart."

The situation made no sense. The killer had disabled her and strung her up for skinning. Why was she waiting for the poison's effects to dissipate?

The assassin stared into Claire's eyes. "You must be special if Daddy wants to speak with you."

Daddy. The word had never sounded more sinister. Daddy called the shots. Was Alpha here? He'd collaborated with Apex in Newburgh. Alpha had known Claire's father. Had her family name deferred her death? The sprout of hope grew toward that sudden ray of light. Claire would meet Alpha. She had to convince him to release her. But how? *Think, Claire. Think! There must be a way.*

Her mind went into overdrive. She analyzed her options. If they met face-to-face, she'd be able to identify him. He'd never risk turning her loose. Claire had crossed swords with psychopaths before. She had a knack for anticipating their thinking patterns. Her cover story would have to persuade Alpha he'd gain more by setting her free. *C'mon, Claire. Think!*

The killer stepped back. "You blinked. Try that again."

Claire did. Slowly, her eyelids closed and reopened. The effort drained her, but her body had responded to her will!

"Good. Move your eyes from side to side. Lift your head."

Claire failed at the last task. Her head was too heavy for her neck. But her fingers spasmed, her lips twitched, and her tongue stirred. It was like waking from anesthesia but without the grogginess.

"That's it. Nice and easy. Now, say something."

Claire exhaled, and her mouth struggled to form words. "Bith," she whispered.

"Try again."

Claire had to learn to speak again. She filled her lungs for a second attempt. "Bitch!"

The assassin grinned. "That's the spirit."

Claire raised her head an inch. "Gonna...kill you."

The grin disappeared. "We'll see about that."

Two minutes later, her captor said, "That's good enough."

She thumbed a button on her phone and held it to her ear. Alpha wasn't present. The Apex ringleader hadn't deigned to show up in person. But a phone call gave Claire more wriggle room. An idea budded in her hopeful heart.

The killer glanced at Claire and spoke into the phone. "Yes, she's here. More or less."

Claire brought her breathing under her control. She shifted onto her toes to relieve the pain in her shoulders. The next few seconds would determine her life expectancy. She'd better make them count. The talk might not spare her life, but it might answer a burning question. *Who is Alpha?* The sound of his voice might be enough.

The woman responded to an inaudible question. "Sure."

She tapped the screen and held the phone before Claire's face. A video feed of her sweaty face filled the screen in real-time. Alpha didn't reciprocate.

The voice that issued from the speakers was unlike any Claire had heard before. Scrambling software had altered the syllables beyond recognition, giving the speaker's words an eerily arhythmic electronic cadence. Alpha might be a man or a woman or an algorithm.

"Ms. Wolfe, we speak at last. You make a lot of noise for someone conducting a secret investigation."

Claire swallowed. "I'm glad I finally got your attention." Her voice still sounded strange to her ears. Her tongue felt stiff. "To be honest, I was expecting a warmer welcome." She gave her captor a dirty look.

"And why is that?"

"Because I'm family, *Alpha*."

The voice didn't reply, so she continued.

"I'm all that's left of Newburgh. William died before he could tell me everything. But I figured it out. You're the reason I moved to Quantico. But you seem intent on destroying everything I've built."

Claire caught her breath. The effort of speaking had worn her out. But she had said her piece. The rest was out of her hands.

Alpha spoke. "Bill Wolfe was a gifted strategist. We worked well together. But you destroyed him."

"He brought that on himself. His pack became sloppy. They lost their edge. And they didn't think big enough."

"But you do?"

Claire's heart skipped a beat. Her ploy had created an opening, and she had to follow through. Her mind raced, and she constructed her story as she went along.

"Why impersonate the FBI if you can have the real Bureau's resources behind you? I've constructed a program called YARI, the Youth At Risk—"

"I know about YARI, Claire. I went to great lengths to end the program. Get to the point."

Sally was right. Apex had targeted Chief Alda to stop YARI.

Claire pitched her idea. "Let the FBI think we're saving unfortunate souls. I'll mold them to our way of thinking. Let me rebuild Apex. We'll be bigger and stronger than ever before."

"That isn't our way. Centralized control is too vulnerable.

Our cells remain separate. Only Bill and I knew of each other's existence. The Apex sign prevented interference."

Alpha had confirmed more of their deductions. Rob and Sally would be thrilled to hear that. But would Claire ever live to tell them? Unless she outmaneuvered Alpha, she'd take those discoveries to her grave.

"How was I supposed to know? Bill and I had barely reconnected. The whole point of Apex is to work together."

"Bill would have told you if you hadn't killed him."

"I didn't kill him. I swore I'd make him proud. So please, stay away from my unit."

The voice on the line laughed, a frightening and inhuman sound. "You claim to serve Apex, but you shout our name to the world?"

Crap. He had her there. Had Alpha intercepted her conversation with Senator Schultz or Moretti or both? How was Claire supposed to explain that away? She couldn't. Maybe she didn't have to?

"Of course! Why cower in the shadows when we can hide in plain sight? Make Apex a household name, right next to Bigfoot and the Loch Ness Monster. Turn our enemies in law enforcement into laughingstocks. Nobody can defeat us if they're embarrassed to speak our name. Slap us on a freaking T-shirt, for all I care."

"As you did?"

Alpha knew about KillerWolfe.com.

Claire shifted her shoulders. "It works for me."

She paused to catch her breath. Claire had gone out on a limb, and the branch creaked beneath her feet. One word from Alpha, and her world would come crashing down.

"You're your father's daughter, Claire. Show us what you can do."

Inwardly, Claire collapsed with relief. She'd live.

The assassin turned the phone around. "Daddy, you can't be serious! We can't trust her."

"That's my choice to make. Don't forget your place."

The killer deflated. "I haven't, Daddy."

She must hate to lose her consignment of human leather, but she didn't dare challenge the leader of the pack. Daddy wouldn't hesitate to destroy her, too.

The electronic voice spoke again. "I have a good feeling about this. Call it destiny. Call it fate. Together, there'll be no stopping us. But Claire must prove herself. Nobody joins the pack unblooded."

Claire blurted, "Whatever it is, I'll get it done."

Within seconds, Claire regretted her words. Alpha couched his order in euphemism, but Claire understood. Her entry ticket to Apex was murder. She had expected nothing less. But she hadn't foreseen Alpha's choice of target.

No, she wanted to cry. *Anything but that. Kill me instead!*

But Alpha had spoken. And refusing his command meant certain death.

assassin lurked behind the door, listening for movement while she attached a silencer to the barrel of a gun.

Rob slid the bedside drawer open and found his sidearm in the darkness. He aimed the weapon at the door in both hands.

The handle turned. The door swung open. A woman stood in the doorway. She flipped on the light switch.

Rob blinked back the bright light and lowered his gun. "Claire! I was worried about you."

She didn't respond. Claire didn't even comment on the weapon in his hands. Instead, she tossed a suitcase onto her side of the bed. She opened the closet door and threw shirts and dresses into the suitcase. Rob hadn't overreacted to their argument. She was leaving him.

"Claire! Please, let's talk." He struggled to his feet and hobbled over without his crutches. "We can work this out. Please, stop."

Claire sniffed and wiped a tear from her eye. "There's no time. We have to go while we can."

We. A second suitcase waited in the doorway. Claire wasn't leaving him. She was packing for them both.

"Go where?"

"Anywhere. Someplace they won't find us."

"Is Moretti after us?"

Claire glanced at him, confused. "What? No. He's not the problem." She upended a closet drawer, raining socks and underwear into the suitcase. "It's much worse." She sobbed like a frightened little girl.

Rob wrapped his arms around her. "Claire. What's gotten into you? Talk to me."

She trembled. This wasn't the Claire he knew.

"She got me, Rob."

"Who did?"

"The assassin. The woman from the hospital."

Rob's breath caught in his throat. While he'd brooded at home, Claire had faced Alda's murderer alone. And the encounter had shaken her to the core.

"What happened?"

"I didn't see her coming. She hid in my car and paralyzed me. I couldn't move, but I felt everything."

Claire had fallen into the web of the cold-blooded killer who had skinned Tony Russo alive. But Claire was here, unharmed and whole. Or was she?

"What did she do to you?"

Claire told him how the killer had transported her to an abandoned warehouse and strung her up. But instead of flaying her, the psychopath waited for the poison to wear off so Claire could speak with her boss.

"You met Alpha?"

"We spoke on the phone."

"Do you know who he is?"

Claire shook her head. "He used voice distortion software."

Rob stared at Claire in awe. "How did you escape?"

"I didn't. They let me go. I told them I'd come to Quantico to find Alpha and use the FBI to recruit for Apex."

Rob laughed in disbelief. "Claire, you're amazing. You'll have access to Alpha. We can root Apex out. This is exactly what we needed!"

Claire didn't seem to share his enthusiasm. Her inside access had come at a price.

"Did she hurt you?"

She shook her head. "It's what they want me to do."

Apex had not simply taken her at her word. They had charged her with an initiation rite, an assignment so terrible it would prove her loyalty to the pack beyond a shadow of a doubt.

"What do they want?"

"I have to kill someone."

"Who?"

"You, Rob. They want me to kill you."

The words erased his excitement like a slap to the face.

Claire fixed him with an urgent gaze. "We have to leave. Right now."

"The Bureau will protect us."

"They can't, Rob. Massoud thinks I'm crazy. And even if somebody with authority believes us, the FBI is in disarray. Apex murdered the director and Chief Alda. Their moles will find us. We have to go off the grid. Maybe Newburgh PD can hook us up with new identities, but even that is risky."

The room swirled around Rob. He had worried he'd lost Claire. Now they both could lose their lives. In the best-case scenario, they'd have to start over from scratch with new names in a foreign place.

He glanced at the plaster cast on his leg. "This'll slow us down."

"Then we'd better get moving. We'll need all the head start we can get."

Rob inhaled sharply. This was too much to take in. "It'll never work. My leg is a dead giveaway, and an invalid won't last long on the run."

"I'm so sorry, Rob. This is all my fault. I had no idea they'd target you." She ran her hand through her hair. "You should go."

"What?"

"Go ahead without me. Disappear. I'll fend them off."

"Claire, what are you talking about?"

"I got you mixed up in this. You don't owe me anything. We're not family."

Felicity's needling had gotten to her. His mother had undermined Claire's confidence in his love for her. He'd set the record straight.

Rob gripped her by the shoulders and looked her in the eye. "You're the family I choose. Like it or not, we're in this together. There has to be another way."

"There isn't. I've had an hour's drive to think it over. The only alternative is to kill you."

She was right. *Yes, that's the key.* He understood what they needed to do.

"Then, kill me."

"That's not funny, Rob. And I'm not a murderer."

Rob grinned. "But they think you are."

CHAPTER 45

Bang-crash! The metallic clatter yanked Felicity Cline from a pleasant dream. She had lazed on a tropical beach, sipping a pina colada with a pink paper umbrella. Azure waves lapped the shore. Her new life was all sunshine and cocktails. The only unsettling detail was her son. On the next recliner, Rob sported black Ray-Bans and a tasteless Hawaiian t-shirt.

He raised his drink. "Here's to you, Mom. You're the best."

What's he doing here? Rob wasn't supposed to share in her retirement. He'd merely financed it. By the time he learned his mother had cleaned out his bank account, she'd left him far behind.

Now the wretched noise had woken her from her warm dream—and soon-to-be reality—in the middle of the night.

Felicity cursed the alley cats and turned over on the hard mattress. She wouldn't have to put up with Rob much longer. Her retirement plans were already in motion. Sometimes her genius astounded even her. Rob wouldn't know what hit him.

Bang-crash!

There it was again—a terrible cacophony, right outside her window. Felicity scrambled to her feet, ready to teach the noisemakers a lesson. A decade ago, she would have stormed outside and wrung the cats' bony little necks. But alas, her strength had waned. She'd settle for a bucket of cold water on their heads. She parted the curtains and peered out the window. Moonlight revealed not cats but a dark-haired young woman.

Ha! Claire Wolfe had come crawling back, and now she was digging in the trash cans. Rob's girlfriend had finally found her niche. *Is she drunk?* If she thought she'd weasel her way back into Rob's heart, she had another thing coming. Felicity would make the gold digger understand she was a *persona non grata* in this household. That bucket of water seemed like a very good idea. *That'll teach her!*

But Claire wasn't searching the bins. She dropped things inside—a bundle of clothing and a pair of men's shoes. *What the devil is she up to?* Claire had backed up her white hatchback alongside the house. With great effort, she heaved a large, black bag into the trunk. Felicity squinted in the dim light. The bag was about six feet long and resembled a body bag.

Felicity gasped. Claire raised her head and looked in her direction. Felicity ducked back inside and clapped her hand over her mouth. Had Claire seen her? *No.*

A shudder racked her body. She'd known Claire was a bad egg, but she'd had no idea she was *that* rotten. Her website, KillerWolfe.com, had proposed theories about covered-up murders, but Felicity hadn't really believed the stories. Now she did. Claire had killed someone.

Felicity thanked her lucky stars. She'd have no trouble severing Rob from a murderer. A whispered word in the right ear would put Claire behind bars for good!

She padded quietly out of her room and down the corridor and knocked on Rob's door. "Rob, dear," she hissed. "Wake up. It's urgent."

Her son didn't respond. Rob had always been a deep

sleeper. She knocked again. He had to hurry, or they'd miss catching Claire red-handed. She opened the door and turned on the light. He wasn't there.

"Rob?"

She checked the adjoining bathroom—empty—and went downstairs. She didn't dare turn on the lights, but she used the glow of her phone. A pungent chemical scent hung in the air. Disinfectant.

"Rob?"

She checked the basement, too. Her son was not in the house. A bucket and mop stood in the corner. Someone had scoured the floor of the hall, using generous amounts of ammonia.

No, she couldn't have. Could she?

A car engine turned over outside. She rushed to the living room window. Claire drove her car off the property. She was alone in the car. The murderer was getting away. *Not if I have anything to say about it.*

Felicity returned to the kitchen and opened the back door. In the dusty patch below her bedroom window, a fire burned. Flames rose from the metal trash bin. She drew near, terrified of what she might find, but the flames drew her like a moth. Inside the bin, the bundle of clothing burned. Felicity recognized the pajamas. Rob had worn them this evening.

"No!" she wailed. She didn't care who heard her. That crazy bitch had ruined everything. Claire Wolfe had murdered her son!

CHAPTER 46

Derek was lounging on the couch, beer in hand, when Karla came home.

He glanced at her, and his eyes twinkled. Could he see that she'd changed, or did he only notice her grandfather's gift, the jacket of untreated brown leather?

Derek leered at her. "I missed you."

The feeling wasn't mutual. He repulsed her. But Karla had returned with a new sense of purpose.

Before her weeks with Ichigouti, Karla had drifted through life, pushed around by the desires of others. Now she knew who she was and what she wanted. And she had a secret weapon.

Karla left her suitcase at the door and walked over to her stepfather. His temples had grayed, as had the hairy paunch that peeked from beneath his shirt and overhung his belt. He was pathetic. How had she let him use her all those years?

Derek ran his hand up her thigh and grinned. "Did you miss me, too?"

She slapped his hand from her leg. "Things are going to change around here."

Karla had rehearsed this meeting in her mind. Revenge was not her goal. The mountain lion doesn't seek revenge on the rabbit. He rips his prey, limb from limb.

Derek grinned. "Things are fine the way they are."

"You'll never touch me again. But you'll pay me. I'm going back to school, and I'll need money for clothes and stuff. A hundred bucks a week will do."

The smile dropped from Derek's face. He rose to his feet, trying to intimidate her with his extra two inches.

"Who the hell do you think you are, little girl?" His breath reeked of alcohol.

Karla didn't flinch. "Do as I say and there won't be any trouble."

He cackled. "Trouble? What you gonna do—tell your mommy?"

"I'll make you regret it. Do you want a taste?"

Derek unzipped his jeans. "I'll give you a taste, Pocahontas. You've forgotten who's in charge!"

Karla moved fast. She pulled a knife from the scabbard on her belt and jabbed his forearm with the sharp edge.

Derek stared at the shallow cut. "What the—?" His face slackened. His body collapsed to the floor.

Karla crouched over him. She'd used a small dose of the poison. The effects would last only a few minutes, but long enough for him to get the message.

She lifted his shirt and ran the blade over his skin. Tufts of gray hair fell from his belly. "I've learned a lot since I've been away. How to slaughter animals and strip their hides. You'll make a great jacket."

His breathing accelerated. He understood the new order.

She aimed the knife at his crotch. "Or maybe I'll cut off your dick and cook it for dinner? I'd call that poetic justice, wouldn't you?"

Behind her, the front door opened.

Her mother shrieked. "Karla! What have you done?"

Karla slipped the knife back into its scabbard and straightened.

Her mother rushed to Derek and stroked his hair and face. "You killed him!"

Karla dragged her suitcase to her room. "Relax, Mom. He'll live."

Derek had learned his lesson. But her mother hadn't. She called the cops.

CHAPTER 47

D r. Sally Fleischer headed for the FBI Academy straight from Ronald Reagan National Airport in DC, Tuesday afternoon. She couldn't wait to speak with Claire and Rob and share her lucky breakthrough.

For the past four days, she'd consulted on a double murder in Irvine, California. Neither she nor the local homicide detectives understood why the BAU had sent her to analyze such an unremarkable case. Sally had gone through the motions, but her mind had remained in Quantico.

Apex survived. The covert pack of psychopaths had assassinated the FBI director and Chief Alda. Did Apex aim to bury YARI? If so, she, Rob, and Claire might be in their sights next.

The suspense and the frustration of being unable to discuss the situation with her BAU colleagues were driving her crazy. *Mentally ill.* Sally smiled. Rob had teased her about using psychological terminology. He'd emerged from his near-death experience with his sense of humor and a childlike sense of wonder. Both would cushion him and Claire during these stressful times.

Sally parked her car and ran toward the FBI buildings. A

minute later, she burst into the YARI office space. Claire slouched at her desk and spoke on her cell phone. Her puffy, red eyelids hinted at sleepless nights and, possibly, tears. Sally's enthusiasm turned to dread. *What's happened?*

Claire shot Sally a nervous glance. "I've got to go, Bella." She put down the phone. "Hey, Sally. Welcome back." Her voice was indifferent and devoid of emotion.

"Thanks."

Sally wheeled her overnight bag to her desk. *Bella.* The name rang a bell.

"Was that Ms. Winters from *The Newburgh Herald* on the phone?"

"The one and only."

Bella Winters had assisted the investigators with serial killer homicides in Newburgh and atoned for her earlier objectionable reporting. Was the newshound sniffing around for new scandals? Had Claire also connected the CIRG bombing to Apex in Newburgh?

"What did she have to say?"

Claire lowered her gaze. "Nothing. Just...keeping in touch."

Sally doubted that.

Claire changed the subject. "How was California?"

Sally blew a raspberry. "Pointless but painless."

Puffy eyes. Evasive answers. Something had shaken Claire since their last conversation. Sally's news would cheer her up.

She closed the door and wheeled her chair over to Claire. "Good news. I found a lead." Her pent-up excitement made whispering difficult. "Apex recruits serial killers, right? So I ran a ViCAP search for our assassin's signature. Guess what I found?"

Claire gazed at her through droopy eyelids. "The flaying homicide in Newburgh. We found that, too."

Claire had beaten her to the punch. "And?"

"Brian O'Leary buried the case. Jessica Long found the files in his private storage unit."

"Perfect! O'Leary tampered with evidence for Apex before. This homicide connects them to Alda's assassin." Why wasn't Claire excited about this?

"That's what I thought, too. I even spoke with Senator Schultz, and he agreed to tell Massoud to look into Apex."

"Amazing! And?" This was the proof they'd needed—the extraordinary evidence Massoud had demanded. Why was Claire acting as though the world was ending?

"Massoud's done nothing."

Sally shrugged. "Give him time. He'll come around. He has to now."

Claire shook her head. "Maybe he's right?"

"What? But you just said—"

"I've been thinking. If the assassin is Apex, why didn't we find any skinned victims at the ranch house?"

Sally squinted at Claire. Wasn't the answer obvious? "Newburgh was a separate branch. The assassin belongs to a different pack. That's why they used the chevron symbols. To—"

Claire raised her hand. "If the assassin is a serial killer, where are her other flayed victims?"

Sally counted them on her fingers. "Tony Russo. The Newburgh case O'Leary covered up."

"Exactly. Only two."

Sally gasped with frustration. "Newburgh might be her first kill. We can use it to track her down. First kills are usually closer to home."

Claire shook her head. "Jess looked into it. The killer left no forensic traces. This was no first kill. And there was no Apex symbol on the corpse."

Was Claire playing devil's advocate? Agent Massoud would,

too. Sally found an easy explanation.

"Maybe Newburgh was a mistake? She didn't intend for the body to be discovered. What if she usually disposes of the bodies completely? This time, she screwed up, and Apex had to lean on O'Leary to close the investigation."

Claire didn't budge. "If O'Leary was a dirty cop, who says Apex was his only customer? Maybe the flayings are related, maybe they're not? Still, Moretti is the simplest explanation."

Sally recoiled. Claire wasn't training her for Massoud's skepticism. She had given up.

That sucks. The ViCAP match had animated her. But Claire had a valid point. Their chain of reasoning was only as strong as its weakest link. They needed more information to build an airtight case.

"Any luck with the assassin?"

Claire shuddered but said nothing. She was hiding something. Why was Claire shutting her out?

"Is everything OK?"

Claire studied her hands. "Yeah."

Her weak voice undermined her claim. Again, Claire's verbal communication contradicted her body language, sending mixed messages. A *double-bind*, in psychological jargon. Rob would be proud.

"How is Rob?"

"I don't know."

That made no sense. "What do you mean?"

Claire paled. *That's it.* Something had happened to Rob. Sally's heart fell. Had Apex gotten to him? Surely Claire would have told her immediately?

"Claire, what's happened?"

Claire's lips trembled. "We had a fight last night."

"That happens in every relationship. Rob's a decent guy. He'll get over it."

Claire inhaled sharply. "His mother moved in a few days ago. She's a piece of work."

So that's what this is about. Sally relaxed. For a moment, Claire had worried her. A laugh escaped Sally's lips, and Claire shot her an injured look.

"I'm sorry. That must be terrible. Mothers-in-law are notorious for meddling."

"This goes beyond meddling. She's pulling us apart. She'd kill me if she could get away with it. Seriously."

Sally stifled an amused smile. She'd never met the woman, but she doubted Rob's mom was a psychopath. "You'll work things out."

"Will we? I hear divorce rates are high among cops. And we're not even married yet."

Sally grabbed the opportunity to brighten Claire's day. "Actually, that's a misconception. Divorce rates for police officers are lower than the general population."

"Really?"

"Yep. People assume the long hours, stress, and exposure to humanity's worst side lead to romantic breakups. But think about it—officers are pre-selected for emotional stability and responsibility. The academy filters out applicants with criminal histories or addiction. The officers' controlling behavior is usually just protectiveness. If they seem overly suspicious, it's because they're trained to assume people are cheaters. That comes with the job."

Claire's mouth betrayed the hint of a smile. "Sounds like you're building a new in-house training course."

"*Marital Bliss for Agents 101.* Not a bad idea. With all the rumored changes, that might help me keep my job."

Claire's countenance darkened again. The hint of imminent layoffs was a downer. *Way to go, Sally.*

"What if both partners are in law enforcement—what are

their odds for staying together?"

This wasn't a typical lover's quarrel. "What happened, Claire?"

"I gave him an ultimatum—his mom or me. Then, I stormed out. I spent the night at a motel."

Sally swallowed. Things must have gotten pretty bad to reach that point. Rob's mom must be a monster.

"What did he decide?"

"I don't know. He won't answer my calls."

Sally touched Claire's arm. "That's not like Rob. He'll find a reasonable solution. I'll call him. I'm sure it's just a misunderstanding."

She searched for Rob's number on her cell phone and hit Connect. Claire lowered her eyes. Sally would sort this out quickly. Rob had no reason not to speak to the unit's forensic psychiatrist.

The number rang. Sally gave Claire a confident wink. Rob and Claire were perfect for each other. They loved each other. Both were balanced and considerate human beings. There was no reason they couldn't work this out.

The ringing continued. An automated voice spoke, and the call ended.

Sally gazed at her phone with concern. "That's strange. His mailbox is full. Hold on."

She hit the Text button and read her message aloud as she typed. "Hi, Rob. Please call me ASAP."

She waited for the double check mark, the sign that Rob had read her message. Five seconds later, she'd still received no confirmation. His phone was last active at 2 AM this morning. Sally's positivity flagged. His unavailability wasn't strange. It was worrying. Had Rob fallen into a dark pit of despair after his fight with Claire? Had something happened to him?

Sally offered Claire a brave smile. "I'm sure he's OK."

CHAPTER 48

Rafiq Massoud stood in the middle of the war room and placed his hands on his hips. "A full week has passed since the bombing, and Senator Schwarz wants results. We need to close the net on Moretti, pronto."

His aides cowered at the table. *Good.*

In a management seminar, an instructor had urged supervisors to mix soft and hard leadership styles depending on their workers' performance. Rafiq ignored that advice. He put the fear of God into his aides every day. This was a demanding job, the stakes were high, and Rafiq was a harsh taskmaster. They'd never satisfy his expectations. Why create false hope?

Rafiq jerked his head at Michael. "Any leads from the hotline?"

The FBI had set up a dedicated tip-off number for the CIRG bombing. The director's assassination had driven every amateur sleuth and his grandmother into a tizzy. As the greenest agent on the team, Michael had landed the chore of diving that dumpster.

Michael swallowed hard. "No, sir. I reviewed over twelve

hundred calls and followed up on fifty-six. None seem relevant."

Rafiq grunted. "Andy, what about the CCTV cameras?"

He'd handed his more experienced aide the more promising task of analyzing the closed-circuit television footage from both within and without the CIRG building. Tony Russo's apartment had produced no actionable evidence. While they waited on search warrants for Niccolo Moretti's properties, the video recordings were the angle most likely to identify the cartel's collaborator within the Bureau.

Andy hazarded a grin. "We found something on the interior cameras."

"Which ones—the hospital or CIRG?"

"Both."

"Show me."

Rafiq walked over to the agent and peered at his laptop screen.

Andy opened a folder of stills taken from the camera footage. "Sentara Medical Center has cameras only at the entrances and a few key corridors."

He clicked an image, which opened in the preview pane. In the wide-angle, overhead photo, a woman stepped from the parking lot toward the camera.

Massoud recognized the subject. "That's Agent Wolfe?"

"Correct. She arrived around one-thirty PM and only left the next morning with Agent Cline. We scanned for women matching the description Agent Wolfe provided for the assassin."

He clicked through multiple images photos. "We've identified two woman entering the Emergency Department. Both are family of patients at the hospital. Unfortunately, there's no camera at the service entrance."

Massoud scoffed. "This is useless, Andy. You said you found something."

The aide clicked another image. "Luckily for us, one of the secondary cameras drifted sideways over time, giving us a view of the service entrance, too. We caught a woman entering at one AM. It's too dark to make out much detail. The cameras don't have night vision and rely on ambient light. This is the best we could do."

Massoud leaned closer and squinted at the screen. The enlarged image was slightly pixelated, but the subject was undeniable. In the shadows, a dark-haired woman walked toward the building. She had a peaked cap over her eyes and a tote back on her shoulder.

Andy clicked the mouse again. "She left the same way five minutes later."

Massoud stared at the screen. "That's our gal." The picture would not help them identify the killer, but it corroborated Agent Wolfe's eyewitness report.

"OK. What about CIRG? Tell me you kept the best for last."

Andy grinned. He opened another folder and clicked on a grainy color video of an office corridor from the point of view of a ceiling camera.

He hit Pause. "Surprisingly, CIRG only has cameras at the entrances and elevator landings."

"Fair enough. They're tracking unauthorized access not double agents."

Andy aimed his finger at the screen. "But this one gives us an angle on the crime scene. In the distance. The second door."

Rafiq grunted again, this time with satisfaction. Toward the end of the corridor stood Agent Robert Cline, his back to the fateful conference room. Andy had found a window on ground zero.

The aide clicked Play, and the conference room exploded.

The door flew off its hinges and slammed into Cline, tossing him against the opposite wall, where he collapsed. Smoke and flames filled the screen. The clip ended.

"And?"

"We found nothing suspicious on the day of the bombing."

Massoud opened his mouth to complain, but Andy continued.

"So, we reviewed older footage going back a week. A number of agents entered the conference room outside of scheduled meetings." Andy toggled to an Excel spreadsheet of names, timestamps, and links to MPEG files. The aide was organized. Rafiq liked that.

Andy read from the list. "Agent Robert Cline was there a number of times between—"

Rafiq interrupted. "Cline's room is down the corridor. Focus on people who have no right to be there and filter out those killed or injured in the blast."

Rafiq scanned the spreadsheet. Claire Wolfe appeared on the list, too. A row with question marks in the name column caught his eye.

He pointed. "Who's that?"

"I'm getting to him, sir. " Andy clicked the MPG link, and an icon spun while the video loaded. "This guy doesn't match any of the agents who work on this floor. He shows up on a few other cameras, wandering the hallways, and he entered the conference room alone the morning of the attack."

Rafiq's pulse thumped. *This sounds like our guy.* The video clip played.

A young, slim man strolled down the hall with a compact black backpack on his slouched shoulders. He looked up and down the corridor, then turned a corner and disappeared.

Andy moved the pointer on the video player's timeline. "He comes back soon."

Sure enough, the man reappeared. He entered the conference room. A few seconds later, he returned the way he came. Andy hit Pause as the suspect neared the camera. The man didn't hide his face.

"He's returned to the scene almost every day."

Rafiq had seen and heard enough. "Check the agent list for the entire building. I want everything on this guy: name, address, background, known associates, favorite color—everything. And put his ugly mug on the board."

"Yes, sir."

Rafiq stared at the still frame of the suspect. With his head of wild red curls, he should be easy to find.

CHAPTER 49

That evening, Claire parked outside Rob's house. Her eyelids seemed to weigh a ton. Her body threatened to collapse into a long hibernation. The sleepless night and constant rush of adrenaline wrecked her body. Worse than the physical exhaustion was the guilt. The lies had depleted her emotional reserves. Claire had deceived Sally, her colleague and friend. She had evaded her new unit chief. *You have no choice.* Somehow, she'd reached the end of the day, and now her heart pounded even faster. A white Toyota Yaris loomed before her, Felicity's rental car. The critical battle lay ahead.

Claire slapped her face with the palm of her hand. *Stay alert.* Claire was flying solo. She had crossed red lines. The heavy lifting was behind her. But to survive, she had follow through. She sucked in a deep breath, got into character, and climbed out of the car.

The lights were on in Rob's living room. Claire unlocked the front door and stepped inside.

Felicity perched on the couch like a pale marble statue, her expression tense but determined. She faced the front door and clutched a kitchen knife. How long had she waited there for

Claire to return? The old crook had nerves of steel. But if she believed she could beat Claire, she was wrong.

Claire tossed her car keys onto the telephone bureau and stared at her future mother-in-law. "You're still here."

A smug smile spread over Felicity's face, hiding her fear. She had defied Claire's ultimatum from the previous night, and that satisfaction emboldened her.

"You have no shame!"

Claire ignored the veiled accusation. "Where's Rob?"

"Don't play innocent with me, *dear*. You killed him."

"What are you talking about?"

The old woman sneered. "I saw you dispose of his body last night. I saw you burn his clothes. You didn't count on having a witness, did you?"

Claire scoffed. But inside, a doubt tugged at her conscience. *How much does she know?* If Claire had made a mistake, Felicity could ruin everything. *Too late to do anything about that now.*

"You're crazy. I want you out of here. Now."

"I'm not going anywhere. I'm Rob's blood. His natural heir. I belong here now. You are the one who has to leave. You're the slut he happened to sleep with before you butchered him in cold blood."

Claire cocked her head at a threatening angle. Nobody said she couldn't enjoy this game.

She smiled, baring her teeth. "That's no way to speak to a killer. Assuming you're right."

Claire parted her suit jacket, revealing her sidearm. "And if you are right, you've brought a knife to a gunfight. Not smart. But I'm tired. I'm going to bed. You'd better not be here when I wake up."

Claire headed for the staircase.

Felicity rose to her feet. "I'll tell the police."

Claire glared at her. "Tell them what?"

"That you murdered my son."

"So, what's stopping you?"

Felicity raised her chin at Claire. "I'll keep quiet for a hundred thousand dollars."

Claire wanted to laugh. She'd been right about Felicity. Narcissists were so predictable. Claire had destroyed her plot to steal Rob's savings, so she leveraged her son's murder to recoup her losses.

Claire stared her down. "You're pathetic."

"I'm being generous. With your father's inheritance and your mother's house, you'll have no trouble raising the money."

Rob must have shared Claire's family situation with his mother during their "bonding." Claire called her bluff and climbed the steps.

"Forget it."

"Eighty thousand. Final offer. I'll call the cops. I swear to God."

"Go ahead. See if I care. Close the door on your way out."

"You'll regret this! I'm dialing nine-one-one."

Claire continued up the stairs to her room. Calling the cops meant Felicity would forfeit her payout.

"Hello, Officer. Yes, I want to report a murder."

Claire closed the door of her room and flopped on the bed. With luck, she'd get ten minutes of sleep before the squad car arrived.

CHAPTER 50

F elicity tapped her foot on the sidewalk. "It's about time!"

The police car had taken five long minutes to arrive. Meanwhile, Claire might have shot her dead. They didn't even used the strobe lights or emergency siren. The officer took his time getting out of the marked cruiser, too, and waddled toward her. He didn't inspire confidence. His beer belly spilled over his belt. Or was that a doughnut gut? The effort of walking seemed to wear him out.

Felicity had played the role of the terrified victim before. But for once, she didn't have to act.

She pointed at the front door. "The murderer is in the house."

Doughnut Gut halted and drew his handgun. At least he was taking her seriously.

"Ma'am, put down the weapon!"

Felicity looked over her shoulder. There was nobody behind her. *Is he talking to me?*

"The knife, ma'am. Put down the knife."

Felicity had forgotten she was still holding the kitchen

knife. "This is for self-defense. I called nine-one-one. I'm the one who needs protection."

"I said—"

He didn't need to ask thrice. She released her grip, and the knife clattered to the sidewalk. But the imbecile didn't lower his weapon.

"Is the attacker still in the house?"

"Yes! That's what I said. She went to sleep upstairs."

"Did she attack you?"

"No, not me. She murdered my son."

His apprehension turned to annoyance. He holstered the gun and spoke into a communications device on his shoulder. "Tell dispatch to call off the backup."

What an idiot! Doughnut Gut had interpreted Claire's need to sleep off her murderous exhaustion as a sign that the danger had passed. His mind was as flabby as his belly!

"Wait—no! You need backup. She's armed and dangerous."

Doughnut Gut gazed past her toward the house.

"Is everything OK, Officer?" Claire said.

Felicity jumped. Claire had snuck up behind her without a peep. Was that how she killed Rob—stabbing him in the back like a coward?

Now was the time for the Doughnut Gut to draw his weapon, but instead, his eyes widened with joy. "Claire? Claire Wolfe?"

"Jimmy!" Claire launched down the steps and, to Felicity's horror, gave the officer a friendly hug. "Good to see you. How are you doing?"

Felicity froze with shock. Claire and the officer knew each other.

"Oh, you know, keeping busy. You're looking good."

"Thank you. And you seem...healthy."

Jimmy patted his doughnut bump and chuckled. "Yeah, I've put on a few. How long has it been—eight years?"

"Yep."

"I heard you made detective. Weren't you in Boston?"

"Moved around. I joined the BAU recently."

"No kidding!"

Felicity cleared her throat. "Excuse me for interrupting your reunion, but a crime has been committed here."

The old friends considered Felicity as if they'd forgotten she was there or why the officer had come there.

"Jimmy and I were at the Academy together," Claire explained as if Felicity cared.

The cop jerked his head at Felicity. "Who's she?"

At least Jimmy had the brains to ask. They might be old pals, but once he reviewed the evidence, the wheels of justice would turn. It was his sworn duty.

"My fiancé's mother. Are you here about the missing person report?"

"What missing person?"

"Robert Cline. My fiancé. He's been missing since last night."

What?! Claire was twisting the narrative to suit her own diabolical ends!

Felicity roared. "Missing person, my ass! She murdered my son in cold blood!"

Claire ignored her. "I filed a missing person report this afternoon. He hasn't answered his phone since last night. This isn't like him. He was recovering at home after the FBI bombing last week."

"He was injured in the bombing?" At least Jimmy Doughnut had heard about that.

"Yeah."

"Are you deaf?" Felicity yelled. "She killed him! I witnessed her getting rid of the body."

Claire shrugged. "Felicity seems to think he was murdered."

Claire spun her finger beside her ear, the international sign for crazy. The officer chuckled. Felicity's rage exploded. Claire had murdered her son, and a local police officer was colluding with her to cover up the crime.

Felicity aimed an accusatory finger at her. "She killed him. He was going to leave her, and she killed him in the night. She washed away his blood with disinfectant. The bucket's inside."

Claire yawned. "She never liked the way I clean."

Felicity pointed at the yard. "She burned his clothes over there, in the trash bin."

The officer cleared his throat. He gave Claire a "bear with me" glance and stepped closer to Felicity. "Ma'am, can you lead me to the victim's body?"

"No, I can't. She shoved his body into the trunk of her car, and I have no idea where she took it."

"But you saw the corpse?"

Felicity hesitated. Claire couldn't have known the police would send her old friend to answer the 911 call. But she hadn't mentioned the missing person's report. Claire was trying to make her sound delusional. *Be careful.* If Felicity exaggerated the details, either Jimmy would dismiss her out of hand or Claire might get off on a technicality.

"She placed a large black bag in the trunk of her car. It was heavy-looking and had the general size and shape of my son."

"I see. I'm sure we can clarify this quickly."

Finally, Officer Doughnut had grown a brain! She shot Claire a victorious grin.

He turned to Claire. "May I search your car for any sign of your boyfriend?"

Why was he asking permission? To her surprise, Claire agreed.

"Sure, no problem. I'll get the keys."

Felicity sensed another trick. But she wasn't stupid. She watched *CSI* on TV. Even if Claire had dumped Rob's body somewhere else, physical traces of him would remain in the trunk—a stray hair, a tiny speck of blood. Claire's old pal couldn't save her from hard evidence. And Felicity would ensure he'd be thorough. She activated her phone's camera and recorded the search.

Jimmy pulled on a pair of disposable gloves, and Claire tossed him the keys. He unlocked the car and popped the trunk. Surprise, surprise, the interior was empty. He bent over, leaning his head inside the trunk for a closer inspection. For a terrifying moment, Felicity feared Claire would shove him inside and add both of them to her list of victims.

The moment passed. He opened the back doors and scanned the interior with his flashlight. Claire waited patiently. After searching the front seats, too, he closed the doors and handed back the keys.

"Everything looks in order, ma'am."

That can't be right. "She must have vacuumed the car."

Claire smirked. "I guess my cleaning isn't so bad after all."

A thought occurred to the officer as he glanced down the street. "Is that your car, ma'am?"

Felicity crossed her arms over her chest. "It's a rental." She preferred luxury sedans when she could afford them. Felicity didn't want the officer to get the wrong impression.

"I should probably have a peek inside, you know, to be thorough."

"Fine! Knock yourself out."

He blinked at her. "The keys?"

Felicity handed them over, and he got to work.

She hovered beside the car. "You're wasting precious time."

He finished with the trunk and moved to the backseats. Fungus moved faster than him.

"There's more evidence in the house. That's where she killed him."

The officer slowed to a stop. Was he dragging out the search to buy Claire time to cover her tracks?

When he emerged from the car, he held a large ziplock bag containing papers and other familiar objects. A sinking feeling cramped her insides. *What did he find there?* Felicity wasn't a fool. She never hid incriminating details in her car.

The officer stared at her severely. "Is this yours, ma'am?"

Felicity recognized the documents and choked up. She'd hidden them well—in the kitchen! What were they doing in her car along with what appeared to be a driver's license, a lock of brown hair...and a dark smudge of dried blood?

"Ma'am, do you recognize these items?"

Felicity gasped. "I have no idea. She put those there."

Officer Doughnut spoke into his device. "We need Homicide on-site and Forensics."

Claire smirked at her. The bitch was framing her for murder. This couldn't be happening. Out of options, Felicity did the only thing that came to mind. She put her hand to her forehead and, like a fair maiden swooning upon hearing bad tidings, she collapsed to the sidewalk.

CHAPTER 51

Rafiq Massoud studied his suspect in silence, Wednesday morning. The agent with the ginger curls and freckles slouched on the stool in the corner of the interview room and gazed back. His youthful, earnest face projected innocence. But even the sweetest of masks can hide a black soul. Rafiq had learned that years ago, and that sad lesson had broken his heart. Was this young man a psychopath, too?

Rafiq offered his hand. "I'm Special Agent Massoud."

They shook. Corey Angel had sweaty palms.

Rafiq wiped his hand on his trouser leg. "We're meeting with a number of people in the building," he lied.

Corey was the only suspect on the list. Rafiq's team had researched his personal history and tailed his car. Rafiq was sprinting toward the end zone of the most important case in his career. This play would end either in a spectacular touchdown or a humiliating fumble.

"Is this about the bombing?"

Rafiq stared at him. *He gets straight to the point.* Was the agent curious about the investigation or trying to deflect suspicion?

Corey's forehead glistened. The charged silence seemed to unnerve him. "You're the CID investigator from Washington, aren't you? You spoke with agents in my unit last week."

Rafiq glanced at his notepad as though he didn't know the suspect's life story by heart. "You're assigned to...BAU-1?"

"Yes. Counterterrorism, arson, and bombing."

Corey grinned as though he was about to say something funny, then thought better of it.

"Do you enjoy your work there?"

"Yeah. It's my dream job. I started two weeks ago, and so far so good. I mean—except for the attack last week. That was horrible."

"Indeed. And yet at the Academy, you requested a different unit."

Corey's smile wavered. Clearly, the questioner knew more about him than he'd expected.

"I applied for BAU-2. Profilers. Chasing serial killers. Who doesn't want that, right?"

"Hm. Did you meet with Chief Madeleine Alda, the head of that unit?"

Rafiq knew Corey had. But easy questions relaxed interviewees and gave them ample opportunity to lie through their teeth.

"Yes, I did."

"Didn't you get along?"

Rafiq was hunting for a cartel infiltrator. But his team considered other possible motives, too, including revenge for rejection or personal insult.

"We did get along. At least, I thought so. I guess the Bureau decided my current unit is a better fit."

Rafiq glanced at his notes again. "Because of your chemistry background?"

"Correct. I have a bachelor's degree in chemistry from the American University."

Corey had offered a lot of free information. Did the details mask a deception, or was he simply a blabbermouth?

"I see. Is that where you met Tony Russo?"

"Excuse me, who?" Corey had evaded the trap elegantly.

"Anthony Russo. You studied chemistry together. Surely you remember him?"

This was the cue for Corey to correct him. Tony was one year ahead of Corey, but they had shared the AU campus for two years—plenty of time for Tony to introduce Corey to his friends in the Italian Mob.

Corey wrinkled his nose. "The name doesn't ring a bell."

Rafiq handed him Russo's file photo. Corey studied the face but shook his head.

"He looks kind of familiar, but I'm pretty sure he wasn't in my class. Are you sure he was at AU?"

Well played. Rafiq shrugged. "Did you meet any of the other agents in BAU-2? How about Special Agent Robert Cline?"

Corey swallowed hard. "Um. Yeah. He's a friend of a friend."

"Is that why you parked outside his home last night?"

Corey's eyes bulged. "What? How do you...?" He wiped the sweat from his brow.

Rafiq charged through his defensive line. "Is that why you keep turning up near his office?"

Corey gasped. "It's not what you think!"

Not such a good liar after all.

"What do I think?"

"That I'm somehow...involved in the bombing. That's crazy!"

Rafiq lunged for the goal line. "I'll make this easy for you, Corey. We have footage of you entering the crime scene shortly before the bombing. Why have you been surveilling Agent

Cline? Do you think he suspects you? Tell us what you know about Moretti, and the judge will take that into consideration."

The junior agent's eyes almost popped out. "Moretti? The drug dealer?" His breathing came fast and shallow.

Rafiq touched the grip of his service weapon. Two armed agents were waiting outside the door to arrest the suspect. This score wasn't going to escape.

Corey found his words. "This is all a big misunderstanding."

"Yeah? Enlighten me."

"I'm not a criminal. I'm..." Corey deflated and hung his head. "I'm in love."

"What?" In all his years as an investigator, Rafiq had never heard such a ridiculous alibi.

"Please, don't tell her."

"Don't tell who?"

"Claire. Rob's fiancée. We went through the Academy together. Back then, I didn't know she had a boyfriend."

Rafiq snorted. *Claire Wolfe. We meet again.* He'd slammed the ball down in the wrong end zone, handing the other side two points.

Corey grabbed fistfuls of his red curls. "I thought the engagement would help me get over her. But I can't get her out of my head."

Join the club, pal. "Does she know about your...crush?"

"No. She thinks we're just friends. We have lunch here and there. She brings me her chemistry questions. I guess I'll have to settle for that."

A vague suspicion materialized. "What chemistry questions?"

"I don't know. The other day she asked about curare extract. It's a—"

"I know what it is. What did she want to know?"

"How to manufacture it." Corey glanced at him with concern. Had he gotten Claire into trouble? "It's purely theoretical."

"Of course."

But the chemist's revelation had sparked a chain reaction in Rafiq's mind. Claire Wolfe had wanted to produce curare extract. Maybe Rafiq's botched play wasn't a total loss? Claire had not lied about the hospital assassin. But had she told the *whole* truth?

CHAPTER 52

Wednesday evening, Nicky Moretti stared at the embers in the fireplace of his home office. He felt like a caged lion in his den. Since the FBI bombing, the world had changed, and his circle of activity shrank. A new predator had invaded his turf. Nicky had tried to adapt. But his tried-and-true strategies had failed him. Yesterday, he'd paid Apex their tribute, and the sacrifice had decimated Nicky's cash reserves. All that remained was to hunker down in this shriveling safe space and await extinction. Thank goodness his father, bless his soul, hadn't lived to see their family name's dishonorable end.

And yet, Claire Wolfe's words refused to leave his mind. The attractive special agent had walked right into the lion's den and shoved a mirror in his face. Months ago, Nicky Moretti had feared nobody. He had eliminated his rivals and developed a mutually beneficial understanding with the Law. He'd taken on the world, and to hell with the odds. Apex had changed him. The savage pack had turned him into a cowering shadow of his former self. Now he longed for the old days—for the old Nicky Moretti.

Then he remembered Tony Russo, and his skin tingled.

Nicky's children would suffer that fate if he rebelled. He had too much to lose. His best men and a horde of private detectives failed to smoke out the extortionists. His contacts in law enforcement, previously so happy to pocket his money, gave him the cold shoulder, and the FBI was tightening the noose around his neck. The barbarians were at the gates, and Nicky was a dead man walking. But still, Agent Wolfe's challenge made him itch.

Knuckles wrapped on the door of the office. "Boss?"

Vinny checked up on him often, nervous that his boss would end his suffering with a bullet to the brain. Nicky didn't blame him. Suicide might be the best way to screw Apex over.

"Come in."

Vinny entered, and the grin on his face won Nicky's immediate and full attention. He hadn't seen Vinny smile so wide in weeks.

"What is it?"

Vinny kept him in suspense. He turned on the TV and switched channels to the news.

A presenter ranted. "... blames inter-party politics for the delays, calling the tactic a filibuster of the worst kind—the kind that costs lives."

On the screen, a red-faced Senator Schultz yelled into a microphone at a podium. The news desk had dubbed over his angry speech while they commented on the event. Nicky read the heading and chuckled.

Vinny joined him. "The Senate called his proposal unconstitutional. They're blocking his legislation. Did one of our friends arrange that?"

Nicky's mood darkened. The cartel had no friends left on Capitol Hill. The Apex girl's words echoed in his mind. *We'll take care of the rest.* Apex kept their promise. They'd hamstrung Schultz's legislation. Gung-ho lawmen wouldn't freeze Moretti's assets or search his properties. But now Nicky owed Apex more than ever. And he loathed their iron grip on his neck.

"No, Vinny. That wasn't us."

His associate shrugged. "It doesn't matter who did it. They won't try that move again."

Nicky's eyes widened. Vinny had talked about the Senate, but the observation applied equally well to Apex. Their operatives couldn't hold that sword over him again. Maybe Nicky wasn't out of options yet?

"Vinny, take my wife and the kids to the villa."

Vinny turned to him in surprise. "Now?"

The Morettis spent a few weeks each summer at his wine farm outside Verona in Northern Italy. It was time the family took an extended vacation.

"Yes, right now."

"What should I tell them?"

"Whatever you like. I need them someplace safe. Something nasty is about to hit the fan."

Vinny's trademark filthy grin returned to his face. His old boss was back. "We gonna screw Apex?"

"Oh, yeah, Vinny. We're gonna screw them hard."

CHAPTER 53

A police cruiser wailed, and Karla ducked behind a bush on the side of the road. *The cop car sped by.* That was close. *She'd spent the past three days off the grid. No buses, free rides, or stores. She'd lived off the land, foraging for scraps in dumpsters. Karla was done with society...and her mother.*

She climbed over a low fence at the edge of the forest. Home sweet home. *This time she avoided the main entrance of Prince William Forest Park. Nobody would know of her return.*

Mom's treachery burned like an ulcer in her gut. She called the cops. *Moments before the officers knocked on the door, Karla had slipped out with her overnight bag.*

She was a fugitive. Friendless. An outlaw. An outcast. But she wasn't alone. One man understood her. Only he could help her.

Karla waded through the scratchy undergrowth and crossed the dirt hiking path. Ichigouti had taught her how to find her way in the reserve. He'd guide her to her rightful place in the world, too.

People didn't understand them. They were the last surviving descendants of a noble bloodline. She and Ichigouti inhabited the peak of the natural order. Their kind had preceded the European invaders. They'd outlive them, too.

Karla spotted the clump of white oaks and adjusted her course. She looked forward to the knowing smile on her grandfather's face. "Forget about those pretendians," he'd say. "We don't need them." She stepped into the clearing of Ichigouti's camp. The hammocks swung in the morning breeze. A ribbon of gray smoke rose from the fire's embers.

"Ichigouti," she called. "I'm back." Where is he? *"Ichigouti?"*

He was probably out hunting. Karla could do with his breakfast porridge. She deposited her wheeled bag on the stony ground and warmed her limbs.

"Never leave a fire unattended," he'd taught her. But Ichigouti had broken that rule.

A burned scent drew her to the suspended cauldron. The stew had dried out and hardened.

The scrape of gravel under boots drew her attention to the edge of the clearing. A woman with a khaki uniform and flat-brimmed ranger's hat approached her.

Karla shot to her feet.

The ranger raised both her hands. "I didn't mean to startle you."

Karla said nothing. Maybe the woman would move along and leave her alone.

The woman lowered her gaze to the overnight bag. "The campgrounds are on the other side of the park."

"I'm not camping. I'm waiting for someone."

The ranger's stare froze. Then she frowned with sympathy. "I'm sorry. But he's gone."

"What do you mean?"

"The man who used to live here. They relocated him yesterday."

That can't be. "Who did?"

The woman hesitated, trying to find the right words. "Social services and the sheriff's office. They took him to Psychiatric."

"Where?"

She pointed behind her. "The Prince William Psychiatric Center."

No! *"You can't do that to him. He has rights!"*

"I'm so sorry. He had controlled substances in his possession. They had to remove him from the park for his own protection."

For his own protection. *Karla wanted to scream, but she held back. Attacking the ranger wouldn't free Ichigouti from custody.* "Listen to me. He's my grandfather. Release him to me, and I'll take care—"

The ranger seemed to remember something. She took a step back and reached for the radio on her utility belt. "She's here. Yeah, at the same spot. Call the sheriff."

Karla swore. She grabbed her bag and sprinted into the trees.

CHAPTER 54

Thursday morning, Claire's boss called her to his office. She had evaded Tom for as long as possible. The seasoned agent knew Rob well and cared about him. He'd take a keen interest in his disappearance. Would he see through Claire's act?

Tom shuffled papers on his desk. "Please, have a seat."

She complied. He clasped his hands and interweaved his fingers. The worry lines on his brow deepened.

"Any word from Rob?"

Claire studied her palms. "Nothing."

Two days had passed since she'd last seen him. Claire was having trouble keeping up the facade. The burden of her secrets crushed her. The tension frayed her nerves. But she and Rob had sworn to tell nobody, not even Sally. Apex had eyes and ears in the Bureau. The slightest involuntary reaction might give the game away—and they'd both be dead.

Any moment now, Apex would contact her. If she'd won Alpha's trust, he'd have more tasks for her. What he'd demand of her, she couldn't guess. But with each communication, she'd inch closer to the criminal mastermind. Then, she'd decapitate the snake.

Tom frowned. "Any word from the local PD?"

As Rob's unit chief, Tom probably received updates about Rob's missing person investigation, too. He knew the answer. By now, Homicide would have taken over the case. Tom didn't do small talk. Was he displaying his concern for his former partner? Or did he suspect Claire hadn't shared the whole truth?

She shook her head. How much longer could she maintain this pretense? She imagined Rob's voice consoling her. *One day at a time, Claire.*

Tom nodded grimly. He seemed to mull over the information. Then, he turned his computer monitor to face her. The screen displayed *The Newburgh Herald* website and the article Bella Winters had written at Claire's request. "FBI Hero Missing, Feared Dead."

Claire feigned surprise. "How d'you find that?"

"Newburgh is serial killer central. The BAU keeps an eye on the place."

Claire scanned the article, dialing up her affect as she read. "What a bitch! This is hearsay. Bella Winters is after her daily fix of drama, that's all."

Tom released a tremulous breath. "I wish that were so. I spoke with the homicide detective in charge of the case. Claire, I won't lie to you. The blood and hair samples found in the mother's car match our data on file for Rob. A full DNA analysis will have the final word, but the handwriting on the loan application clearly isn't Rob's. Considering his mother's history of check fraud and child abuse, the facts aren't looking optimistic."

Claire averted her eyes. He was trying to break the news of Rob's death to her gently. But Rob was alive. She had planned his disappearance with him. Claire had driven him overnight, avoiding any CCTV, to a safe place and planted the incriminating DNA samples and documents in Felicity's car. But their strategy hadn't factored in the impact his murder would have on the people who cared about him.

Had Claire's mother read Bella's article, too? Would Diane cut her cruise short and hurry back to comfort her bereaved daughter? Her ties of family and friendship threatened to sever her only lifeline.

Claire bit her lip. She hated the lies, but she couldn't share the truth with Tom. Not yet. Too much was riding on this deception for her to fall apart now. Instead, she doubled down on her performance.

"I don't believe it. Felicity is an irredeemable narcissist, but she isn't a murderer."

"Claire—"

"She isn't physically capable of overpowering him."

"Claire, Rob's injuries incapacitated him. She could have drugged him, too."

She raised her voice. "Rob wouldn't fall for that. He's a trained FBI agent. Besides, killing him would jeopardize her plot to steal his money."

Tom shrugged. "Maybe she didn't plan to kill him? Not at first. Maybe he discovered what she was up to and confronted her?"

Claire channeled her very real angst into tears. "I should have been there. How could I leave him alone with that monster?"

Tom offered her a box of Kleenex. "It's not your fault, Claire. You had no way of knowing what she was up to."

She wiped her tears. "How much did she try to take?"

Claire already knew the answer.

"Four hundred grand."

Again, she feigned shock and disbelief. The police officers

had arrested Felicity that night. Claire had almost felt sorry for the old hag. *Almost.*

Tom observed her closely. Did he suspect Claire knew more about Rob's disappearance than she was letting on?

"I've been thinking about what you and Rob told me earlier." He lowered his voice. "Your theory about Apex."

She swallowed. A few days ago, she would have welcomed his interest in her suspicions. But Alpha had expressed his displeasure with her bandying about the Apex brand. She'd obey his will until she sprang her trap.

Claire slumped on the chair. "I don't know what I believe anymore. Maybe Massoud is right and Moretti is behind the bombing? The Senate shelved Senator Schultz's bill against organized crime. Moretti has more power than I thought. Maybe I've been reading Apex into everything?"

"What about the assassin at the hospital? She murdered Alda."

"That doesn't prove Apex is involved. It won't bring Rob back either."

She covered her face in her hands.

Tom let her sob for a while. "I'm sorry you've had to go through this. Rob was a good man. Why don't you take a few days off?"

Claire wiped her cheeks and pulled herself together. "No, I'd rather work. It'll keep me busy."

Tom nodded. "We have a backlog of cold cases that need review. I'll send you a few."

Claire stood. "Thank you."

"Claire?"

"Yeah?"

"Watch your step. Massoud doesn't like you, and Rob's disappearance won't go unnoticed. Keep your head down. Stay out of trouble. You hear?"

"Yes, sir."

Claire returned to her office and nodded at Sally. The psychiatrist smiled at her quickly, then focused on her computer. Ever since Rob's disappearance, an invisible wall separated Claire and the psychiatrist. Did Sally sense Claire's secrets? Was her guilt printed on her forehead in large black letters?

She checked her generic Gmail account. An automated message suggested she follow up on her unanswered email to The Level Field Initiative. Claire had forgotten about that lead.

A New Email notification popped up for her work account. Tom had sent her a link to a cold case. A few clicks later, Claire studied the crime scene photos of a series of rape and murder cases in Milwaukee. She stared at the battered dead girls. Were the crimes related? Did Apex have a hand in these, too?

Sally stretched her arms. "I'm getting an early lunch. Want to join me?"

"Go ahead. I'm not hungry."

Sally shrugged and left the room.

Keep your head down. After Claire's conversation with Tom, pursuing leads on Apex had become even riskier. She closed the door and called Jess's work number on her cell phone.

"Investigations Bureau," a man said. "How may I help you?"

Claire recognized the quirky detective's voice despite his fake Irish brogue. "Mahoney?"

"Sergeant Wolfe, how lovely to hear your voice. Are you calling to invite us to the wedding?"

Jess had updated Newburgh PD's Investigations Bureau about Apex in Washington, and Bella's column, which *The Herald* had limited to the online edition.

"Not yet. We're still figuring out the details."

"Don't forget the open bar."

"We won't. Wait. Isn't this Jess's extension?"

"She's out. The ME's assistant keeps calling her, so I've become her official call screener."

"Among your many other talents."

"Hm. I sense a favor on the horizon. What do you need?"

Claire asked him to research The Level Field Initiative and identify the operators of their scholarship program.

"Is this related to He Who Must Not Be Named?"

Claire smiled at the Harry Potter reference. Alpha was her own personal Voldemort. "Yes."

Her phone vibrated, announcing the arrival of a text message. "Thanks, Mahoney. Got to go."

She clicked the message notification. The sender had used a private number. Had the deception finally yielded results? Was Alpha reaching out to her?

Claire read the message, and her breath caught in her lungs. The contents consisted of two details: a street address and a time. Tonight, she'd get her answer.

CHAPTER 55

Felicity Cline bawled her eyes out in the interview room. "My son! My son is gone!"

She pulled out all the stops to spell things out for the officer. The lanky homicide detective at the Prince William County Police Department seemed incapable of understanding that she was the victim in this case. She was surrounded by idiots!

Sergeant Arnold White stood with his hands on his hips. Her tears made no visible impression on him. Her fainting stunt had failed to move Officer Doughnut Guts to sympathy, either. These cops had hearts of stone.

With a world-weary sigh, the detective lowered his tall, thin frame to the seat on the other side of the table.

"Ms. Cline, we are aware of your criminal history." He flipped through a thick sheaf of printed pages. "Check forgery. Mail fraud."

"Those charges were dismissed, Sergeant."

White raised a disapproving eyebrow at her. "On technicalities."

He'd done his homework. *Rats!*

Sergeant White turned another page. "Then there's the incident in which you impersonated a..." He squinted at the document. "Veterinarian?"

"That was a tragic misunderstanding."

Fortunately for her, no legislation outlawed that type of identity misappropriation, but a vengeful group of pet owners had reported her to the authorities all the same.

"It's a long story. I won't bore you with the details." She hoped that warning would discourage further prying.

In her six decades of independent living, Felicity had remained within a hair's breadth of the law and relied on plausible deniability to avoid prosecution. On the occasions when temptation pushed her over the edge, she deployed her formidable acting skills to save the day. Living by one's wits required bold action, and a girl had to eat. But this time, none of her usual techniques sufficed. It wasn't her fault. Claire Wolfe had set her up, and local law enforcement danced to their colleague's tune.

The detective returned to the matter at hand.

"The blood found in your vehicle matches that of our missing person. We also discovered his personal effects in your possession."

"I certainly didn't place them in my car. They were planted there by the real villain."

The detective stifled a smile. Had she laid it on too thick?

"By villain, you mean Special Agent Claire Wolfe, your son's fiancée?"

"Girlfriend. Ex-girlfriend, in fact. He had broken up with her the previous night, and good riddance." She sobbed. "If only I'd been able to stop her from taking her bloody revenge!"

"Ms. Cline, things will go easier with you if you cooperate."

"But I am cooperating!"

"Let's talk about the victim's body."

"I already told you—"

"All I'm asking is that you point us to its location. That kind of cooperation will help you later."

"Later? When you charge me with murder?"

The sergeant wanted her to supply the rope for her hanging. She wouldn't fall for that lame trick!

"Your testimony is the only indication that a homicide took place. No corpse, no crime."

The sergeant was a sneaky devil, she gave him that. If she were twenty years younger, she'd offer to reward his lenient handling of her case with special favors. Then again, if she were twenty years younger, she wouldn't be in this mess.

"If I knew where she buried my son, I would've told you already. Why don't you question *her*? *She* dumped his body. Claire is the murderer."

"We have questioned Agent Wolfe. She cooperated fully."

"Did she reveal where she buried the body?" *Ha!* She had him there. "Why the double standard? You're covering for her. I won't stand for this injustice, this..." She raised her voice. "Police brutality!"

The officers outside the room would assume he'd manhandled her, and they'd cut short the interrogation. But Sergeant White didn't take the bait, and no indignant officers burst through the door to rescue her.

He raised his eyebrows again. "Agent Wolfe believes her fiancé is still alive and well."

"Of course she does. What else would she say? 'Oops, I murdered him. My bad.'"

The sergeant sighed again. He was losing his patience. What was she supposed to do? The police had closed ranks to protect one of their own. The system had turned against her. Nobody wanted to hear the truth. At least, not that truth. Perhaps she could sell them another story?

"This isn't only about my son's disappearance."

The cop's eyebrows rose a third time. "It isn't?"

She knew what he was thinking. *What has the crazy old lady cooked up this time?* She'd show him.

Cogs spun in her mind. Felicity had held a drinking glass to the thin bedroom wall to better eavesdrop on Rob and Claire. She'd overheard their discussion of an internal FBI investigation. The information had meant little to her and promised no foreseeable payout, but now the tidbits wove a colorful tapestry.

"This is only one in a series of related crimes. The bombing attack at the FBI last week. Did you know that Rob was injured in that blast, too?"

The eyebrows rose higher. She'd captured his attention.

"Claire had a hand in that, too. But that wasn't her first mysterious explosion. There was another. Three young innocents, blown to smithereens. Children. No! Students. And a man. Yes! A man with ties to a drug cartel." She strained her memory, but the name danced out of reach. "Something Italian."

Sergeant White straightened on his chair for the first time. She'd hit the jackpot. Everybody had heard about the daring attack on the heart of the FBI. Felicity bet the local police department itched to learn the gory details.

Her memory retrieved another overheard word—the perfect hook for her new narrative. "One name connects the crimes. One secret criminal group. Remember this word, Sergeant. *Apex!*"

CHAPTER 56

Special Agent Rafiq Massoud marched down the corridor toward his meeting, Thursday afternoon. The CIRG building had become his second home. As the investigation dragged out, the nauseating scent of frustration clung to its halls. Wherever he turned, obstacles rose in his path. An assassin killed a potential witness in her hospital bed. A drug lord skinned his chemist alive. Self-serving politicians stalled Senator Schultz's Organized Crime Bill. And now, Prince William County PD spouted conspiracy theories. All the setbacks traced back to one source—Claire Wolfe.

At first, Rafiq had dismissed Claire as an annoying but harmless distraction. The BAU recruit spun wild speculations from recent events to satisfy her thirst for drama and attention. Her history as a high-profile homicide detective supported his assessment. Her claim to cure psychopathy only added to his contempt for her.

But Agent Wolfe didn't know when to stop. Her interference with his investigation had culminated with blatant insubordination when she had sidestepped Rafiq and contacted Senator Schultz directly.

The senator had convinced Rafiq to reboot his attitude. After all, Claire had discovered that Alda's death was a homicide, and Rafiq's team found corroboration for the assassin Claire had sighted. But a series of highly suspicious facts eclipsed her positive contributions to the case: repeated attempts to control the investigation; grandiose theories about a cabal of serial killers; her interest in manufacturing curare; the mysterious disappearance of her fiancé and the arrest of her future mother-in-law for his suspected murder.

Was Claire simply an overzealous detective with spectacularly bad luck, or was there more to her than met the eye? Was she the invisible hand that had sabotaged his investigation? Now that was a conspiracy theory he'd embrace! But recent events whispered that Rafiq was running out of time. Rafiq had to remove that obstacle from his path, today, before matters spiraled out of control.

He knocked on the unit chief's door and entered.

Tom Brown looked up from his computer monitor. "Agent Massoud, I was about to call you."

His Southern twang grated on Rafiq's nerves.

"Then I've saved you the trouble."

Brown scrutinized his guest. His stormy entrance had set off warning bells, and rightly so.

"Please, have a seat."

Rafiq closed the door behind him and sat. "You first."

He owed his host that courtesy. Did the unit chief have concerns about his new agent, too? Managers tended to fight external interference. Rafiq preferred to skip that battle.

"I've been thinking about your investigation."

Rafiq hugged his midsection. Brown had triggered his defenses, too.

"I'd be happy to hear your insights," he lied.

Brown grinned. "I was hoping you'd feel that way." His

ironic delivery undercut his words. "I'd like you to reconsider the role Apex might have played in the bombing."

Rafiq chuckled and stared at the ceiling. *Here we go again.*

Brown mistook his laughter for ridicule. "It sounds like fantasy, I know. But I wouldn't underestimate them. I've seen firsthand what they're capable of. We shouldn't dismiss them out of hand."

"She put you up to this, didn't she?"

"Who did?"

"Agent Wolfe. She planted that idea in Senator Schultz's mind as well. Prince William County PD is frothing at the mouth. And now she's entangled you in her crackpot ideas, too."

"I assure you, Agent Massoud, nobody *put me up to* this. In fact, Agent Wolfe told me to drop the Apex angle."

Rafiq scoffed. *Of course she did.* That's how manipulators worked. *Make it seem like the other guy's idea.* He'd heard enough.

"Please, Agent Brown. I reviewed the Newburgh files. Apex was a small-time operation in a Massachusetts backwater. Over here, Apex is a distraction."

"A distraction from what?"

"From the real culprit—Nicky Moretti."

"Why would Agent Wolfe help Moretti?"

"I've been asking myself the same thing. Claire Wolfe is one big question mark, isn't she? She leaves town the day of the bombing, although she only started work there the previous week. Her fiancé survives the blast, then mysteriously disappears days later. Her unit chief is assassinated while she's spending the night at Sentara Medical Center. She sees the killer leaving the scene but doesn't stop her. Wherever she goes, she leaves a trail of corpses in her wake. Doesn't that strike you as odd?"

Brown shrugged. "I wouldn't sit next to her in a lightning storm, but that doesn't make her an accomplice to murder."

"It doesn't. But you'd think she'd learn to stop poking her nose where it doesn't belong."

"Considering what she's been through, that's understandable. Her concerns aren't pure paranoia. She battled Apex in Newburgh. She fears they survived and hold a grudge against her and her new program."

"There it is again. Apex. The criminal masterminds who leave no trace. How convenient."

"Why would she lie about that?"

"Because she thrives on the attention. Or she used the chaos to get rid of her new boss."

Brown laughed. "You think she killed Alda?"

"The thought did occur to me. Maybe she figured she deserves the promotion? Or her fiancé."

"What do you think now?"

"She's a smoke screen, a distraction from the real culprit, Niccolo Moretti. Maybe he admired her work? Moretti transferred large sums of money in the past weeks. Maybe he made her an offer she couldn't refuse?"

Agent Brown grunted. "To eliminate a hardline FBI director?"

Massoud nodded. "Moretti's up to something. He's moved his family overseas. I get the feeling his big finale is near. And Agent Wolfe's distractions are slowing us down."

"There's only one problem with that theory. Agent Wolfe changed her mind. She thinks you're right. Moretti is our man."

The revelation knocked Rafiq speechless for three seconds. "What? No more Apex? No more bogeymen? Just good old organized crime?"

"As of this morning. But I don't believe her."

"Why not?"

"She's afraid. I think she went digging for Apex, and what she found scared the crap out of her. And Claire Wolfe doesn't scare easily. We should sit up and listen."

Rafiq huffed. Brown seemed genuinely concerned about his agent, but Rafiq wasn't buying her act. Was the about-face another attempt at muddying the waters or was she backpedaling to throw Rafiq off her case? Claire Wolfe was a riddle wrapped in a mystery inside an enigma. Whatever her game plan, she was dangerous.

"Well, I'm listening now. And watching. I suggest you keep a close eye on her, too, Unit Chief Brown. If she keeps throwing a wrench in the works, you'll have to explain her behavior before the oversight committee. And they're already convinced the Bureau needs to cut some flab."

He let the threat hang in the air.

"Is there anything else?"

"I'm done. Thank you again for your cooperation."

Agent Brown sneered. "Always a pleasure."

CHAPTER 57

In her Washington apartment, the killer mixed the black paste with a new wooden stirrer. Frank Sinatra crooned from the Bluetooth speakers. The music helped her focus. This procedure demanded her full attention. As with her leather-craft, she used only the best equipment for her professional work. Laboratory-grade glass beakers. An electronic Bunsen burner with a digital display. Protective goggles and tear-proof rubber gloves. Precision was critical in her industry. Errors might be fatal. She had studied the chemical composition of her poison and experimented with its dosage and delivery. Today, she'd raise her capabilities to a new level.

Sinatra sang her favorite, "I've Got You Under My Skin." She had old-fashioned taste in music. The Chairman of the Board reminded her of Daddy. Did she have a thing for older men—a father complex? Her mind drifted to Daddy's new pet.

"Claire, Claire, Claire. What am I to make of you?"

She knew exactly what she'd make *from* her. A black leather miniskirt with silver studs. She'd never introduced metal into her creations before. They'd add a badass touch that suited Claire. The thorn in her side would serve a better purpose in her wardrobe. Wasn't that what people wanted in life—to find a purpose?

The killer let the paste settle and grabbed a handful of silver pellets from the flat, round tin. She lined them up on a plastic tray filled with putty—a dozen lead projectiles with hollow points.

She'd known the FBI agent would cause trouble. But now Claire had become a clear and present danger. Claire had slipped through her fingers—the second target to do so in a row. That trend was ominous enough. But the circumstances of her survival troubled the killer more.

Daddy had overruled her misgivings and let Claire go. Why had he sided with this stranger?

The killer drew the dark paste into a plastic pipette and dripped the substance into the pellets, filling the tips to the brim. Then she heated her soldering iron to three hundred degrees Celsius and melted globs of tin solder wire over each pellet, sealing the curare payload.

She didn't trust Claire. She didn't believe that she supported Apex either. Claire was a cop and an FBI agent. She was their enemy. And her revelations unnerved her.

The killer had been to Newburgh, but she'd never heard of other Apex branches. *Daddy has secrets.* What else was he hiding?

She set aside the pellets to dry and retrieved the previous batch. She prodded the tips with tweezers. The tin coverings had hardened. *Perfect.* One by one, she inserted the hollow points into the ten-chamber Gamo Quick-Shot. Each time she scrubbed her thumb along the edge of the round magazine, an empty chamber panned into view and the counter incremented.

Yes, Claire Wolfe is our enemy. Why else had she contacted

Nicky Moretti? Daddy was getting soft. *Claire wants to steal Daddy's heart and take my place in the pack.*

The killer had news for Claire. She'd lost two father figures before. She wouldn't lose a third.

Her playlist switched to the next song, Sinatra's "The Way."

She reached for her new Gamo Swarm Maxxim Air Rifle and inserted the magazine into the slot at the base of the barrel. Amazon had delivered both purchases to her doorstep.

The killer had considered other distance weapons. Arrows and blow darts were intuitive but unreliable, inconvenient, and frankly, ridiculous. Fits of laughter would disable her opponents before the poison hit their bloodstreams. Air rifles offered easy aiming and quick reloading. Considered non-lethal, they didn't require a firearms license. Pellets fired at thirteen hundred feet per second penetrated clothing and pierced human skin. The hollow points flattened on impact, providing her with a delivery mechanism for paralyzing doses of neurotoxin.

Thanks to Claire, she had upped her game. She was ready for all eventualities. She'd make Daddy proud.

Her cell phone rang. The special one. *Speak of the devil.*

She answered. "I was just thinking of you."

The digitized voice answered. "I'm flattered."

She and Daddy never bothered with hellos or goodbyes. Their connection ran that deep. Claire didn't have a chance. She'd obviously failed at her mission, and Daddy had called to order her assassination.

"Is this about our new friend?"

"It is. Congratulations. You have a new partner."

Her lips parted with surprise and irritation. "What do you mean?"

"She exceeded our expectations."

The killer gasped. Claire Wolfe had killed her fiancé. She

didn't think Claire had it in her. Now Daddy had welcomed her into their family. The killer swore under her breath. The balance of power had shifted.

"I don't believe it."

"Are you jealous?" Despite the electronic garbling, a note of amusement had crept into his voice. Daddy was needling her.

"No. But I don't trust her. And neither should you."

"Strength lies in numbers. You'll learn to like her."

The killer disagreed. She had collaborated with Daddy's other children, and that experiment hadn't ended well.

"We don't need her, Daddy. We're doing fine without her."

"Together, we'll go further."

"But she killed her father."

Surely that raised questions about her trustworthiness. What if Claire betrayed them, too? Didn't that bother Alpha?

"Sometimes we hurt the ones we love."

Was that a warning? Had she become expendable?

Daddy mistook her silence for acceptance. "Our Italian friend has disappointed us. It's time to bid him farewell."

Nicky Moretti's time was up. Daddy had signed his execution order.

"Understood."

Moretti was a well-defended target. He wouldn't go easily. Finally, she'd found a worthy challenge...and an excuse to play with her new toy.

"Take your partner along. You'll need her." He was right. Claire had access to Moretti.

The killer swallowed her pride. "Fine. But don't blame me if she trips up."

"Fair enough." He ended the call.

She brightened. Her new mission had provided her with an unexpected opportunity. She'd extract the thorn in her side and solve her daddy issues.

She screwed the carbon dioxide cartridge into the rifle to the satisfying puff of releasing gas and cranked the barrel downward to load the first pellet. Then she raised the weapon, pressed the butt to her shoulder, and peered through the sights.

The crosshairs hovered over the photo on the corkboard at the far wall. She pulled the trigger. The firing mechanism clicked, and the rifle fired without a fuss. *No silencer necessary.* She inspected her target, a candid photo she'd snapped on the street. A small round hole pierced the head of Claire Wolfe.

The killer smiled and sang along with Frank Sinatra. "I did it my way."

CHAPTER 58

The white dome of Capitol Hill glowed brightly that evening when Claire parked her car on the street. She checked the Washington address in the anonymous text message. The symbol of justice wouldn't save her tonight if she was walking into a trap.

She crossed the street. A chill breeze sent ghostly fingers through her hair and goose bumps over her skin. Did Alpha believe she'd dispatched Rob, or was his assassin waiting for her in a dark alley? Once again, the specter of Tony Russo's flayed corpse floated in her mind. Claire shuddered. She'd experienced the terror, too, but escaped with her life. Next time, she wouldn't be so lucky.

The patter of her shoes echoed off aging office buildings.

Apex had eyes and ears everywhere. If they learned of her deception, she'd have nowhere to hide. Claire shook her head to clear the thoughts of torture and death. She had beaten Apex before. She'd outsmart them again. Claire had to. The only path to survival led onward.

You can do this. Alpha had started Apex with William Wolfe. Claire, William's daughter, would shut down their murderous project. *Call it destiny. Call it fate.* Alpha had gotten that part right. Claire would stop them. But to decapitate that snake, she had to locate its head.

Claire put her hand in her jacket pocket and activated her digital recorder. If Alpha showed his face, she'd capture what she could. His voice signature might be enough to track him down. But was the recording worth the risk?

The text message had surprised her. The sender had provided no details and little time to plan. She was on her own. If she blew her cover, Rob wasn't here to rescue her. She'd never felt so alone.

At home, she'd strapped on her Coolmax Pro covert vest. The bulletproof lining sat underneath her clothes. Rob's gift had saved her skin before. She hoped it would bring her the same good fortune tonight.

Claire halted on a street corner. She'd reached her destination. The alley sank into inky darkness. The stench of spilled trash and urine assaulted her nostrils. Red warning lights flashed in her reptile brain. A lone woman, no matter how well-trained, entered this space at her peril. *Just a bit further. You're almost there.* Like a casino addict, she went all in, hoping, against the odds, that this last gamble would pay off.

The closed space amplified her footfalls. Did she have company? She drew her firearm. Trash cans and piles of discarded packing boxes emerged as her eyes adjusted to the dark. She passed two large trash cans and scanned her peripheral vision for threats. Finding none, she charged ahead.

Alpha had selected a public but secluded area for their meeting. Did he still doubt her loyalty? If he'd discovered her trick, she'd never leave this place alive.

The alley ended in a brick wall. Had she come to the wrong place? Crap! She couldn't afford to miss her rendezvous.

"You made it," a man said behind her.

She spun around. He stepped from the shadows. In the dull reflected moonlight, Claire recognized his sarcastic grin.

"Vinny."

Nicky Moretti's aide flashed his crooked smile. "For a while there, I didn't think you'd make it."

Claire deflated. Alpha hadn't called the meeting, Moretti had. Or was the cartel henchman a secret Apex operative? She never thought she'd be relieved to encounter a Mafia thug in a dark alley.

"Nice place. You sure know how to impress a girl."

He chuckled. "Mr. Moretti sends his apologies. He figures it's better you aren't seen together in public. Not twice. People might talk."

He had hinted at her indiscretion at turning up at the Moretti residence in Berkley, and he had a valid point.

Hope kindled in her chest. "Has your boss reconsidered my proposal?"

"As a matter of fact, he has."

Claire smelled a catch. "Why the sudden change of mind?"

"You made a good impression."

Claire laughed. Moretti had declined her pitch in absolute terms. She doubted he'd risk his life because she asked nicely.

"This is about the OC Bill, isn't it?"

Vinny shrugged. "Circumstances have changed. Mr. Moretti would like to help the FBI keep our streets safe." He was enjoying this game of make-believe.

Claire cut to the chase. "When can we meet to record his deposition?"

"We're one step ahead of you." Like a stage magician, he produced a flash drive from between his fingers. "Mr. Moretti recorded a full declaration on video. Everything you need to know."

Claire reached for the drive, but Vinny whisked his hand away. "Not so fast. First, Mr. Moretti needs insurance."

"I don't offer dental plans."

Vinny lost his sense of humor. "The FBI must assure his well-being. Safe houses. Immunity from prosecution. Security around the clock. The whole shebang."

"He already has security."

"Not like the Feds."

Claire scoffed. Nicky Moretti didn't want to risk his people on the front lines. FBI agents were his cannon fodder. He knew what he was up against.

She put her hands on her hips and pretended to mull the suggestion over. Moretti could never learn she was walking a tightrope without a federal safety net. Once she showed Moretti's testimony to Tom and Massoud, they'd pull the necessary strings...probably.

She held out her hand for the flash drive. "That won't be a problem."

Vinny grinned. "Good. Mr. Moretti will hand this over personally at his safe house."

Claire was screwed.

He handed her a small flip phone. "This is your direct line. There's one saved contact. Call when you're ready."

She pocketed the device and smiled. "Will do."

"Then, we're done. Never thought I'd say this, but it's nice doing business with the Feds."

Claire's panic attack began on the drive home. She needed a safe house and a ton of luck. Her timing had to be perfect. Get Moretti's recording. Call in the big guns. Keep Apex in the dark. But first, she needed a safe house. And the only one she had was occupied by Rob.

She longed to talk with Rob. But they had agreed to cut off

communication until their mission concluded and Apex was no longer a threat. Breaking that rule might endanger Rob and blow her cover, too. Two days since his disappearance, Claire had no ID for Alpha or his assassin. She'd uncovered no new information about their activities. The BAU could provide zero assistance. She didn't know who to trust. And she featured prominently on the Apex radar. How was she supposed to pull this off on her own?

You don't. Claire wasn't alone. She had friends at Newburgh PD. She'd mobilize them and construct her own safety net. Rob's home would have to double as a safe house, at first. Moretti wouldn't be happy when he realized she'd turned witness protection into a cottage industry. If anyone paid her an unscheduled visit—Tom, Massoud, or Felicity—her house of cards would collapse.

Claire squeezed the wheel. She couldn't breathe. She pulled over in the highway emergency lane and forced her lungs to fill with air. *Calm down.* Nothing would happen until she called Moretti. For now, she controlled the flow of events. She had time to think and explore all options. Moretti's data might lead her to Alpha or at least to the assassin. Claire had better prepare for that possibility, too, and leverage the element of surprise.

She drew three more deep breaths and joined the flow of traffic. Claire needed a long jog to clear her thoughts and a good night's sleep to recharge her batteries. She'd neglected her health since the bombing, and her fatigued body already showed signs of decline.

Claire parked outside Rob's house. *Their* house. The lights were out. Felicity's rental car was nowhere to be seen. Forensics had impounded the vehicle. *So far so good.*

She unlocked the door, turned on the lights, and jumped. A

woman in a black sweatsuit lounged on her couch, her legs stretched on the cushions. She'd tied back her jet-black waterfall hair in a ponytail.

The assassin gazed at her, deadpan. "I let myself in. I hope you don't mind."

CHAPTER 59

Remain calm. Act casual. Claire lobbed her car keys onto the credenza. She fixed her uninvited visitor with a cool glance. "I see you've made yourself at home."

The assassin appeared to be unarmed, but the police academy had imprinted the Plus One Rule into Claire's brain. When searching a suspect, never assume you've found all their concealed weapons. Found a gun? Look for another. Found a second? Look for a knife. If Claire were to hold this killer upside down and give her a shake, a dozen deadly implements would litter the floor. And her arsenal included blades spiked with curare. Was she here to kill Claire? If so, she hid her intentions well.

"Acid?" the assassin asked.

Claire wrinkled her brow at the seemingly random question. "Excuse me?"

Is she high? Was she offering Claire drugs or soliciting?

"I hear the police didn't find the body. Did you use acid?"

Claire relaxed. The woman wasn't tripping. She was scratching an itch. The assassin had contacts at the Prince William County Police Department, or she'd read Bella's article in *The Newburgh Herald*'s online edition. Either way, she wondered how Claire had disposed of Rob's body.

Claire folded her arms over her chest, as though reluctant to reveal the secrets of her trade.

"Maybe."

The assassin grunted. "Use white vinegar when working indoors. It clears the smell."

"I'll keep that in mind next time."

They shared a quiet and creepy moment of professional camaraderie.

Sally had speculated about why ViCAP's database didn't contain more flaying victims. *What if she usually disposes of the bodies completely?* Sally's suggestion was on the money. The assassin dissolved her victims in acid, leaving no trace of her sick crimes. Would she dispose of Claire that way, too?

The killer vented a resigned sigh. "I'm Karla. Welcome to the family."

Claire blinked at her. The woman wouldn't skin Claire alive. Not tonight. She'd dropped by to confirm Claire's entry into the pack.

"Karla who?"

"Just Karla. We'll be working together."

Claire's gut tightened. She couldn't arrange Moretti's protection or set a trap for Alpha with the assassin breathing down her neck.

"I work alone."

Karla twisted her mouth into a commiserating smile. "Same here. But these are Daddy's orders."

Claire grunted. She couldn't expel her new colleague without raising suspicion. Maybe she could turn this unexpected visit to her advantage?

"Do you want a drink? There's vodka and—"

"I'll take the whiskey. Straight."

Karla had searched the house. She stared at Claire, daring her to complain.

Claire nodded and moved to the kitchen. She wiped two glass tumblers clean with a kitchen towel. Her fingers trembling, she poured shots of Jack Daniel's. The assassin's presence induced an involuntary terror response. Claire's traumatic ordeal as Karla's defenseless prey had conditioned her, searing neural pathways into her brain that threatened to expose her deception. The thought of breathing the same air as the killer revolted her. She resisted the urge to stir rat poison into her guest's drink.

Keep your eyes on the prize. Karla had murdered Chief Alda and Director Warren, among others, but she was only a footsoldier. The key to defeating Apex was Alpha. If Claire attacked Karla now, she'd win a battle but lose the war. The murderous army would regroup and claim more innocent lives. Claire had to capture the commander in chief.

She returned with the drinks.

"How long have you known Alpha?"

"Long enough."

She presented both glasses, allowing Karla to choose. If Claire was trying to poison her, she'd left their fate to chance. Karla selected a glass. Claire settled on the armchair. The assassin watched her but didn't touch her drink. She didn't trust her. Claire had faced the same dilemma in Nicky Moretti's den.

Claire sipped her whiskey. "What's he like?"

The killer studied her tumbler, then took a gulp. "Cautious."

She'd reveal nothing. Not intentionally.

Claire tried a different angle. "What were the others like?"

"Others?"

"The college kids. You worked with them, too. I've done my homework." Claire had presented her educated guess as fact.

Karla glared at her, then relented. "I didn't mind them. But they didn't seem to like me. I guess I got under their skin." She laughed.

Claire forced a smile. "That's understandable."

Karla sobered. "I'm sorry about...the other night. I had my orders." She looked contrite. The sociopath realized she'd broached a touchy subject and tried to make amends. "You made a good impression on Daddy."

Her lips twitched.

Claire didn't fall for the compliment. She'd invaded the killer's turf. Karla resented her rival and would get rid of her at the first opportunity.

The assassin winced. "We'll both have to get used to running with a larger pack once YARI gets going."

YARI. Daddy had adopted Claire's suggestion to recruit Apex members through the new BAU program. But Karla's words also implied Apex was smaller than Claire had imagined.

Crush one tentacle, two more take its place. Nicky Moretti had thought Apex teemed with psychopathic devotees. Had the warehouse bombing depleted their human resources? Did that explain why YARI had posed such a dire threat? Claire had stumbled upon the criminal group during a period of critical weakness. Destroying them might be easier than she'd thought.

"How many are we now?"

"Don't worry about our numbers. Daddy prefers quality over quantity, and he has big plans for your recruits."

Big plans. She slotted more details into place. *Is that why Alpha needed Moretti's money—to bankroll his next grand scheme?* Claire aired her thoughts, hoping to goad Karla into filling in the blanks.

"The college kids were studying political science, public policy, law and criminology. Apex already has moles in the police force and FBI. The students were destined for similar roles in local and national government. Like the plan for Sara Malik."

"Who?"

Claire seized the opportunity to share information and build rapport. "Malik was the pack's candidate for mayor in Newburgh. She would have won the election if my colleagues hadn't screwed up."

Her thoughts drifted to The Level Field Initiative. Did scholarship funnel illicit funds to groom Alpha's army of political infiltrators?

Karla knocked back her drink and set down the glass. "Only Daddy has all the puzzle pieces."

Did she resent Alpha for keeping her in the dark? Could Claire use that bitterness to turn Karla against Alpha?

The assassin dashed her hopes. "Don't take it personally, Claire. Daddy does that for our own protection. He says we're like a starfish. Cut off one arm, the others survive. Later, it'll regrow the lost limb."

Claire nodded. "I'll start YARI as soon as the dust settles. When do I meet Alpha?"

"You don't."

"I only work with people I've met face-to-face."

"Do your job well, and he'll grant your wish."

"What does that mean?"

"Daddy has a new task for you—a high-profile target. This one should be easy, seeing that you already have access."

The blood drained from Claire's face. Who had Alpha marked for death now? Her unit chief, Tom Brown? Or Senator Schultz? Fabricating their murders would be exponentially more complicated than Rob's.

"Who?"

"Your new friend, Niccolo Moretti."

"Are you crazy? I'm supposed to take on the Mafia?"

Inwardly, Claire sighed with relief. The drug lord would soon step willfully into her custody. Faking his death could be a part of his witness protection plan. She'd have to inform Vinny about the deception, or the cartel's hitmen would hunt her down.

Karla rolled her eyes. "Not if you're smart. Isolate him. Daddy wants to pull the trigger himself."

Alpha would join them in the flesh. This was Claire's opportunity to capture him and decapitate the snake. Claire might actually pull this off. But she'd need to keep Karla at a distance.

The killer smirked. "Should I tell Daddy you're not up to the task?"

"Tell him I'll take care of it."

"*We'll* take care of it, Claire. Daddy wants us to work together, remember? I'll be by your side every step of the way."

CHAPTER 60

F riday morning, Detective Jessica Long heaved two brown paper grocery bags from the trunk of her car. Despite sunny skies and a spring breeze that rustled the leaves in the trees overhead, the two-level house in Pine Hills made her skin crawl. Chilling memories haunted Claire Wolfe's childhood home. A deadly shootout had taken place in there. For the past year, the place had stood empty, a For Sale sign in the front yard. Well, almost empty.

Jess had stopped by the address every day since Tuesday. A bulk grocery delivery would have saved her time and effort. But her daily visits served an additional purpose—to provide the current ghost with some human company.

She shifted the bags in her arms, fished for the house key in the pocket of her suit jacket, and unlocked the front door. Jess never knocked. Nosy neighbors should never learn about the residence's occupant. The secret was a matter of life and death.

She swung the door shut with her foot. "It's me."

Jess offloaded the groceries onto the kitchen counter and unpacked her trove.

"We've got milk and eggs. Tuna fish in water, not oil, as

requested. Fresh fruit and veggies. They're out of avocado—sorry. Oreos. Pringles. And dark chocolate. Oh, and this time, I remembered the can opener."

Halting footfalls on the staircase announced the ghost's arrival. "Thanks, Jess. I appreciate it."

Special Agent Rob Cline grinned at her. In his pajamas and sporting three-day stubble, the special agent looked scruffy but fetching. *He's Claire's fiancé, remember!* Last year, Jess and Rob had spent quality time together while chasing leads to identify a morgue-load of unidentified homicide victims. He'd helped her ease into her detective role when she'd felt insecure about her new job. Now she could return the favor.

She beamed at him. "Any special requests for tomorrow?"

"No, this is perfect. You're a lifesaver. Literally, without you, I'd starve."

Jess chuckled. Since his official "murder," Rob was forbidden to leave the house. Sightings of the missing special agent would compromise Claire's secret operation and place her in the sights of a homicidal maniac who skinned her victims alive. Only a handful of officers at Newburgh PD knew the truth about Rob's disappearance, and Jess was honored to number among them.

His humor failed to hide the anxiety in his eyes. Jess resisted the urge to give him a comforting hug. She should have brought more chocolate.

"I should get going."

"Any news from Claire?"

Rob's lockdown demanded absolute radio silence, too—no telephone calls or internet chats. He had access to video streaming and books to stay sane, but Jess was the only human being he'd interacted with in days. The isolation would drive most people stir-crazy. But Rob also shouldered the burden of knowing his fiancée faced constant mortal danger. The worrying and helplessness must be unbearable.

Jess produced a brave smile. "Nothing yet. I'm sure she's fine. We'd know if anything went wrong. No news is good news, right?"

He nodded but remained forlorn.

"Claire's a tough cookie. She'll get them."

Them. Apex had survived, and the group's poisonous tendrils had reached Washington, DC. But Claire's team still knew little about the murderous organization's size or activity. How long would Rob have to stay locked up like a lone survivor of a zombie apocalypse? Judging by his hangdog expression, the same gloomy thought occupied his mind.

Jess's phone buzzed. Her new partner, Detective Lucas Gomez, was calling.

"You like to travel, don't you?" he said.

"Um, sure."

"Good. We've got plans for the weekend."

Jess whispered an apology to Rob. "What's going on, Gomez?"

"Claire lifted Psycho Girl's fingerprints from a drinking glass, and we found a match."

Psycho Girl. Gomez had invented the fitting if unimaginative moniker after hearing Claire's unsub skinned her victims alive.

Jess smiled at Rob. "That's great news!"

"Captain Washington approved a trip for the two of us to Washington. Ha! Get it? Washington...is sending us...to Washington. I've got it all planned out. We'll start with the Lincoln Memorial, then head up to Capitol Hill—"

"Whoa," Jess interrupted. "Slow down, partner. I'm sure Captain Washington didn't have sightseeing and guided tours in mind for us."

She asked him for the details and hung up.

Rob stared at her, hungry for information. "What happened?"

"Claire got the assassin's fingerprints. We have her name and home address. Gomez and I are going to Washington. Apex ordered a hit on Moretti, and Claire thinks this is our chance to catch Alpha."

Rob's eyes brightened. "That's amazing. Excellent!"

"I know!"

"I'm coming with you."

"What? No, no, no! You need to stay here."

"Claire has no Bureau resources. She'll need all the help she can get."

Jess could kick herself for telling him. "It's OK, Rob. Apex is smaller than we thought. Moretti wiped out most of them in the bombing. The assassin and Alpha are one of the few operatives left."

Rob scoffed. "I've heard that before. Never underestimate these psychos. I'm not going to let you face this alone."

Jess spread her hands to hold him back. "I'm sorry. I shouldn't have said anything. Forget it all. You're supposed to be dead. You have to stay here."

Rob clenched his jaw. "Try to stop me."

CHAPTER 61

The moment Sally Fleischer walked into the BAU room, Claire put her phone down. Again.

"I'll call you back," she muttered and pocketed the device.

Secret phone calls. Mysterious absences. Zero communication. Claire had changed since Rob's murder.

Suspected murder. Sally had reviewed the forensic evidence but refused to accept the conclusion. *Denial*, Rob's voice said in her mind. *Use the technical term.* Had Claire turned her back on reality, too?

Sally empathized. Rob and Claire were engaged to be married. They had planned a new life together. Claire had changed careers and moved out of state for him. The sudden loss of a loved one could crush any human being. But Claire's erratic behavior went beyond the five stages of grief.

Prince William County PD had arrested Rob's mother for his homicide, but Claire didn't comment on her guilt. She hardly said a word to Sally. Had depression silenced her, or did Claire know more about Rob's disappearance than she let on? He had gone missing while Claire had investigated Apex's involvement in the CIRG bombing. Ever since, Claire had shown no interest in probing deeper. Had Apex executed Rob? Was Claire hiding the truth to protect Sally?

Sally sat at her desk. "Claire?"

She looked up. "Mm?"

"Are you OK?"

Claire nodded and averted her gaze. There it was again— the opaque secrecy. Did Claire blame herself for Rob's murder?

Sally waited for Claire to open up. She didn't.

A haunting wave of déjà vu swept over Sally. At Columbia, she'd shared a room with a pensive New Yorker named Liza Murray. After a bad breakup, Liza had turned to drugs for comfort. Her addiction cast her into an abyss of isolation and self-loathing.

Sally had noticed Liza's unusual behavior. She'd asked her, repeatedly, what was wrong. But Sally had been too buried in her studies to act on the warning signs, and one morning, Liza didn't wake up. Sally, the gifted psychiatry student, had failed to prevent the psychological meltdown in her own dorm room. The irony—and the guilt—had never left her. Sally wouldn't repeat that mistake.

She wheeled her seat next to Claire's. "You know you can talk to me, right?"

Claire grunted but continued to study the police report on her computer monitor.

"I can only imagine what you've been going through. First the bombing. Then Chief Alda. Now Rob. Speak to me. You aren't alone. People care about you. *I* care about you."

Claire winced, then glanced at her. "I know, Sally, and I appreciate that. But Rob will turn up, eventually. We have to have faith and let the police do their job. There's nothing to say."

Sally didn't believe that for a moment. She lowered her voice. "Did Apex contact you? If they're behind Rob's—"

Claire raised her hand to cut her short. "Maybe Massoud is right. I've been obsessed with Apex for so long, I see them everywhere. I need to let go and move on."

"What about the Apex symbol on the bomb casing? We didn't imagine that. What about the Newburgh homicide? That's bound to lead us to Alda's assassin."

What drove this sudden change in attitude? Why was she shutting her out? Didn't she trust her anymore?

Claire touched her arm and gave her a meaningful look. "I need to deal with this in my own way. Please trust me."

Sally studied her friend's eyes. Claire always told the truth. She'd never betrayed her, even though, to Sally's eternal shame, she'd once doubted Claire's sanity and inadvertently put her life at risk. Now Claire was asking her to be patient. Sally owed her that much.

"OK. But if you need anything—anything at all—I'm here for you."

Claire glanced at the closed door and whispered, "There is one thing."

A refreshing breeze dispersed the clouds of gloom and doom. Sally's friend was opening up.

"Sure. Name it."

"I need medication."

Sally chuckled. "That I can do. I didn't spend twelve years studying and slaving away for nothing." Sally returned to her desk and found her script pad in the drawer. "What do you need? Sleeping pills? Antidepressants?"

Claire told her. The dark clouds returned. Sally associated the drug with eating disorders and alcoholism. How was this related to Claire's current medical and psychological condition?

"Claire, that's powerful stuff. The side effects can be horrible. Large doses can be fatal."

Claire shrugged. "So are too many sleeping pills."

Sally blinked. Did Claire intend to poison herself—or somebody else? Sally could lose her license.

"Are you sure you need that?"

"Yes, Sally. It's critical."

Sally swallowed hard. She'd offered help, and Claire was asking her to trust her.

"OK."

She wrote the script, stamped the page with her medical practitioner's seal, and signed her name. Sally was placing her career in Claire's hands. She hoped she wouldn't regret this.

Claire held the script in both hands as though she'd received a cashier's check for a million dollars. "Thank you, Sally. I'll explain everything later, I promise."

Claire grabbed her bag and jacket and headed for the door. "Don't worry, Sally. I'll be fine."

Sally smiled. Another wave of unsettling déjà vu soaked her with dread. *I'll be fine.* Those had been Liza Murray's last words, too.

CHAPTER 62

Saturday morning, Jess stared at the apartment block in downtown Washington, DC, from the passenger seat of the rental car. Her eyelids threatened to slam shut. She shook her head vigorously to stay awake. *Watch the entrance.* Behind the wheel, Gomez snored softly. Jess resisted the temptation to poke him in the ribs. This wasn't the sightseeing adventure he'd promised. Jess demanded a refund.

A man groaned in the backseat. Rob's disheveled head reflected in the windshield. He was waking up.

"Good morning." She hoped she sounded more alert than she felt.

Rob yawned. "Morning."

He probably regretted joining their road trip. His plaster cast made sleeping on the backseat difficult.

Jess shifted her tingling legs to restore circulation. The six-hour drive from Newburgh and overnight vigil had taken their toll on the three of them. But at least Jess could step out of the car and stretch her legs. Rob, the dead man, could afford no such luxury.

He rose from the seat and blinked at their surroundings.

"What did I miss?"

"Nothing. Here, have some breakfast."

She tossed him the last sealed package of Oreos. Empty snack bags littered the floor of the vehicle, testimony to the makeshift meals the officers and agent had enjoyed over the past sixteen hours.

The black-haired assassin had arrived home at 8:15 PM last night. The lights in her apartment had cut out around ten.

Thanks to Claire, they knew the assassin's home address and her name, Karla Deloria, aka The Flayer, aka Psycho Bitch. She'd gone to bed early ahead of the big day.

Today, Nicky Moretti would enter his fictitious witness protection program, and Karla would lead the detectives to Alpha. Rob would get his life back. Claire, her fiancé. And Jess would enjoy hours of glorious sleep in her bed. *Good times.*

But first, Jess had to stay awake long enough to spot Psycho Bitch leaving her apartment or the assassin would slip away and, probably, kill them all. *No pressure.* Jess wouldn't screw this up. Claire's life depended on her, too.

Rob read his wristwatch. "It's after eight o'clock. She should have left already."

He was right. Was Karla sitting this one out? If Alpha dropped by to surprise Claire, all hell would break loose.

"I'll call Claire."

Jess dialed Claire's number. They had discussed their communications protocol yesterday. No answer would mean Claire had company. But she should still be available. Her meeting with Niccolo Moretti was only in fifteen minutes. The number rang.

Claire answered on her car's hands-free and skipped the hellos. "Any movement?"

Jess thumbed the speaker button. "Not yet. She must be inside still."

"It doesn't feel right," Rob said.

After a shocked pause, Claire said, "Is that who I think it is?"

"He wouldn't stay home."

Claire swore. Jess had feared Rob's presence would stress Claire out. She had enough on her mind today.

"Stay out of sight."

Rob looked sheepish. "I will. Good luck."

"I can't talk now, they're here." She ended the call.

Jess cleared her throat. "She's not happy with you."

"Yep."

Gomez jerked awake. "Why are we still here?"

"No sign of her yet."

"Hm."

Rob said, "Quantico's an hour's drive. If we stick around, we'll get there too late."

Gomez disagreed. "We can't let Psycho Bitch slip through our fingers. She's the reason we're here. If she flies, we're screwed. You'll never sleep peacefully again." He peered into the empty tin of Pringles. "Who ate my Pringles?"

Rob shook his head. "We can't sit around. We need to make sure Claire's safe."

"Claire can handle herself."

"They almost killed her a few days ago. That bluff won't work twice."

Gomez sighed. "Tell you what. I'll see if anybody's home. I need to pee anyway. If she's gone, we'll move on. Sound good?"

Rob nodded, and Gomez opened the door.

"Wait," Jess said. "What if she walks out the building while you're inside?"

"Follow her. I'll catch up with you later."

He got out of the car and swaggered toward the apartment block.

Jess climbed over the transmission block and slipped into the driver's seat. Gomez glanced up and down the street, then entered the building.

Behind her, Rob drummed his fingers on the armrest. "I don't have time for this."

He opened his door.

"Hey! Are you crazy? You can't go walking around here. Somebody might see you."

"Don't worry, Jess. I'm in disguise. Nobody will recognize me."

With a moan of effort, he stepped outside and leaned heavily on his walking stick. His dark glasses and black ski cap fooled nobody.

Jess rolled down her window. "Claire going to kill me."

He grinned at her. "How do I look?"

"Ridiculous."

"Perfect. Call me if anything happens."

"What about your leg?"

"I'll hail a cab."

"That's not what I meant!"

He hobbled off. Both men had bailed, leaving her alone in the car.

She swore. This was not a part of the plan. *Sorry, Claire. We're screwing this up.*

CHAPTER 63

Nicky studied his reflection in the hotel's bathroom mirror. The navy jumpsuit seemed appropriate for the occasion. He'd miss his mansions and their creature comforts. But the Morettis were fighters. They did what they must to survive. And survive he would.

"What do you think?"

Vinny hovered beside him and scowled. "I told you, boss. This is a bad idea."

"I meant the jumpsuit. Who knows when I'll change clothes next, huh? This is comfortable and casual. Nobody will say, 'Hey, look over there. That's Nicky Moretti!' What do you think?"

Vinny sighed. "It's fine."

Nicky patted him on the cheek. "You worry too much, Vinny."

"That's my job."

"And you do it well. I want you to know, whatever happens today, the Morettis will take care of you and your family."

"Thank you, Mr. Moretti."

"Now, let's get moving."

They took the service elevator to the parking lot and hit the street in a Jeep SUV with tinted windows. Nicky soaked in the views of his beloved Washington one last time. Who knew where the FBI's witness protection program would take him? He had grown up here, consolidated his father's empire, and extended into new territory. Had he gotten too big, too ambitious? His prominence had drawn Apex's attention. It didn't matter. Maybe he'd get the better of them, too, maybe he wouldn't. He'd had a good run and lived the good life. But he sensed Nicky Moretti's story wasn't over. This was the beginning of a new chapter.

He allowed himself a sentimental moment. "It's just the two of us now, Vinny."

"It's not too late to back out, sir."

"What's eating you, Vinny?"

"I don't trust Claire Wolfe. There's something about her."

Over the years, Nicky had acquired an intuition for people. Who to believe? Who to bury? You didn't survive long in this business without that instinct. Nicky believed in Claire Wolfe.

Nicky grunted. "She's a complicated woman with a complicated past. But I think she's honest."

Was he trying to convince himself? He was entrusting his life to a stranger. Dramatic times called for dramatic measures. But the further he traveled from his old life, the faster his early confidence dissipated.

They reached a seedy part of town. Abandoned warehouses with broken and shuttered windows gave them the evil eye. Vinny turned a corner and slowed to a stop.

"There she is."

An old white hatchback idled in the shadows between cracked cement walls. The door opened, and a woman in a cheap suit emerged from the driver's seat. Claire Wolfe leaned against the car. Not quite the armor-plated cavalcade Nicky had imagined, but this would have to do. One didn't outsmart Apex by lounging at the spa all day. Nicky had set the wheels in motion. There was no backing out now—not with his empire and his honor intact.

He rubbed his hands together. "Let's do this."

CHAPTER 64

Claire's pulse thumped in her ears while she drove Niccolo Moretti across state lines. Vinny had left in the Jeep, entrusting his boss's life to her. *You know what you're doing. Everything will be fine.* The mantra looped in her mind. She'd coordinated the operation with Newburgh PD, and they'd arranged their activities to avoid a head-on confrontation with Apex. But few things in life went to plan.

Detectives Long and Gomez would stake out Karla's apartment and tail her. They'd warn Claire in case the assassin arrived early. With luck, Karla would lead them to Alpha. The detectives would arrest both criminals and collect incriminating evidence at Karla's apartment. Moretti never had to know she'd used him to bait the killers.

Claire had prepared for less favorable scenarios, too. But she hadn't prepared for Rob. His presence complicated things.

Karla hadn't left her apartment yet. Had she spotted him and discovered Claire's bluff? "Fake it 'til you make it" wouldn't save Claire—or her high-profile asset—from Alpha's wrath. Claire followed the plan and headed home.

She scanned for suspicious vehicles in the rearview mirror. "Did anyone follow you?"

Moretti shook his head. "Nope. Not that we noticed."

"Did you leave home last night?"

"We followed your instructions to the letter."

"Good. Cooperation is the key to your survival."

"Understood."

The crime boss had slipped into his state witness persona smoothly, although he looked like an aging hip-hop singer in the jumpsuit. At least Nicky Moretti wouldn't give her any trouble today.

"Where's the rest of the team?"

"Were you expecting a red carpet?"

"No. An armored car or SWAT team—yes."

"This is witness protection, not special forces. The idea is to keep a low profile. The government can't mobilize an army for one witness."

Nicky shifted on his seat. Did he regret leaving behind his small militia of henchmen? She'd need to win his confidence to avoid unnecessary conflict.

"Don't worry. You won't be in the program long."

Nicky snorted. "That sounds ominous."

"We've launched a sting operation. My associates might have the remaining Apex operatives in custody by the end of the day."

"No kidding?"

"If we're lucky. There are no guarantees in this kind of operation."

Nicky chuckled. "And I was starting to worry that you're a one-man band."

If you only knew.

He wiped his brow. "Do you want the flash drive now or later?"

"Now."

He handed the memory stick over, and Claire slipped it into her jacket pocket. "We'll record another session at a safe house to make sure we have all the details the prosecution needs."

"OK."

The hint of an organized schedule seemed to calm him. The deposition served to pass the time, too. Claire had to wait in silence until Jess let her know if their trap had sprung. She focused on the highway.

Where are you, Karla Deloria? The Apex assassin's menacing presence haunted Claire's dreams. Last night, the killer had paralyzed her again and plunged her skinning knife into Claire's immobile body. The terror of Claire's absolute vulnerability had forced her upright in bed. She'd rather kill herself than repeat that experience. Claire had prepared for that scenario, too.

Claire took the Quantico off-ramp. Moretti had lost his appetite for conversation. Jess still hadn't called with an update. Were the Newburgh detectives in hot pursuit of Karla and her "Daddy?" *Time will tell.*

She turned onto her street. A neighbor's car parked across the road, but Claire found no sign of unexpected visitors. The waiting game had begun.

Their fate was in the hands of Jess and Gomez. *And Rob.* She understood his need to follow the operation from up close. He was only trying to protect Claire. But even if all the operation's unknowns fell into place, his presence risked blowing her cover and destroying everything.

Claire pulled over.

Nicky gazed at the house through the passenger window. "Is this it?" He didn't hide his disappointment.

"It's a waiting station. Leave your bag in the trunk."

They got out of the car. If the team lost sight of Karla, Claire would have to find a new hiding place for her star witness, pronto. At least she wouldn't need to pack his bag.

"What do we do now?"

She found the house keys in her pocket. "I've set up the video camera in the basement. We'll take your testimony and deliver it to the right people."

"Got it."

Claire unlocked the front door, stepped inside, and tossed the keys on the credenza.

A rustle of fabric drew her attention to the corner of the living room.

Claire's heart skipped a beat.

A figure aimed a hunting rifle at Nicky Moretti's chest.

Claire reached for her Glock. "No!"

Nicky raised his hands. "What the...?"

The intruder fired the rifle, and Nicky Moretti hit the floor.

CHAPTER 65

Special Agent Rafiq Massoud wiped his sweaty palms on his trousers and unfolded the search warrant. The fortified walls of Niccolo Moretti's Berkley mansion looked less impregnable this morning. Rafiq's hard work had paid off. He'd gotten all his ducks in a row. The moment of truth had arrived.

Sergeant Devon of DC Metropolitan Police swaggered over to Rafiq's car. At least, Rafiq assumed the SWAT officer was Sergeant Devon. His protective helmet, bulletproof padding, and tactical vest packed with ammunition made identification difficult.

"Agent Massoud, we're in position."

Rafiq nodded. He recognized the voice. *Sergeant Devon it is.* Rafiq hoped his other assumptions would prove right, too.

A wave of unreality gripped him as he led the heavily armed officers to the gate. Rafiq had tracked the cartel boss for years. He was obsessed with the criminal's plans and motives. But the Mafia godfather eluded his grasp. Moretti's file photograph had taunted him from the corkboards. "You can't touch me," his smug smile seemed to say.

The CIRG bombing was Rafiq's lucky break. Finally,

Moretti had slipped up. Senator Schultz interceded with a Washington judge to push the search warrant through the sea of red tape. No longer untouchable, Nicky Moretti would answer for his crimes. But when Rafiq neared the fist of armed guards at the gates, a bizarre sensation surprised him. The operation didn't feel like a raid. To Rafiq, it seemed he was meeting an old friend.

The guard—a bald, neckless thug with reflective sunglasses—stood his ground.

Rafiq waved the signed document in his ugly face. "Special Agent Rafiq Massoud, FBI. We have a warrant to search the property."

The guard nodded at his companion, who called the house from a landline.

Rafiq looked forward to seeing Nicky Moretti's smug smile disappear. The crime lord would plead innocence. He'd play the victim and accuse Rafiq of harassment. But a dozen pieces of evidence connected the cartel to the bombing, and the search party would collect more today. *Moretti, you're going down.*

An electric whine announced the arrival of a golf cart and a suited thug. Moretti had sent Vincent "Vinny" Marino to welcome the Bureau. The cartel boss couldn't refuse the warrant, but he could delay their entry to buy time. *Go ahead, Nicky. Delete your files. That'll only make them easier to find.*

The digital forensics lab would make short work of the cartel's disc drives. After flaunting the law for years, crooks grew complacent. They developed a false sense of invincibility. But the small details got them every time. Eliot Ness nabbed Al Capone for tax evasion, and Rafiq Massoud would unthrone Nicky Moretti using modern forensic science.

Vinny sauntered through the pedestrian gate and gloated at the investigator. "Agent Massoud, how may I help you?"

The Morettis knew his name. *Nice.* But that wouldn't save Nicky from justice. Massoud would soon wipe that cocky smile from Vinny's face, too.

"We have a warrant to search the property. "

Vinny received the document and studied the text. His brow wrinkled. *Well, what do you know? The thug can read.*

But instead of scowling and protesting, the henchman handed back the warrant and grinned. "Be my guest."

He nodded at the guards, who opened the gates. The SWAT team marched onto the premises, trailed by Rafiq's aides.

Rafiq lingered with Vinny. "Tell your boss he's welcome to make a statement."

The cocky smile returned. "Mr. Moretti isn't here."

Rafiq scanned the henchman's eyes. A surveillance unit had watched the mansion since early morning. Moretti hadn't left the property.

Rafiq took the bait. "OK, I'll bite. Where is he?"

Vinny shrugged. "I was about to ask you the same thing."

The henchman grinned, obviously enjoying this game, but Rafiq lost his patience.

"How should I know? He's *your* boss."

"Didn't you get the memo? Mr. Moretti is a guest of the FBI. He joined witness protection this morning."

Witness protection? Rafiq's cheeks burned.

Vinny laughed. "I guess that arrangement is above your paygrade, Agent Massoud."

The thug wasn't pulling his leg. Moretti had known the Feds were coming. This raid was a waste of time. Some Bureau smart-ass had undercut Rafiq's hard work.

"Who brought him in?"

Vinny cackled. "Wow. You really don't know? That must hurt. But if the FBI figures you don't need to know, who am I to interfere?"

The henchman swaggered back toward the mansion. Moretti's men had known they were coming. They'd sanitized their records ahead of time. And whatever the Feds found couldn't be used against their boss. Defense attorneys would accuse the Bureau of double-dealing, and a judge could disallow today's findings as Fruit of the Poisonous Tree.

Rafiq swore under his breath. He could guess who had ruined his raid. And she'd pay for this dearly.

CHAPTER 66

S aturday morning, Sally Fleischer did the right thing. *Finally*. She hoped she wasn't too late.

Last night, she couldn't sleep. She'd tossed and turned in bed. Claire's face floated in her mind, and her voice looped in Sally's ears. *I'm fine*. Claire was not fine. Her avoidant behavior was a cry for help. But to assist Claire, Sally had to betray her.

7 AM arrived, and she surrendered to wakefulness. Her apartment rental in Stafford came with a large shared swimming pool, and Sally did lengths to calm her mind and ease her conscience.

Claire had a good head on her shoulders. She wouldn't harm herself, would she? But trying situations drove smart people to rash decisions. Passing clouds of depression often had terrible, lasting consequences. Claire had moved to Virginia and changed careers, then lost her fiancé. The lack of stability in her life intensified her grief. Would she seek a quick escape during a moment of desperation? Despite what she said, Claire needed a friend now. Unlike in college, this time, Sally wouldn't stand idly by.

She climbed the ladder of the pool and wrapped her body

in a towel. Sally showered, dried her hair, and headed for the nearest Starbucks for a mocha latte, her weekend treat. *You need to get out more.* Sally enjoyed her routine—before the bombing had thrown her work schedule into disarray.

Sally came to a decision. She had to tell Tom about Claire. Had he noticed her inner turmoil? Probably not. He was buried in work and struggling to fill Chief Alda's shoes. Was Tom aware of Claire's secret investigation? Duty demanded that Sally share her concerns with her boss. But, true to form, she procrastinated until ten o'clock.

Tom answered with typical irony. "You do realize today is a Saturday morning, right? I hope you didn't turn up at the office, wondering where everybody is."

Sally laughed. "No chance of that, Tom. I mean, Chief."

"Don't rub it in." He lowered his voice. "Now Mary thinks we can afford Botox. This promotion will be the end of me."

Tom had cheered her up already. Maybe he'd throw new light on Claire's behavior, too?

Sally trusted her intuition. "This isn't strictly a business call. It's probably nothing, but Claire's been acting...strange lately?"

"Since Rob disappeared? That's to be expected."

"Yes and no. She's secretive and avoidant. I thought maybe you'd know what was up with her."

Tom sighed. "She had raised a theory about Apex being involved in the bombing."

Sally didn't publicize her involvement in that theory if Claire hadn't. "What do you make of that?"

"I don't know. At first, it seemed like a long shot. Now, I'm not so sure. Claire backtracked on that anyway. She thinks Massoud is right and the Moretti cartel is to blame. Well, I'll be. That's Massoud calling on the other line. Hold on."

"OK."

The line went silent. Why was Agent Massoud calling Tom

on the weekend? Had his investigation made a breakthrough? The agent clearly didn't want the BAU's help. Sally's wasted weekend in California proved that. He'd crossed swords with both Sally and Claire. The floor fell out of Sally's stomach. Had Claire gotten herself into trouble with Massoud?

When Tom spoke again, he cut their conversation short. "Something's come up. I have to go."

"Is everything OK?"

"You were right about Claire. She's gotten herself into a mess."

Sally knew it. "Can I help?"

"No, I'll handle it. But I don't think this will end well. I can't protect her anymore."

CHAPTER 67

Jess's knuckles whitened over the steering wheel. Gomez had gone after the missing assassin. Rob had limped off in search of Claire. Neither had reported back during the past ten minutes. Jess felt alone and useless, and her leg had fallen asleep again. The operation had not gotten off to a promising start.

She closed the windows, turned on the air conditioner, and started the engine so she wouldn't drain the battery. Gomez worried her the most. By now, he should know whether Karla Deloria was home. Had the assassin attacked him? Was she flaying his conscious but immobile body while Jess sat there like a crash test dummy? Calling Gomez might draw attention to him when he needed stealth, and abandoning her post might allow Karla to escape unnoticed. Jess had to stay put and hope for the best. Should she call in reinforcements?

Newburgh PD had notified the DC Metropolitan Police Department about their activity in their jurisdiction but without releasing compromising details. They were pursuing a lead on an old homicide and had processed a search warrant with a local judge. The visiting officers would update the local

PD if they needed assistance. DC was happy to let Newburgh work freely, having more than enough work on their hands. But the situation on the ground was spiraling out of control.

Her phone rang. Gomez was calling—or someone in possession of his phone. Jess answered but said nothing, just in case.

Gomez said, "Did she leave the building?"

Jess glanced at the entrance. "No. Isn't she home?"

"There's no answer at the door. Either she slipped out or she's hiding inside. I'm hoping for option number two. We should go inside and check. Grab the vests and meet me on the second floor."

"On my way."

Jess sprang from the car, only too eager to stretch her legs and make herself useful. As she popped the trunk and pulled on her black Kevlar vest, her skin tingled. She was about to confront a psychopathic killer responsible for multiple grue-some homicides, a woman who turned human beings into fashion accessories. *Are you up for this?* Jess had almost fainted at a murder scene in a Newburgh hotel. Was she ready for the sights and smells of another?

She pushed the thoughts from her head. Gomez was counting on her, and so were Rob and Claire. The team hadn't planned on using the bulletproof vests, but she was glad they'd brought them along.

Jess hurried through the double doors of the apartment block and scanned her surroundings for the target. The elevator stood empty, so she took the stairs. Jess drew her Glock in case she bumped into the assassin. She didn't.

Gomez waited on the second-floor landing. Wordlessly, he put on the second jacket and led the way to apartment 213. A young couple passed them and rushed away. Jess and Gomez let them disappear down the corridor before continuing.

Gomez drew his gun. "I'm primary."

Jess nodded, gladly waiving the "ladies first" rule.

Gomez stood to the side of the door and knocked once. "Karla Deloria, this is the police. We have a warrant to search your property. Open the door now."

They waited. The assassin didn't respond.

"Last chance. Open the door or we'll force our way in."

Jess and Gomez exchanged a glance.

Gomez stepped back and prepared to kick in the door.

"Wait," Jess hissed. "She killed the bomb maker, right?"

"Yeah."

"She stole his explosives and planted them at the FBI?"

"Cut to the chase, Jess."

"What if she rigged the place to explode?"

Gomez raised his eyebrows. "And blow the building to pieces? This is a residential block."

"Do you think she cares?"

Gomez still had trouble thinking like a sociopath. Worryingly, Jess didn't.

He waved her off. "Step back. Just in case."

Jess edged further away from the door. The vision of a fireball incinerating her partner halted her retreat.

"Shouldn't we call a bomb squad?"

"There's no time."

Before she could raise more objections, he slammed the heel of his shoe into the door. The frame cracked, but the locking mechanism held. The impact probably would have detonated a booby trap. Gomez kicked the door again. With a crunch, metal tore through wood, and the door swung inward.

Guns aimed low, flashlights on, they entered the dark apartment. Gomez flicked on the light switch. The living room and kitchen were empty. They swept the apartment, room by room checking under the beds and behind the shower curtain.

Jess holstered her Glock. "She snuck out."

Gomez opened a closet door. "And she took all her stuff. She left only the furniture."

Jess voiced the obvious conclusion. "She knew we were coming."

While they had waited outside, the assassin had made her move. Did she know Claire was on their side?

Jess found her phone. "I'm calling her."

Gomez watched her like a convict awaiting sentencing.

The call cut to voicemail. "She isn't answering."

"Try Rob."

Jess did. He answered on the third ring. Jess caught him up to speed.

"That's not good," Rob said. "She knows where Claire lives."

Jess had that sinking feeling again. "Claire isn't answering her phone. How far off are you from her?"

"Another half hour, at least."

Jess cursed her wasted hours. "We're on our way."

She and Gomez ran for the car. They'd search the apartment later. Time was against them. They had to reach Claire before the killer did.

CHAPTER 68

Nicky Moretti knew he was still alive. Death would hurt less. He lay flat on his back with his eyes wide open and stared at the ceiling of the safe house. Cobwebs bridged a corner. *Somebody should dust those.* He clung to the random thought, which diverted his attention from the terror of his present condition.

He'd recognized the black-haired young assassin during the split-second before she'd pulled the trigger. The rifle shot had floored him. By the time his head hit the floor tiles, his body had gone limp. He couldn't move a muscle. Not a bullet, then; a tranquilizer dart. The American Indian had downed him like a poacher dropping a lion on the savanna. His frozen body might seem dead to the world, but his heart pounded and his five senses remained almost painfully alert.

Special Agent Claire Wolfe yelled at the assassin, "What the hell are you doing?"

The Apex girl kept her cool. "What does it look like?"

A mechanism shifted loudly, the sound of a shotgun reloading, and a flat metallic surface connected with the floor. The shooter had put down the rifle.

This was Agent Wolfe's cue to arrest the attacker. But she didn't.

"You aren't supposed to be here yet."

Yet. Claire knew the assassin. She'd planned for her to be here.

Hands grabbed his ankles and dragged him along the wooden floor.

"Change of plans."

Claire had set him up! Vinny was right. He should never have trusted her. The legendary Moretti instincts had failed him. She was working for Apex, just like the other bitch. And now the psycho killer was towing him, the stunned animal, to the slaughter. *This isn't happening. It can't be.*

Claire raged on. "You have to speak with me first, Karla. What if somebody saw you?"

Karla. The assassin had a name.

She dropped his feet and towered over him. "I had to move things up. There's a carload of cops watching my home. You wouldn't happen to know about them, would you?"

"Cops? Of course, not." Claire changed the subject. "Where's Alpha?"

Cops. Alpha. What were they talking about? Was Claire trying to lure the Apex boss to the house? Maybe Claire hadn't double-crossed Nicky? He cursed her all the same. She'd used a lion for fishing bait!

Karla stood with her legs apart and her arms akimbo. "Like I said, change of plans. Moretti has to go. We'll dispose of his body. The cartel thinks he's under FBI protection, and the FBI will assume he's gone underground. That'll keep everybody quiet for a while."

She's right. Nobody would know Nicky was dead. Nobody would mourn or avenge his death. Apex had wiped him off the map. His blood boiled. *When I get a hold of you...* But he wouldn't, would he? His words were meaningless. The Moretti legacy would sputter out today.

The assassin gripped Nicky's ankle again. "Come on, give me a hand. We're a team, remember?"

Claire walked over and took hold of his other ankle. They hauled his body through the living room. A door opened, and the floor fell away. His head and back knocked against the sharp, hard edges of a staircase. *Thump, thump, thump.* His arms flapped uselessly at his sides. The bitches were towing him into the basement.

Fury exploded in his pulsating heart. The trapped lion roared. *Nobody treats Nicky Moretti like this! I'll rip you limb from limb and feed you to the fish!* But nobody heard him, and he was powerless to execute his threats. With one squeeze of the trigger, the Apex girl had turned a cartel lion into a dead jellyfish.

He found only one consolation. He'd disappear forever—nobody would ever know that two young women had dispatched the great Niccolo Moretti like a plate of spoiled seafood.

The steps ended, blessedly, and the bitches released his legs. A light switch clicked, and bright light flooded the basement and assaulted his open eyes.

Karla stared at the far side of the room. "What's with the video camera?"

"I told him we'd record his statement."

"Why go to the trouble?"

"You and Alpha were only due later. The safe house had to look authentic."

Karla chuckled. "Is this how you offed your boyfriend?"

Claire glared at her. "My *fiancé.*"

A tense moment passed between the two women, and Nicky hoped they'd fight each other to the death. But two seconds later, they laughed. This was just another day at the office for them.

"I set up shop here. I'm sure you don't mind."

"You can't skin him in here!"

"Go upstairs if it bothers you."

Gooseflesh broke out over Nicky's body. The photo of Tony Russo's skinned corpse rose in his mind. The assassin would do the same to him.

"I have money," he pleaded, but his lips refused to move. "Loads of money. Take it all. Please don't do this. I'm begging you. Please!"

Reality hit Nicky over the head like a blacksmith's anvil. He'd heard these words before. Desperate men had pleaded with him for mercy, too. Nicky hadn't spared their lives. No, he'd never leave this basement in one piece. He'd never see his kids again or his wife. They'd never know he had died. The story of Niccolo Moretti was coming to a close. *Beg and plead all you like. Nobody cares. You're a dead man. No, worse. Dead men feel no pain.* Nicky's world of suffering was only beginning. In comparison, the quick deaths he'd meted out were mercy killings.

"It doesn't *bother* me," Claire said. "But the Feds are watching me. I don't want Moretti's DNA all over my basement."

"Relax, I know what I'm doing. Be thankful I didn't drill a hole in the ceiling."

Karla leaned over Nicky and stared into his eyes. She smiled.

"Don't worry, Nicky. You're in good hands. It'll all be worth it. Nothing beats genuine Italian leather."

She was enjoying this. The sick bitch was looking forward to torturing him. A tear slipped from Nicky's eye. Warm pee soaked his boxers and soiled his new jumpsuit.

Nicky projected his thoughts. *Kill me. Just kill me. Please. If there's one iota of human decency in you. Kill me now and be done with it.*

But the killer had lost her humanity long ago. She glanced at his groin, and her smile widened.

"Oh, Nicky. Did you wet your pants? Don't be ashamed. A lot of guys finish too soon. Around me they just can't keep it in."

Karla moved out of sight. A zipper opened, and metal tools clinked. When she returned, she held a butcher's knife in front of his face. The sharp blade glinted in the incandescent light.

"Let's see what you're made of, Nicky."

She lowered the blade to his neck.

"That's enough." Claire's tone was harsh and commanding.

Karla turned around. In Nicky's peripheral vision, Claire stepped into view. She aimed a gun at the sadist's head.

The killer's voice was a low growl. "Think very carefully about what you're doing, Claire."

The agent ignored the warning. "Put the knife down, slowly, or I'll blow your head off."

What was happening? Was Claire arresting her Apex partner? Nicky wished he could raise his head and thank her.

Claire took another step closer. "It won't be the first time I've shot Apex scum dead. Drop the knife and put your hands in the air. I won't ask again."

Karla let go of the butcher knife and raised her hands over her head. But from her tense fighter's stance, Nicky knew the danger hadn't passed. This killer wouldn't go quietly.

CHAPTER 69

Rob stepped onto the metal gate with his good leg and heaved his body upward. Obstacle courses were his least favorite part of training, and today he tackled the challenge with a broken leg. The plaster cast weighed him down like an anchor. In his mind's ear, Tom's critical voice chided him. *Here's another fine mess you've gotten us into.*

The plan for neutralizing Apex had not included scaling walls. Rob had no choice. If a stakeout crew saw his face—Apex or FBI—Claire was as good as dead.

Karla, the Apex assassin, had slipped through Newburgh PD's net. Intercepting her and Alpha before they got to Quantico was no longer an option. Now Claire wasn't answering her phone. Rob's premonitions intensified.

Had the psychopaths discovered Claire's betrayal? Apex's punishment for turncoats was swift and deadly. Rob had learned that last year in Newburgh and almost lost Claire. He wasn't going to let her walk into a trap again, whether she liked his interference or not.

To get a handle on the situation, Rob needed eyes on the ground. So he'd instructed the cabbie to stop one block from his destination. Rob would spy on Claire from the backyard of the property behind his. He'd never met those neighbors and hoped they weren't home.

With almost superhuman effort, Rob lifted his broken leg over the gate. The cold metal rod pressed into his glutes as he straddled the frame. Then, he lowered his body slowly so the fall wouldn't break his healing bones. The muscles in his arms objected loudly to the task, but eventually his feet touched down on the other side. *The eagle has landed.*

He limped along on a tidy stone path beside the house and into the backyard. Judging from the freshly cut grass, the owners were not on an extended vacation. The wall at the back of the yard was taller than Rob had hoped. He glanced around for a ladder, then moved a metal chair from a white garden table set to the flower bed at the foot of the wall.

Rob stepped onto the chair, and slowly, peered over the wall. He had never pictured his house from this angle. Compared to his neighbor, Rob was a shabby housekeeper. When this was over, he'd hire a gardening service, replace the ugly metal trash can, and order furniture. But before Rob completed his suburban dream house, he had to ensure Claire's safety.

Through the windows of the living room and the upstairs bedrooms, he detected no movement. Was Claire recording Nicky's testimony in the basement? At least Rob was nearby and ready to charge if Claire needed backup. He wasn't looking forward to climbing that wall. The house blocked his view of the street. If Karla Deloria arrived with Alpha, they might enter without Rob's knowledge.

His phone vibrated in his pocket. He gazed at the neighbor's home. This was no time to get caught trespassing.

Rob answered and lowered his voice. "Jess, what's going on?"

"Are you with Claire yet?"

"No, but I'm nearby. Everything seems quiet. What about you?"

"Fifteen minutes out. She still isn't answering."

Rob came to a decision. "I'll go inside and see what's happening. We'll have to move Moretti. Apex will know to look for them here."

A loud metallic click drew Rob's attention behind him. "Hands where I can see 'em," a man said.

"Rob?" Jess's voice carried from the phone.

Rob ended the call. Slowly, he raised his hands and turned around. The bearded man with the gray pajama trunks and Havaianas sandals aimed a shotgun at Rob's chest. *Perfect.* Of all Rob's neighbors, he'd chosen the trigger-happy Apocalypse prepper. Luckily, he'd removed his sunglasses and ski cap in the taxi.

Rob smiled. "Hi, I'm Robert." He cocked his head toward the wall. "That's my place. We're neighbors. Nice to meet you."

The bearded man glanced at Rob's holster. He shifted the shotgun to one arm and reached for his phone. "I don't care who you are, I'm calling the police."

Rob had no time for this. "Good, do that. They'll tell you I'm with the FBI. I'll show you my ID. Someone's broken into my property. If I walk in the front door, they'll be waiting for me."

The neighbor's finger paused over the phone's touch screen. "Show me that ID."

Rob extracted his wallet from his pocket and tossed his card to the gunman.

The neighbor read aloud. "Behavioral Analysis Unit." His eyes widened. "The *Mindhunter* guys?" Not a prepper, then—a crime thriller junky. *Saved by Netflix.*

"Exactly."

Bearded Man jerked his head at the wall and handed the ID back. "Are we talking serial killers?"

Rob put his finger to his lips and pocketed the ID. "Not so loud."

The neighbor lowered the shotgun and grinned. "Aw, man! Can we do a selfie?"

"Sure. But don't share it for at least two weeks. This is an ongoing investigation."

"No problem!"

The man whipped out his phone again, and Rob stepped off the chair for a quick photo.

"Thank you, man! That's awesome. What can I do to help?"

"Trust me, you don't want to get too close. If this killer sees you, she'll come after you."

"She? A female serial killer!"

"What's your name?"

"Jake."

"Just sit tight, Jake. If you hear gunshots, call the police."

Jake swallowed hard, and his Adam's apple bobbed. He nodded gravely. "You can count on me. Good luck."

"Thanks. Nice meeting you."

"Yeah. Me, too."

Jake steadied the chair while Rob checked that the coast was clear. He clambered over the wall and stifled his groans of pain. "Don't embarrass the Bureau," was the FBI's unofficial motto, and Rob didn't want to burst his neighbor's bubble either.

He landed softly, crouched at the foot of the wall by extending his broken leg, and listened. Then, he stepped quickly toward the side of the house. Rob pressed his back to the wall and edged toward the kitchen. He peered through the window. Nothing. No movement.

Rob removed the backdoor key from the chain in his

pocket. Millimeter by millimeter, he slipped the key into the lock, then turned the bolt with as little noise as possible. He drew his gun, twisted the handle, and stepped inside. The refrigerator hummed in the corner of the kitchen.

Muffled voices came from within. He followed the sounds, scanning the living room as he passed the doorway. A hunting rifle rested against the armchair. Claire didn't own a rifle. Had Nicky Moretti come armed? Why had they left the weapon here? The voices led Rob to the basement door. He drew closer until he could make out the words.

"Where is he?" Claire said.

"I don't know," a woman replied. "And if I did, I wouldn't tell you."

Rob's pulse throbbed in his neck. *The Apex assassin is here, with Claire.* It seemed Claire was calling the shots. Was Moretti with them? Were they talking about the Mob boss or Alpha?

He peeked through the open door. Claire held the black-haired killer at gunpoint. Rob could help Claire with the arrest. But a hurried entrance might distract her and hand over control to the killer.

"Claire," he said. "It's me."

The door swung open under his hand. Niccolo Moretti lay on the floor, his eyes and mouth open. Was their witness dead or temporarily paralyzed?

The killer's slanted eyes widened, and she snarled. The game was up. Karla knew Claire had fooled her.

"Rob," Claire said. "What are you doing here?"

Taking advantage of the distraction, the assassin lunged forward. A knife materialized in her hand, and she stabbed Claire with all her might.

CHAPTER 70

Pain seared between Claire's ribs. The force of the blow knocked her off balance, and she toppled to the floor.

Rob clambered down the basement steps. "Claire!"

Claire rolled over. Karla pounced on her, knife in hand, a grimace twisting her face.

Rob raised his Glock. "Stop or I'll shoot!"

He didn't need to. Claire slammed her gun into the scowling face. The hard casing connected with Karla's temple and threw her sideways. The assassin had not expected such furious resistance after the knifing.

Claire rose to her knees and aimed her weapon at her stunned attacker. "Try that again and I'll put you down for good."

Sprawled on the floor and nursing her bruised head, Karla panted like a wild-eyed beast. Rob joined Claire. They trained their guns on the killer.

Karla glanced from the bloodless blade on the floor to the hole in Claire's blouse. The padded, white surface of her Kevlar vest showed through the torn fabric.

Claire kept her eyes on her target and spoke to Rob. "That's the second time you saved my life." He'd given her the protective vest as a gift after she'd recovered from a bullet wound to the shoulder.

"Third time. But who's counting."

The gun trembled in Claire's hands. "Cuff her."

Claire didn't want to go near Karla. The scars of her close encounter with the psychopath hadn't healed.

Rob holstered his gun and secured their prisoner.

Karla glared at Claire. "I knew you were a faker."

"Tie her legs, too. There are zip ties and rope in the bag."

Rob nodded. "Karla Deloria, you're under arrest for the murder of Madeleine Alda and Anthony Russo, among others. Anything you say can—"

"Save it," Karla growled. "You're dead meat. Both of you. You'll pay for this when Daddy doesn't hear from me. And I'll enjoy ripping you to shreds."

She was right. The game was up. Claire had blown her cover to save Moretti even before Rob had arrived. Karla would go to prison. But if Claire and Rob didn't expose Alpha's identity soon, they'd need a witness protection program, too.

The same dark thoughts seemed to trouble Rob. "Did you record Moretti's deposition?"

"No. She drugged him the moment we arrived. The air rifle upstairs has curare pellets. Nice touch, by the way," Claire said to their prisoner. "But you'll never use that again."

A sudden worry struck Claire. Would Moretti ever recover from his paralysis?

"How much curare did you put in him?"

Karla smirked but said nothing.

One glance at Moretti reassured Claire. "He's breathing. A larger dose would have stopped his heart like Chief Alda's. It'll wear off eventually."

Rob tied Karla's ankles and stood over her. "Who is Alpha?"

"Wouldn't you like to know."

"What's this big operation he's planning?"

She laughed. "Why don't you ask him yourself? He'll be here any second."

Rob turned to Claire. "Will he?"

Claire shrugged. "Maybe? We have an hour, tops, before he figures out there's a problem. If he isn't already on his way."

"Then we'll prepare for the worst." Rob dialed a number on his phone. "Jess, I'm with Claire." Rob described their predicament. "We need to move Moretti to a safe location. Alpha might be here any minute. When will you get here?"

Rob hung up and gave Claire a foreboding look. "They're still ten minutes out. We'll have to move him and hope for the best."

The flood waters of panic rose within Claire. Their plan had failed miserably, and she had no idea what other aces Alpha hid up his sleeve.

"We need more than hope." The seed of an idea sprouted in her mind. "What if we could buy more time? If Alpha thinks we got rid of Moretti, he won't suspect anything."

Rob frowned. "How do we do that?"

"Karla has a burner phone, a direct line."

Karla scoffed. "Dream on. I won't help you."

Claire ignored her. "She doesn't have to." Claire smiled at Rob. For the first time since Karla shot Moretti, Claire believed she could win. "We'll call him ourselves."

Rob parted his lips when he caught on. He smiled. "The encrypted phone. The app garbles their voices. Alpha won't know it's not her. Brilliant!"

Claire sprang into action. "I'll check her pockets. You search the bag."

Rob extended his broken leg, dropped heavily to one knee,

and unzipped the black equipment bag. Claire patted Karla down and found the bulge in the back of her jeans.

"Got it! This is the phone she used to call him." Claire touched the screen. "It's unlocked."

Karla cried out. "Help!"

Claire waved her gun at their prisoner. "Keep it down!"

Karla called her bluff. "Cline is alive! Wolfe betrayed us!"

Rob ransacked Karla's bag and found a thick roll of silver duct tape. When he tried to seal her mouth, she bit his finger.

"Ow! Behave or I'll use the air gun."

That did it. Karla sulked in silence, and he taped her mouth shut.

Claire opened the phone's history log. "She's called only one number."

Rob copied the number into a text message on his phone. "We can ping his number and triangulate his location. I'm still officially dead. Newburgh PD will have to help out with that."

Claire nodded. She called Jess and explained what they needed. Then she switched to Karla's phone. The device seemed as forbidding as a scorpion.

She glanced at Rob. "Ready?" They were about to call Alpha.

He nodded.

Beads of sweat prickled her brow. "What do I tell him? If he figures out it's us he could destroy his SIM card and split." Claire ran her hand through her hair. She saw no way to avoid that risk. "Keep it short. Moretti is dead. Mission accomplished. Then we track Alpha down."

Claire stared at the phone in her hand. She had a direct line to the man responsible for countless deaths, the man who had conspired with her father to create Apex. If he realized she wasn't Karla, he'd disappear. Claire and Rob would never be safe again.

She moved closer to the steps to improve her cell phone reception and inhaled a deep breath.

"Here goes."

The number rang. Claire nodded at Rob. Her pulse throbbed in her head like a battle drum. The number rang again. *He can't hear your real voice. He won't know it's you.* But what if the garbling worked in one direction only? What if Karla had disabled the voice encryption in case Claire took her phone?

There was no third ring.

Claire blinked. "It cut out. He ended the call. Why wouldn't he answer?"

Rob frowned. "Maybe he has company?"

Behind them, Karla sniggered.

A dark pit seemed to open beneath Claire's feet. "What if she's right? What if he's onto us?"

"*I'm* onto you," a man said.

The intruder stood atop the basement steps, and he held a gun.

CHAPTER 71

Jess pressed her phone to her ear and gripped the passenger seat with her other hand. The Newburgh PD car gunned down I-95 South toward Quantico at breakneck speed. Verizon's forensic department had put her on hold, and she hoped she'd survive long enough to hear their answer.

She raised her voice over the growl of the engine. "You drive like Claire."

Detective Gomez raised his eyebrows. "Are you saying I drive like a girl?"

Jess laughed. "C'mon, Gomez. Don't be a chauvinist. Claire's one of the best drivers on the road, male or female."

And the fastest.

"Now that you put it that way—thank you."

"You're welcome."

It felt good to joke around. The calls from Rob and Claire had lowered their tension levels considerably. Rob had joined Claire, and they were both safe. They had arrested the Apex assassin, and Jess had contacted Verizon to locate Alpha's phone signal. Now Jess and Gomez had to extract Moretti and Karla in case the Apex leader showed up.

Gomez weaved through traffic. "I was thinking..."

Jess snorted. "Uh-oh. Now we're in trouble."

Captain Washington was still in the habit of putting down his former partner, and the other detectives had followed suit.

Gomez didn't seem to mind the playful verbal abuse. "I figure if we wrap this up soon, we can still visit Capitol Hill."

Jess chuckled. "You're optimistic. Once we get Alpha's location, we won't have time for sightseeing."

Gomez frowned. "Nah. Karla's in custody. Claire and Rob can handle Alpha. They'll call in the FBI, and we'll get our weekend back."

"I hope you're right." Jess sighed. "Geez, how long does it take to triangulate a phone's location?"

The phone vibrated in her hand. Another call was coming in.

"I need your phone. Mahoney's calling."

"Put Verizon on hold."

"I don't want to miss them. Your phone—hand it over."

Gomez unlocked his phone with the fingerprint scanner. "OK, OK. But no peeking at my Instagram. It'll scar you for life."

Jess snatched the device. "Now I have to check it out."

"Hey!"

"Just kidding." Jess called Mahoney back. "It's me, and you're on speaker. My phone's on hold with Verizon. What's up?"

"Is Claire with you?" Mahoney asked.

"We're on our way to her now. Why?"

"I couldn't reach her."

"Yeah, she has her hands full."

"Tell her I hit pay dirt with the scholarship fund."

"Any key details?"

"A shell company owns The Level Field Initiative. I couldn't get more on that, but I did find another beneficiary, besides the first three."

Jess and Gomez exchanged meaningful looks. *Was another Apex agent running loose?*

"Go on, don't keep us in suspense."

"The fourth student is dead, so it's probably not a top priority."

Gomez lost his patience. "Mahoney, man! Spit it out already."

What Mahoney told them chilled Jess to the bone.

"Geez," Gomez said.

He and Jess traded another worried glance.

"Detective Long?" said a woman. Her bored, nasal voice reminded Jess of the secretary at Hannover High.

"Got to go," Jess told Mahoney. "Verizon is getting back to us. Speak later."

Jess put down Gomez's phone and unmuted hers. "Right here."

"Thank you for holding."

"Do we have a location?"

"Yes, the phone is online. But as I told you, please remember—"

"Yes, I know. I'll send you the court order within three business days. Where's the phone?"

"I'll text you the coordinates. We traced the recent tower signals to North Stafford in Virginia."

Gomez swore.

"Excuse me?" the woman asked.

"Nothing. Thank you!" Jess hung up. "That's near Rob's neighborhood."

"I know. Are you thinking what I'm thinking?"

Jess was. "I'll call Claire." Seconds later, Jess swore, too. "Voicemail."

Gomez stepped on the accelerator, and Jess gripped her seat with both hands. And she knew they were both thinking, *Massoud is Alpha, and he's already at Rob's house.*

CHAPTER 72

Claire stared at the gunman. He observed the scene and blocked the basement's only exit. What was *he* doing here?

Special Agent Rafiq Massoud chuckled. "What do we have here?"

He leveled the gun at Rob. "Agent Cline—back from the dead." The gun barrel moved to the man on the floor. "Nicky Moretti, out of commission. And the infamous Claire Wolfe." He scoffed. "I had pegged you for a cartel mole. I guess you and Nicky fell out. Or were you a triple agent from the start?"

Claire placed Karla's phone in her pocket. "I can explain."

Her explanation would depend on why Agent Massoud was here—and his true identity. He had blocked her investigation at every turn and dismissed her theories. Did Massoud simply dislike her or was *he* the elusive Alpha?

Rob glanced at her. He seemed to be wondering the same thing. Claire studied Karla's expression for the hint of an answer, but the assassin's face was blank.

Massoud aimed the gun at Claire. "Don't bother. I think I've figured it out on my own. Humor me."

Claire dug her hand deeper into her pocket and curled her fingers over a small remote control. Her JVC camcorder sat on a tripod in the corner of the room. She pressed the remote's Record button, and a small red dot glowed on the video camera.

Massoud descended the steps slowly. "Agent Wolfe, you offered your services to Nicky Moretti. You planted the bomb at the CIRG, killing Director Warren. But you covered your tracks. You left town that day. That's a solid alibi. *And* the blast injured your fiancé. I don't know how you pulled that off—unless Agent Cline is a party to the deception. Yes. His miraculous resurrection makes that highly probable. But the bombing served a second purpose, didn't it? Chief Alda had to die, too. Unfortunately, your boss survived the explosion, so you poisoned her"—he jerked his head toward Karla—"with your accomplice. Was Alda onto you, or did you just want her job?"

Claire couldn't let that pass. "I didn't plant the bomb, and I didn't kill Chief Alda."

Was Massoud trying to make sense of the scene or was he creating a narrative to frame the agents who had exposed him? That story would end with Massoud shooting them both dead in self-defense.

Massoud reached the basement floor and halted. "But you did collaborate with Moretti. That didn't work out well for him. Did he refuse to pay? Did you raise your price? I admire your sense of humor, though." He snorted. "*Witness protection.* How long did you think you'd get away with that?"

"I wasn't getting away with anything."

Massoud pointed the gun barrel at Karla Deloria, bound and gagged on the floor.

"Were you going to pin everything on her? Does she know you ratted her out from the start?"

"She killed Chief Alda and Tony Russo."

"What about Agent Cline—did she kill him, too? Whoops! Here he is, alive and well."

He turned to Karla. "Are you OK?"

Karla nodded.

He waved the gun at Claire and Rob. "Drop your weapons, both of you."

Rob spoke up. "You're making a mistake."

"I'll be the judge of that. I've got you on obstruction of justice and, by the looks of it, seizing and confining, too. Are you going to come quietly or do I have to shoot you?"

Claire and Rob made eye contact again. Could they trust him with their lives? Would he murder them once he'd disarmed them? Together, they might overpower him. But would he kill them in the process?

Slowly, Rob bent over and lay his gun on the floor. Claire hesitated. Massoud had blackballed her from the start. He'd opposed YARI. But was this gunman Alpha or just a crusty old investigator? Was she prepared to kill an innocent man? *Another* innocent man. Claire had made that mistake once before, and the fatal error still haunted her.

Claire placed her Glock on the floor. Rob had chosen a path, and she'd follow him, in life and in death.

"Whoa!" somebody said. "Am I late for the party?"

Claire's heart almost exploded with relief. Tom Brown grinned at them from the top of the stairs. He held the air rifle loosely in one hand. She'd never been so glad to see him.

"Looks like you started without me. Agent Massoud, why are you pointing a gun my agents?"

Massoud scowled at him but kept the gun trained on Claire and Rob. "You knew he was alive? You're in on this?"

"I had my suspicions. I'm sure he and Agent Wolfe had their reasons." Tom hefted the air gun. "Rob, you shouldn't leave weapons lying around the house like that." His tone hardened. "Lower your weapon, Massoud. We're all on the same team."

"I'm not so sure about that."

Tom hopped down the steps one at a time. "Then let's talk this out. Set the record straight. After that, you can shoot whoever you like."

Slowly, Massoud lowered his gun. Claire breathed at ease. Cooler heads had prevailed. Tom reached the basement floor, but Massoud didn't holster his weapon.

"Watch out for him," Claire said. "He could be Apex."

Massoud chuckled. "Here we go again. The phantom group strikes again."

Tom joined Massoud. "But what if she's right?"

Massoud blew a raspberry. "Don't tell me you still buy that nonsense. I told you to keep her under control. Now she's kidnapped Moretti and screwed my investigation."

Tom glanced at Karla, cuffed and bound. "Who's this young lady?"

Claire said, "Karla Deloria, the Apex assassin."

Massoud said, "Or Agent Wolfe's accomplice...and scapegoat."

Tom frowned. "I'll take Claire's word on that."

Massoud huffed. "Let's hear what Karla has to say. You two, stay down."

He walked over to Karla.

"Watch out," Rob said. "She bites."

Massoud helped Karla to her knees. Claire cringed. *This is a mistake. He'll free her. Then they'll attack us.*

He peeled the duct tape from Karla's mouth. "What's your role in all this?"

The killer hung her head. "Claire betrayed us. She protected Moretti."

Claire tensed for action. Karla had burned her cover. If

Massoud was the Apex kingpin, he knew Claire was his enemy now. Would he drop his mask in front of Tom or exact his vengeance later?

Agent Massoud studied Claire and Rob, then turned to Tom. "Betrayed who?"

Tom shrugged. "You tell me."

The scent of imminent violence carried in the air. Adrenaline tore into Claire's bloodstream. Her muscles tensed, ready to spring. She had to draw her weapon before Massoud and Karla silenced them forever. But that weasel of doubt gnawed on her conscience. *Is Massoud truly Alpha?* What if she was wrong?

She shifted her hand in her pocket. Claire had owned a phone like Karla's years ago. She found the call button with her finger and pressed it twice to dial the last number.

Massoud questioned Karla again. "Betrayed who? Who do you work for?"

If he was Alpha, he was putting on a good show. Had Claire misjudged him?

A phone vibrated. The familiar sound broke the tense silence like a jackhammer. Rob gazed at Claire.

Slowly, she extracted Karla's burner phone from her pocket. "I called the number."

Rob understood immediately. Alpha was in the room. Rob tilted his head, trying to locate the source of the noise.

Massoud stared at her, confused. "What number?"

The buzzing didn't come from him.

Tom extracted a flip phone from his breast pocket. He pressed a button to cancel the incoming call. Then he raised the rifle and aimed at Claire.

CHAPTER 73

K arla watched her mother's apartment from across the street. The TV painted the thin drapes in flickering colors. They were home. This is their fault. Derek had destroyed Karla's innocence, and her mother had turned a blind eye. When Karla had finally stood up for herself, Mom had sent the police after her and condemned Ichigouti to a mental institution. Derek and her mother had ruined her life. She tightened her grip on the butcher knife. You are next.

Her grandfather wasn't crazy. Karla had scouted the Prince William Psychiatric Center from the tree line. The low, long building of gray windowless concrete seemed more like a prison or military installation than a medical facility. Karla was a fugitive. Busting him out wasn't an option. I'm sorry, Ichigouti.

Karla had hiked back toward Washington, avoiding main roads. A grim understanding consolidated in her mind. Predatory men. Stuck-up schoolgirls. Judgmental teachers. Oppressive institutions. Ichigouti was right. Society is hostile. It persecuted her kind. Karla would use her last days of freedom to avenge those wrongs. People would read about Karla in the newspapers. They wouldn't understand her actions. But they'd fear her.

She hid the knife under her leather jacket and crossed the street. Her heart pulsed with anticipation. She imagined their pleas and screams, their futile attempts to escape her wrath. Karla pictured the carnage: prone bodies on the floor; the blood; the triumphant silence. She felt alive.

Karla climbed the exposed stairwell, lifting the carry-on bag into the air. Maybe she wouldn't kill them right away. She could drug them and take her time. She'd peel off their skin. Yes. They deserved that.

On the second-floor landing, she rested her suitcase on the grimy tiles quietly. Karla withdrew the butcher knife from under her jacket to switch it for the penknife dipped in curare—when a man spoke.

"I wouldn't do that if I were you."

Slowly, she turned around. The smiling stranger in the plain brown suit had streaks of gray hair at his temples and a gun in the holster at his waist. He didn't look like a cop. His amused Southern accent made his threat sound like fatherly advice.

Karla stood there. She hadn't done anything wrong. Not yet.

"Oh yeah?"

He stepped closer and seemed unafraid of the naked blade she wielded.

"If you proceed with your plan"—he waved a dismissive hand at the apartment—"you'll feel better for a few hours. But you'll die in prison. Are they worth it?"

Rage built within her. His cocksure pep talk wouldn't stop her.

"You know nothing about me."

The man grinned. "Let's see. Stepdaddy abused you. Mom called the cops—on you. And now they sent Granddad to the loony bin. I understand why you're here, Karla. And I admire your...special talents. But if you do this—here and now—you're finished. Game over."

Karla clenched the knife. He knew too much. He was a cop. She'd carve him up, too, if she had to. "You won't stop me from killing them."

He snickered as though she'd said something funny. "Now why would I do that?"

CHAPTER 74

R ob Cline stared at his former partner in disbelief. "Tom?"

His unit chief's incoming call was a strange coincidence. *It must be.* Or the burner phone wasn't his. Tom used an iPhone. He'd discovered the device upstairs along with the rifle. *That explained it.* But as Rob's relief set in, Tom aimed the rifle at Claire.

His former partner grinned. "Surprise."

No. This can't be. Rob had served with Tom for years. They had hunted killers across the nation. Tom couldn't be Alpha.

Karla spoke. "She's wearing a vest."

Tom lowered the barrel to Claire's legs.

Rob's stream of justifications ran dry. *He's going to shoot Claire!*

"No!"

Rob lunged forward. Tom fired. The bullet tore through Rob's shirt and pierced the skin beneath his rib cage. He crashed to the floor, landing on his shoulder. *He shot me!* The plaster cast banged against the basement tiles. Waves of agony burned down his leg.

Tom cranked the loading mechanism and fired another round.

Rob reached for his gun and scrambled to his feet. Or tried to. His body had gone limp. He slumped onto his back and lay there, motionless and inert...but fully aware of his surroundings. *Not a bullet—a curare pellet!*

Claire's body thudded to the floor behind him. Her arm flopped over his waist.

Rob's brain demanded action, but his muscles ignored the urgent calls. He stared at the basement ceiling and listened to the soundtrack of his impending murder.

Massoud cried out. "Hey, what are you—?"

But he'd reacted too late. Tom noisily cranked the mechanism again and clicked the trigger. Another body collapsed to the tiles like a puppet whose strings were suddenly severed.

Karla pleaded. "I'm sorry, Daddy. She betrayed me."

Daddy. The word sent tremors of shock through Rob's mind. *Tom lived a double life.* Rob had known the grumbling FBI agent and family man who served the law. But Tom had led another, covert existence. His dark side had raised a very different family—a pack of murderous criminals. And Rob had suspected nothing.

Tom stepped into view. He leaned the rifle barrel on his shoulder.

"Don't be so hard on yourself, Karla. She tricked us both."

He gazed toward Rob and Claire. "For what it's worth, Claire, I'm impressed. You pulled the wool over our eyes." He tutted. "Such talent. What a waste. Bill Wolfe must be turning in his grave. He always believed you'd see things his way. I succumbed to the same delusion. Even after Bill's death and the demise of the Newburgh pack, I reserved judgment. Maybe you didn't want to live in his shadow? Maybe you wanted to eliminate the competition and build your own pack? The truth had to come out eventually. It's a shame you chose the losing side."

Claire could hear Tom's confession. Massoud, too. There was no way Tom would let them live. Rob wanted to kick Tom's legs from under him, to beat him senseless with his bare fists. But the poison had transformed Rob's body into Jell-O. Jess and Gomez were their only hope for survival. *Go on, Tom. Gloat.* The longer he talked, the better.

Karla spoke. "We need to move fast. Some detectives from Newburgh are on their way. Claire and Cline spoke with them on the phone."

Rob wanted to strangle her. But the damage was done. Her words spurred Tom to action.

Tom walked out of view and released Karla. He unzipped the duffel bag and pulled on latex gloves. "Put her in the chair over there. Have Moretti sit opposite."

Claire's arm slipped from Rob's waist as Karla dragged her body away. They were staging the murder scene.

Tom had decades of forensic experience under his belt. He and Karla would position their paralyzed victims and fire their weapons using their unresisting hands. They'd remove the air gun pellets and obliterate the entry cuts with bullet wounds. Gunpowder residue. Blood spatter. Ballistic angles. Time of death. All the details would match.

The homicide detectives who studied the basement's gruesome contents would find a clear, simple story. Niccolo Moretti had bought Claire, as Massoud had suspected. Her fiancé discovered her treachery, but she subdued him. When Massoud confronted them in the basement, they killed each other in the shootout. The investigators would find no sign of Apex or the curare pellets. No trace of Tom or Karla would remain either.

Tom moved back into view and stared at Rob. How many

perfect murders had he staged during his long career? How many killers had he protected—and nurtured—on the FBI's dollar?

Tom shook his head at Rob. He seemed disappointed.

"Rob, Rob, Rob. I warned you not to get too close to Claire. You never listened, did you?"

He glanced at the corner of the room. "Karla, take that video camera when we're done, too. It's still recording." Tom waggled his finger at Claire. "Nice try, Ms. Wolfe."

"What about him?" Karla asked.

"Put him in the corner. Tie his arms and legs."

Karla hovered over Rob. She grabbed him under his armpits and hauled him away. His head lolled forward. Tom followed them. Karla dumped Rob against the wall and fetched cable ties.

Tom dropped to his haunches and smiled at Rob.

"You and Claire, together in life and in death. You like that, don't you, Rob? You were always a romantic."

Rob wanted to punch him in the face. He wanted to scream and shout. But Rob shared the blame. He'd been so close to Tom for so long. How had he not known? *So this is how it feels, Claire?*

Karla secured Rob's wrists and ankles, the hard plastic biting into his flesh.

Tom snickered. "I bet you're wondering, 'Why didn't I figure it out?' You are, aren't you? I know you too well, Rob. Well, the truth is, you should have. The writing was on the wall. Go on. These are your last seconds in this life. Use them."

Rob searched his memory. There were so many cases. They had shared the same motel rooms, for crying out loud. But still, Rob drew a blank.

Tom studied his eyes. "No bells ringing? I'll spell it out, just in case. The dead girl's house in Newburgh, when Bill's young female accomplice escaped on the roof. She left another set of footprints in the garden. I stepped on them."

Karla dragged Massoud's body toward the basement stairs.

Tom snapped his fingers. "Later, I tried to terminate our endless investigation in Newburgh. But you kept coming back and sniffing around. You thought I was a lazy old fart, didn't you? Ha! You found their graveyard eventually. And I'd almost given up on you."

Again, he snapped his fingers. "Remember when you rushed to Diane's house to save Claire from Johnny Norton's trap? I tried to talk you out of that, too. But no, you had to go running in. Always the hero."

He sighed. "I got tired of taking out Newburgh's trash. Let them crash and burn. They're only one arm of the starfish. But I drew the line at YARI. The juveniles are the future of Apex. Pioneered by Bill, perfected here at Quantico. The time was ripe. Moretti had become more trouble than he was worth. He almost wiped us out. Karla and I were the last Apex agents in the field. The solution was beautiful in its simplicity. Bury Moretti and YARI in one glorious blow. Sadly, Rob, that meant an end to you and Alda, too. I enjoyed working with you. But nothing lasts forever."

Rob's breathing accelerated. *Tom planted the bomb at CIRG. He murdered Director Warren!*

Tom lost his sense of humor. "Then, Alda snubbed you at the director's meeting. What a bitch. She was going to take all the credit...and all the shrapnel. I kept you in the kill zone for as long as possible. But explosions are so unpredictable. Both you and Alda survived."

He pointed at Rob. "You faked your death well. I'll give you that. I know, that was mostly Claire's doing, but you get points for not screwing that up. *Leverage YARI. Hide in plain sight.* She had us going there. And as the new unit chief, I was well-positioned to take full advantage. I hadn't planned for that, by the way." He pointed upward and smirked. "I guess someone upstairs is looking out for me."

Karla stepped up behind Tom. "Daddy, we're ready."

Tom got to his feet. "Our time is up. This is goodbye, Rob. The scene is straightforward. Massoud surprised Claire and Moretti. They shot each other up. Sadly, you took two bullets to the gut, too, and bled out. Not a nice way to go. It'll hurt. But to be completely honest, Rob, you annoyed the crap out of me all these years. You should have seen this coming."

Rob listened for distant sirens. He strained his ears for the footfalls of Jess and Gomez. *We need you. Now!* In a few seconds, the four immobile bodies would become corpses, the unlucky actors in another Apex production. Tom was right. *I should have seen this coming. I should have prevented this!*

Karla handed Tom a gun, and they walked toward Massoud.

There was a sudden movement in the corner of Rob's eye.

"Did you see this coming?" a woman said.

Claire rose from the chair. She held her Glock in both hands and aimed the gun at the killers.

CHAPTER 75

Claire's fingers tingled. Her head spun. She gripped her Glock tightly and struggled to focus on her enemies. Tom and Karla gaped at her in silence. Claire knew what they were wondering. *How had she withstood the poison?* The truth was—she hadn't. Not *entirely*. They had no idea how unstable she felt. *Don't let it show.* Claire faced two sociopathic killers alone. If the wolves smelled weakness, they'd eat her alive.

Claire jerked her head at Tom. "Lay your weapons down. Slowly."

Tom gazed at her but surrendered neither the rifle nor his sidearm. "I hear you're an excellent shot, Claire."

He was right. Claire had achieved a near-perfect score in marksmanship at the Academy firing range. She had trained to pick off multiple targets in short succession. But today, she wasn't her usual self.

Curare coursed through her veins. Curare and another powerful chemical compound. She had retained control of her body, but her reflexes were far from peak performance. If the killers rushed at her together and she misfired, her gamble would fail. Claire had to disarm them and keep them here until Jess and Gomez arrived. Three lives depended on her bluff.

Karla turned and bolted up the stairs. Claire fired a single shot at the assassin's legs. The bullet ricocheted off the cement wall and pierced the wooden door of the basement. Mistaking the miss for a warning shot, Karla stopped in her tracks and raised her hands.

Claire slowed her breathing. "The next one goes in your head."

She trained the gun on Tom. "You. Last warning. Lay down your weapons, slowly, and put your hands in the air."

Tom did as he was told, his eyes never leaving hers.

He curled his lips into a knowing smile. "You win, Claire."

Tom was buying time, too. He'd turn the tables on her. Not Tom. *Alpha*. The Apex grandmaster. Claire had to select her moves carefully to outsmart him. *Offense is the best defense.*

Claire exerted her control of the situation. "Seems your daughter tried to abandon you. Ouch. That must hurt."

Tom shrugged the fact off. "I'd do the same. We all know what you're capable of, Claire."

He moved one step closer to her.

Claire aimed at his heart. "One more inch and you're a dead man."

"How did you do it, Claire? The pellet hit you." He pointed at her thigh, but she didn't take the bait and avert her gaze. "You're bleeding. The poison entered your body."

There's no harm in telling him. Time was on her side. "Pyridostigmine. The pills block nerve agents such as curare."

"Ah." Tom chuckled. "Brilliant, Claire. Absolutely brilliant. I should expect nothing less from Bill Wolfe's daughter." He searched her eyes. "Feels good, doesn't it? You were born for this, Claire. To wield power."

Claire sneered at his desperate attempt to corrupt her soul.

"This isn't *Star Wars*, and you're no Darth Vader. You won't seduce me with the Dark Side."

Karla descended a step, moving closer to Massoud's prone body. She eyed the gun in his holster.

Claire aimed her Glock at her. "Don't even think about it, Karla. Keep your hands up."

Tom continued. "Apex doesn't have to end here."

"Yes, it does."

"Apex is your family. You said so yourself."

"I lied."

"Did you? Be honest with yourself. There's truth to what you said. More than a little. People fear you. Always have. Always will. Because you are superior to them. They don't understand you. How could they? But we do. We are like you."

"I am nothing like you."

"Your father started this. Apex is his legacy and your destiny. We are your true family."

She laughed. "Then I disown you both."

This did feel good, but not in the way Tom probably imagined. Claire had held this conversation before with William. Since then, she had feared she was damaged. Were psychopathic thought patterns hardwired into her DNA? Now she grasped the truth.

"You don't get it, Tom, do you? Bill didn't understand either. Why won't I destroy lives to serve my purposes? He couldn't see the answer, and neither can you. Human life. Empathy. Trust. You're blind to them. You and your kind aren't superior to anybody. You're defective."

The smile dropped from his face. He could imitate human sentiment up to a point. Beyond that, he reverted to animal self-interest.

"There's two of us, Claire, but only one of you. The numbers are in our favor, and we're not going to prison. You can't beat us. Let us walk away. Save yourself and your friends. That's what you want, isn't it?"

Claire shook her head. She knew how this worked. If she let them leave the basement, they wouldn't disappear. They'd ambush her and her friends and murder every last one.

"Apex is done, Tom. And so are you. You just don't know it yet."

Her hands trembled. Her attention drifted. Claire pulled herself together by sheer force of will.

Tom grinned. "Pyridostigmine. Didn't those pills give us Gulf War syndrome? How are you feeling, Claire? A little wonky?"

"I feel great," she lied.

During the first Gulf War, US soldiers in Iraq took pyridostigmine bromide in case Saddam Hussein attacked them with the nerve agents in his chemical weapons arsenal. Side effects of the medication included weakness, stiff muscles, and impaired cognitive functioning. The symptoms became so common among veterans, the condition became known as Gulf War syndrome.

Claire filled Sally's script yesterday and took a pill every six hours. She hadn't noticed any physical reaction to the drug. Had curare interacted with the antidote to trigger Claire's fuzzy mental state?

"On your knees, Tom."

His gaze shifted to her hands. "What's the matter, Claire? Is the poison kicking in?"

Karla moved down another step. Claire had to follow through on her threat. She aimed the Glock at her.

Tom took advantage of the distraction. He dived toward the firearms at his feet. Karla reached for Massoud's gun. Claire squeezed the trigger. Karla squealed. Tom raised his service weapon. Claire leaped sideways and pumped the trigger repeatedly. Tom's shoulder jerked twice. Metal tore through his chest and neck.

Claire hit the floor, her gun still raised. Tom fell to his knees, then keeled over, his eyes open and vacant.

Another yelp reminded Claire of the second danger. Karla limped up the stairs, her jeans soaked red at the thigh. Claire lunged forward and grabbed the rifle on the floor. Karla reached the basement doorway. Claire took aim. With a satisfying click and whoosh of gas propellant, the curare pellet struck the fleeing assassin between the shoulder blades. She dropped, face-first on the threshold.

Exhaustion washed over Claire. She dropped the air gun and sprawled on the cold floor. Her heart pounded. With a groan of effort, she pulled her phone from her pocket. She dismissed the notification for ten missed calls and dialed a number.

"We've been trying to reach you," Jess said. "Alpha's in North Stafford. We're almost there."

Claire had no energy for details. "It's over," she said. "It's over."

CHAPTER 76
THREE MONTHS LATER

F elicity grabbed a glass of champagne from a floating tray and almost tripped on her fancy high heels. The new shoes and evening gown had maxed out her credit card, but they were worth every borrowed penny. She blended in with the crowd at The Hannover Hotel. The staff hadn't asked to see her invitation even though she'd missed the ceremony. At least she hadn't missed cocktail hour. Felicity downed her drink in one gulp to steel her nerves. She'd never crashed a wedding before. So tonight, she had dressed to kill.

Her blood still boiled at the news. She had learned of the wedding the way she'd discovered Rob still drew breath—from the media. While released on bail from the Prince William County Adult Detention Center, Felicity had received a Google Alert notification in her inbox. Not only was her son alive, but Rob had arrested the criminals behind the FBI bombing. His apparent murder had been an elaborate hoax constructed to fool the culprits. The news article didn't mention that he'd sent his mother to jail for his phony death. Some hero!

A second alert had reached her two months later in Boston, where she had retreated to lick her wounds. Rob and Claire were to be married in Newburgh, Massachusetts. *The Newburgh Herald* gushed about the fairy-tale romance between the local detective and the dashing federal agent who had reconnected two years ago to chase a serial killer. Rob hadn't bothered to inform his mother about his upcoming nuptials, never mind invite her. Yes, Felicity truly had failed as a mother. But it wasn't too late to teach him to honor his parents. Plenty of fairy tales ended tragically.

She scanned the sea of guests but recognized none of them. The bride and groom had yet to conclude their post-ceremony photo session. Felicity waited. And she drank.

A man spoke into a microphone and herded the guests to the banquet hall. A band of men in white tuxedos played a mambo rhythm, and a woman in a sequined dress sang "Sway" by Michael Bublé. *When marimba rhythms start to play...*

Felicity lingered outside. She hadn't come here to dine. None of the little tags on the tables bore her name, anyway. She cracked her handbag open and checked on her concealed weapon.

She'd purchased the Sig Sauer from Bert, her regular drug dealer, and he'd shown her how to use it. "You're not going to blow your brains out, are you?" Bert had asked.

Felicity had laughed. "Don't worry, my friend. You won't lose a loyal customer. The gun is strictly for self-defense." This was true. She was defending her rights as a mother and a human being. Rob and *that woman* had violated both. They'd gone too far. But Felicity would have the last laugh.

She closed the bag. The hall crawled with plainclothes police officers. She needed another drink.

At the bar, she ordered a double whiskey.

"Bride or groom?" a man asked her.

The forty-year-old had a mop of sandy hair, a pronounced belly, and spoke with an overdone Irish brogue which he seemed to think was charming. He reeked of alcohol. *Definitely a cop.* As a rule, Felicity steered clear of police officers. They had no money, and to seduce them was to court disaster. Besides, this chump was out of her age range. But that didn't mean she couldn't have some fun.

"Neither. I'm divorced."

He jabbed a stubby finger in the air. "Nice! I have to remember that one."

Felicity's whiskey arrived. "What about you?"

She always asked questions. Get people talking about themselves, and they never notice anything suspicious. The tactic had served her well for decades.

His eyes drifted to a point behind her, and his grin faded. "Soon to be divorced."

A woman walked over and grabbed him by the arm. "Brendan Mahoney, haven't you had enough?"

Her shrill voice sent a shudder down Felicity's spine. She almost felt sorry for him.

Mahoney deadpanned, "Yes, I have had enough."

His wife gave Felicity an apologetic frown. "I'm sorry if he's been bothering you." She pulled him away. "Come on. They're back."

As if on cue, the master of ceremonies spoke over the loud-speakers again. "Ladies and gentlemen, join me in welcoming the bride and groom."

The guests clapped, and Felicity glanced over her shoulder. Sure enough, the happy couple walked hand in hand through the throng of well-wishers. Rob looked dashing in his spotless tuxedo. Claire's strapless dress of white satin accentuated her shapely figure.

Felicity scoffed. White was the color of purity and inno-cence. Did the newlyweds honestly think they could use

Felicity and throw her away? She'd wipe the smiles from their faces.

A thrill of adrenaline sparked within her. Felicity knocked back her whiskey and slipped her hand into her bag. *It's time to bless the bride and groom.*

CHAPTER 77

Claire felt weightless. She seemed to float on white, puffy clouds. Was she dreaming? Could reality contain such intense joy?

The ceremony passed in a warm and fuzzy haze. The pastor's voice hummed in her ears. People filled the lavish hall behind her. But Claire had eyes and ears only for the man beside her. Rob gazed into her eyes and smiled. In his immaculate tuxedo, he seemed to have stepped out of a romantic comedy, the kind that ended with a wedding. Claire pinched her finger under the bouquet in her hands. She didn't wake up. She'd left her nightmarish past behind, and for once, the dark veil of gloom and doom had lifted. Claire was free at last.

She savored every sensation: the aromatic scent of the flowers; the deep rhythm of Rob's voice when they exchanged vows; the warmth of his hand on hers; the cool touch of the gold band on her finger; the soft press of his lips as he kissed his bride.

They turned to face their guests. Diane beamed at Claire from the front row of chairs, happy tears moistening her eyes.

Frank stood beside her, grinning beneath his mustache and clapping. Even Cynthia and Edward Hannover looked overjoyed. Claire had caught their daughter's murderer last year. In gratitude, the billionaires had insisted that Claire and Rob celebrate their nuptials at The Hannover Hotel, Newburgh's finest, free of charge. No longer on Newburgh PD's payroll, Claire had accepted the offer.

A surprising number of FBI agents and Newburgh PD's entire Investigations Bureau had turned out for the event. Claire mouthed hellos to many of them. Jess and Sally, her maids of honor. Gomez. Mahoney. Nakamura. Captain Washington.

Chief of Police Charlie Emmerso smiled from ear to ear. *You're not just a colleague or friend. You're family.* At her farewell party, Claire had doubted his words, but he'd stood by them. Detective Ned Evans, Claire's mentor from Boston PD, had walked her down the aisle. Even Bella Winters was in attendance. Claire and Rob felt the comforting embrace of their growing network of family-by-choice. Soon, she and Rob would start a family of their own.

Special Agent Rafiq Massoud stood at the back with his wife, Nasim. Claire had met her at the Emergency Room after the shootout in Rob's basement. When the paralysis had worn off, Massoud had corroborated Claire's account of the events that day.

Nasim had choked up. "Thank you for saving my husband's life."

"You're welcome." Claire glanced at Massoud. The agent had suspected her of heinous crimes. But Claire discarded her grudges. "We were both just doing our jobs."

Massoud bowed his head. "I'm sorry for doubting you."

Claire shrugged. "I would have done the same."

"No, you wouldn't have."

Massoud's face seemed to crack with anguish. "We had a son, Amir—our firstborn. By the time he was five, we knew something was wrong with him. Broken. He would steal cash from us and set fire to people's property for fun. We caught him red-handed, but still, he denied everything. He lied to our faces." Massoud shook his head. "I thought I could fix him. Maybe he needed more attention? Maybe I hadn't set the right example? So I covered for him. I pretended he'd grow out of it. I pulled some strings to get him into a good college. But I couldn't fix him."

Claire nodded but said nothing. She sensed the story had a tragic ending. Massoud had opposed YARI not out of bigotry or ignorance. He'd experienced psychopathy firsthand and struggled to cure the aberration. YARI's claim to treat antisocial behavior had poured salt on his wounds by highlighting his failure to protect his family.

Massoud exhaled a tremulous breath. "He died in a hit-and-run two years ago. Later, I found out he'd been dealing drugs on campus."

Claire swallowed hard. "I'm so sorry."

In the weeks that followed, the new FBI director approved YARI's budget. Claire hoped their program would provide hope for youth like Massoud's son.

Claire and Rob had interrogated Karla Deloria while she'd awaited trial, but the assassin had no idea what Alpha had planned to do with Moretti's money.

"Maybe there was no grand plan?" Rob had suggested. Tom's betrayal had shaken him to the core, but Rob still retained a fragment of his post-bombing optimism.

"Maybe."

Claire didn't believe that. She also didn't believe Niccolo Moretti when, after the ordeal, he swore he'd change his ways.

But with Alpha dead and Apex dismantled, it was time for Claire to let go.

Photographs done, Claire and Rob headed to the banquet hall for their grand entrance. Claire was ravenous. Hopefully, they'd get a bite to eat before their first dance.

They didn't. After the dancing and welcome toasts, waiters served dinner. Claire and Rob mingled with their guests, then made for their table. *Food, at last!*

Sally intercepted them, her face serious. "We have a problem." She tipped her head. "Follow me."

Claire eyed Rob with suspicion, but he shrugged.

"If this is a wedding day surprise," Claire whispered, "can it wait until *after* we eat?"

"This is news to me, too. Maybe Sally put something together for us."

Sally led them through the cocktail area to an office. She knocked on the door and entered.

Inside, two Newburgh detectives flanked a woman in a glittery champagne evening dress.

Claire's heart skipped a beat. *She has a lot of nerve showing up here.*

Felicity Cline swept her arm in a melodramatic flourish and almost fell over. "Well, if it isn't the happy young couple." She slurred her words.

Rob inflated his chest. "What are you doing here?" His voice was calm but stern.

Felicity feigned insult. "What am I doing here? I belong here. The question is why the groom didn't invite his mother to his wedding?"

Detective Nakamura said, "We caught her breaking open the gift box to steal the checks. She had a gun in her bag, too."

Felicity raised her hand to speak. "Unloaded. The gun is only a precaution—for self-defense."

Nakamura didn't accept her BS. "Self-defense, my ass. More like armed robbery."

"Thank you for stopping her," Claire said.

"Thank Mahoney. He's the one who spotted her."

The red-nosed Mahoney grinned with satisfaction. "I may be tipsy, but my detective chops are still sharp. And she stole my wallet at the bar."

"I did not!" Felicity raged. "He planted it in my bag. This is entrapment!"

She's pathetic.

Rob shook his head. "You're drunk, Mom. So much for rehab and turning over a new leaf."

Felicity aimed an accusatory finger at him. "That money is mine. Everything you have should be mine. You owe me! You and your bride from Hell sent me to jail. How dare you frame your mother for murder? Didn't anyone teach you to honor your parents?"

Rob kept his cool and stood his ground. "You can't demand respect, Mother. You have to earn it."

Felicity snarled. "You ungrateful little idiot! After all I've done for you—"

"Shut it," Nakamura said. "Or I'll book you right now. Claire, do you want to press charges? I'm pretty sure that gun isn't registered either."

Felicity clasped her hands together. She fell at their feet and grovelled. "No! Don't do that. Please! This is all a big misunderstanding."

Rob looked to Claire. *What should we do?* Felicity had tried to rob them and spoil their special day. She deserved to answer for her crimes.

But court cases dragged out. The procedings would tie them to Felicity for months to come. And Claire didn't want her future mother-in-law's incarceration on her conscience.

She shook her head, and Rob smiled. He clearly liked their decision.

"Nah," Claire said. "Let her go. She doesn't get to spoil our evening."

Mahoney raised his whiskey tumbler and grinned. "I'll drink to that."

EPILOGUE

L ate that night, Claire and Rob retired to the Honeymoon Suite on the top floor of The Hannover Hotel and put their bridal bed to good use. Then they shared a steamy shower...and ended up back in bed. Who said weddings were overrated?

Claire lay between the soft, silky bedsheets while Rob showered again. She reached for her phone. It was 2 AM, but she was too pumped to sleep.

She browsed the catalog of a flower delivery website. She and Rob should send Detective Mahoney and his wife a token of their appreciation for saving the day. Roses for the wife and a crate of whiskey for Mahoney.

Claire opened her work inbox. Mahoney had emailed her the day of the shootout, and she'd overlooked his message during the manic aftermath. She opened the unread message. The detective hadn't identified The Level Field Initiative's scholarship administrators, but he had discovered a fourth beneficiary. *Amir Massoud.* Rafiq and Nasir Massoud's psychopathic firstborn. The hairs on the back of Claire's neck bristled.

I pulled some strings to get him into a good college. Massoud had gotten his son into the same scholarship program as the three Apex students. That's not all the beneficiaries had in common. *He'd been dealing drugs on campus.* A coincidence? What strings had Massoud pulled? Did he know the fund administrators? Did it matter? Both Alpha and Apex were gone.

She put down her phone. A gift basket, overflowing with goodies, sat on the counter below the flat-screen TV. Claire hadn't noticed the delivery when she'd dressed for the wedding. She got out of bed, threw on her pajamas, and studied the basket's high-end contents. Godiva. Moet & Chandon. Caramelized nuts and dried fruit. Had the Hannovers sent them complimentary snacks?

The showerhead fell silent.

Claire raised her voice. "Who sent the gift basket?"

Rob spoke through the bathroom's wall of translucent glass. "What basket?"

"The one by the TV."

"Beats me. It wasn't there when we checked in."

Claire tore open a pack of roasted pistachios and munched away. *Finally, something to eat.*

The nuts had hidden a small, square envelope of high-quality paper. The short message on the embossed card read, "Congratulations to us both." She turned it over. Two capital letters marked the back of the card: A. S. *Who could that be?*

She searched the basket for clues. A folded *Washington Post* lay beneath the box of chocolates. The front-page headline ran, "Election Bombshell." Claire skimmed the article. She checked the date. This was tomorrow morning's paper. How had a Washington daily, hot off the press, shown up in her gift basket? *Is this a joke?*

She grabbed the TV remote, settled on the edge of the bed, and flipped to a news channel. CNN's "breaking news" banner announced an "election game-changer."

A political reporter gushed about the surprising development.

"The new candidate has completely upturned the electoral apple cart. Known for his tough handling of organized crime and his rehabilitation of the FBI after the Quantico bombing, the senator has officially tossed his name into the ring for the upcoming primaries. He launched his campaign tonight from his home in Washington, DC."

The screen cut to a shot of a familiar white-haired man behind a podium. Senator Arnold Schultz spoke into a fist of microphones.

"This country deserves better—a clean sweep and a fresh start for our great nation."

A chill spread over Claire's skin. *No, it can't be.* Tom Brown was dead. Bill Wolfe had called him Alpha. Karla Deloria had called him Daddy. By any name, the Apex mastermind was gone.

But Alpha had isolated each arm of the starfish. He had used voice garbling software to hide his true identity from his troops. Karla had no idea who was on the other end of the line. What if Daddy and Alpha were two separate people?

Tom's words echoed in her mind. *Karla and I are the last Apex agents in the field.* Was Alpha no longer *in the field*?

Senator Arnold Schultz stared at the camera to address the viewers. He seemed to speak directly to Claire.

"With your help, we'll raze the old guard to the ground and start anew. Call it destiny. Call it fate. Together, there'll be no stopping us."

Claire lost her appetite. Her breath caught in her chest. She had heard those exact words before—from a psychopathic criminal mastermind, Alpha.

The truth hit her like a speeding freight train. Tom was dead. Alpha had survived. *He* had sent the gift basket. Again,

Tom's voice replayed in her head. *Someone upstairs is looking out for me.* The gift note was signed, A. S.—Arnold Schultz. *Alpha.* And he knew where she was.

Claire's pulse pounded in her ears. A burning sensation ballooned in her chest. Was she having a heart attack? She'd eaten from his offering. Had Alpha poisoned her?

She drew deep breaths. Slowly, the panic attack subsided. The food wasn't toxic. He didn't want her dead. *Not yet.*

The revelation sent her thoughts into overdrive. A murderous psychopath lurked in the US Senate. *I pulled some strings to get him into a good college.* Senator Schultz, Massoud's patron, stood behind The Level Field Initiative, too. Now the senator had set his sights on the presidency. But a campaign required deep pockets, and Schultz wasn't the only promising new candidate on the horizon. Before his death, FBI Director Douglas Warren was rumored to be on the cusp of a presidential bid. The Quantico bombing had eliminated the competition from the race and helped Schultz pocket Niccolo Moretti's millions. Alpha's master plan stretched before Claire in all its diabolical horror. But she could prove nothing.

Why had he contacted her? Did he think she was on his side? *No.* He knew Rob was alive and that Claire had deceived him. Was his message a threat—a warning for Claire to keep her distance? Not exactly. *Congratulations to us both.* This gesture was far more twisted—a menacing hat tip between fiendish rivals. *I see you. You see me. Now, Claire, what are you going to do about it?*

ACKNOWLEDGMENTS

Behind every novel there is a long line of very talented and supportive people.

My team of awesome beta readers provided valuable comments and corrections. They are: Maura Bauwens, Heather Bryant, Candice Lutz, Jennifer Medina, Lara Morrison, Roger Proctor, Roxx Tarantini, Billie Wichkan, Kai Wills, and Beatrice Yeow.

My excellent editor, Emmy Ellis, made the novel shine.

Teresa Collins, my trusty and talented proofreader, ensured the final manuscript is error-free and ready for publication.

I thank you all from the bottom of my heart.

~ Jamie Millen

ABOUT THE AUTHOR

Psychopaths. Stalkers. Narcissists. Killers.

Jamie Millen writes about the people you hope never to meet in real life...but probably already have.

If you enjoy crime thrillers packed with nail-biting psychological suspense, unforgettable characters, and breathtaking twists, you've come to the right place.

Visit JamieMillen.com/Claire to download free stories, sneak peeks, advanced chapters, and more.

Printed in Great Britain
by Amazon

36463619R00219